DAISIE'S ARK

DAISIE'S ARK

Grace Thompson

WTA

2034315121

This first world edition published in Great Britain 1994 by
SEVERN HOUSE PUBLISHERS LTD of
9–15 High Street, Sutton, Surrey SM1 1DF.
First published in the USA 1994 by
SEVERN HOUSE PUBLISHERS INC., of
425 Park Avenue, New York, NY 10022.

British Library Cataloguing in Publication Data
Thompson, Grace
  Daisie's Ark
  I. Title
  823.914 [F]

  ISBN 0-7278-4651-5

Typeset by Hewer Text Composition Services, Edinburgh.
Printed and bound in Great Britain by
Redwood Books Ltd, Trowbridge, Wiltshire.

4963

To Topsy and Lynn Evans
For all their help and encouragement.

1

Daisie Clements looked out through the ill-fitting door into the gathering greyness of evening. Her long hair was in two plaits hanging down her back; red in colour it looked dull and lifeless, only when the sun glinted on it did it show the possibilities of beauty. Her face was thin and pale, with the blueish, transparent look of the undernourished. Her hands, fiddling with a skein of wool she was trying to untangle, were red and, even in the warmth of summer, chapped and red.

Yet there was a spark of spirit showing in the large blue eyes, a hint that, given the chance, she would soon escape the life she was forced at present to lead and find a niche for herself with the promise of better things. She was watching for the first sign of her father returning from The Swan so she could slide the kettle from the hob onto the fire and make him a hot drink. Although, she thought with a wry smile on her young face, drink was the one thing her Dad wouldn't need. Not with him being in The Swan since midday.

On the hob to keep warm was a saucepan in which she had cooked some vegetable soup with the bones of yesterday's chop to flavour it. She had eaten her share, savouring the warm and tasty food with the enthusiasm of youth. Daisie Clements was only ten and in South Wales in 1906 life was difficult when there was no Mam to keep things going.

She wished her father would hurry, the smell issuing from the saucepan was making it more and more difficult not to take another bowlful of his soup for herself.

"Dais, you in then?" a voice called, and Daisie left the doorway and ran to greet her friend Tommy Thomas. A year younger than Daisie but twice as worldly he showed her the large empty bag he was carrying with an expression of pride. "Sold all I had! I borrowed a cart and walked through the village with them and sold the lot. Here, I saved some for you."

In the brown paper bag Daisie found three stale cakes and ate one with enthusiasm as she and Tommy went inside to sit by the fire. Daisie looked longingly at the other two cakes that were somewhat squashed but were filled with fruit and smelled delicious. "I ought to save one for Dad – "

"Wouldn't bother if I was you, Dais, the state he's in he wouldn't know the difference between a fancy cake and a crust that's too hard for the crows. I reckon they'll need the barrow for him tonight."

"That bad?"

"That bad!" Tommy confirmed, his weak eye winking at her.

Like Daisie, Tommy Thomas had red hair but his was short, cut jaggedly by the family who had taken him in when his parents had died. His eyes were almost as blue as hers, too, but a weakness made the left one wink involuntarily: an impression of friendliness quite misleading at times.

Tommy had soon realised that he wasn't loved, or even wanted, by anyone. Instead of this making him sad and resentful it had created in him a determination that made every day another step on the way to his wonderful future. Apart from blaming the fates for depriving him of his parents before he could even remember, he concentrated every thought on making money. One day he would have to be taken seriously. He would have a house with the toffs up on Pleasant View where he could look down on the town of Cwm Manachlog and be someone to be listened to, someone to respect. Until then, he devoted his energies and wit to making money.

He sat with Daisie for a while, making the skin around her large blue eyes crinkle with merriment as he told her of his adventures. Daisie's face was made for laughter; a scowl or the lines of discontent did not sit well on it.

"I scrounged the stale cakes from the baker, see, Dais. I made almost one shilling and sixpence by selling them to

2

houses where there are large families. At three for a penny they didn't worry about how hard they was!" He thought it better Daisie didn't know that some of them came out of the ash bin behind the bake-house.

As he stood to leave, Daisie emptied the crumbs from his bag and put them in an enamel dish to feed the birds the following morning. It was one of her greatest pleasures, watching the birds alight on the branches around the door and wait for her to throw out the odd scraps she had saved during the previous day. As soon as she re-entered the house they would swoop down and clear the food, drink from the clean water she provided, before flying off to other prospective handouts.

Daisie watched Tommy go with regret. He was whistling cheerfully, his hands rattling the coins in his pockets. His socks fell in wrinkles around his ankles and his short trousers were too large, hanging wide of his skinny body by his braces, like those of a clown. The clown image was exagerated by the spiky red hair and the ancient boots which were several sizes too big.

She sat on the bench outside the door with a sigh. She had so little company these days. The three school friends, Daisie, Gillian and Megan, were inseperable during most of the year, but for the past week Daisie had been on her own. The school was on summer holiday and Megan and Gillian were both unavailable. Megan, the shy and gentle girl who the other two had befriended, was sick with a fever. Lucky Gillian, whose parents were wealthy by most standards, her father being in regular work and her mother taking in lodgers, was still on holiday with her aunt in Somerset. As in previous summers, Gillian's parents had put her on a train in care of the guard and arranged for her to be met at Bristol by an aunt. What an adventure Daisie thought with a pang of envy.

Gillian wore newly bought clothes and never needed to walk to school without shoes. Megan's mother bought second-hand clothes for her only daughter and unpicked and re-made them so she also had clothes that fitted. Daisie wore much repaired items that others had no further use for. She was grateful if they fitted, philosophical if they did not.

Gillian was very pretty, with dark eyes, almost black hair and small, perfect features. She had a flair for dress and made even the simple skirts and pinafores they had to wear for school into something flattering and charming. Daisie wondered if Megan's mother would lend her an iron again to freshen up her school blouse and the white frilly pinafore that she had boiled in the copper and that was such a devil to press properly. Tomorrow she would visit Megan and ask.

Behind her in the one habitable room in the house that was little more than a shed, was a small bed, now hardly long enough for her, so her thin legs hung over the end like those of a heron. She vaguely hoped that something would happen before winter or her chilblains would be worse than usual.

Her father, Dan Clements, slept on the couch that stood against the far wall. A curtain had once been drawn across the room at night for privacy but, since Mam and the boys went and it had been singed by sparks spitting from the fire, they hadn't bothered.

She dozed, sitting on the fire-side stool, relishing the warmth, enjoying the heat of it on her cheeks. The crumbs of Tommy's last cake were scattered around her mouth. She'd let Dad have them all next time she promised herself guiltily as she succumbed to temptation and swallowed the last piece.

The rumble of wheels alerted her and she stretched and stood up to see if it was the wheel-barrow, pushed by the pot-boy from The Swan, bringing her father home at last. Then she realised that besides the wheels she could hear the clip-clop of horses hooves and she sat down again. It would be the milkman going to collect the evening's milking from the farm. Perhaps if she waited by the lane he might stop and give her a drink. She picked up the enamel jug and stood waiting.

The air was still warm, the evening filled with that special hush of summer disturbed only occasionally by a bird or the rustle of a small animal in the grass. The month of August had been a good one, sunshine day after day. Crowds had gone to the beaches she'd heard. Perhaps next year Dad would be well enough to take her. She tightened her grip on the jug hopefully and looked along the lane. It was her father who arrived first and, with regret, she put aside the jug and went to help him into the house.

When Dan had been settled on the couch to sleep off his excesses Daisie undressed, washed in the enamel bowl, and climbed into her own bed. She wasn't tired but there wasn't anything to do. She lay for a long time without sleeping, remembering how different her life had been before Dad's accident.

Dan Clements had spent his working day underground hewing coal in a warm, friendly valley until an accident had made it impossible for him to continue. He had collected their few belongings into bundles and, with his three children and his wife, had set off to walk to the next town in the hope of employment for himself or his wife and sons. There had been none and he and his family had been unwelcome, the locals accused them of trying to steal what work there was from those who lived there.

The five-mile walk had become fifteen, then fifty, then over a hundred as they treked to and fro, sleeping where they could find somewhere dry, all the time searching for a place where they would have work and a home. Eventually they had stopped on the outskirts of the small town of Cwm Manachlog, 'Valley Of The Monastery'.

It seemed a busy and relatively prosperous little place, the roads were constantly filled with the sound of horses and carts and people walked along the clean pavements wearing good quality clothes. The houses were neat with front gardens tended and carefully fenced to prevent the sheep from the mountains close by and that wandered through the town from trespassing on their flower beds. They learned there was a market held in the main street on Saturdays bringing extra trade to the well-stocked shops. There were farms all around with the possibility of at least seasonal work.

It was so different from the place they had been forced to leave. There the shops were boarded up, tradesmen were owed more money than they were paid and they had no prospect of seeing debts cleared. People were not dishonest but they couldn't give what they didn't have. Groups of defeated men stood on corners, filling the air with the smoke from shared cigarettes and murmuring about better times. They stood and waited for time to pass in the hope that the morrow would offer hope of a fresh start to at least a few of them.

The sight of Cwm Manachlog had given Daisie's parents the hope that their tomorrow had come. Three days passed without Dan finding work but he knew it would be pointless to continue walking in the hope of some marvellous 'end of the rainbow'; there was nowhere else to go in search of it. They must stay here in this market town and succeed or starve. They slept those first nights in what had once been a pig-sty, well built of brick, cleaned of all unpleasant odours and used as a store for root-crops, on which they dined.

The work Dan eventually found was farm work, labouring, poorly paid and with only an abandoned, tumbled down house in which to live. His wife soon refused to accept the lowly state he had brought them to. Daisie shrank inside when she remembered the rows. "I'm not staying. I can do better on my own!" her mother had shouted again and again as her father had tried to reason and persuade her things would improve.

The house they had been given, originally boasted two rooms, but a leaking roof and a broken window made one of them unusable. They crowded in the one room with hardly enough space to sit. The door was always open so they could extend their living space and Daisie wondered how they would fit in when winter came. She was reassured with exciting stories of how it would all be made good. Dan was going to mend it, fix everything and make the place a "little palace" but somehow he never found the time. Work or The Swan, which he passed on his way home, took every waking moment.

The building was of stone with a roof of corrugated iron which was rusting and in need of replacement. The timbers were split and distorted. Perhaps, Dan said, in a rare burst of enthusiasm, it had once been a good thatch and one day, he had promised, when he felt stronger, he would earn the money to have it thatched once again.

In those first few weeks, relieved at having settled, glowing with a sense of achievement even though they were no better off than if they had stayed in their home village, Dan had become quite animated about their future. Through his spoken dreams, young Daisie saw the house as it would one day be; white-washed and neat, with proper windows and that beautiful, wonderful golden thatch, all set amid gardens glowing with the vibrant colours of summer flowers. Daisie was the only one who believed it.

The days passed with Dan spending more and more time at The Swan and less and less at work. The farmer was intolerant of the man to whom he had given work at the expense of a local family and, after six weeks, told him to go.

Encouraged by verbal beatings from his wife, Dan found an even more poorly paid job helping the road-mender. The weeks of wandering had unsettled his wife and, as things showed no sign of improving, she became less inclined to argue with him and her anger simmered inside and gradually became plans.

Dan came home from work one day to find Daisie crying, the fire out and no meal on the hob. Unable to hold back the tears to explain she handed him a note left by her mother. Dan read the few words telling him his wife had gone and stared at the ten-year-old Daisie as if she could explain.

Dan's wife had been tempted away to follow a group of men who had wandered through the town and stated their intention of walking all the way to London, "A magical place where there was plenty for all". She had taken their sons, leaving Dan and Daisie to cope as they could. With the little girl to look after they would have found it impossible, without her there was at least a chance.

"Best I light the fire, Daisie," was all Dan said. "Then we'll go and buy some bread and cheese."

The only possessions they had were a couple of chairs, the two makeshift beds and, hidden away for when Daisie was "grown up", Mam's ring. The ring had two diamonds and had belonged to Mam's own mother. It was, Dan told Daisie, an heirloom, to be handed down daughter to daughter and would never be sold, no matter how dire their situation.

To the young Daisie in those dark days following the departure of her family it seemed something akin to the Crown Jewels, although its value was probably little more than ten shillings. Somehow they would get themselves a decent place to live, money to spend on as much food and as many clothes as they could want, so long as they didn't part with Mam's ring. It was a talisman, a promise given by the fates that if they cared for it they would be repaid.

The pedlar's tray was Daisie's idea. She remembered seeing a man walking along the lanes, knocking at doors to sell small items from the tray he carried and she had persuaded Dan to obtain a licence and some stock and try his luck.

Now he walked the streets, visited the farms and the big houses, often with Daisie beside him to encourage sympathy, and sold bootlaces, elastic, pins and needles, darning wools and earning sufficient to save them from real hunger but dependent on health and good weather: a precarious living.

The walking aggravated Dan's wounds and Daisie quickly learned that if she were to feed them and replenish his stock, and buy oil for the lamp and coal for the fire, she had to persuade him to part with a few pennies before he went to The Swan. Today she had failed, tomorrow would be a lean day.

She woke the next morning to the sound of the milk cart passing on the way to the farm for the morning's milking. Dan was snoring on his couch near the ashes of the fire. She washed and dressed herself, put out the crumbs for the waiting birds, and went out into the lane. The enamel jug was on the bench and she picked it up hopefully and waited. She knew the cows had been milked because she could see them making their slow plodding way up from the milking shed, over the stream, out into the green field.

Ivor Price, who suffered under the nick-name "One and Sixpence", saw her and pulled up the horse with a smile.

"Thirsty are you, girl? Go on then, go and fetch a jug, I can spare a lickle drink for a pretty maid this fine morning." A small man wearing a jaunty cap on his head, a waistcoat of gaudy green and trousers that looked like corkscrews they were so stiff and creased with spilt milk. He jumped down from the cart and lifted the lid of the fifteen gallon churn that rode with him on the back step. With a half pint measure which he carried with several others hooked on the side of the cart, he filled her jug and handed it to her.

"Thank you 'till you're better paid," she said politely, repeating words she had heard her mother say on similar occasions.

Ivor waved away her thanks. "Your dad, all right is he? I heard he was a bit, well, you know, fach, a bit more under the table than on it, last night."

"He's sleeping," Daisy said defensively. "It's his injury, he has to drink to ease the pain. Hurts something awful at times it does."

"Pity for him." A curl of the lips that was not sympathy wiped the smile briefly from Ivor's amiable face. "Still, you'll be leaving that school and starting to earn a bit yourself soon, won't you?"

"There's a few years to go yet, Mr Price," she sighed. "I thought I'd try for a bit of cleaning at The Swan when I do leave. Handy for home and for looking after Dad, see."

"I'll have a lickle word when you're ready, listen to me they will. My sister Ethel Trip does a bit of cleaning for Helen and Desmond Prewitt, she does. You'll get work if Ivor-the-milk recommends you."

The horse had been slowly moving along the hedgerow seeking his favourite leaves, pulling at them with his great long tongue and snorting in pleasure. Putting down the jug, Daisie pulled some grass and fed him, laughing at the sensation as he puffed and snorted into her wide open hand before gently taking her offering.

"It's a pity you can't get work with animals, young Daisie. Work like that would suit you a treat. Still, the world wasn't designed to suit our wants, not the likes of us. Cheerio, fach."

Daisie carried the milk inside, covered it with a crocheted cotton circle against the flies then set off for a walk along the stream which crossed under the main street of Cwm Manachlog, and went through the farm where Ivor Price had just collected his churnful of milk. Apart from the humming of insects the morning was almost silent, then she heard a loud splash, followed by the sound of someone running. Curious, she hurried in the direction of the sound and saw a figure that she thought was Tommy Thomas. She called, but he didn't stop.

At the place where she stopped the stream was not at its deepest. Near the centre, where a bank of mud reduced the depth further and probably the cause of the splash, was a sack. She was barefoot and, without bothering to lift the skirt of her thin cotton dress, she waded in to see what had been thrown away.

The sack was wet and her fingers were clumsy, but a movement within the sack made her hasten and when she had opened the double knot she gave a huge cry of anger. Inside were two puppies. Hurrying to the bank she placed them on the grass and at once one of them began whining and trying to lick her hands, the other was clearly dead.

Crying, her wet dress clinging to her legs, her red hair as yet uncombed, she looked a sorry sight when she reached the house. Leaning against the door was Tommy.

"Tommy," Daisie shouted between sobs. "How could you do it?"

"Do what? And what have you got there? Carrying a dead dog about, you'll be sent to the lockup if you carry on like this, Dais."

"I saw you, throwing the poor things into the water," she challenged. "Saw you, so don't deny it!" she lied. She had to find someone to blame, to be the recipient of her anger.

"Chuck 'em in the stream? Not me."

"I heard the splash and saw you running away." She spoke with less certainty. She didn't want it to have been Tommy.

"I ran away all right, Dais. But I don't know nothing about no puppies. I saw Ivor-the-milk and we owes him, see. So I ran as fast as I could."

"Help me, Tommy," she said, too concerned about the

10

puppy to argue. "I have to get him warm and I haven't even lit the fire yet."

"Give it here to me." Tommy took the puppy and glanced at the dead one. "All you can do for that is bury it, Dais. We'll have a funeral later."

They lit the fire and found a box to put the puppy in to keep it warm, and Daisie gave the small creature some of her precious milk. Then, with the puppy tucked inside her cardigan, she helped Tommy dig a hole and bury its dead brother. They said a prayer and covered the grave with flowers gathered from the hedgerow.

"I want to keep it, Tommy, but how will I feed it?" Daisie looked to Tommy hopefully, her blue eyes pleading. Surely he would be able to help. Never lost for an answer was Tommy, or so everyone said. "The cats-meat man comes to the market regular, but I haven't the money to buy from him."

"Feed it? There's no problem there, Dais. Enough stuff chucked out in this town to feed a hundred little scraps like him. I'll have a word with the butcher, and there's often fish thrown away from the fish-stall at the market on a Saturday. Feed him? That'll be easy. I'll make sure you keep him fed, Dais." He looked at her, grinning, his head on one side, his left eye winking madly. "What you going to call him then? Neptune?"

"Is it a boy or a girl, Tommy?"

Tipping the puppy onto it's back Tommy studied it's belly seriously. "It's got one of them things like boys have, but it's in the wrong place, so I think you've got yourself a girl dog."

"Then she'll have puppies?" She smiled her wide and charming smile. "Thank you, Tommy," she breathed, as if the sex of the puppy had been decided by her friend as a gift.

They chose the name Alexandra after the Queen, Alex for short. Tommy left Daisie happily nursing the puppy and as he walked away he touched the pennies in his pocket. He had been given the coins to drown the puppies and he wondered if the owner would now demand the money back. Then he shrugged. How could he help it if, after he had thrown the

11

things in the water, someone had come along and taken them out again? He'd done what he'd been paid to do, hadn't he?

And what a lot of pleasure Daisie would have minding the one that had survived. He had satisfied all three people involved: pennies in his pocket; a woman rid of the puppies she didn't want; and Daisie with something to make a fuss of. He felt quite noble, feeling he had done the world a few favours, and what was wrong with winning himself a couple of pennies at the same time? Conscience appeased he set off briskly for home, whistling contentedly, his left eye winking in time.

Daisie spent a happy day looking after the puppy who cried the moment she was out of sight, flattering her with its need of her. She fixed a rope around its tiny neck and walked with it to Megan's. She must be out of bed by now. She could show her the puppy, talk a while, then borrow the iron to fix her clothes ready for school. She could also find out when Gillian would be home from Somerset. On impulse she went to Gillian's house first and to her delight Gillian was back, looking paler than she expected, but obviously fit and well after her holiday.

Gillian, at ten years of age, was already a rather vain child. Having heard the view that it was "common" to allow the sun to tan a woman's skin, she had spent the summer holiday frantically avoiding the sun's rays. A floppy hat, made by her aunt to match her best cotton dress, had been worn constantly, and although her arms and hands had browned and freckled her face, with its dark eyes and perfectly proportioned features, was as pale as winter. She was wearing a dress made of muslin which her aunt had embroidered with flowers, her white summer shoes were immaculate and, to the down to earth Daisie, she seemed more like a doll than a person.

"God help us, Gillian, you look like a picture. You ought to be floating about on a flower-covered swing!"

"Like it, do you? Auntie says if you want to be a beautiful woman you have to start young." She gasped then as the puppy charged into view, leaping at her with delight, believing now that everyone was her friend. "Daisie! What have you got there?" Gillian stepped back as the puppy attempted to jump up. "Keep it off my skirt, it's muslin and I don't want it ripped!"

Daisie picked up the squirming animal and smiling said, "Take it off and put on something proper. You can't sit there wearing that bit of nonsense all day!"

"I'll do what I like, Daisie Clements!" Gillian practiced her pout and looked with disapproval at the animal wriggling to be released. "Where did you get it? You aren't keeping it are you?"

"I saved her from the river, tied up in a sack she was, mind. She's called Alexandra and yes, I am keeping her."

"What did your Dad say?" Gillian moved further away from the fussy little animal, brushing at imaginary marks on her full skirt.

"He doesn't know yet, but it's all right," Daisie added hastily. "Tommy will help me feed her."

Daisie had to admire the new clothes Gillian's aunt had bought for her: white buckskin ankle-strap shoes; leather sandals for the cooler weather; three new and expensive dresses such as Daisie had never seen; there were pouch bags to match each dress and ribbons and pretty hand-painted bands for her hair which, her aunt had insisted, must be rolled in rag curlers every single night. Gillain's mother offered to iron Daisie's school blouse and apron. Tomorrow was the first day back after the holiday and everyone wanted to look smart. After Gillian had changed into a grey skirt and linen blouse, the two girls went to find the third member of their trio, Megan.

Inseparable since they had met on Daisie's first day at the school, the three girls were unalike in looks and temperament but seemed to tolerate their differences without any conflict. A respect for each other had been born at the moment they had decided to be friends.

Megan was small, slender and with fine, light brown hair that seemed to float about her face, giving her an ethereal look as if she were about to fade completely into the shadows. Her slight stoop and the hesitant way she looked around her revealed her shyness. When asked a question she weighed up every word, checking in her mind before she opened her mouth to make sure she wouldn't give offence.

Her gentle and kindly nature made Daisie and Gillian protective of her. Small, apologetic and easily frightened, Megan had been the butt of jokes and teasing and had been given the nick-name of Crying Mouse, but since Daisie and Gillian had befriended her the teasing had ceased. Boys who found Gillian fascinating, with her extravagant gestures and her slinky way of walking, tolerated the nervous Megan to be near her. Daisie, too, attracted a lot of followers, her outspokenness and the way she always defended the weak made her popular with boys and girls. When Daisie and Gillian had become her friends, Megan's life had changed overnight, and now she was envied for her position with the ebullient Daisie and the attractive Gillian.

As pale as Gillian but from illness not choice, Megan's light brown eyes widened with delight as her friends appeared in her bedroom, dragging the exhausted puppy.

"Your mam said it was all right to come up," Daisie said, picking up the puppy and throwing her on the bed for Megan to admire. Megan always wore brown dresses and skirts and, Daisie was hardly surprised to see, her nightdress was also a fawn colour. She seems determined never to be noticed, Daisie thought affectionately. I wonder if she would change if her mam dressed her in pink or blue? Or bright red!

"Your mam said you'll be getting up tomorrow, so we'll come and see you after school, won't we, Gillian?"

"Of course," Gillian's reply was vague, after waving her greeting at Megan she was standing in front of the long wardrobe mirror pulling her long dark hair into a pile on her head, twisting, turning and swaying to see the effect.

"Get her!" Daisie laughed. "Give over, Gillian. School we're going to, not a fancy-dress ball!"

Giving her hair a pull of disgust, Gillian returned to the bedside in a parody of a seductive walk. "I wish I was older," she sighed. "There's so much fun to be had, and I want to start finding it."

"I don't mind school," Megan smiled, "not since you became my friends. I don't relish working in a shop, being told off all day by some bad-tempered woman who won't give me time to learn anything before expecting me to be perfect."

"You're going to work in a shop?" Daisie was surprised. "I never thought of a shop. It's skivvying for me, no one would take me on for anything else, now would they?" She lifted her feet, in their ugly boots and attempted a mock curtsy. "Yes, madam, I'll show you our latest fashions, walk this way." She walked with feet splayed to the wardrobe and pretended to open the door.

"You'd be all right, Daisie, once you got something decent to wear," Gillian laughed. "My auntie says beauty's all a matter of clothes, confidence and character."

Daisie picked up the puppy who was chewing the tassled corners of the bedspread. "Three more years before we can hope to leave school. Fancy making us stay till we're thirteen!" The others chorused their dismay.

"Three years before we're grown up. I'll have Mam's ring then," Daisie confided. "It seems a long time before I can work and earn some money and have a nice dress." She looked down at the cotton dress, faded so the pattern was all but invisible and wrinkled at the hem where she had waded in to rescue the puppies.

"I don't intend to work for long. I'm going to find myself a husband with plenty of money," Gillian said.

"Huh, get her," Daisie teased.

Megan just smiled. "I bet you will, too, Gillian. Snapped up you'll be as soon as you're grown up."

A few days later, Daisie was walking along the bank of the stream with the excited Alex making choking noises as she tried to run on ahead of the rope that held her. Daisie turned away from the water to avoid the spot where someone had tried to drown the two puppies, pushed her way through the sloe bushes, and nearly fell over the recumbent figure of a man. She picked up the dog and began to tip-toe away, thinking the man was most likely a tramp. But a quirk of memory suddenly revealed what she had seen more clearly and she gave a gasp of fright. The figure lying either dead or unconscious was wearing what she recognised as her father's long mac.

Hands to her face, as if preparing to cover her eyes against an unacceptable sight, she crept back. His pedlar's tray was beside him, the flaps closed, the shoulder straps neatly folded: it looked as if it had been carefully placed rather than dropped. He must have come over all tired, she thought, and laid down for a rest.

She tied the dog's rope to a tree and knelt down to look at her father's face. He was snoring peacefully. Then she saw that the linings of his pockets were showing and a brief examination revealed that they were empty. If Dan had had any money left from what he had earned that day, someone had helped themselves while he slept.

She tried to wake him. She didn't think she could lift him and help him home without assistance. Slowly and patiently she woke her father and persuaded him to stand: then, with the pedlar's tray under her arm, the puppy struggling on ahead, she guided him home. Her mind battled with the prospect of feeding them without any money. If only she could work and earn money.

When Daisie was twelve she found herself a job. With only a few months to go before she was allowed to leave school, she went to The Swan and offered to do some cleaning. It was harder work than she expected, previously having only to brush the floor and wash the bedding of her primitive home. When she finished on her first day she was met by her friends, Gillian and Megan. "How d'you get on, Daisie?" they chorused, and with the intention of making them laugh she exaggerated the boring tasks until they were envious of her exciting life. She was still smiling when she reached home. Then, seeing her father sleeping on the couch, his tray fallen, the contents spread and ruined having been chewed by the latest of Alex's puppies, she began to sob.

16

Her father woke and stumbled to his feet and, seeing the mess, he tried to gather the tangled bundles of darning wool and the skeins of elastic, his hands scratching on the scrap of linoleum in the centre of the floor.

"Sorry, Daisie, don't cry. I didn't mean to lose it, love. I think someone robbed me again." *I didn't mean it* or *I couldn't help it* were his usual cries when he returned without money. But to Daisie's sharp ears this sounded different.

"What d'you mean?" she asked. "What have you lost?" Not waiting to be told she ran to the small cupboard where they stored the birth and marriage certificates and opened the small box. "Mam's ring! You've lost Mam's ring!"

"Not lost, Daisie. Stolen it must have been. It was in my pocket and on the path someone pushed me over, held my head down, and emptied my pockets."

"Why was it in your pocket? You promised it would be mine, when I'm grown up." Two more months, she thought bitterly. Two more months before I leave school and become a grown up and he has to lose it now.

"Sorry, I was going to pawn it, see, like I've done before, but the shop was shut and . . ." He turned and smiled apologetically. "It was for you, Daisie. I wanted to buy you something smart for when you start work proper."

He was lying. He hadn't been knocked down and robbed, he had sold her ring. She knew he was lying, but she also knew he couldn't help it. Easy to be truthful when there was something in your pocket, the price of a meal and a drink with your friends. When your pocket-linings were pulled out white and stark, it was a different story. She grieved about the ring but tried to accept its loss. There was nothing she could do to get it back.

So it was with disbelief that she recognised it in the palm of a customer's hand as she wiped the tables in The Swan a few days later.

"Where did you get that?" she demanded.

Desmond and Helen Prewitt who ran The Swan came over to see what the noise was about as she and the man began to argue about the ownership of the ring.

"Daisie, calm down," Desmond said, his round face puckered in alarm. "Tell me what has happened. This man has something belonging to you?"

"Mam's ring, that's what he's got. Got my gran's initials inside it has. It was stolen from my Dad! He was knocked down and robbed while he was on his way home!" Her dad must have been telling the truth after all.

"I'll see to this, Daisie," Helen said quietly.

"I want Mam's ring!"

"Leave it to Helen and me, we'll sort it, I promise." Desmond was firm and Daisie was sent to wait in the back room among piles of dishes and glasses waiting to be washed, while Desmond, Helen and the customer sorted things out.

When the man had been appeased and had agreed to accept money and return the ring, Desmond came into the room and handed it to her.

"Helen and I bought it back for you," he said. "You can pay us out of your wages when you start work full-time. Is that all right?"

"Thank you. But shouldn't that man be punished?"

"He says he bought it from someone and I don't think we'd be able to convince the police of his guilt."

She was grateful to have the ring returned but the thought of debt frightened her. She hadn't started work properly and already she owed money. Five shillings Desmond had paid. To Daisie it was a fortune.

She sat in the decrepit old house later that evening and watched for her father's return. One day she knew he wouldn't come back. Like her mother and her brothers he would be gone from her. She shivered even though the room was over warm. To be alone was her most frightening thought. She cuddled up the the fat puppy and squeezed her eyes shut in a fervent prayer: "Please, God," she said aloud. "Please help me to find a family and never face living alone." A movement at the door disturbed her as she sat there thinking about the lack of a family. A small shadow emerged from the darkness behind the open door and waddled towards her. A duckling, ignoring the dog, walked up to the bowl of water she had prepared for washing herself and drank. Its leg was twisted and the wing was hanging at an awkward angle. She reached over to where she had the crumbs ready for the birds breakfast and scattered them on the floor. If she couldn't have people, then animals would do.

"Welcome to Daisie's Ark," she whispered.

2

The summer Daisie was twelve was a warm one and although she still attended school she also worked for a few hours each evening at The Swan. Most of her time there was spent in the back room of the busy public house, apart from gathering the empty plates and glasses for washing. But she began to know the regulars, of whom her father was one. She became more and more irritated by the fact that her father spent as much as she earned on the other side of the bar.

"It isn't fair," she grumbled to Gillian and Megan. "I hate the work, it's lowly and uninteresting and all I'm doing is giving Dad the excuse to drink more."

"Leave home," Gillian advised. "Staying makes you a martyr. I don't approve of martyrs, Daisie." She swished back her long hair to emphasise her indignation. She always managed to "lose" the ribbons that held her beautiful hair in sober plaits before morning break time. The teacher's disapproval was ignored.

"She can't leave her father with no one to look after him!" The gentle Megan was shocked at her friend's suggestion. "You have to honour your parents, whatever they do."

"Listen to her!" Gillian laughed. "If my dad expected me to skivvy just to pay for his beer he'd be very disappointed." She shook her black hair that lay about her shoulders like a shawl and stuck her pretty nose in the air. Daisie and Megan shared a glance of amusement. They were used to Gillian's demands on life.

It was Saturday and they made their way to the High Street where the market was in progress. Daisie's two dogs followed,

Alex and the last of her latest batch of puppies, both less playful now in the intense heat of high summer.

Helen and Desmond Prewitt usually persuaded Daisie to help out at The Swan on this their busiest day, but today she had refused for reasons of her own. The heat of the sun seemed to bounce back from the pavements and in her thin-soled shoes, Daisie thought her feet were beginning to cook. The dogs stopped frequently and lay panting in whatever shade they could find.

That morning, with the sun already making the tin roof of the coal-house too hot to touch, the thought of The Swan's dark kitchen with the never-ending arrival of dirty dishes had been too much. Even the lowliest has to rebel sometimes to keep what little self-respect they have, she told her friends. The kindly Megan was worried about her letting Helen and Desmond down on a market day, but Gillian cheered her decision.

The street was crowded with horses and carts used by families to transport them locally. A number of the carts were tilted onto their shafts, the horses taken away. Many carts and waggons were already filled with parcels and bags and boxes of shopping. Customers were examining the produce with looks of disapproval on their weatherbeaten faces, determined to go home loaded having spent as little as possible. Everyone searched for a bargain.

Sheep wandered around the feet of the stall holders and their customers. They, too, wanted a bargain. Perhaps some freshly bought cabbage or tasty cauliflower. Cats and dogs, too accustomed to the sight to bother to chase them, lay in the shade of the canvas coverings and panted.

The three girls bought home-made toffees from the old lady who made it in her kitchen and chewed determinedly as they walked around. They waved to their friends and made faces at those who did not "belong". One of the people they disapproved of and treated to one of their tongue-poking, face-curling glares, was Arthur Huntley-Davies.

Mrs Huntley-Davies was the wife of the local estate agent, a lady who regarded the less fortunate as beneath contempt.

Shiftlessness and idleness were the only reasons they weren't as fortunate as herself; or so she believed. With her over-weight, over-indulged son, Arthur, she walked around with her face registering disapproval and sent her servant, Mattie, to buy the items she chose.

Arthur was the same age as the girls, but they rarely saw him. He went to a private boarding school and was a rare visitor to his home town. He turned and looked back at them with a wistful expression.

"Look at Arthur, he'd like to talk to us, but his mother won't let him," Megan said.

"Talk to him? Rather have a rat for company!" Daisie retorted. Gillian nodded her agreement. For differing reasons, the Huntley-Davies's were beneath *their* contempt. The *crachach*, the toffee-nosed, the swanks; they were only there to be laughed at.

In late afternoon the market benefited from a new surge of business. As evening approached the stalls were still attracting custom, the pavements filled with people who had waited, hoping for a bargain. Prices were dropping and there was a rush of customers pushing and shoving, arguing and bargaining, with business almost as frantic as the early morning when boarding-house keepers and hotels sent out for fresh vegetables for the lunchtime trade. Many of the present crowd searching for bargains were those same servants who had returned to by cheap leftovers for the weekend.

The summer scene was colourful. Several of the women who still wore hats anchored to their plaits and buns with hat-pins fierce enough to be classed as offensive weapons, were shedding coats and revealing their arms and easing the neckline's of their dresses, blowing down the fronts in an attempt to cool themselves. There was a lot of noise as vendors shouted to compete with their neighbours.

The cats and dogs, including Alex and her puppy, skulked among the stalls searching for fallen scraps, avoiding the feet and the occasional kicks of the impatient crowd. The green-grocer, Dicky Daniels, was waving his arms about shouting the praises of his greens, extolling the beauty of his apples and pears and bananas, the freshness of his salads, his eyes nearly popping out of his head as he strained to shout above the cheeky barrow-owner parked near by who's presence had already caused two fights.

The girls watched with amusement as the green-grocer's son who went under the name of Little Dicky, went around the back of his stall and up-ended the barrow amid shouts of laughter, anger and sing-song jeering. The market's "Toby" came to settle the argument but, as he was blamed for allowing the stranger to deal so close to a regular stall-holder in the first place, was also the subject of jeering and was pelted enthusiastically with the fallen fruit and vegetables.

Laughing, the girls helped themselves to a couple of Worcester apples from the ruined barrow, wiped them on their long skirts then, chewing happily, went to watch the china seller and his assistant, Tommy Thomas.

All the stalls had a fascination for Daisie but to her the china stall was the best and the one she always left till last, savouring the anticipation of that first glimpse of the seller, Phil Johnson. For a start the man was young, probably only six or seven years older than herself, she guessed, and he was beautiful. He usually wore a tennis shirt under a white apron and on his fair, almost white, hair sat a white hat that was neither chef's hat or ice-cream sellers but something inbetween. He was powerfully built and handsomely tanned. His arms seemed to reflect light, the pale hairs, bleached by summer, a contrast to the brown skin.

High above the crowd on his platform he performed his act, and seemed to belong to a different world, the world of entertainers. He had greeny eyes which Daisie always thought of as devilish. Now they shone, telling the world he enjoyed every moment. Life is fun, they seemed to say. Just looking at him sent shivers down Daisie's spine.

"There he is," Gillian whispered as they left the sweet stall having bought a second piece of toffee. "Go on, ask for a cup and saucer, your dad broke yours, didn't he?"

"I can't spare the money," Daisie hesitated, remembering

23

the way her father had stumbled a few nights before and smashed their last cup.

"Go on, Daisie." Even Megan helped to persuade her. "He's sure to let you have them cheap."

"Here, mister, she wants something." Megan and Gillian pushed the hesitant Daisie forward and, blushing to the roots of her red hair, she asked for a cup and matching saucer.

"For you the best I've got, little lady," Phil said, encouraging his audience to cheer. And, before handing a set decorated with violets to Tommy for wrapping, he kissed the cup where she would drink from it, smiled at her, bowed to the applause and took her shilling.

Daisie pretended he didn't talk to all of his customers like that and savoured the words and the special smile. In her excitement she forgot her change and had to go back, blushing even more furiously than before, her eyes an intense blue against her rosy cheeks.

They stood for a while admiring Phil's expertise as he placed a bread-plate on his large hand then slid plate after plate around it, then the saucers, and finally, to gasps of admiration and expectation of disaster, he threw the whole display in the air, "Once, twice, and three times for luck!" he shouted.

They waved at Tommy Thomas and shouted for him to try it as well. He was wearing a hat similar to Phil's and a sacking apron in which there was a large pocket to hold the money. He was whistling and winking at the crowd as he came forward with boxed sets and handed them to those in the crowd who raised their hands to buy.

Chewing on the home-made toffee, the three girls watched as Phil then began to juggle with glasses, throwing them into the summer air so the sun glinted on them creating an occasional rainbow of colour. All the time he chattered non-stop, watching for those showing an interest in buying, hardly pausing in his breathless liturgy, hypnotising the crowd with his patter and, all the time, directing the cheerful Tommy to take goods to people in the admiring crowd and gather their money.

"I hope Phil keeps an account of what he sells," Gillian

laughed. "Can't trust that Tommy with a farthing, let alone all that cash!"

Daisie chose the food she needed and haggled with the rest of the customers to make sure she didn't pay more than necessary. They filled two paper carrier bags with meat, bones and vegetables, missing out the fruit to compensate for the expense of the cup and saucer. As the crowd dispersed and the stalls were gradually emptied of their goods, Gillian suggested a walk through the town to the stream.

"We can paddle and cool our feet," she encouraged.

"No, I think I'll – I'd better get home in case Dad's there," Daisie said.

"Come off it, Daisie. You're planning something. Let us in on it. We're friends, aren't we?"

"I just thought I'd poke my head around the doors of a few pubs and see where Phil Johnson drinks," Daisie whispered.

"Why?"

"Well, he doesn't drink in The Swan. I'm just curious, that's all.

"Ask Tommy," Megan suggested. "Tommy Thomas knows everything that goes on in – " She gasped as a young man stumbled against her and knocked her staggering against the window of a shoe shop.

"Oh, I am sorry. I nearly tripped over this dead cat and I lost my balance. Is your friend all right?" he asked Gillian.

Gillian helped Megan to regain her balance and stared at the boy who had caused her to stumble. She smiled slowly, admiring his neat clothes and slicked back hair, the way his eyes sparkled with interest.

"It's all right," Megan said, "I'm not hurt." She looked around. No one seemed to have heard her, or if they had they didn't care. The boy and Gillian were smiling at each other and Daisie was on her knees examining the cat curled against the wall below the shop window.

"Bring your friend inside and Mam will get her a drink of water," the boy said, still staring at Gillian. "My name is Waldo Griffiths. My parents own this shoe shop."

Megan found herself escorted past racks and displays of

shoes and rows of seats. Waldo led them beyond the sales area to where there was a comfortable living room. Daisie followed, nursing the cat who seemed to be regaining consciousness.

Apparently unaware of where they were, Daisie sat beside the self-conscious Megan and murmured, "Been knocked by a cart I think. It's bruised but I don't think anything's broken. Oh, Megan! I wish I had some money. I'd take it to the vet."

"Let me see." The boy tore his attention from Gillian with reluctance and took the cat from Daisie. "I'll get the vet to look at it, but I can't keep it."

"I can!" Daisie said at once and an hour later, the three girls, with the dogs following and the cat safe in Daisie's arms, set off along the stream to Daisie's house. The duck heard them coming and limped, as if in sympathy with Megan's injury, along the path to meet them.

They wandered at a leisurely pace and for a while walked in the stream, the cool water giving a luxurious silky sensation after the heat of the streets. They were unusually silent; Daisie watching the still drowsy cat, Megan limping slightly from a bruised ankle and Gillian dreaming of Waldo Griffiths, wealthy Waldo Griffiths whose parents owned a shoe shop.

When they reached Daisie's house they all went inside to have a drink and see the cat settled in its new home. Dan was on the couch and the sight was so normal they did not comment on his sprawled, unconscious figure. Daisie thought vaguely that it was early for him to be home and sleeping off the excesses of drink but presumed he had met friends who had been more than usually generous. Market day sometimes had that effect on people, they treated it like a holiday.

The cat gradually recovered from its ordeal and managed to drink a little milk and Daisie spread butter on its paws following the superstition that if it knew it had been adopted by a generous household, it would never stray. They laughed as they watched its anxious attempts to clean itself of the sticky mess.

*   *   *

26

On Sunday morning, while most of the inhabitants of Cwm Manachlog were preparing themselves for chapel, Tommy searched through the rubbish left from the market picking the best of it to offer to those to whom a small crack or chip was unimportant. He found a cup with only a small chip that matched the one Daisie had bought and, separating it from the rest of his treasures, he set off to find her.

The streets were full of people but the mood was completely different from the previous day. It was Sunday and best clothes were displayed. Most of the men wore three piece suits, lapels on both jackets and waistcoats. The shirt collars were wide and stiff, giving a slightly offended air to the men who had to hold their chin up to prevent their throats being cut but the sharp crease. Many wore long white scarves with either flat caps or bowler hats and watchchains and polished shoes which winked in the bright sunshine. Others wore the latest long jackets with only the top button fastened, the watch chains still visible and proudly worn, moustaches bristling on red, sweating faces.

The women all wore hats – regardless of whether they wore suits or long coats – which were works of art, decorated with feathers and ornaments that filled the brims and hid the deep crowns, each trying to outdo the rest. Their long coats were far too warm for the day, yet they were fastened as tightly as if it were winter. Beneath the outerwear, there was underwear of calico and linen and stifling corsets desperately pressing them into the approved shape.

Tommy touched his cap in a polite salute to those he recognised, but several did not respond. Tommy was not popular, considered much too "fly" for most, too ready to grab a bargain, too quick to see a way of making money, too good at getting in first! Success was not admired in Cwm Manachlog, apart from those born to expect it.

When he reached the shabby house near the stream he heard laughter and at the doorway he stopped for a moment to watch the three girls playing with a ball of wool and the now lively cat.

"God help us, Dais, what you done to its fur then?"

"Buttered it to make it stay," Megan laughed. "He was left

for dead but Daisie cuddled it and it recovered so she's going to keep it."

"I found this in Phil's junk, d'you want it to match the other one?" He offered the cup to a delighted Daisie then lay on the floor with them and admired the cat. After a while he asked, "What's the old man say about you bringing in another mouth to feed, Dais?"

"I haven't told him yet. He's still sleeping it off from yesterday, as usual. I'll wait till he wakes."

"She's calling the cat Slipper," Megan said with a chuckle. "Because she was found outside the shoe shop."

Tommy stood up and leaned over Dan, then he spoke in a strangled whisper.

"Here, Dais, I think you'd better fetch the doctor, If I'm not mistaken, he isn't going to wake. I think he's been an' gone an' died."

All Daisie could later remember about that day was Tommy holding her tight and allowing her to cry until she was exhausted. She was comforted by the feel of him, the special scent of him and by his soothing words.

Megan went to fetch the doctor who was premptory in his examination and stopped only long enough to tell her who would lay the old man out, where to find the undertaker and how to arrange for a pauper's funeral.

Gillian took her to her parents once the crying had stopped and together they had sat through the night, talking about Dan and his sad life, the impossibility of finding Daisie's mother so she could be told and the bleak months ahead.

Daisie savoured the memories of belonging to a family. Since leaving the valley and all their friends, the lack of people around her was an ache that couldn't be soothed. Her brothers, their companions, her parents' friends and the kind-hearted neighbours, had filled their small house from morning until night. Since they had moved on, with only a drunken father for company, she often lay awake dreading the time when he failed to return. Loneliness was her worst nightmare. Anything else she could cope with, but not being alone.

In the days following the death of Dan she hardly slept,

afraid to close her eyes on the familiar room, fearing intruders, who would find nothing of value but who would search for the little she had. In her solitary bed, with only the animals for company, the world seemed large and she so very small. She couldn't live alone, she would be constantly in a state of panic. But where could she go? She hugged Alex tighter and thought miserably that she had no one and no where to go. She was too frightened to cry.

The funeral was a small one with only a few of Dan's drinking companions following the coffin. Gillian, Megan and Tommy stayed with Daisie in the empty house that, with the departure of Dan, seemed more tumbled down than before. It was as if his presence had somehow hidden the squalor of the rotting walls and the sagging iron roof.

"You can't stay here, Daisie, not on your own," Megan said tearfully after the funeral party had left. "I know your dad wasn't exactly company, but it'll be worse now there's no one."

"Tell me something I don't know!" Daisie said shivering at the thought.

"Can't you find someone to take you in?"

"I'm going to stay here until I finish school at Christmas and then I'll start work proper at The Swan. Helen and Desmond Prewitt have promised me a room of my own."

"But it's months. You can't stay on," Gillian argued. "Look at it!" She waved her arms expressively. "One good storm and it'll be gone! I'll ask Mam if she knows of anyone. You could share with me but Mam has enough to do with her lodgers."

"I'd love you to share with me, but I don't think Mam would agree either," Megan said with genuine dismay.

"I'll be all right," Daisie insisted. "There's the animals, remember. I can't expect to find a room where they'll allow me to keep them. And besides, I don't earn enough to pay for a room. With what I earn at The Swan I'll manage for food as long as I can stay here. Wood is plentiful to make a fire and the stream's close by for all my needs. Alex and her puppy will look after me. They're all the company I need." she added with a bravado she didn't feel.

"There must be somewhere," Megan said.

"I don't want to go into the Home for Waifs and Strays, do I? Just shut up about it or someone will try and get me out of here into one of those places and goodness knows when I'll be able to get free of them." She glared at her friends then, her eyes narrowing to slits, warning them she was determined. "It's only a couple of months before I'm thirteen and can leave school. I'll be grown up then and able to please myself. It's only five months. If 'they' get their hands on me it'll be until I'm sixteen or even longer."

Subdued by the thought of their friend being locked away and looked after like the children they sometimes saw walking in a crocodile to and from church on Sunday, Megan and Gillian said nothing more.

"And Tommy will help," was Daisie's final word. "He said he'd keep an eye, sort out any difficulties. I'll be just fine. Take more than a few weeks on my own to frighten me." She turned away so they wouldn't see the fear in her eyes.

Daisie stayed in the house just three weeks. She grew thinner and hollow eyed as sleep evaded her and she was too unhappy to eat properly. She had a runny nose and a persistant cough and her eyes were reddened with exhaustion. She attended school less and less regularly and when the inspector came to see why she was so frequently absent he was horrified at learning how and where she lived. In a panic, Daisie ran to The Swan and pleaded with Helen and Desmond to take her in.

"I can't go into that place," she pleaded. "It's only weeks now before I can leave school, can't you let me have my room a bit early? I'll work before and after school, scrub the yard, help with the barrels." Her blue eyes were wide as she tried to persuade Helen and Desmond of her sincerity.

"Helen and I will discuss it and we'll let you know. All right?" Desmond smiled. "We'll come and see you tomorrow after school."

"No, it's all right, I'll come and see you," Daisie said in alarm. She was afraid that if they saw the shambles of a home they wouldn't think her capable of keeping a room decent.

She huried home from school the next day, took off her white, frilly apron and hung it against the door and knelt to light the fire. The place smelled of damp and rotting wood. She fed the new flames with fuel and knelt back to watch them grow. The dogs sat near looking hopefully from her to their dish and the cat purred about her knees in ecstasy. She was about to feed them when footsteps approached.

Helen Prewitt looked into the room, the bright autumn sun making her eyes slow to react. She saw the flames, then the silhouette of the girl and her pets and as the rest of the poor room came into focus her heart lurched with pity.

"Come to fetch you I have," Helen said, although that had not been her plan. "Desmond and I have a small room at the top of the house and it's yours so long as you do a few hours work each day."

"What about the dogs and Slipper the cat and the duck?" Daisie looked anxiously at Helen, afraid that the animals would make her withdraw the offer of the room.

"There's a shed at the back, they can sleep there so long as they aren't too much of a nuisance," Helen smiled.

Helen was always dressed formally. She had on a long tweed skirt and a jumper almost the colour of her iron-grey hair which she pulled back into a severe bun. At thirty-five, Daisie thought she was very old. But since Daisie had worked at The Swan she had come to recognise the kindness and surprising gentleness of the woman who, without raising her voice, could empty the bar room of anyone causing an argument, lifting them by an arm and escorting them through the door with ease. Helen was, Daisie decided, a capable woman. In the euphoria of the woman's kindness, Daisie wanted to grow to be the same.

When they reached the back door of the public house Helen told Daisy to wait while she exchanged a few words with Desmond. Daisie tied the two dogs to a fence and, carrying the anxious cat, with the duck quacking amiably behind her, she walked up and down the field while she waited to be told she could enter.

Desmond had lived in The Swan all his life. His parents

had lived there before him and his grandparents before them. It had begun as a small private house and had been enlarged when the grandparents had bought the ajoining houses. Now, a little overweight, balding and looking older than his thirty-five years, he was content. He had never wanted any other life. He was a quiet, well-spoken man who on first acquaintance appeared reserved. He nevertheless got on well with his customers, joining in with their games and accepting with his aimiable smile the regular teasing that was part of life at The Swan. He looked at Daisie now with a slight frown on his round face. After a few more whispered words with Helen he came forward and took one of the bundles that held all her worldly goods. The other square parcel she held tightly and insisted on carrying herself.

"Come on, then, let's get you settled, Daisie Clements," Desmond said and, looking doubtfully at the mewing cat, he led them up the stairs to the top of the house.

There were three rooms on the top floor, all without floor-covering and all but one completely empty. The third held a bed and a small cupboard. Daisie put her bundle on the bare mattress and uncovered it carefully.

"It's Dad's pedlar's tray," she said. "I don't want to part with it."

"Keep what you like so long as you make sure your room is always tidy and clean. I don't want your being here to make extra work for Helen. You're here to help her, right?" Desmond said. "And that cat will have to stay downstairs." He took the animal from Daisie and left Helen to sort out bedding and the few extras Daisie would need. But Slipper had other ideas. As soon as Desmond released her she was at the window of Daisie's room, her pink mouth wide in its demand to be let in. Helen looked at Daisie and laughed.

"I think you'll be easier to train than Slipper," she said sliding up the window.

That night when she undressed Daisie felt like a duchess: her own room and a full length bed with three blankets and clean calico sheets and a pillow, crisp and white and smelling of soap. It was dream. On a washstand in the corner stood a large china bowl and jug which Helen had filled so she could wash before going down to breakfast. Beside the washing bowl was the cup and saucer decorated with violets, still unused and still with Phil's kiss on the rim.

There was a rail on which to hang her clothes, empty now but one day, she promised herself, one day it would have decent dresses and a proper coat hanging there.

The kind-hearted Helen had even provided her with a small rug and a mirror. But best of all she had privacy, a door to close and a curtain to draw across the window. She shivered in her nightdress as she stood at the window and looked at the back yard of The Swan far below. Beyond, although it was too dark to see, she knew there was a field, with the stream emerging and heading for the farm, and in the distance the cottage, now empty. She might be able to see the farm where Ivor Price the milkman went twice each day with his churns.

Slipper was curled up already sleeping, her tiny mouth showing a slit of pink in the wavering light of the candle. Smiling happily, Daisie slid in beside her, the sheets cold but luxurious.

After a few moments relishing her good fortune, she rose and opened the door and drew back the curtains. She felt too cut off from everyone. With the door wide open, strengthening the feeling she was no longer alone, she slept better than she had for weeks and woke refreshed, to begin her new life.

Helen insisted Daisie went to school and Daisie found a calendar on which she marked off the days until term ended. She longed for the moment when she could say goodbye to the routine of lessons which she felt had no relevance for her. She knew what she wanted to do, work at The Swan for the rest of her life. Helen and Desmond would teach her all she needed to know.

"What's the point of swimming lessons, balanced on a chair in the classroom?" she complained to Megan and Gillian one day when rain had sent them in from the playground. "And Drill, standing in rows waving our arms about!

What use is that to anyone? Why can't they teach us book-keeping?"

"Ironing is what we've got after playtime," Gillian moaned. "I have to iron the lodgers' shirts, sheets and pillow cases for Mam, I could show the teacher more than she can teach me! It would take all day if I did it the way she showed us!"

"Then on Friday mornings there's hygiene," Megan laughed. "Who would believe it! There's teacher talking to us about washing properly and having a weekly bath. And how many of us does she think has a bathroom? I ask you. Where's the sense in it? And cleaning teeth. There's half the class never had a toothbrush in their lives!"

"If your Mam doesn't teach you then it's pointless the teachers trying to make you," Gillian said. "I know I have to look after my teeth, I want my smile to be devastating."

"Devastating, now there's a word," Megan laughed.

Daisie said nothing. She hadn't owned a toothbrush until Helen had given her one and shown her how to use it.

Daisie settled into the routine of The Swan with very little trouble and soon made herself indispensible to Helen and Desmond. They treated her more like a relation than an employee and she relaxed into the wonderful warmth of belonging.

The two dogs, the cat and the duck made the place their own and were soon accompanied by two chickens, given in exchange for a debt and which Desmond hadn't the heart to have killed, and two rabbits which rapidly became seven. Daisie was needed and had animals who needed her, she thought she could not be happier, apart from the fact that Phil ignored her completely.

Even that didn't spoil her days, she only had to be patient and wait until she grew into a woman, and her body was already showing signs of that. When Helen allowed her to serve in the bar and wear less childish clothes, then Phil would take notice, of that she was certain. She sighed with contentment as she chopped up the stale bread and threw it out for the birds waiting in the trees.

3

Helen had helped Desmond Prewitt to run The Swan for more than fifteen years. As Desmond's parents grew old she swiftly took over the day to day running of the busy place and since then there was never a moment when she wanted any other life. With a boy to help with the heavy work and having Daisie living in for the past five years, everything ran smoothly; Helen organising the days so there was never a hitch and no sign of how it was achieved.

Little had changed at The Swan except for perhaps a few fresh curtains and the replacement of the rag rugs that partly covered the floor in what they called the "select" bar. This was a small room where businessmen could meet their clients and discuss their arrangements in comparative peace. Mr Huntley-Davies met prospective house-buyers there, Peter Griffith, who owned the shoe shop, called in occasionally for a quiet drink. There was a hush about the room that Helen found less pleasant than the big room. The prices were higher but they made little money there.

The larger, more popular bar room was unchanged. Its slate floors and the battered tables, benches and chairs had been there since Desmond's grandparents owned the place. The friendly room had seen the male population celebrating all the important events in the town, both happy and sad. Funerals and weddings had been discussed, racing results mourned over and the clacking of dominoes was as much a part of the scene as the crackling of the fire and the ticking of the big clock. The room had memories. The air rang with the sound of voices every Thursday evening as the Male Voice Choir practised their award-winning melodies. If the town has a heart, Helen thought, it's here, not in the select but in the big bar of The Swan.

In a sentimental mood, she stopped and looked around the empty bar room, redolent with the scent of pipe and tobacco smoke and the wood-smoke of a thousand fires. In the early morning when she first entered she enjoyed the sense of friendliness and laughter that seemed always to linger in the still air. If anyone asked if I were happy, she thought with a contented smile, I would have to say yes, utterly.

She bent down to begin clearing the ash-trays from the wooden tables, emptying the debris into a small galvanised bucket. She was not a large woman but there was a strength in her easily overlooked by those who did not know her well. Working from early morning until long after the pub closed its doors was a hard life, yet her temperament never changed throughout the day. At eleven o'clock at night she appeared as calm and energetic, as ready for a joke or a tale of woe, as at eleven in the morning. She knew she could not be called pretty, in fact with her angular features, the rather non-descript grey-green eyes, small in the rather heavy face, and the thick short hair she was almost manly. Loved for my personality rather than my fragile glamour, she used to joke to Desmond. He always assured her that to him she would always be his capable and beautiful love.

She turned to greet Daisie whose footsteps she had heard coming down the stairs. The girl's face and figure were filled out after five years' living at The Swan. Her complexion was creamy and with the rich red hair falling in curls around her shoulders she attracted many an eye. Helen felt proud of the girl as if she had created her from the sad little waif who had come to help after Dan Clement's death. At the age of seventeen, Daisie Clements was becoming a real beauty.

Daisie's appearance in the bar had increased the takings at The Swan considerably. Her quick wit and often down-right rudeness had customers laughing and coming back for more. The worse the insults she threw at the men the more they enjoyed it. She made even the most elderly, defeated, tired old man feel "a bit of a lad" by picking him out for special mention. The younger men all invited her out, but in vain. In spite of her sense of fun and lively manner Daisie refused them all. She was waiting for Phil Johnson to notice her.

"Morning, Daisie love. Ready for the grand clean up? Never changes, does it? Every morning we clear up the dregs of last night then open the doors so they can come and mess it up again." Daisie smiled widely in response to Helen's greeting. "Looking pleased with yourself. Got off with one of the customers, did you? See to the fires and the floors then you can get out this morning if you want to. Do you good to get out and do a bit of flirting, it's about time."

"No, it's all right, Helen, I'll go to the market and fetch the vegetables and what fruit I can find. Even in the cold month of January there's usually something worth having."

"You want to go to the market instead of sending the boy? Again? Oh, I see, it's Phil Johnson is it?" Helen teased gently.

"Of course not. Too old by far he is and set on that barmaid from the Horse and Hounds!"

Helen saw from the blush of colour rising from Daisie's throat that her teasing had hit the mark. "Go on then, get the fires lit and you can go. It's bitter cold so we'd better get this one blazing early or the room'll be like a morgue and the market crowd will be in before we know where we are." She watched as Daisie tied a coarse sacking apron around her slim hips, tightening the strings, emphasising her trim waist and allowing her rapidly developing breasts to swell above it. Daisie was growing up fast.

"Talking about Phil Johnson, we could do with some fresh plates. See what he's got for me, will you? You can buy if you think the price is right. Plain white is best, saves trying to match the ones we break." She stole a glance at Daisie and held back a chuckle. Oh, what it is to be young and in love, waiting for every glance, arranging meetings and pretending they are accidental, reliving every word and gesture, lying in bed unable to sleep, dreaming of what "he" will say when they eventually find themselves alone.

The clock struck seven, time to go and wake Desmond.

She always allowed him an extra hour in the morning as he stayed up at night to finish the glasses, empty the till, "out" the fires and lock up. Yes, she sighed as she placed the rubbish where Daisie could throw it onto the back of the fire as soon as it was blazing, life was good and she was one of the fortunate ones.

"The money for the shopping is on the counter, love," she called as she went through the door to the stairs. "But we'll have breakfast first, mind. You can't go out without something warm inside you."

"Thanks, Helen, I won't be long finishing this."

"And put on your scarf and heavy coat, mind, it's freezing out there."

Helen went up the stairs swiftly, it was an ingrained habit to run from room to room along the chilly passages with the few fires becoming oases of comfort. In the winter mornings the whole house was cold until the fires were going. She opened the bedroom door and leaned over the sleeping form. She always relished this moment, watching Desmond in sleep. His brown hair was peppered with white and had already retreated well back on his head. This year he would be forty and she was planning a very special surprise.

She had thought for a long time about the most exciting way to mark his birthday but had discussed it with no one; besides the few necessary to its purchase, not a single person even knew she was thinking of buying him anything. She wanted it to be a real surprise. She sat and imagined his face when he saw it and was bursting with the need to tell someone, or even hint to Desmond that there was something on its way for him, but she held back. It would be more fun if he suspected nothing.

She touched his forehead with her cool hand and waited as his brown eyes opened, then watched them half close with the smile he always gave her. She bent lower and kissed his mouth.

"Another wonderful day, my darling," she said softly.

Daisie cleared the breakfast table, washed the dishes, then

set off for the market. She carried two baskets, one on each arm, and she sang as she walked, her long red hair waving about in the cold wind. The scarf Helen had insisted on was hanging out of a pocket. She was vain about her hair which had curled as she matured and with regular attention shone like well polished copper. Even on a morning as cold as this one she didn't like covering it.

There were already a large number of people in the street, stall-holders were still arriving, some on carts pulled by ponies and horses and even one recalcitrant donkey, others pushing their produce on hand-carts, sweating as they forced their way to where the Toby was allocating spaces, not wanting to be among the last. The shouting, the bargaining and enthusiastic claims of the sellers were already vieing with each other and between the china stall and a newcomer trying to sell thick cups and saucers labelled Frentonbury Hotel, there were ructions. The Toby was shouting for the man to shift himself, Phil was threatening to smash the discarded hotelware and Tommy was quietly tilting the man's display so the china was wavering on the edge of collapse.

As Daisie watched, preparing to enjoy the fun of a fight, she saw what was about to happen to the incomer's china. She saw Tommy Thomas dart away as the Toby marched around the back of the pile. She ran to help as the china swayed more and more precariously and the crowd echoed her sigh of relief as they succeeded in preventing its fall.

"What you doing that for, Daisie?" Phil demanded. "Interloper he is and belongs at the furthest end, not here, next to my quality lines."

"Poor dab, he's entitled to earn a crust, Phil," she retorted and received a grateful look from the incomer, a poorly dressed man of about fifty.

She helped the man to re-pack his china and watched him walk off following the Toby to his allotted position, amid the displays of second-hand jumble. He turned and waved his thanks and she smiled. At least he had made Phil notice her.

"We need some china for The Swan," she said when there

was a lull in Phil's serving. "None of your rubbish, mind. And no fancy prices, either."

"Come up here and look for yourself," Phil invited, offering her his hand. "See what you want and we'll discuss the price."

"Watch him, Dais," Tommy called. "He offers reductions for kisses and favours."

Phil growled good naturedly for Tommy to get on with his work and began lifting plates from boxes for Daisie to examine. "If it's white you want I can give you twenty of each size for a good price, especially if you'll promise a kiss," he said. "Tommy's right, I'm a fool to myself when a pretty girl is concerned. You're growing into quite a beauty, young Daisie."

Laughing, enjoying the flirting that was making her breathless, they discussed prices and finally agreed. "You'll have to deliver them today, mind," Daisie said as Phil helped her down from his platform. "So don't sell them all if you get the chance, then expect us to wait until next week."

She was glowing with excitement as she set about finishing her shopping. If only there was someone to tell of the exciting encounter. Gillian rarely came to the market these days, she and that Waldo Griffiths from the shoe shop were courting steady and she no longer had much time for her friends. Megan might come, her mother usually gave her the weekend shopping list, but that would be much later.

There was still the meat to buy and she looked at her baskets almost filled with vegetables and the seville oranges she had bought cheaply to make marmalade. Shuffling the bags around to make the baskets look full, she went back to The Swan. She made the excuse that she couldn't carry any more and after unpacking what she had bought set off again for the noisy, bustling street.

The meat for pies and bones for soup plus the off-cuts and lights she scrounged to feed the dogs and cat filled the baskets again and she stood looking for Megan. She chose her position with care. While looking down the street past the cavalcade of shoppers she could see the corner around which Megan might appear and at the same time she could see Phil. He could also see her.

A newspaper-seller walked along the road, avoiding carts and the occasional car with a nonchalance that was almost suicidal. "Death at the North Pole," he was shouting. "Scott and the rest all dead." His words penetrated the noise of the crowd and there was a momentary hush of shock and regret.

Daisie felt in her pocket for a penny and handed it to the man. Beside her several others swooped towards her to do the same. So anxious were they to read about the death of one of Britain's heros, she was pushed from the kerb and would have fallen if someone hadn't grasped her waist firmly and held her.

"Worse than a rugby scrum, isn't it, Daisie," Phil said, still holding her. "Why do they all have to push and shove as if there isn't a minute to lose?"

"Thanks," she said. "I'd have been killed in the rush if you hadn't held me back. But," she added with a saucy grin, "you can let go now."

Phil didn't want to release her, her small waist with the swell of her burgeoning figure above it was deliciously tempting. While he had been seeing her every week he had not noticed how she had changed from a thin little ragamuffin into a desirable young woman. He gave her a final squeeze, wondering if she was yet old enough and, turning her around to smile into her eyes said, "I'll get you another paper, the mad lot have crumpled yours." He went to where a crowd had gathered around the seller and returned with a fresh copy. "Sure you aren't hurt?" he asked, his eyes bright with admiration.

"I'd best get back with this meat or Helen will be wondering where I am." She moved away from him and, after one final glance, she walked slowly back to The Swan. His attentions had changed her. She just knew she looked different. A bubble of excitement grew in her throat, life was beginning to be fun.

What a pity there was no one to tell. She wished it was an afternoon when she was free so she could wander along the stream and day-dream about him, or better still go again to

41

the market with the excuse of looking for Megan. Helen, not privy to all her hopes and dreams, gave her the task of boiling and cutting up the fruit ready for the marmalade instead.

The steady stream of customers demanding drink and food swelled towards midday. Dicky Daniels the green-grocer ran in, ordered and drank two pints, and ran out again, having left Little Dicky in charge of his stall. Tommy came in and drank, pretending to be old enough. Desmond served him and pretended to believe him. Billie Beynon the butcher stayed a while, leaving his wife to serve the lunchtime straggle. Daisie, Helen and Desmond were kept busy supplying their needs. Ethel Trip, the wife of the coalman, called in to borrow a loaf and stayed to serve for more than an hour.

Matt Prosser had to be wheeled home in the drunks barrow that stood in readiness outside the pub's back door, the vehicle in which Daisie's father had often ended his day.

Daisie kept watching the door in the hope of seeing Phil although she knew it was unlikely, even after the interest he had shown that morning. Tommy was his delivery boy and it would be he who came with the boxes of china.

"Come on, Daisie, I'm not invisible, am I?" a fat man complained, waving his empty glass.

"No, more's the pity, what an improvement on the scenery that would be if you disappeared, Henry Bishop!" Daisie snapped, "And The Swan would be more peaceful, too, without you bellyaching all the time."

Billie Beynon, in the straw hat and white-and-blue-striped overall of a butcher laughed and banged his glass on the counter. "Damn me if I don't complain to your boss about you," he said.

"Don't threaten me, Billie the Butcher. Bigger than me you might be but it's mostly gristle, not much brain!" The crowd laughed and Billie joined in.

"What are you laughing at Mick-the-post? We all know where your brains are!"

As Daisie was handing Billie his foaming glass the door opened and Phil Johnson walked in, struggling with a card-board box. Daisie spilled some of Billie's ale and he was

42

about to complain but stopped when he saw how Daisie was staring.

"Where d'you want this, Mrs Prewitt?" Phil asked. "There's another on the cart outside. Drives a hard bargain does your little girl. Nearly bankcrupted me this morning, mind! Where is she, then? Promised to draw me a pint with her own fair hands she did." He stood for a moment and looked at her and to Daisie it seemed as if the whole world was staring at her, not just one pair of the palest blue eyes.

She no longer felt able to torment the customers. Phil's presence enfeebled her wit and weakened her voice to a murmur. The room took on a sombre silence as she efficiently attended to the men's requests. He stayed for an hour before telling them he had to get back to help Tommy with the final flourish of business. "Can't trust that Tommy Thomas for long," he said to Desmond and Helen. "Good worker is Tommy, mind, but his hands get busy in the till give him half a chance." He walked over to the bar where Daisie was washing glasses and whispered, "What time d'you finish, Daisie? Any chance of meeting up later for a chat?"

"Hardly. I don't stop until the place closes and that's gone eleven on market day."

"Tomorrow, then. I'll meet you where the stream comes out beyond the street. Oh no," he said, before she could answer, "not Sunday, unless it's early?"

"I'll be taking the dogs for a walk about nine," she said.

"Bring dogs, cats, anything you like as long as you come. Thrilling you are, Daisie Clements. Thrilling."

"He's very nice but a bit old for you, love," Helen said when Phil had gone. "Sorry, but I couldn't help over-hearing. Seventeen you are and him at least twenty-five."

"What does age matter?" Daisie coloured up, angry that her meeting with Phil after all the long waiting and dreaming should be spoilt by someone as old as Helen knowing. What could she know about love?

"Up to you, of course, but be careful, won't you?"

"Only taking the dogs for a walk!" Daisie snapped. Then, as Helen nodded and left the room she felt mean. Helen was only doing what a mother would, protecting her and caring.

She washed the bar top and thought about how Helen had changed her life. From the ragged, ill-fed child, Helen had coaxed her to take more care of herself, had bought her the first decent clothes she had ever owned and had given her pride and confidence. Everything she was, everything she owned, she owed to Helen Prewitt. Throwing the cloth aside she ran after and hugged her. "Sorry, Helen. I was a pig. I know it's because you care."

"I don't want you to make the usual mistake, love. Phil is a grown man and skilled at loving. You know what can happen, I've explained as best as I can. I want you to be careful and make sure you don't end up unhappy and with a child in tow to hold you back. You can do better than Phil." She pushed Daisie's thick red hair back from her face and smiled affectionately. "Lovely you are, you can have the pick of the bunch when you're a bit older."

There was ice in the wind that blew across the fields, the mountains in the distance were shrouded in a blue mist that darkened as she watched. A storm was on its way and would probably bring snow to blanket the fields before the day was out. Against the metalic blue-grey of the clouds the roofs of the houses in Cwm Manachlog seemed to have changed colour, and Daisie always associated that with the approach of snow.

The dogs ran on ahead of her, sniffing the ground, their tails wagging in unison as if the same scents were discovered at the same time. There were three of them now, the third was a stray that Tommy Thomas had brought to The Swan, in need of love and care. Daisie tightened the thick coat that had once belonged to Helen around her shivering body and wished for once that she had put on a scarf. The cold air hurt her forehead and set her scalp tingling unpleasantly. Even the anticipation of seeing Phil and talking to him alone for the first time wasn't enough to make her forget the cold.

He was standing near the edge of the stream, throwing

small sticks into its slowly moving water. He looked different without the clothes he wore for the stall. Not ordinary, she mused, but more attainable somehow in his navy suit, long overcoat and long white scarf. She felt childhood slipping from her like cold water flowing down the waterfall further along the stream.

He didn't hear her coming and only stepped back when the dogs burst past him. As she watched him he sensed her presence and looked up to smile and offer his hand. He was tall, surprisingly fair and, even dressed against the weather, revealed an elegance in the way that he stood and moved that seemed out of place in a man who worked the markets for a living. Most of the stall-holders were poorly dressed, whether from necessity or to invite sympathy, and were, in Daisie's opinion, very ordinary. Phil was different from any one else she had known.

The shyness she felt as they met was partly due to Helen's warnings and she was stilted in her replies when he spoke, but after only a few moments the strangeness faded and they were talking non stop about everyone and everything. He made her laugh and think and most of all he made her feel like a beautiful woman.

"We must do this again, Daisie," he said when they returned to the start of their walk. "Soon," he added softly. In a state of euphoria Daisie went back to The Swan and didn't notice the first flakes of snow touching her face. She was glowing and thought she would never be cold again.

The Swan closed on Sundays together with all the other public houses in Wales, but it was far from an idle day. The routine cleaning there wasn't time for on weekdays was done. Cooking for themselves and making pies ready for Monday was important or the meat bought on Saturday would go off, even in the coldest days of winter. She had finished most of her chores by three o'clock and, after feeding and cleaning the animals, Helen said she could go and meet her friends. So at six o'clock she went out again, this time to the church.

Megan attended regularly and would be sure to be coming out of the evening service. The church was a little way out of town along a country lane with hedges of hawthorn, blackthorn and holly on either side. The evening was already dark. Swirling snow was blinding her, distorting her sense of direction and already covering the edges of the grass verge, obliterating familiar signs. She began to wonder if she had lost her way as the road went on without a sight or sound of the grey stone building. But the sound of singing led her to the gate and she trampled the snow that hid the grass with the enjoyment of a child, her boots leaving huge impressions more like a giant than a young woman.

The singing ceased and as she reached the porch the doors opened, spilling light onto the shining snow. A chattering group emerged, each shaking the hand of the vicar in his white surplus made yellow by the light and the stark white of the snow. She called when she saw Megan huddled in her brown cloak and then shouted again when she recognised Gillian walking beside her.

As usual, Gillian was fashionably attired and apparently unaware of the weather. She wore a long skirt with frills of artificial flowers at the hem, a white lacy edged blouse and a velvet-trimmed jacket, over which she wore a cloak, the hood of which was large enough to cover her fussily ornamented hat. She stopped in the doorway to scoop the cloak around her, oblivious to the complaints of the people she held back. Gillian always made an entrance and an exit, Daisie thought with a chuckle. And Gillian, she decided, would never dress "sensible"!

"Daisie!" Gillian shouted as she emerged from the ancient door. "Waldo Griffiths and me, we're getting married!"

Megan and Daisie pushed their way back into the porch defying the complaints of those trying to get out. A tall, rather austere young man saw their difficulty and moved easily through the crowd to assist. He held back the protesting people with a raised arm and allowed the three girls to get safely inside. His parents waited for him beyond the porch but he stood for a moment and watched. Megan pulled her coat more tightly around her and turn slowly in his direction, her mouth moving in shy words of thanks. Then she was swept into the arms of Gillian and Daisie to share a gaggle of whispered confidences and he gave a half smile before following the last of the worshipers through the door into the spinning snow.

The vicar nodded to them as he left, after genuflecting towards the altar. The great door closed, blocking the view of the darkness and, although the church was hardly warmer than outside, they were cheered by the impression of comfort.

"Who is that man?" Megan asked. "The tall one who helped us push our way back inside?"

"Never seen him before that I can remember," Daisie frowned. "Boot-faced and haughty he looked, you'd have a job to get a laugh out of him."

"You know him, Daisie," Gillian said impatiently, she wanted to begin talking about herself and Waldo. "That's Arthur Huntley-Davies. They live up on Pleasant View. Pots of money they've got. His father is an estate manager and seller of houses and all that stuff." Irritation growing she added, "You do remember him."

"So it is! Fancy him getting so tall." Megan continued to stare at the closed door. "Where's he been all this time?"

"Please listen to me," Gillian groaned.

"Away at school," Daisie said to Megan.

"Oh. No wonder we haven't seen him."

Daisie touched Megan's arm and grinned. "Remember how we used to rag him when he walked past, all swanky, dressed up like a sailor boy?"

"For goodness sake!" Gillian groaned. "Can't we forget Arthur Huntley-Davies and his fancy clothes? I want to tell you about me and Waldo!"

"Tell us all about it, Gillian," Megan begged, dragging her eyes from the door. "How did he propose?"

Deflated by having her own news so firmly surpassed by Gillian's engagement, Daisie found it difficult to enthuse, but with Megan now a willing listener and happily feeding her with questions to illicit more and more details, Gillian didn't notice.

The three friends huddled together in the hollow-sounding

church and discussed their thoughts for the future. Daisie waited for a lull and then said as casually as she could, "I went out with Phil Johnson this morning. Walked the dogs along the stream we did."

"You what!" It was Gillian's turn to be surprised.

Daisie smiled at her friend's reaction. "*And* we're meeting again next week. And besides, I'll see him at the market. I go regular now. Helen says I do much better than the boy."

"I'm freezing. Come back to the house where we can talk," Gillian suggested. "Mam and Dad won't mind."

So, traipsing through the deep snow in a world so silent and empty they could have been the only inhabitants, they walked along the lane and sat in Gillian's parlour and talked about boys.

Megan was the quiet one. She allowed the chatter to go on around her, smiling occasionally, nodding her head when it was expected. She was thinking about Arthur Huntley-Davies. It was nice to dream, even someone like her had to play "let's pretend" now and then. Pretend was all it would be, she knew that. She was never noticed by girls let alone boys, and at the tender age of seventeen accepted that she would die an old maid.

"I don't want to get married," she said when there was a brief lull in the excited exchange of news. She said the words with the conviction of regular use, although she knew Gillian and Daisie guessed her reason for saying them. Best to pretend you don't want what you know you'll never have.

"I'd say yes to Phil Johnson tomorrow if he asked," Daisie sighed.

One day when snow again made the town a patchwork of white and grey, the three friends were in a cafe sipping tea when Arthur Huntley-Davies came in. He sat at a table near them and every time Daisie turned her head he was staring at them, but, she realised quickly, he was staring not at her or the attractive Gillian, but at Megan.

"He's watching you, Megan," she whispered.

Megan shook her head. With sad honesty she whispered

back, "Not me, Daisie. How could he notice me with Gillian and you beside me?"

Arthur Huntley-Davies was facinated by the quiet girl talking to her strikingly lovely friends. Her gentleness and submisive manner warmed him. What a charming companion she would make. Such a change from the rather brash behaviour of some of the girls his mother paraded before him in a constant stream.

He had noticed her in church and by surreptitious questioning had learned that she worked in a small office dealing with the rents of local houses. A cautious man, Arthur decided to watch her for a while before making any approach. The last thing he wanted was a troublesome woman wailing about his abandonment of her if it didn't work out after a few weeks of courtship.

Unaware that his attention was firmly on her, Megan began to dream of a marriage to a man like Arthur, a strong important man capable of sheltering her from everything unpleasant and making her feel safe. It was only a dream, not something she could ever imagine in real life.

In church she watched him and when she dared, offered a hesitant smile, unaware that the shy and friendly greeting turned his heart over.

Arthur waited for Sundays with surprising pleasure, dreaming of holding her hand and kissing her soft mouth. She was such a gentle girl and would certainly make him a loving wife, he was sure of it.

Daisie watched the growing attraction with dismay and a sense of foreboding.

4

It was Desmond Prewitt's fortieth birthday on 29th of February. So, as 1913 was not a leap year, Helen arranged his surprise for the 28th. She didn't even take Daisie or Ethel Trip into her confidence, making all the preparations on her own. She had to tell Tommy, of course, he was the one who had helped arrange the surprise.

"Are you sure it will be here first thing in the morning?" she asked as he showed her the illustration for the third time. "And you're certain he'll be able to drive it without any trouble?"

"Simple as falling out of bed," he assured her. "These new motor cars are a damned sight more controllable than horses. Ever thought how puny we are compared to a horse? If he doesn't want to stop all we can do is pull on the poor thing's mouth and shout at him. A mechanical thing is different. Tell it what to do and it does it without argument."

"You're sure he'll manage it?"

"I learnt in half an hour while that Huntley-Davies was having a fitting for a new suit," Tommy bragged. "I drove it round the lane to the church and back without him even knowing."

"The brakes, they're reliable?"

"They can be a bit slow to stop sometimes, mind, bit like a horse there. It's heavy, see, and you can't expect it to stop within inches, doesn't make sense to expect that. All you have to do is shut your eyes and hope when there's something in the way. Oh, and there's a wooden chock to put under the wheels when you stop on a hill, just in case, like."

"Sounds dangerous to me. And difficult to learn."

"Nonsense. Just take the brake off, start the engine and off you go. Er, no . . . the engine first, specially if it's on a hill." He grinned to show he was joking, his eye winking furiously as he watched her anxious face. "Honest, Mrs Prewitt, he'll have it licked in five minutes, a smart man like your husband, lucky bloke that he is. Why can't I find a wealthy woman to buy me a car? Clever beyond, that Desmond Prewitt. The most I get out of a girl is a promise, and those never kept."

"Go on, Tommy, I bet you could afford a car if you wanted one badly enough. You've been making money and stacking it away ever since you could walk."

"It's true I'm not short, but it's not for wasting on luxuries. Not yet. It's to make more, Mrs Prewitt, I'm not where I want to be yet. I'll be rich one day, mind. Rich enough to buy a house up on Pleasant View *and* make everyone up there sit up and take notice, you just wait."

"I believe you," Helen laughed. "Meanwhile, when do I pay the remainder of the money? I'll need time to get to the bank without Desmond wondering where I'm going."

"Why not give me a cheque? I'll take it along when I pick up the car for you."

"No, I don't like the idea of a cheque."

"Why ever not? Modern that is, paying by cheque. All the nobs do it."

"No, I'll get the money and give it to you, all right?"

"All right by me, I just thought a cheque would be simpler. Having your hair marcelled for the party this afternoon, aren't you? Do it then, I'll go round straight away and settle it all. But next week or the end of the month would do, good name you've got, Mrs Prewitt."

Helen sat after he'd gone, the final "Mrs Prewitt" lingering on the air. She hoped she was doing the right thing, parting with all her savings. It was her security. A woman needed that today. If she and Desmond ever separated it would be a disaster to be without money. But why should they part? Life was good and they were as content now as the day they had first decided to make the relationship permanent. She went into the kitchen and gave a box of balloons to the boy to blow up. Time to start decorating the bar.

Thursday, the day before the party, was a day Daisie had arranged to meet Phil. He had no market on that day and once the lunchtime customers had departed and the kitchen cleared ready for the evening, Daisie was free for a couple of hours.

On this Thursday she was feeling a little apprehensive about seeing Phil. She was as enamoured of him as ever but he was pushing her to do more than kiss and his urgency frightened her. What frightened her more was her willingness to surrender. The fear of having a child held her back. She and Helen had discussed what happened between lovers and Daisie knew that if the dreaded situation arose and she and Phil made a baby, her life would be ruined. Life in the derelict house with a drunken and defeated father was still a clear memory, and Daisie was determined that she wouldn't risk losing the comfort and prestige of her life at The Swan, even for Phil.

He might marry her, but she was shrewd enough to guess that he might not, and she could never face a return to a life alone and shunned by everyone. She would try to keep that thought uppermost in her mind, refuse to succumb to the temptations of the flesh, as the vicar called them. Then a picture of Phil came into her mind, pale blue eyes admiring her and revealing his need of her. Thrilling, he called her. Phil, so passionate and so beautiful, and she doubted if she were strong enough to think of anything but him once she was in his arms.

February was a wet month, February-fill-dyke her mother used to call it, with constant rain and the torrents of melted snow pouring down from the mountains and making a river of the gentle stream. But now the weather had changed, the day was dry, the ground hard with frost, and a wind blew across the fields from the distant sea, lifting over the hills and bringing air with an edge like a knife.

Phil was waiting for her at the usual place on the bank of the stream, watching its muddy turbulent passage. He smiled a greeting and she ran to him, impatient to be in his arms.

He kissed her and pressed her close, then stroked her long red hair with gentle hands.

"Oh, Daisie, you're beautiful! It seems an age since last week. Can't you stay longer this time? An hour once a week isn't enough of you. I'll never have enough of you, thrilling you are," he whispered.

Was he walking faster than usual and with more purpose? She looked up at him and saw that the smile had stiffened, then he looked down at her face and relaxed.

"It's bitter cold," he said. "Let's go somewhere where there's a bit of shelter."

She realised quickly that his intention was to go to her old home. He didn't know how she had lived before coming to The Swan? Few people did and those who had known her as the ragged girl with the drunken father had long forgotten.

The place was in a far worse state than she remembered, and memories flooded over her and she felt sick with the horror of it. The roof sagged over half of what had once been her living room but remarkably, her bed was still there, the springs covered in rust, mattress stained with damp and half covered by dead leaves that had blown in through the sagging door that would no longer shut, and the whole thing decorated with mould. Surely he didn't expect her to –

"I'll take my coat off and we'll share it's warmth," Phil said, easing the thick overcoat from his shoulders. "That way we'll get the benefit of two bodies."

She was tense and anxious, afraid of where this would lead, thinking of the terrifying prospect of having to return to this, her only home, if she had to leave The Swan in disgrace. Phil had relaxed and seemed the same as always, talking to her about his customers and making her laugh, doing no more than place an arm around her shoulder and hold her close to him. The dampness of the bed seeped through the coat and their warmth released sour smells.

Soon the surroundings no longer mattered. She was alone with Phil and they both had loving on their minds. She felt his hands caressing her and easing the clothes from her warm body. His lips touched her throat and she was on fire, unaware of the cold, no longer caring about the awfulness of the situation, conscious more and more of his nearness.

He kissed her suddenly and urgently on her lips and her insides melted. She was soon lost in the joy of him. The consequences no longer of importance, all she wanted was for him to continue to do these wonderful and previously unimagined things to her.

As he eased the rest of her clothes away from and stared down at her full blown womanliness he gave a shuddering sigh that brought desire flooding to empty her mind of every vestige of worry. She encouraged him with her eager arms as he pressed his warm body against hers. The filthy hovel became a summer palace, the sound of the stream a melody, her heart was filled with utter bliss. This was such enchantment it couldn't be wrong.

He eased himself away from her. Was it minutes later or hours? She didn't know and didn't care. But when they had separated, her body slowly returning to earth, she knew that no matter what happened in the future they now belonged together. For always.

The euphoria faded as suddenly as Phil's kiss had begun it. He stood up and began to pull the coat from under her, smiling, kissing her occasionally but determinedly planning to leave.

"Come on, Daisie, love, time we left. Don't want anyone to see us, do we?"

"But, why not?" Alarm returned and there was a buzzing of danger inside her head that was still woolly from loving.

"Don't want people to talk, do we?"

"Why not? I don't understand? You and me, we're – "
She was about to say together now, but a glance at his face, pale in the semi-dark of the old room, stopped her. The loving expression had gone. In its place was an impatience to be gone. She became frighteningly aware once more of the cold.

"Hurry now, people will be walking back from the shops about now, getting dark, too."

"I'll be a moment," she said in a surprisingly calm voice.

"You go on and I'll tidy myself up." The relief on his face almost made her choke on the words, but she managed to add, "You haven't got a comb have you?"

He handed her one, then, with a final kiss on her flushed cheek, he left her. It was as if he had taken all her warmth with him and her body, hot from the exertions of the previous moments, shivered in the cold air. She fell back on the foul-smelling bed and stared up at the cobwebed ceiling. What had she done?

Sick with fear, trembling with the emotions of the past minutes, she rose and straightened her clothes. She was aching and unclean. And worse, Helen would only have to look at her to know. She had to hurry, she'd need a wash before going down to the bar.

It was choir practice tonight. After the rehearsal in the chapel room the men would fill the bar and sing some more. Many of the locals came to hear them. It was one of their busiest nights. Perhaps she'd need to do more food. She hoped Desmond had tapped the new barrel. Thoughts spun around as she tried to think of anything except what had happened. She looked around at the once familiar room and shivered. What she had just done might sent her back to a place as awful as this. She could see herself bringing up a child in circumstances worse than those she had experienced, and all for a few beautiful moments.

The path home was deserted. It wasn't the weather to entice people out without purpose. Evening had moved in early, bringing an icy mist that covered the mountains and changed the water in the stream to a dark grey line, dissolving the grasses into strange shapes.

She still had an hour before starting work in the kitchen. She slipped in without Helen hearing her and ran up the stairs. Her legs felt leaden and she was followed by the dank, earthy smell of that awful place.

Easing the clothes from her aching body she washed herself in cold water in the icy room before dressing in fresh clothes. Blue with the cold she went down stairs and began cutting bread into slices, cubing the cheese and slicing the onions to soak in vinegar. On the side tables were dishes and plates of food ready for the following day's party. Today the fare was ordinary, tomorrow would be different. She didn't want to think about tomorrow. How many tomorrows before she had to face the consequences of today?

Tommy went to the "Cycle and Motor Stores" and handed the owner the money for Desmond's new car.

"You'll find it all there, Mr Jenkins," Tommy said, thumbing the large white five pound notes. "Less my commission, of course." He patted his pocket. It wasn't as if he'd diddled Helen Prewitt, she wouldn't have asked and he had, discount for cash he had told Jink Jenkins, a phrase he had heard somewhere and remembered.

"Sorry an' all, boy, but the car isn't ready like," Jinks said sorrowfully. "It won't be here for another few weeks."

"What? Mrs Prewitt'll kill me! Why isn't it here? You promised!"

"So I did and the traders promised me, but the fact is there won't be a delivery for a couple of weeks, sorry to my heart I am to disapoint the lady but there's nothing I can do."

Tommy snatched the money back from the man and hurried out. What could he do now? The party was on for tomorrow and Helen planned to have the car delivered in the middle of it. Damn it all, why weren't people reliable? He went to the bank and put the money in his account, arranging for interest to be paid on it and went to tell Helen Prewitt.

"He's awful sorry, Mrs Prewitt, but he's been let down. He'll get it, but there'll be a delay." He looked guiltily at Helen's sad face, then offered, "I know! I know what you can do!" He smiled as he tried to think of a way to console her. "You can delay the party and say nothing. He doesn't know about the car, does he? Then in a couple of weeks we can surprise him just like you planned. The money's paid, there's nothing for you to do except wait. Clever woman you are, Mrs Prewitt, keeping it as a surprise, like. Must have known things might not work out as planned. Damn me, I could murder that Jink Jenkins for doing this to you. Promised faithful he did, mind."

Helen's mouth had been opening and closing trying to get a word in. When Tommy finally stopped talking she only nodded. "Let me know as soon as you have a date, will you?" She walked away feeling as breathless as Tommy should have been.

It was disappointing but Tommy was right, she had only to wait. Everything was delayed that was all and a couple of weeks would soon pass.

Tommy Thomas was up bright and early the following morning. He went to see the people who were selling the stock of a small book and stationery shop whose owner had met hard times. He had been asked to pass the news on to Matt Prosser. Although it was not his usual line, Tommy knew he would find customers. Everyone needed stationery and, even if it took a while to move, he wouldn't lose.

He used a shed on the road to Brynteg as a store room and soon filled it with the boxes of luggage labels, envelopes and writing pads and all the hundred and one items the shop had once sold. The books he didn't want. Those he bought and passed on to Matt Prosser leaving himself a margin of profit.

"Just to cover the cost of transporting it," he explained. Matt, too fuddled with drink to fully understand, thanked him and piled up the books in his porch and tried to wake himself sufficiently to get to his stall. His wife had gone to market having failed to rouse him and was awaiting his arrival with a glowering expression that didn't bode well for the weekend.

Tommy smiled and offered sympathy on Matt's poorly head. He would made a good few pounds out of this transaction and no one would know how he had cheated Matt Prosser to do it.

Before The Swan opened its doors that Saturday morning, Tommy called and asked to speak to Daisie. "Come to ask for some help I have," he announced, taking the glass of beer Daisie drew for him. "Can you help next Wednesday at the market over in Melinbanc? I've got the chance of a load of bedding and such very cheap. If I can get rid of most of it on Wednesday at Melinbanc then I can sell off any that's left here next Saturday."

"I've never served on a stall, Tommy. I wouldn't be able to shout like you and Phil do. I won't have the nerve!"

"Course you would, Dais. Take to it like a baby takes to milk you will. Besides, someone as gorgeous as you will bring the customers flocking to the stall. Go on, Dais, say you will." He stared at her, red hair standing untidily on end, his weak left eye winking encouragement.

"All right, but only if Helen agrees." She liked the idea of learning to deal with market customers. After all, if she and Phil were to marry, she'd have to help him, wouldn't she?

Wednesday was early closing in Cwm Manachlog and Helen gave Daisie the day off. She caught the bus at the end of the road and half an hour later was standing near the area put aside for the market in the small town of Melinbanc.

Tommy Thomas was already there and in charge of a heavily laden cart. The horse was being led off by an ostler from the local inn and Tommy was arguing about the position he had found for himself.

"Paid for this spot I have, you ask the Toby," He was shouting. "Plenty of space for you without you wanting me to shift to the far end. Piddling little market this is anyway. Doing you a favour I am, coming here with quality goods like I carry."

"Whatever is the matter, Tommy?" Daisie asked, standing between the two men who were already dropping into the stance of those about to fight.

"Watched me he did, watched me unharness the horse and start to shape up my display. *Then* he tells me I can't stand here!"

"You did get permission from the Toby?" Daisie asked suspiciously.

"Damn me of course I did. Two stalls I've got and all arranged proper."

Daisie turned to the protestor and shrugged prettily. "Sorry, but it seems you were mistaken."

Grumbling in a low voice and turning back occasionally to glare at a now smiling Tommy, the man lumbered off.

"Now that's settled, hold on here for a mo while I go and sort out the payment for the horse and get my other stall underway will you, Dais?" Without waiting for her agreement he ran off whistling happily.

Daisie followed him and saw that the other stall was selling stationery. That was not Tommy's usual line, but she knew that if it would make a profit there wasn't anything he'd refuse to handle. She returned to the linen stall and began to look through the various boxes and plan the best way of showing what they had to sell. Raised voices made her look up and she saw that another argument had begun. One of the dissenters was the same man who had tried to pick a fight with Tommy. To her delight the other was Phil Johnson.

"Phil!" she called in delight. He turned to see who called and the man he was arguing with took the opportunity to swipe at him with a fist. Phil staggered off balance for a few steps then turned to retaliate.

"Thanks, Daisie!" he shouted between blows. "Great help you are!"

"Damn me, Dais, don't say you're refereeing another fight! What did you have for breakfast?" Tommy leant forward, hands on knees, watching the moves of the two men with great enjoyment. The Toby, a small irrate man in a long overcoat, gaitered legs and a tall hat, came up and pushed him out of the way.

"Come on you two. Stop this or you'll both leave. Right?"

Phil faced the Toby, arms wide in suplication, ready to begin his defence when the other man danced in front of him and landed another blow on his nose.

"Out!" the Toby demanded waving a finger. "Out now this minute and don't bother to come back. There isn't a place for you here now or any other Wednesday, right?"

"I don't want a place," the man said happily. "Only wanted a fight. He crouched, fists ready, as if to start on the Toby then ran off laughing.

Tommy watched as Phil was led off by the Toby to clean

his face, plead his case and be given his usual spot. "You've always liked Phil Johnson, haven't you, Dais? I hope you don't like him too much."

"What d'you mean, too much?"

"Well, look over by there. "He pointed to where a rather boldly dressed young woman was setting out jars and buckets of flowers. "She and Phil, they're, well, you know, Dais. I just thought you ought to know, like."

Sickness almost overwhelmed her. She knew she couldn't be the first woman Phil had taken to bed, he was twenty-four after all and few reached that age without experience. But surely he didn't need anyone else, not now she had –

"Used to be," she said with a conviction she didn't feel. "She used to be his girlfriend, but not any more."

"If you say so, Dais." Tommy looked troubled. "Look, you go and get a cup of tea at the stall while I sort out this lot, then we'll work like Phil and I do, I'll do the patter and you can hand out the stuff and take the money. All right?"

The temptation to go and take a closer look at the girl Tommy had pointed out was too great to resist. The market was a bright scene, the flower seller the brightest of all, with a dark red skirt spangled with gold ornaments, a scarf on her head and another around her shoulders which also shone with the disks and circles of gold and silver sewn on in great numbers.

In the cold of the February morning she was barefoot and seemed to dance as she moved around her stall reaching for various requests. She attracted customers by shouting in a sing-song way about the freshness of her flowers and several people were around the stall. Daisie noticed that Phil was staying away from them both.

Buying two cups of tea and some buttered scones, Daisie turned her thoughts away from Phil and the facinating flower seller and carried them to where Tommy was already doing a fair business. She was soon involved with his routine, caught up in the enthusiasm of Tommy's skillful persuasions.

Pairs of sheets made of cotton, calico or twill sold well at the reduced prices he shouted without pause, and the piles of terry and huckaback towels, pillow and bolster cases, antimacassars, dados and chair backs reduced steadily. The selling became automatic and all the time Daisie watched to see if Phil visited the flamboyant girl on the flower stall.

Around the middle of the day trade eased off and several of the stall-holders left their stalls in the care of a neighbour and went to find refreshment at the local public house. Daisie was on her own when the girl left the flowers and walked past her. She was walking through the stalls in her sensuous swaying manner, talking to a girl who sold lengths of dress material.

"'Thrilling you are, Polly,' he tells me," she was saying as she passed Daisie. "That's what he says, 'thrilling', and now he's hardly looking at me. Men! Dose of salts they want if you ask me." Laughing, the two friends disappeared in the direction of the food stall. Phil followed a few moments later without looking in Daisie's direction. She left the stall long enough to see them standing very close, Phil's arm around her elegantly clad shouders.

What a fool I've been! Daisie told herself as she straightened a pile of tapestry cushion covers. I shouldn't have given in so easily. If I'd been stronger and made him wait I'd have been more likely to keep him. But it's only a setback. I'll still marry him one day. But even though her thoughts were brave, she didn't really believe them.

When Tommy came back from his lunch he intended to tell Daisie that Phil and the girl were sharing a meal, but seeing the miserable swollen-eyed expression on her face, he decided she no longer needed telling.

"Come on then, Dais, let's get these shifted. Take a penny off everything over a shilling and we'll soon get rid."

"I've put some of the best pillow cases and sheets in the corner for Gillian. She and Megan are saving for their bottom drawers," she said pointing to a blue tissue-paper wrapped parcel.

"And you should do the same, Dais, never too early to start gathering your future home together. Look, take these pillow cases as a gift to start you off."

She thanked him and held the crisp white pillow cases to

61

her face, breathing in their sweet freshness. New linen was a luxury.

These might be her only luxury she thought, as fear of a baby came back to worry her. She thought of the clean crisp bed Helen gave her and then went back in time to the old house. There she had been used to grey sheets that had been cut lengthwise then sewn together, sides to the middle, the weaker centre piece thrown away. And the patched pillows filled with any oddments she could find, including dry grass. The scratchy blankets made from knitted squares, repaired again and again. Times which she had thought had gone for ever might still return.

Worse, she could find herself alone in her poverty. Chapels scorned a fallen woman and named them from the pulpit as a warning for others. Her shame would be spoken of all through the town. Whispered by friends, said loudly by others fortunate enough to have escaped her fate, gloating voices enjoying her disgrace. What chance of marrying then?

She put the pillow-cases Tommy had given her on to the pile for Gillian. She wouldn't need them. She would never marry. How could she when the man she wanted didn't even acknowledge her? When this very minute he was probably with another willing and gullible fool, telling her she was "thrilling"?

5

Tommy was at the Cwm Manachlog market the following Saturday. It was raining and everyone was faced with the dilemma of showing their stock and at the same time keeping it dry. The street was thick with mud brought by walkers as well as the carts and waggons and cars carrying produce for the market. Water from one of the small streams that wandered through the houses before joining the larger one that crossed under the road, had flooded one of the fields and spread to the verges.

The Toby was watching the rising water and hoping it wouldn't come far enough up to flood the road. It had happened once before in his memory and he knew that if it did, it would happen fast. As a precaution he wore waders that reached his thighs and added to the alarm by his obvious anxiety.

He prepared for the possibility by making some of the stall holders move their carts further up the road, and he loftily ignored their complaints, strutting around pointing his finger and demanding they move as directed. If there was a flood he wanted to be able to shift every last one, not see them wallowing in mud up to their axles.

Tommy wasn't helping Phil, he was running his own stall. The remainder of the linen supplies were augmented with boxes of stationery and greetings cards. Besides birthday cards, some of which were beautifully decorated with lace and dried flowers, there were postcards with room on the back for brief messages. The sending of post-cards was extremely popular, not only for those fortunate enough to go on holiday but between people who could rely on the postman to deliver a message sent before noon to a friend in the same town by evening. Tommy, never slow in seeing a way of making money and encouraged by the success of selling the bankrupt stock, had bought the hand-cart full of similar items from a man who had intended getting himself a stall and disposing of what he had bought, himself.

"You don't want the fuss and bother of selling at the market in weather like this," Tommy had said when he stopped to help the man heave his cart out of a sea of mud. "Ruined it'll be before you've sold the first birthday card. I'll take it all and keep it back to sell on a better day, how's that then?"

So a deal had been struck and now Tommy was now offering it at "bargain prices" which were in fact higher than they had sold at before. No one had seen him do the deal with the prospective market trader or he might have been in trouble. Forestalling – buying off traders before they get to the market and selling on at higher prices – was frowned upon and the Toby might have refused permission for him to sell it.

The rain continued all through the morning and the water from the stream was beginning to show at the edge of the road. The heavily dressed customers bought what they needed and headed for home, there was no casual strolling about. The envelopes and cards were beginning to curl and Tommy wondered if he had been too clever, buying such stock on a day likely to ruin it all.

He saw the boy from The Swan purchasing the vegetables and the bread needed for the lunch-time trade and asked, "Why isn't Daisie doing the marketing today? Not afraid of a little drop of rain is she? She's not sick?"

"No, no." The tall thin old man who gloried under the title of "boy" because of the work he did at The Swan, shook his grisled head. "Not sick, just sick of shopping, or so she says. Scrubbing the floor as if it was the face of her worse enemy she is, and it was scrubbed proper only a couple of days ago. Temper if you ask me, mind. She's giving that floor a real going over."

A man stood on the edge of the throng with some wicker

baskets in which he had some day old chicks for sale. A pile of cardboard boxes held others, a dozen to each box. The Toby had given permission so long as he didn't attract too large a crowd and block the pavements. As superintendent he would be held responsible if the stall-holders didn't allow pedestrians and traffic free passage. Tommy gestured towards where the man had opened one of the baskets and, under the shelter of a neighbouring canvas cover, was allowing the fuffy yellow chicks to walk up and down his arm.

"I hope he feeds them," Tommy said doubtfully.

"The trouble with animals," the Toby said, "is that they make a crowd gather to utter their ooo's and aaah's and cause a blockage and lead to complaints from the other traders as well as the police. My eyes have to be everywhere, this is a big market to be responsible for, one of the biggest in this part of Wales."

"Best thing about the market," Tommy said winking cheerfully at the boy from The Swan, "there's never two days alike. You never know what'll happen next."

"Lucky Daisie isn't here, she'd be sorry for them chicks and probably buy the lot!" the boy grumbled, heaving his baskets onto his skinny arms and draping his overcoat across to protect the contents. "Damned animals. She had me chasing some lads yesterday, said they were aiming stones at her wounded duck. Went at them bald 'eaded she did. I'd give it duck. On a plate it should be, surrounded with gravy and a few roast potatoes!"

Daisie finished washing the floor and threw the dirty water over the rhubarb clump outside the back door. Hanging the galvanised pail on the wall beside the bath, she rubbed her bleached hands on her sacking apron and wondered how long they would take to lose the wrinkles caused from such long imersion in soapy water. She wished she had been able to go to the market.

It was Phil who made her change her routine. She had believed their affair to be a growing romance, like Gillian's and Megan's, but the weekly visits to the old house and the

65

accidental meetings during which they exchanged glances, the fun of a secret that she daily hoped he would proudly reveal, was fading into a situation in which she felt used.

She hated their meeting at the derelict house. Phil didn't know it had once been her home and she daren't tell him. She had protested about its awfulness, but his insistence was the kind that she couldn't break down. The fact that he didn't listen to her, or even attempt to find somewhere more pleasant, made their meetings more sordid than ever, but hope of better things stifled her doubts. It was surely only a matter of time?

In his absence she created fantasies of beautiful love, but after their meetings she felt dirty and unclean. The affair should be ended, she knew that, and she even planned how she would tell him, but the need of him was too strong. As always she was afraid of being alone and even the pretence that he loved her was better than emptiness.

He was definately less interested in her. Once their loving was over he seemed in a great hurry to leave. The last time he hadn't waited for her to straighten her clothes but had moved away after a kiss as casual as cousins, then walked at a great rate along the path, soon out of her sight as she stood at the door of the filthy house watching him.

She shivered in the cold damp air and closed the door against the rain, the gloom of the darkened room engulfing her in sadness. How could she ever go to the market again? How could she look at him without wondering where else he was going for his loving?

"Daisie, love," Helen called and, forcing her features into a smile, Daisie went to see what Helen wanted.

"Just done the floors again, the rain's made it into a right pigsty and it's taken a lot of scrubbing to get it right," she said, removing her coarse apron.

"Will you go to the market and find Tommy?" Helen asked. "Ask him to come and see me, there's a bit of business he hasn't sorted."

"Can't the boy go?" Daisie asked in alarm. "I really have a lot to do, and – "

"Had a quarrel have you?" Helen asked in her quiet way.

"No, it's just that I'm getting a bit tired of Phil. He's dull really for all his handsome looks." Best to pretend rather than look foolish when he says goodbye, Daisie thought with a gulp of dismay. "I don't really want to see him yet."

"All right. If you'll keep an eye here, I'll go."

Helen stood on the edge of the crowd and watched Phil for a while; he certainly attracted plenty of adoring women, she thought as he blew a kiss at a lady who had just put her hand up to buy a tea set. Ignoring the rain, he wore a short sleeved shirt and Fair Isle pullover. Everyone else was draped in macintoshes and thick coats and he was like a ray of bright sunshine with his white apron and white shirt.

Pale yellow hair and pale blue eyes, sounds anything but exciting Helen thought, but she could see by the faces of those watching him that the combination of his build and colouring, the strong arms on which the fine white hairs shone in the lights that decorated his stall, and his way of flirting with them all, were having their affect. She wondered how many of the buyers really needed what they bought or just used a purchase as an excuse to make contact with the seller. Poor Daisie, she muttered to herself as she passed on, searching for Tommy.

She heard him long before she saw him. He, too, had a crowd of women around his horseless cart. He had fixed up a covering of rubber sheeting he had scrounged from a trader who had dodged the Toby and left early. There were boxes of cards left from the stock he had bought and a few oddments of linen.

"If you've come for a bargain, Mrs Prewitt, you've left it a bit late," he said. "But – " and here his wink seemed apposite, "there's a few cards left and to you they're half price." He held up a fan of postcards. "Look at these. Beautiful they are. Covered in good luck charms. Four leafed clovers, lucky imps, and a chimney-sweep's brush and all for twopence each, how's that for a bargain?"

"It isn't cards I want, Tommy," Helen whispered, "it's a car. When can I expect it?"

"I was coming to see you after this lot's sold. Found out what happened to the car you ordered. I went to one of them posh families up on Pleasant View. Arthur Huntley-Davies wanted one and of course he couldn't wait so we had to. Damned cheek."

"But I've paid for it!" Helen looked alarmed. All her savings gone to buy a car for Desmond was one thing, but to lose it without anything to show –

"Two more weeks, maybe three, and we'll have it. Don't worry, Mrs Prewitt."

"Don't worry? How can I not worry." She looked at him doubtfully. "It will be all right, won't it? All that money."

"I know what you're thinking, I'm not the most honest of men, is that it? Well, all right, in this world when you're born disadvantaged you have to make things happen for yourself, I'll admit that, but I wouldn't take money from someone like you and certainly not this amount. D'you think I want to go to prison? Kill me that would being shut up in a small room and with no latch on the door. No, I went around yesterday and demanded an explanation. It'll be all right, I promise, Mrs Prewitt."

To make matters more frustrating, a car like the one she had ordered, passed her as she returned to The Swan. The darkly handsome Arthur Huntley-Davies was driving and beside him, shrunken with nerves and shyness, was Daisie's friend Megan. She was dressed in a ginger-brown coat with large lapels that seemed to smother her small frame. On her head a large bedecked hat held in place with a gold silk scarf put her face in shadow. Shadow, Helen thought, was where the poor girl wanted to be, not stuck up there for all the world and his wife to gawp at. What was she doing with a man like Arthur Huntley-Davies?

Helen's feet were getting wet as water began to roll down the street. She ran up the few steps and into The Swan and was gratified to see Arthur step out in the downpour and hear his struggles to get the engine started again.

At lunch time, when stalls being flushed away by the storm was an imminent possibility, the rain stopped. The mountains appeared out of the heavy dark clouds and within fifteen minutes, the sky was an unbelievably bright blue. Traders came for refreshment and sat as close to the fire as they could. The Swan was soon filled to capacity with the complaining men discussing whether this was the worst storm or only the second worst. The bar room steamed.

The streets shone, freshly washed and sparkling in the bright sun. Water still ran down the gutters and gurgled into overtaxed drains but the threat of a flood had receeded. Traders shouted themselves hoarse trying to be rid of their goods. It had been a bad day and the perishables would be useless by the next market day, so even a few pence was better than throwing the stuff on the rubbish heap for the rats.

When the market finally closed, Tommy noticed that the man who had been selling chicks had left a few boxes behind. When he investigated he found that two of the boxes still contained chicks. A number were already dead and the rest were gasping for lack of water, which after the rain they had experienced seemed inexcusable. He reported his find to the Toby who promised he wouldn't allow the man to deal there again.

"Like you, I don't want to see animals treated so uncaringly, Tommy," he said. "Best you finish them off, almost dead by the look of it, no need to prolong their agony."

"I think I'll take them to Daisie at The Swan, she might save a few. Always a sucker for animals is Dais."

With Tommy's help, Daisie fixed up a temporary shelter in the kitchen for the ten surviving chicks with a feather pillow covering a hot water bottle to give them some warmth, and food and fresh water. The motherly dog, Alexandra, sat near them and allowed the boldest to hop onto her soft warm fur. Making certain that Slipper was locked out for the night, Daisie thought they were as safe as she could make them and after thanking Tommy for his thoughtfulness went back to the bar.

Phil didn't appeared in the bar that evening and she tried to persuade herself she was glad. When she climbed the stairs to her bed, Phil was under the sheets waiting for her.

*   *   *

Several more weeks passed, the six surviving chicks were now odd creatures with spiky feathers poking through the down growing daily and still being watched over by the dog.

One morning when the bar was beginning to fill up Tommy came with news that the car would be delivered on the following Saturday. He came bursting into the bar full of excitement then, as he saw Desmond, controlled himself and asked casually if Helen were about.

"What is it?" Helen poked her head around the doorway from the kitchen and raised an eyebrow in silent query.

"Oh, I just wondered if you want to buy my last few pillow cases, Mrs Prewitt, Got them outside if you want a look."

"A lot of excitement over a few pillow-cases," Desmond laughed and touched his head then pointed at Tommy, sharing a grin with Helen. "*Twp* he is. Sure as eggs are eggs."

"Twelve o'clock next Saturday I'll be bringing it," Tommy said in a whisper. "Pity we can't make it the evening and have another party, isn't it?"

Helen was smiling when she went back inside. "Where are the pillow cases?" Desmond asked with a puzzled frown.

"Stitching's poor," Helen said with a dismissive wave of her hand.

"Something's going on."

"Time's going on and Daisie's been too long with her menagerie. She should have the food ready by now!"

"Daisie's Ark they're calling this place," Desmond chuckled. "She'll have to marry a farmer, or a very rich man."

"A farmer? He'd have to be too simple to kill anything," Tommy added, returning to the bar. "Soft-hearted to a fault is Dais."

Tommy no longer helped Phil, he had his own pitch with a load of goods to sell that differed from week to week. Most Saturdays he would arrive with a cart filled with something he had bought cheaply. The horse would be led off to spend the day in the field behind The Swan and the cart would become the centre of the market's activities. Phil missed having Tommy to help him, but only

70

once did he protest. That was when Tommy had a load of glassware.

"Too much like what I'm selling *and* you're too close," Phil complained. Tommy gathered a swarm of helpers and heaved the cart cheerfully from his usual pitch to one near the farthest end of the street and proceeded to attract the greater crowd away from the rest.

On the Saturday he was to deliver the car, he had very little stock and he found a boy to deal with it for him and went to find Daisie. To his surprise she was not at The Swan. Neither Helen nor Desmond knew where she had gone.

"I hope she's back soon," Tommy sighed. He had planned for Daisie to be sitting beside him when he drove the new car around and delivered it to Desmond Prewitt.

"But are you sure?" Gillian was saying to a sobbing Daisie. "I've heard you can misscount the days as easy as anything." With her wedding to Waldo approaching, Gillian had been taking advice about how to avoid having a child. She didn't want a baby to ruin her slim figure, or have a child to ruin the life she planned to enjoy as Mrs Waldo Griffiths, the wife of a wealthy shoe-shop owner.

Megan was silent, such talk embarrassed and worried her. If she and Arthur were to marry she would have to be prepared for all this and she didn't think she could cope.

"I thought I was so clever." Daisie's voice was hoarse with crying, her blue eyes bright in the moist, reddened face. "Thought I was modern. Thought I knew it all. He said what we were doing was safe. Promised me he did. Moved from me before I could come to any harm, he said."

"Who is it, then? Aren't you going to tell us? Not Tommy Thomas is it?"

"Tommy! Get you! As if I'd be seen dead with Tommy Thomas as a boyfriend!"

"Tommy says you've been seeing Phil regular. Doing more than walking out, have you?"

"I'm not saying." How could she say until she had told Phil and found out if he would marry her. "I'll talk to

– the person, and when we've discussed it, then I'll tell you."

"You don't think he'll marry you, do you, Daisie?" Megan whispered. "Oh, to do that and then be turned away. I think I'd die."

"I'll manage. It'll take more than this to send me to my grave." Daisie spoke harshly and in that moment she knew that whatever happened, however the problem was resolved, she wouldn't leave The Swan and go back to her previous poverty. Whatever she had to do, nothing would make her accept that again.

Daisie returned to The Swan just as Tommy drove up in the shiny new car. Being Tommy he had decorated the bonnet with a huge bow of ribbons and a bunch of Spring flowers lay on the back seat. Helen and Desmond were in the doorway, flanked by their customers. Tommy handed the flowers to Helen and bowed dramatically to Desmond. "Happy Birthday, you lucky sod, and sorry it's late." Desmond stared at Helen, a slow smile widening on his round face. A blush of pleasure spread up to his balding head and a look of disbelief clouded his eyes. "Helen, my love, you bought this for me?"

Tommy waved the keys in front of the bemused man's face and then went to open the car door. "Come on, then, let's see how you look."

With the crowd getting in the way and laughing at everything that happened, Desmond succeeded in lurching his way up and down the street between shoppers and market stalls and the disapproving looks of the local policeman. As dusk fell, Tommy and an exhausted Desmond parked the beautiful car behind The Swan and staggered into the bar.

There were balloons and a good spread arranged by Helen and Daisie. A large number of the Male Voice Choir were there and David Power, who had once played the chapel organ on Sundays, but was now one of the boys, surprised them by accompanying the increasingly bawdy singing on the piano. When, plied with too much drink, he fell off the stool, Daisie took over and in an amateurish manner, thumped out a melody of sorts and sang with gusto.

Billie Beynon the butcher tried to do conjuring tricks and failed miserably, his large hands fumbling and causing good natured laughter. Tommy Thomas recited. Daisie surprised them by singing several music hall songs. One man did a sword dance using pokers from the hearth. Choruses swelled as even the quietest joined in the well-known melodies. The songs changed as inhibitions relaxed; saucy songs and, as the evening lengthened, sentimental ballads changed the mood of the crowded bar.

Desmond was laughing at everything, his face red and shining with perspiration. After the first hour he was utterly speechless and unable to stand.

There was a false gaiety about Daisie that evening, a greater than usual confidence and boldness. She threw insults faster than Desmond and Helen pulled pints and was, for a time, the centre of everyone's attention.

When Daisie later went to open the door of the Select bar in case there were glasses needing to be washed, she heard voices and stopped. Helen's she recognised and the other she did not know.

"You bought him a car for his birthday?" the voice was saying. "That's a lot of money. You and Desmond must be well off for you to afford to give him a car."

"It's money Mam and Dad left me," Helen explained.

Daisie had intended to move away but she was unable to resist stopping to listen further.

"I kept it all these years as a precaution," Helen confided, "in case anything went wrong and Desmond and I separated. But now, well, we're happier than ever and him being forty, well, it doesn't frighten me any more."

"Why haven't you married him?" the voice asked and Daisie was startled. But then she grinned in the darkness. Fancy the two of them living over-the-brush all these years and no one knowing!

"We just sort of drifted into living together and for a while we thought we'd make it legal, now it doesn't seem important.

73

If Desmond dies before me he'll see me all right. That's why I decided to spend the money on a car. Desmond will always look after me."

Daisie tiptoed away without revealing her presence. Best Helen didn't know her secret was out. She smiled again at the thought of old Desmond living "tally" with Helen. At forty he should know better! And the vicar never knowing what black sheep he had in his congregation.

The party reached its peak and then began to slow down. Even the most energetic slipped into a stupor. Matt Prosser had to be taken home in the drunk's barrow. Billie Beynon was arguing incoherently with the small wiry vegetarian coalman about the need for meat to built up a fighting man.

It was late when Phil came into the bar and Daisie was playing a quiet tune on the piano. With a slight incline of his head he indicated that he would be waiting upstairs. Daisie closed the lid of the piano. She made up her mind to face a different sort of music. The cheerful and rowdy scene faded and became a distant echo as she went to join him in a corner of the room.

He cut at her confidence at once by pretending their conversation was only that of barmaid and customer as he nonchalantly handed her his empty glass without looking at her.

"I have to talk to you, Phil," she said close to his ear as the noise was so great. He moved away and rolled his pale eyes upwards, towards her bedroom far above.

"It wasn't talking I had in mind," he mouthed silently, a hand hiding the words from others.

It was no use delaying. Daisie pulled him close again and urgently whispered, "I think I'm going to have a baby, Phil. Now d'you see why we have to talk?" Her beautiful eyes were beseeching him not to turn away from her. Rosy in the firelight, her face was so lovely and her hair, rich coppery red in the reflection of the dancing flames from the fire, framed it so perfectly that for a moment Phil faltered. Then he put the glass down on the table and, looking away from her, shook his head.

74

"Nothing to do with me, Daisie. Sorry, but you can't pull that old trick. I've always been careful so just think again. Try one of your other blokes. Got it?" He turned to stare at her briefly and eyes that had reduced her to jelly seemed those of a stranger. Wide with determination and edged with what she interpreted as fear, they tried to stare her protests down before she spoke them. His gaze left her then, wandered jerkily around the room, at the floor and up at the dark corners of the ceiling high above them before coming to rest briefly again on her striken face.

"It's no, Daisie. Understand? No one's seen us together and I've got a steady girl who'll swear I spend all my nights with her." He pushed his way through the bar and out into the dark street, the door slamming behind him signaling the end of Daisie's hopes.

The way Phil had refused to even consider helping her out of her dilemma hardened Daisie's heart. She had to have a father for her child and a respectable marriage. Her heart thundering within her, her eyes revealing her fury, hurt and despair. She looked around the crowded room. Most of the male population of Cwm Manachlog as there, even Gillian's fiance, Waldo Griffiths, was sitting close to the bar with his father and a few friends. Surely someone among them would marry her? She sipped at the drink Waldo had bought her, the second that evening, and poured herself another.

"Anything the matter, Dais?" Tommy asked. "Phil upset you has he? Just tell me if he has and I'll get someone to sort him out. Too big for me he is, mind!" he said, trying to make her laugh.

"I'm just tired that's all," she told him. "Just tired."

"Seems you aren't the only one, Dais." He gestured with his thumb.

Helen was slouched in a wooden settee at the side of the fire, her mouth dropped open, an empty brandy glass about to fall from her hand. She was fast asleep, a sleep induced more by the spirits she had swallowed than fatigue.

"Daisie, give me a hand to get Helen upstairs, will you?" Desmond, who seemed in almost as bad a state as the woman he was trying to help, went to gather up Helen and, with Daisie's assistance, carry her up the staircase.

"Just let me throw this lot out and lock up first," Daisie said, and calling insults to see them on their way she quickly emptied the bar.

"Gwilym Rees, get that ugly mug of yours out of here and go home before your wife locks you out again, sensible woman that she is. Jimmy, off with you and don't breathe on the milk, you'll turn it sour." She pointed to David Power slumped in a chair, his jaw wide open and emitting loud snores. "Tommy, pick David's chin off the floor and get him out of here before someone kicks his teeth down his throat. It's the drunk's barrow for him tonight."

Daisie's head swam. She rarely drank although that evening, it being a celebration for Helen and Desmond if not herself, she had accepted a few from regular customers. Unlike most, she discovered that the unaccustomed alchohol made her miserable not merry. With Desmond it was different. He had been carelessly celebrating the gift of the car with all his customers and was at that state of inebriation when everything was uproariously funny.

It was funny trying to lift a lifeless Helen from the settee. Her foot caught in the linoleum and he laughed. They almost dropped the unconscious woman on the first landing and Desmond had to put his burden down as giggling weakened his muscles so he could barely stand.

"Mar'lous birsday this's bin, Daisie," he said as they at last managed to place Helen on the double bed.

"I'd better help you down the stairs again, Desmond, or you'll fall," Daisie said. "There's the clearing up to do yet. We can't leave it all until tomorrow."

Desmond looked at her with that straight look that a drunk occasionally achieves and said, "Lovely girl you are, Daisie my swee'eart, don' know wha' we'd do wi'out you an' – an' – thasafact!"

"Come on, you silly old fool," Daisie smiled and they began to head towards the stairs. "We've still got work to do."

"No, Daisie, I got to 'elp *you* up stairs now. Goroo look

after my Daisie. S'my job to look after you." In his confused state Desmond imagined he was looking after her and seeing her safely to bed as he had Helen.

When he changed from the weak-limbed drunk to the fiercely strong and determined lover, Daisie couldn't quite remember. One minute he was fondling her shoulder as she supported him, trying to turn him round the corner of the landing towards the room he shared with Helen, and the next he had pushed her through the door into her own bedroom.

She wasn't frightened at first. He was confused, that was all. His hands were fondling her thinking she was Helen. She kept pushing them away with more and more force. This seemed to enflame him. His hands her began to hurt her. She began to whisper urgently for him to behave before Helen heard him. Then the laughter faded. His face was tense and his eyes looked at her with frightening intensity. He was pushing her towards her bed. She struggled then, trying not to wake Helen, not wanting her to be upset by what was obviously a bit of drunken tomfoolery going too far.

"Desmond," she pleaded. But in a sudden movement he had forced her back on the bed and was tearing her clothes from her body. She pushed and struggled but her efforts only added to his fury. He pressed her down and, heaving himself upon her, plunged into her, thrusting painfully, gasping with the urgency of it until with a final gasp he fell and was at once asleep.

She couldn't move, his weight was on her in such a way that she couldn't escape. She wailed then, a low keening cry of a child, rising to a screaming sobbing. In the doorway, framed in the light from the landing Helen appeared. She pulled Desmond from Daisie's naked body with a scream as distraught as Daisie's and hit the unconscious man with her hands until her strength gave out.

6

Helen somehow managed to heave the battered and confused Desmond up off the floor and drag him out of the room. Daisie was still sobbing and she looked in vain to Helen for comfort. Helen left him on the landing and closed Daisie's door. She didn't say a word about what had happened, but the way she glared at Daisie left the girl trembling.

After stripping her bed, Daisie washed in cold water and dressed. She didn't put on night clothes. She had a need to be ready for the day. Sitting on the floor, unable to go near the bed, she tried to think about what had happened. She would definitely be homeless after this. Helen was certain to blame her, had already shown her so with that inimical look. She tried the think of a plan. All she needed was somewhere to stay and work to enable her to buy food. It didn't seem a lot to ask of life but even those paltry needs were likely to prove difficult to attain.

As dawn lightened the skies she heard Helen coming up the stairs and Daisie's heart thumped like small explosions as she waited for the door to open. "You little bitch," was all she heard. Sobs broke out anew but if Helen heard she paid no heed.

Helen ran back down the stairs and out into the field behind The Swan. She was trembling and, in these first hours, as much worried for herself as hurt. Where could she go? What would she do? That damned car! Why had she spent her savings? After all these years of feeling safe and secure, why had this happened now when she had just given away all hope of getting a place of her own? "Fool! Fool! Fool!" she scolded herself. "Vain, overconfident, fool!"

The dogs barked, wondering what was the matter, their heads held low, preparing to roll over to be tickled. Pulling at the end of their chains they watched with curious eyes as Helen passed them by without a word. They seemed to understand she was distressed and wanted to comfort her.

Three cats walked casually across the grass, approaching at an angle, with that slinky walk suggesting they are only being polite, not pleased to see her. The duck waddled up to the wire of its enclosure amid a flutter of clucking chickens. Helen saw none of them.

She walked through the field and out to the bank of the stream. She saw no-one. The milkman returning along the road from the farm which ran parallel to the stream shouted a greeting, his measures rattling a cheerful accompaniment to the trotting hooves of his horse, but Helen was unaware of his passing.

She had not yet combed her hair and it fell about her face in a wildness that matched her mood. She felt old, a discarded and useless "thing". Her humiliation grew as self-blame faded. It was Desmond's fault. He had betrayed her in the most cruel way. This could hardly be the first time, not in all the years since Daisie came to live with them.

The image of Daisie's face returned to her. The wide blue eyes had been large with tears. She had looked at Helen as if trying to judge her reaction. Beside that almost quizzical stare there was a hint of shame at being caught. That was it! They must have been carrying on for months. And she, poor stupid fool that she was, continued to adore Desmond and spend her nest-egg buying him a car. For a while, blaming Daisie gave her comfort, but it soon faded. Desmond was a grown man, Daisie, in spite of her confidence in the bar, was still little more than a child.

Where could she go? What would become of her? She couldn't walk back into The Swan as if nothing had happened. Sitting down on the cold bank she stared into the water as if a solution would miraculously appear on the silvered surface. Or, below it.

*   *   *

79

In the small bedroom on the top floor of The Swan, Desmond stared at Daisie as if she were a ghost.

"What the hell was I doing here?" he asked. "What the bloody hell happened last night?"

"You followed me up and . . . you wouldn't go away." Daisie felt sobs building up again. Desmond looked creased and red-faced and bewildered.

He stumped down the stairs, calling Helen. Then Daisie left her room and went down to start lighting the fires. Until Helen came back and told her to go, she'd best carry on with the daily routine. Whatever the result of last night, business at The Swan would continue as usual.

Desmond was frantic. What had got into him? He remembered nothing about following Daisie. Why had he drunk so much? After Helen had given him that magnificent gift he had become so incapable he had got into the wrong bed and ruined them all. He remembered making love, but was certain it had been Helen he had held, Helen he had told of his undying love.

He released the dogs from their chains and they went haring off in the direction of the stream. Yelling in anguish for Helen he raced after them.

The stream wasn't deep enough to drown in with any ease. Helen had slipped into the water and found that her face was not covered. She tried to wriggle further into the middle but the cold hurt her skin, made her muscles stiff, slowed her thinking so she became confused as to what she had to do. Her resolution lessened but she knew she mustn't give up. She had to do it.

She seemed to be dreaming, the urge to cover herself in the water only half understood. It was a problem she had to overcome. The best way was to roll until she was face down. Her body was so heavy and it wouldn't do as she wanted. Oh, why was she so useless? It was all her fault. But what was it she was guilty of? It tired her to think.

As she succeeded in heaving herself partly on to her side, strong hands lifted her, a warm face touched hers and warmer tears took the place of the icy water of the stream.

"Helen, my only love, what have I done?" Desmond sobbed.

Helen was ill for several weeks, weeks of utter misery for both Desmond and Daisie. They continued to run The Swan; partners almost without speaking to each other. Daisie hated Desmond. He had almost caused Helen's death. Desmond was too ashamed of his drunken conduct to face her. Once when they found themselves together, each needing help to haul another barrel from its place to where it could be tapped, Daisie said quietly, "You did know it was me, didn't you Desmond?"

"I – I don't know what I thought, Daisie, I want us to forget it if we can."

"But you did know it was me," she insisted quietly.

"I was weak and foolish, but yes, I suppose I did. But I won't admit it to Helen. What I did was wrong but I won't lose Helen over this. There was no harm done and she's more important than a few moments of . . . I'm truly sorry, Daisie. It won't ever happen again. If you want to leave I'll give you a written character and make sure you get a good place."

"She won't see me yet, will she?" Daisie pleaded hopefully. "I miss her so much."

"She won't even see me on some days. I have to put her food outside her room and just hope she'll eat it. Often she doesn't touch a thing."

"She will get well though? When does the doctor say she should come down and take part in the daily routine again? Surely that would help to make her well?"

"Doctor can't say. He says she'll face it one day, then she'll start to get well again. At the moment she doesn't . . . doesn't want to live." He broke down and hurried from the cellar.

Daisie tried several times to see Phil Johnson but each time he managed to avoid her. There was a row of cottages down at the far end of the town on the way towards Pleasant View and the mountain road. Phil rented a room in one of them and Daisie went every day to see if he would talk to her. She would beg him to marry her if need be. Anything to get away from The Swan.

He had a small pony and trap that he used to transport his goods to and from the various markets and on Sundays it was nowhere to be seen. She might catch glimpses of him running through the fields behind his lodgings to avoid seeing her on other days, but on Sundays he was never there. No one knew where he went, not even Tommy Thomas who knew the routine of practically everyone in the town.

"Can't be church or chapel can it, Dais?" he said, when she discussed Phil's mysterious absences. "Tried to follow him once I did. Led me round and round the lanes and ended back here with a grin on his face you could sell pictures of. Whatever it is he gets up to, he doesn't want anyone to know about it."

The beautiful new car stood at the side of The Swan unused apart from Tommy's regular visits to run it around the town to keep the battery topped up. Tommy and Daisie met beside it one morning when Daisie was walking the dogs, followed as usual by the cats and the duck.

"What about coming for a ride in the car this afternoon?" he invited. He could see she was unhappy and guessed it was caused by Helen's strange illness. "Get out for a hour and let the breezes blow through that flaming hair of yours. I don't think you've even been to the market since Helen went mental, at least I haven't seen you there."

"She *isn't* mental!" she snapped angrily. "Depressed she is, that's all, and there's no knowing how long she'll be kept to her bed." She glared at him.

"Come out for a spin, Dais, take your mind off it."

She shook her head. "I can't, Tommy. It's Helen's place to sit beside the driver. It's her present to Desmond and no one else should ride in it until she's well enough to go with him." Besides her stomach was queasy, especially in the mornings, although she had succeeded so far in keeping her sickness from Desmond and Helen.

"Come with me to the market, then. Be my partner for the afternoon, Dais. Come on, it'll be a laugh."

"I've got to be here for when Helen gets up," she excused, shivering involuntarily, aware that when Helen was able to take charge once more her first action would be to tell her to leave and the battle for her place would start.

"Did you know Helen and Desmond aren't married proper?" he said. She nodded disconsolately. His eye winked furiously. "Well, there you are then. That's what the trouble is. If Desmond and she were hitched she'd stop worrying. Shamed she is, Dais, for sure. But why, I wonder, after all these years?"

Daisie learned from the "boy" that Phil no longer appeared at the Saturday market in Cwm Manachlog. Tommy told her he had found a place at another town further away, nearer the coast, where locally caught fish attracted a larger crowd and hotels and summer visitors were frequent customers for his china and glassware.

"Got Phil's old pitch myself," Tommy told her with glee when once again they met on the banks of the stream. "Contacts in the china manufacturers dealing with seconds quality were easily found. Though Phil wouldn't help, mind! And with Billie Beynon the butcher next along, yelling his fat head off and attracting both regulars and casual trade, I'm doing very well."

"What d'you want to do, Tommy?" Daisie asked. "With your life, I mean. What are you working and saving for?"

"Something real grand." His eye winked with enthusiasm and he saw a dream in his mind's eye, a dream that was hazy as yet, but which he knew would be just wonderful when he got there. He scratched his spiky red hair and shrugged. "I don't know but it'll be great. One day you'll see me dressed up to the nines, talking posh and more 'ikey' than that Arthur Huntley-Davies."

"So you want to be posh, like those up in Pleasant View. But what then? What do you want out of life, Tommy? Really want?"

"Enough money for it to earn a living for me. Yet I don't

want never to have to make more. Making money is like a game to me and it's one I can't see me ever tiring of. But I want to make it my way." He shuddered, his blue eyes slits, his mouth pursed in horror. "Gosh, Dais, I couldn't sit in an office all day looking out through a window at the sky and green fields. Having to stay locked up would be the greatest unhappiness. Having enough money to do what I enjoy and eventually having a house with a woman to keep it looking nice and cooking my meals – " He frowned, his eye winking furiously as he thought of how to describe his thoughts. "I don't know, Dais, it's all vague at present. I want freedom I suppose, and enough money to please myself."

"When we were kids you'd do anything for money. Are you still the same?"

"Well, if everything is going great it's easy to be reasonably honest, isn't it, Dais? It's when life comes and kicks you where it hurts most, then you find your conscience slipping out of sight." He looked at her sad face. "You all right, Dais? You seem a bit down, like."

"I might be leaving The Swan. I'm wondering what to do. I don't have the skill for making money that you have, so I don't have many choices."

"'Course you have, Dais! Good barmaid you are and you've been running The Swan while poor Helen's been mental – er – ill. Get a job anywhere you would."

"I don't know if anyone'll have me – " she almost blurted out the reason for her misery but held back at the last moment. Instead she swallowed her unhappines and said more positively, "I don't know if I want to work in a public house all my life, Tommy."

"It's what you do well, Dais. But you have to decide what you really want and make sure you go full pelt to get it. But don't move on 'till it's right for you. Don't be persuaded to change anything till you're ready, mind. If there's a problem with Desmond or Helen, don't let them make you move on to something you won't like. There's always a way to get what you want, Dais, and people like us have to be prepared to grab whatever weapon that's to hand. And use it."

Tommy's final words echoed in her head as she walked back to start preparing food for the evening. Perhaps he was right. She knew that in similar circumstances Tommy wouldn't let affection for Helen become a barrier, keeping him from what was best for him.

The sun warmed her head and made her long red hair gleam as she strolled slowly home along the bank. The water was almost solid with frogspawn, the tiny parents were occasionally to be seen swimming, so neatly and expertly, just below the surface in the few places where the water was still free of rafts of their eggs, their eyes like jewels in the spring sunshine. She had always watched the seasons through the changes in the stream, enjoyed the flowers that grew at its edges and the animals who came to drink. But now she almost hated the place. She would like never to have to walk along its banks again, but it was such a convenient place to walk the dogs and the cats who always accompanied them. The duck sometimes walked this far, too, as it liked an occasional swim.

There were places she couldn't pass without shivering. The place where someone, Tommy she suspected, had tried to drown the puppies, and now further along the spot where Helen had tried to solve her predicament by drowning herself. The ruin of the house where she and her father had once lived in squalor was another reminder of unhappy days and more recently of Phil. Each winter she hoped that the gales which swept through the mountains and tore through the town would one day demolish it completely. The vegetation was doing its best to hide its ugliness but the chimney pot on the soundest end of the roof still made a silhouette that was visible when she walked the banks of the stream.

March passed with Helen occasionally recovering for a few days, then retreating into the dark unhappy world where no one could reach her. Desmond hardly spoke to Daisie, yet he was grateful for the way she coped with the extra work and helped keep the business going. In fact the takings increased considerably as she served drinks and food, shouted cheek and insults at the customers and was occasionally persuaded to sing and thump out a heavy accompaniment on the piano for others to sing with her.

The Swan had two separate and utterly different centres; one, the silent unhappy bedroom where Helen spent her days with Desmond a regular although unacknowledged attendant. The other was the bar with its laughter and noise and the gathering in of money.

Desmond knew he should get extra help. Daisie had so little time for herself. She rose early and went to her bed late, filling in the hours with a dozen different tasks. The only moments she could call her own were the early morning walks along the stream with her animals.

One morning towards the end of April, coming into the kitchen of The Swan after the bright sun, Helen's voice made Daisie start. "Daisie, love, can we talk?"

"Helen, are you well enough to be up?" Relieved by the apparently friendly sound of Helen's voice, Daisie was off balance. She had expected to be told in as few words as possible to pack her belongings and leave.

"Of course I am."

"There isn't anything wrong in the kitchen is there? I've tried to do everything the way you like it done, Helen. I haven't been slacking, just taking the dogs for a walk, I met that Tommy and you know how he talks." Daisie gabbled to hide her fear.

"About what happened. We're wondering if you'll forget it? I know it will never happen again. Desmond isn't a man for the ladies and it was the drink and the celebration. It got him confused, he says he thought he was in bed with me and, well, I'm inclined to believe him, Daisie. Could we, *can* we carry on as before d'you think?"

It was now or never. She had to tell Helen she was carrying a child. She had managed to hide the early morning sickness that had tormented her so far but Helen would soon guess. It would be cruel to have overcome the situation with Desmond to be told only weeks later that she must leave. Better to get it all settled now. "It's what I want more than anything in the world, Helen," she whispered, her head low, her shoulders dropping in dismay. "For us to get back to how it was before. But I might have to leave The Swan. Shamed I am to say it, you see, I believe I'm going to have a baby."

She caught Helen as she was about to fall and called for the boy to help her back up the stairs.

"What did you say to her?" Desmond demanded when he returned from the wholesalers to find the doctor in attendance. "What have you done now to upset her?"

"She came down and said we could pretend it hadn't happened and I'm sorry, Desmond, I really am, but I had to tell her it wasn't possible, not now. There'll be a baby before the end of the year."

"No! Lying you are, you wicked girl. Lying!"

"I wish I was. I wish everything was back as it used to be."

Her tears and her wishes were genuine. It was only then that she realised both Helen and Desmond had presumed the child was his. Tommy's words slipped insidiously into her mind. "There's always a way to get what you want, Dais," he had told her, "and people like us have to be prepared to grab whatever weapon that's to hand. And use it." Was this a weapon? Could she use Desmond's lapse and allow him to think the child was his? She shook her head angrily. After what Helen had done for her she couldn't be so cruel. But Desmond didn't give her the opportunity to deny or insist so the matter was left unexplained.

To their surprise, Helen didn't suffer a setback. Once over the shock she dressed, came down, and took her place at the bar without further signs of distress.

"Desmond's so excited to have her back in the bar you'd never believe. The way he fusses, he's like an old hen with one sick chick!" Daisie told Gillian and Megan when she was finally able to take an afternoon off.

The three friends walked along the bank of the stream with the intention of continuing past the farm and into the next town and catching the motor-bus back. But instead they sat on the bank and talked.

Daisie evaded any deep discussion of either her own

predicament or Helen's illness. It was easy to persuade them to talk of other things. Megan and Gillian were full of their wedding plans, although Gillian seemed the most ebullient and confident of happiness.

"What's the matter, Megan?" Gillian asked. "You don't sound very excited and there's you marrying one of the richest men in Cwm Manachlog!"

"I suppose it's because I'm not really involved," Megan explained. Gillian and Daisie stared at her, their faces breaking into smiles.

"Not involved? And you the bride? How much more "involved" d'you want to be, for heaven's sake?" Gillian laughed.

"Arthur's mother is making all the arrangements, she says my family wouldn't have the know-how," Megan explained patiently. "I did chose my wedding dress. Sort of. But Mrs Huntley-Davies came with me and persuaded me to have one much grander than I'd have bought. She's so kind and they're paying for everything, even the honeymoon."

"Get her! A honeymoon, like the nobs!" Daisie gasped.

"Waldo and I will be going on honeymoon, too," Gillian said proudly. "Torquay would you believe."

"Get you!" Daisie laughed. She said nothing of her own situation. Time enough for further talk of her baby when a decision had been made.

"I wonder which one of us will have a baby first, Gillian," Megan said, her pale face shining.

"Not me!" Gillian said firmly. "Definitely not me. I've been to talk to the doctor and I've got advice from a few people besides. I don't want to spoil my figure with a baby!"

"But doesn't Waldo want a son?"

"He can want all he likes but what he wants and what he gets are two very different things."

Daisie said nothing. Nature had a way of persuading women to change their mind, and of surprising them with the unexpected!

To the regulars at The Swan, everything seemed the

same as it had always been. The food was good and the atmosphere warm and relaxed and friendly, but beneath the surface, trouble simmered. Daisie interrupted frequent hissed conversations between Helen and Desmond, many of which were far from friendly.

Daisie felt an almost painful need for her mother, a figure half forgotten yet whose absence still caused heartbreak. It was to a mother girls ran when life threw out serious problems. She had no one. Not even Helen any more.

Saturday was always the busiest evening with the market-stall owners coming in throughout the evening until business was declared finished. Then they would expect a sing-song and a few drinks to relax them and send them home content with their day. Daisie was called from behind the bar and encouraged to sing and play. For some reason the evening was a good one.

When the doors finally closed Daisie was still laughing. The evening had confirmed what she already knew, that the bar was the place where she would be most suited to spend her life. If only Helen and Desmond would say something about the future of herself and baby, she would be able to enjoy it even more.

Unable to feel anything but happy, having managed to cut herself off from everything except the present, she sang as she carried out the last of the glasses to wash them. Helen and Desmond followed her. In the flickering light from the gas jet on the stone walls of the kitchen, Daisie thought Helen looked old. Her hair, never her best feature, was grizzled with grey and carelessly combed so it fell in disarray about her lined face.

"We have come to a decision, Daisie," Helen said quietly. Daisie felt the colour rise on her cheeks. This was it. The moment she had been dreading. A glance at Desmond's solemn face convinced her she was being told to leave. Well at least she would know her fate.

Then panic overcame her. Her legs began to tremble. Where would she go? What could she do to earn a living for herself and a child? Between them Phil and Desmond had destroyed her. She found herself taking a deep breath as she prepared for Helen's words of dismissal.

"Desmond will marry you." The words seemed part of someone else's dream, half heard, half invented. "Marry me! But he's already married to you." No need to tell them she knew differently.

"Helen isn't my wife. Now she never will be. She wants me to accept responsibility for the child and bring it up with my name."

If she accepted, she would have to sleep beside Desmond, allow him in her bed. Memories of the night he had forced her returned and an involuntary shiver slipped down her spine. She would have to share his life completely, in every way. For the only time in her life she felt like fainting, shutting out the prospect of being Mrs Desmond Prewitt and sliding into unconsciousness.

"But, you don't love me and – " In a way it was an answer to her prayers, security, a way out of all her troubles. But like all dreams, the achievement of this one was not as perfect as imagined. "I can't – "

"Our mind is made up, Daisie, it's the only solution for us all."

Telling Gillian and Megan was better. Her wits gathered, she had prepared a story that made her adventure sound like the most romantic love story anyone could invent.

"So it was old Desmond Prewitt who was your secret lover all this time!" Gillian said. "And there was me thinking it was Phil Johnson."

Daisie didn't disabuse them. It was best that any thoughts of Phil Johnson remained locked in her heart.

"Poor Helen," the kind hearted Megan said. "All this coming out about them not being married, and now having to stand by and see him marry someone else."

"Silly Helen more like!" Gillian laughed. "Asking for trouble that is, living tally all these years and not persuading him to lead her up the aisle."

Daisie went back to The Swan to be told that Helen was moving out.

"Please don't, Helen." She panicked at the prospect of Helen being absent from the house, it made the future as Mrs Prewitt frighteningly real. "Please don't go. The Swan is your home."

"It's the only thing to do," Helen said, quietly determined. "Do you really imagine I could stay here after this? All change bedrooms like some children's game of hide and seek? Desmond has bought several of the small cottages on the edge of town, out towards Pleasant View and I will live in one of them. And," she added to clinch the argument, "I've already found a job in a cafe."

"Helen, you can't do this." She pleaded for Helen to stay. Fear of the reality of marriage to Desmond, a man older than her by twenty-three years, was suddenly quite terrifying. She hadn't thought clearly. Fear of loneliness and her determination to find a father for her unborn child had turned her mind. She had listened to Tommy Thomas when she knew his way was not hers. She stared wide-eyed from the tearful Desmond to the calm faced Helen, feeling trapped by a predicament of her own making.

"It's Phil's baby," she blurted out. "Phil's. Not Desmond's." She held Helen's shoulders and pleaded again, "Just look after me, that's all I want," she pleaded. She wasn't believed.

"It's all decided." Helen's voice was level as if chanting something painfully learnt. It was as if Daisie hadn't spoken. The reference to Phil being the father brushed aside as an attempt to put things back as they were for them all. "Desmond will go into the registry office this afternoon and arrange everything. I am moving out now, in a few minutes."

"Please, Helen, don't go and leave me." Daisie's pleading was to no avail.

So the first time Helen rode in the beautiful car she had bought for Desmond's special birthday present was as she left The Swan, with all her possessions around her and Tommy sitting in the driving seat.

Ethel Tripp the coalman's wife came in to help clear up and

she saw Daisie's face and asked, "What's the matter, then? Something making you unhappy? I thought everything was sorted?"

"What's happiness, Ethel?" Daisie asked.

The older woman frowned and said, "Happiness isn't a constant state, whatever story books tell you. I suppose it's brief moments when problems are temporarily solved. Simple things can make you happy, like catching a bus you thought you'd missed, sitting comfortably in your seat as the bus glides up the street you thought you'd have to walk."

"What if you're sitting there all pleased with yourself and you find you're on the wrong bus!"

Ethel shook her head. "Now you're getting too deep for me, young Daisie."

The announcement that Daisie and Desmond were to marry was a day of forced jollity. Daisie bought a new dress and although it was hardly a normal engagement, with Helen moving out and the barmaid moving into her place, Daisie's friends did all they could to make it special, and many of the customers turned out to wish them well.

From the smatterings of overheard conversation around her Daisie knew their wedding was a joke that would keep the local wags amused for months. There was only one thing Daisie could do, that was join in the joke.

Every time she heard a joke she would cap it with one of her own. She sang songs about surprise babies arriving at the church and shocking some and amusing others. She hated doing it. It put Desmond in a bad light and would hurt Helen even more if she heard of it, but it succeeded in stopping the jokes. Within weeks, her new position was hardly mentioned.

Until the date set for the wedding Daisie decided to stay in her own room. It was a small act of decorum and probably a stupid one, but Desmond went along with it, in the hope that the wedding day would have some relevance to them both.

Phil did not appear in Cwm Manachlog. He seemed to have vanished completely and Daisie used the time before her wedding thinking of how he had used her and let her down. She thought of ways to strengthen her dislike of him, hoping that he would support her in her lie by showing dislike or at least indifference when they did eventually meet.

But her strongest emotion at that time was anxiety for a future built on a lie. An untruth she had tried, without much perseverance, to correct.

7

The Swan was quiet on Sundays and after Helen left the day was a difficult one. Daisie kept out of Desmond's way as she went about her usual tasks. If Desmond was in the cellar she worked in the kitchen, but if he came to do something there, she went out and spent time with the animals. They ate at the same table but in silence. She felt bereft without Helen and wished something would happen to make everything all right again.

What she had done to Helen was a pain that wouldn't go away, yet she had no thought of owning up to the fact that the child was Phil Johnson's, unless he miraculously accepted that the child would be his and promised to marry her. There was no point in even trying to see him today. On Sundays he was always absent from the town. She still carried the faint hope he would have a change of heart and come to see her, but days passed and she heard nothing.

She didn't show her unhappiness to anyone. Resisting the impulse to lower her head and creep about with her guilt and misery clear to see, she showed the world a tall, pretty, confident woman, in charge of her own destiny.

Phil had not been seen in the area since she had told him of her condition. Others manned his china stall in Brynteg and Melinbanc and, if he drank in Cwm Mananchlog, it was not anywhere near The Swan. Daisie decided that before she became Mrs Desmond Prewitt she would try once more to see him. If he could be persuaded to marry her then there was a chance, albeit a slight one, of sorting this mess. She decided to ask Tommy to help. Like many of the stall-holders Tommy rented a room in Cwm Manachlog and a storage barn outside of the town. Tommy, with his sharp eyes, knew where everyone lived and many details of their lives. The room he rented was not far from Helen's new home and next door to Helen was the house in which Phil rented a room. Tommy told her the most likely time to find Phil at home.

"Want me to come with you, Dais?" Tommy offered when she met him on her way to try once more to talk to Phil. They had met in the High Street that looked bare without its Saturday stalls. The wide pavements and the almost empty road waited for the next market day with a forlorn air.

"I wouldn't mind your company, Tommy, but I want to talk to Phil alone," she said. She looked at his face with its fringe of red hair, similar in colour to her own. Did the blue eyes dart a look at her waistline? Did he suspect?

"All right, Dais. I'll walk with you and then wait at the corner. Right?" As they approached the row of small cottages with their colourful gardens behind stone walls, he glanced at her with a hesitant expression. "Dais, d'you want me to knock at the door? If you and Phil have had a row, he might open the door if he thinks it's me and not you?"

Daisie stopped, her hands on her slim hips, and glared at him. "You've guessed, haven't you, Tommy-knows-it-all-Thomas?"

"Guessed, Dais?" He grinned. "Guessed what? Come on, we'd best get on or he'll be off out for his dinner time pint."

They walked around the back lanes to the rear of the house and walked up the path between rows of last year's vegetables and, while Daisie stood behind the rain-water barrel, Tommy knocked on the half-open door.

Phil opened the door wide, saw Tommy, smiled, then as Daisie appeared the smile faded and he blustered, "Just off out I am, you two. Can't stop. Nice of you to call, anything important was it? See me another time, is it?" Struggling to pull his coat from the arm of a chair near the door, he pulled it on and shut the door.

"Well, that's that, Dais." Tommy caught hold of Daisie's arm and pulled her gently away.

They walked in silence for a while, their footsteps echoing

in the narrow lane between the high garden walls of the terraced houses. Tommy was whistling cheerfully, unable to decide what to say to comfort her. It was clear to him that Daisie was going to have a child and that Phil was the father. Perhaps he'd better make her talk about it. She needed someone to listen to her fears.

"There's a rumour, started no doubt by the boy in The Swan, that the reason you and Desmond are getting married is because you're going to have a baby, Dais. True, is it?"

"He talks too much, that boy. I'd have him out of there if I were in charge," Daisie whispered, close to tears.

"True though, is it?" She didn't answer him and he went on. "It's Phil's, isn't it? And him too much a swine to accept it? You've somehow convinced that Desmond it's his and found a way of finding a safe place for yourself and the baby."

"I had to, Tommy. I couldn't go back to living like a wild animal in that old house."

"Good on you, Dais, for making the best deal out of poor pickings," he said with a grin. "You and me we've got to take what we can in this world, haven't I always said it?"

They had walked around the back of the High Street. Before they turned into the field behind The Swan Tommy stopped and looked back along the stream towards the farm. "That house, Dais, it's still a nightmare for you, isn't it? Why don't you burn your boats, then it won't trouble you any more."

"What you on about, Tommy?"

"Well, the Vikings used to burn their boats when they were no longer any use. Viking funerals they called it. I read about it once. Damn me, that old house would go up like a torch dipped in tallow. Let's set it going and see an end to it, what d'you say, Dais?"

"One day," she said, studying the lone chimney pot that stood out above the blackthorns and hawthorns, the willows and alders. "One day we'll do just that."

Daisie chose Tommy Thomas as witness to her wedding three weeks later. Gillian and Megan came, too, each wearing their prettiest dresses and carrying a bunch of flowers. Megan brought a white, leather-covered prayer-book which she pressed into Daisie's hands to make the ceremony more of a religious occassion. Daisie trembled so much she almost dropped it.

After the brief ceremony they paused momentarily at the door. A few passers-by had paused in their morning's activities to watch the solemn group emerge. Daisie clearly hear one woman say, "Definitely another 'case'." Her friend nodded doubtfully, before they walked on with disapproval in their faces. "Only one reason for a young girl to marry an old man and at a registry office instead of doing it proper in church," was the parting shot.

The small group separated immediately. There was to be no celebratory wedding breakfast. Megan went to her future in-laws where she was to have a fitting for her wedding dress, Gillian to the church where a rehearsal for her own wedding in a few weeks time was arranged. Tommy hurried off to the Brynteg market where he had a cart-load of flannel shirts and long-johns to sell.

Side by side, like strangers walking the same way by accident rather than intent, Daisie and Desmond returned to The Swan for business as usual. No one else had been told the time and place, although Daisie guessed from what Tommy had said that the boy had spread some lively and embellished rumours of what had been going on at The Swan.

The departure of Helen seemed to be put down to her long illness and once a few days had passed most customers seemed to accept her departure without comment. The fact that Desmond and Daisie were married had worn itself out as the source of amusement long before the actual marriage, so little more was said.

Desmond and Helen had been together for so long people had presumed them to be Mr and Mrs Prewitt. Most had actually called them that and had not been corrected. Now, with Daisie soon to have his child, Desmond had faced the gossips and told everyone he and Helen had never married. Derision and laughter had filled the air for weeks but now they said as little as possible and waited for it all to settle.

There were further embarrassments for Desmond outside the public house. He decided that, as his wife, Daisie should no longer do the cleaning. So he advertised for a daily help. When he agreed to employ Bessie Morgan, a thirty-year-old unmarried woman from a poor family, her mother arrived at The Swan, pushed her way into the crowded bar room and demanded he keep away from her daughter.

"Not safe she is, or any other young girl either, with the likes of you in the same house!" she shouted. Desmond looked horrified and stared at Daisie aghast.

"Thank you, Mrs Morgan, that will be enough of that! Nothing but a lot of old lol it is and you know it. Young girl?" Daisie looked around the room, smiling for support from her regulars. "Thirty if she's a day, wouldn't you say, boys? *And* no better than she should be!" There was a murmur of approval as Daisie added. "We don't want that sort in The Swan and that's for sure! Respectable we are round here."

Daisie guided the woman to the door and pushed her, none too gently, down the steps into the street. She returned to the room, smiled encouragement at Desmond, and offered free pints to ease the situation. She soon had the regulars criticising the Morgans and supporting Desmond.

"It'll be far worse for Helen," Daisie exclaimed when Desmond began to talk anxiously about this latest embarrassing moment. She spoke sharply, Helen always a tender subject between them. "Best for her if she'd stayed here and pretended I'd been loose with some casually met man so I'd have faced the shame. She did nothing wrong and she has to face as much, if not more, than us. I should have borne the brunt of all this, not Helen."

There were nights when she lay awake wishing she had done just that. She missed Helen dreadfully. Helen had been kinder to her than her own mother who had walked away treating her like an unwanted burden.

"Don't think it wasn't discussed. I wanted to let you face it, mind, I'll be honest. I tried to persuade Helen to agree.

It was she who persuaded me to do the honourable thing by you."

Desmond was tense. Now he and Daisie were man and wife he wanted to suggest they shared a bed, but in the month since Helen had left and a week after the simple and private marriage service, Daisie still went to the top of the house to her familiar room.

The field behind The Swan was a regular part of Daisie's busy day. Each morning, as soon as she, Desmond and the boy had eaten breakfast and the kitchen was clear to begin the lunchtime preparations, she went out to attend to the animals.

She opened the shed and released the duck, fed the hens and the tiny newly-hatched chicks that looked like giant honey bees, then unleashed the dogs, called the cats and walked alongside the stream. She frequently met Tommy who told her of his latest bargain buys with which he planned to build up his fortune and of the girls he occasionally took out.

In May, when the heady smell of the hawthorn blossoms gave the air a tantalising perfume, she was unaware of the beauty of the morning. She hardly noticed the tall elegant flowers on the horse chestnuts or the pale pyramids of blossom on the holly. She didn't notice the grey heron standing like a statue in the grasses at the edge of the water waiting for his breakfast to swim past, or the beautiful kingfisher offering expert competition. Her thoughts were on Helen.

The previous day she had called to see her and, as before, Helen had refused to open the door. She had slipped a note through the letter box and waited until she saw it pulled inside. At least she knew that Helen was on her feet.

No one had seen Helen since she had left The Swan, except Tommy, who was the kind never to give up. He'd bang on the door, shout through the letter box and generally make a nuisance of himself until she opened up and spoke to him. At her request he began to buy a few items for her from the market and later, from the town shops, so he was able to report to Daisie that although she was still low she was, "alive and taking nourishment", as he cheerfully put it.

On the morning after Daisie's most recent attempt to talk to Helen, Tommy could see she was unhappy. Taking her arm he pointed to the old house. "Come on, Dais, let's burn it down."

She smiled at him sadly. "Still think burning the past will improve the future?"

"'Course it will, Dais." He patted his pocket then produced a box of matches.

"Pointless to do it now. The morning's so bright it wouldn't be exciting."

"Tonight then, after the pub closes. I'll meet you back here and we'll make a bonfire of your past. Right?"

It was easy to leave the house on the pretext of checking on the animals. Desmond hardly spoke to her apart from the necessities of business and, leaving him to count the takings in the back room beyond the Select, she put her coat around her shoulders and went to meet Tommy.

In the small living room Desmond heard Daisie leave. He rose, gathered his coat, and set off to follow. Time this dalliance with Tommy was stopped. Soon there would be further excuse for gossip. There had been enough jokes and teasing without Tommy adding to his humiliation!

The night was as black as could be. A wind disturbed the trees and caused a low whine as he felt his way along the path. He wished he could use a torch as his feet kept slipping on the uneven ground. He only had the sound of the stream to keep him on the path. The gas lights along the High Street were hardly visible so far from the road. Daisie was able to find her way without any hesitation. Knows the way to Tommy from regular use, Desmond thought with growing anger.

In spite of the wind rippling through the tall grasses and rushes, he heard the whispers as Daisie and Tommy met, and cautiously increased his pace to get closer. He wanted her to give herself away completely, then he could tell her to move into his bed or go. Divorce wasn't an impossible thing, he could afford it, and while he waited he and Helen could return to their previous happy state. He would willingly face more gossip to achieve that happy end. He willed Daisie and Tommy to fall into each other's arms.

He saw the couple reach the cottage that had once been Daisie's home and turned off the path. So that was their love-nest. What a sordid way to carry on. Then he saw them go into a huddle and, although he couldn't hear what they said, they were obviously amused at something as their stifled laughter came back on the stiffening breeze to increase his anger.

The whoose of flames startled him and he stepped back and just recovered his senses in time to hide as they came back along the path to stop close to where he was hiding and watch as flames took hold of the old building. What on earth were they up to?

Then wild screams rent the air and two figures stumbled out of the ruin, each seen clearly in the bright light from the newly made flames. The woman was naked, the man with his trousers about his ankles. Each was screaming in rage and fright. Who could they be? And what were Daisie and Tommy doing? Attempting murder?

The man hopped about, his trousers preventing him from running as he was valiantly trying to do, indifferent to the girl's predicament in his panic. The girl was covering her backside then her front, arms waving ineffectually as she tried to decide on the most advantageous use of them.

"What the hell?" Tommy gasped. "Who is it for heaven's sake?"

"Phil," a young woman's voice wailed pitifully, "find my dress! I can't go home like this or Mam'll kill me!"

"Phil!" Tommy shouted, his voice coming out like an explosion as the humour of the situation overwhelmed him. "I'm sorry. We didn't dream anyone would be in there." He collapsed into laughter and, after a moment, Daisie joined him.

Desmond saw their faces and found that the shock followed by the ludicrous sight of the two escapee lovers was too much for him and he began to laugh too, stifling his giggles with

101

his hands as he staggered backwards away from the intense heat of the conflagration. Whatever Daisie and Tommy's intentions had been, it couldn't have been loving.

"Venus rising from the ashes," Tommy chanted between bouts of laughter. "God 'elp us, Dais, this is better than any bonfire night I've ever known."

The heat of the furious fire forced them back and the five people, three laughing helplessly, one crying and Phil swearing without repeats for longer than Tommy believed possible, stood watching as the house fell in on itself and completely buried the girl's clothes and any hope of dignity.

Suddenly Daisie leaned closer to Tommy and whispered urgently, "Tommy, there's someone else here, over by the bushes."

"I can see him, Dais. Let's pretend we've known all along, shall we?"

"Who is it?" Daisie asked.

"Hello, Desmond," Tommy shouted, "glad you didn't miss this. Better than washing up glasses, eh?"

The two lovers were performing a grotesque dance as the woman tried to take Phil's trousers to hide her nakedness and Phil determinedly hung on to them. "Let *me* have them, I need them more than you do!" the girl shrieked.

"Don't be daft. I can't walk home like this, I live in the High Street for heaven's sake, woman!"

"One hand! That's all *you* need to keep yourself decent! One hand! I can't cover all I've got with only one hand!" She lunged at him and heaved on the disputed garment.

"Ger'off!"

"Give them to me!"

"You'll have me in the stream in a minute, you daft ha'porth!"

"Selfish bugger!"

There was a real danger now as the flames began to lick across the space between the house and the surrounding trees and the five people began to walk, then run, back along the path towards The Swan.

Tommy had recovered sufficiently to hand the furious girl

102

his coat. Unfortunately, when the girl put the jacket on, she found it was a short one which reached no lower than the bottom of her spine, leaving a great expanse of white flesh exposed. With the coat making the top half of her invisible, she fought on for possession of the trousers. Unsympathetic, Daisie clung to her own, longer coat and ignored the girl's pleas for a more dignified garment.

The girl, following after Phil who was impatient to put as much distance between himself and the sorry affair as he could, disappeared behind the High Street towards the far end of town.

"You can't let her go like that," Desmond said, catching up with Tommy and Daisie after a final glance at the disappearing backside.

"Serve her right," Daisie said firmly, trying not to think of the times she had been in the girl's situation herself.

Before they reached the door of The Swan they could hear the bell of the fire-engine on its way to deal with the fire, and Tommy wished them goodnight and went back to watch the battle against the flames.

Desmond ushered Daisie in doors and at once demanded, "What's going on between you and that Tommy Thomas? It has to stop, d'you hear?"

The laughter threatened to turn quickly to tears, the sight of Phil had been both funny and tragic, but Daisie stood upright and forced her voice to be low and level and said, "I've been very unhappy. Tommy understands, that's all. He thought that burning my past might help me settle for my present situation and learn to accept it."

It was quite a speech for her and Desmond was confused by it. "But why are you unhappy? I thought you *wanted* to marry me and have a name for your – our – child?"

"I'm grateful, but I miss Helen. I think she's suffered the most and, oh, Desmond, I feel so guilty."

"It was my fault, you were only a child," Desmond said stiffly. "Now we must make the best of things, for the baby's sake and for Helen's," he added wisely. "We can't let her go through all this for nothing, can we?"

"Do you want to take me to bed, then?" she whispered. And suddenly she wanted it, too. An end to the humiliation of Phil's rejection and an end to the loneliness of the weeks since they parted.

Desmond offered her his hand and together they climbed the stairs to the big bedroom above the bar.

Tommy was troubled. There was an opportunity to make a lot of money if he took a chance and with almost a thousand pounds in his bank account and several hundred more hidden away in boxes and stone jam-jars, he felt weak at the prospect of losing it all and having to begin again. He had been making money since he was still at school and now he could buy some good houses, live modestly on the rents while he continued to make more, and Cwm Manachlog would see him as a respectable businessman.

If this latest deal came off he would be able to buy twice as many properties and live twice as well. He might even consider finding himself a wife then he'd really feel he'd "arrived". The trouble was the deal necessitated borrowing money and it involved getting help from Phil. After the debacle of the night they had set the old house on fire he doubted if Phil was in a frame of mind to assist him!

He knocked at the house along from where Helen still lived quietly and rarely seen. Phil opened the door and to Tommy's relief, gave him a crooked grin.

"Come in if you promise to leave your matches outside!" he said. "What d'you want? The name of my companion of that night?"

"Sorry to my heart I am, Phil," Tommy spluttered, trying to control his laughter. "I was only trying to help Dais to put the past firmly in the past. Not harmed were you?"

"Only our dignity, boy. Only our dignity." He gestured to the kettle singing on the side of the fire. "Want a cup of tea?"

"I want a favour," Tommy said bluntly. "I want to borrow your warehouses for a couple of weeks. Pay you I will."

"What d'you expect me to do without storage space?"

104

"China wouldn't hurt in any old shed. What I have to store won't take kindly to damp. Probably won't be for longer than two weeks. What do you say?"

"I say tell me more."

What Tommy had been offered was the contents of a department store, from the basement china and kitchen ware through ladies and gentlemen's clothes and hats, to bedding and linen. Even small items of furniture. It was far more than he had ever dreamed of handling and would take several weeks to clear, but at the price he was negotiating, he would become a wealthy man in the process.

"The building is falling apart, see," Tommy told Phil. "Wood is rotten, concrete crumbling and the metal work is rusted right through. Been neglected for years it has. Now it's in real danger of collapsing and it has to come down before it falls down. Desperate they are to find someone to take the lot. They haven't time to sell in dribs and drabs, see."

Tommy glanced at Phil to see if he was as excited about the prospect as he had been. "What d'you think, then? It's a risk, you don't have to tell me that." His eye winked wildly as he waited for Phil's response.

"What if I buy half of it from you here and now?" Phil offered. He tried not to sound too eager but the deal could be a further step in his plan to open a shop to sell china and glasswear. The two men glanced at each other, each trying to appear casual. "The china and glass I'll want for myself, mind, so we'll have to do a deal bearing that in mind." Eyeing each other like two warring dogs, they eventually came to an understanding.

"Come and look at it this afternoon," Tommy said. "And if the price you have in mind agrees with mine, we'll trade." As an extra incentive he added, "We can go in Desmond's car. I take it out every week since he can't bring himself to either sell it or use it."

That afternoon, Tommy completed the deal. The bank had forwarded a loan, Phil had agreed his use of the warehouse and had bought half of the stock, some of which would be for his new shop. They had less than a month to settle the details.

Phil loved the markets but he had been thinking recently of getting a shop in the main street of Cwm Manachlog and putting in a manager. He thought at once of Helen. She was old enough to be reliable and young enough to be capable of hard work. That she was honest he did not doubt.

He knocked on her door a couple of days later and called softly for her to let him in.

"Mrs Prew – Helen," he called. "It's Phil, can I have a word?"

"I'm busy right now, Phil, won't it wait?"

"Not really, I'm in need of help and you're the first one I thought of, being next door an' all." After a lot more persuasion Helen opened the door and looked through the gap. Phil was shocked to see how old and sick she looked, but he pressed on with his intention, forcing the door wider, and getting inside.

The place was a mess, with boxes and cases opened and half unpacked. The fireguard was drapped with clothes obviously just washed and steaming in the heat of the fire. The room was unbelievably hot, the fire built up almost to the throat of the fire-back, unnecessary on the warm June day.

"Leaving or just coming?" he joked and to his relief she smiled at him.

"I've been sitting here all these weeks refusing to accept that this is now my home. Fool that I am. I should consider myself lucky. At least I've got a home. Now I'm starting to get things straight."

"Want a job?" Phil asked. "I'm opening a shop in the middle of the High Street where the hat shop used to be. I'll be selling china and ornaments just like on the stalls. You'd do a treat as my manager."

"You'd want a man, surely, for a job like that?"

"One day, when the business is grown maybe. But for now I'd like you to run it for me." He waited as she considered it. She frowned once or twice as if about to refuse, then she looked at him and nodded.

"All right, Phil. I'm your new manager. Now, what about wages?"

*   *   *

106

The goods bought by Tommy and Phil were quickly sold. The warehouses they rented were filled and emptied three times, protected by a guard dog called Mot.

The stores were finally cleared and the dog returned to its owner. Tommy and Phil each made more money in a month than they usually made in a year. They sold a lot of it to people in the big houses on the outskirts of the town and more to hotels and tea shops. Phil dealt with the *Crachach*, the well-to-do and wealthy, and Tommy sold to the less favoured members of the public. They worked without rest, day after day, until the bulk of it was safely sold and the money in the bank or in one of several hiding places.

Tommy and Phil both rented extra stalls and used them to dispose of the less saleable items. To Phil's delight and surprise Helen offered to take on a stall and sold kitchen items and, when they were gone, hats. Even the clothes had all been sold before the month was out. News of the reduced price bargains spread and people came from towns and villages further and further out and went home loaded with shopping their purses empty, their satisfaction showing in their smiles.

The Toby of Cwm Manachlog market was so overwhelmed by all the extra business he had difficulty keeping the pavement free and allowing access through the High Street. There was such a confusion with the cars and charabangs that he hired a field to be used as a temporary car park, and boasted that it must be a first for a market to have to do such a thing. "It was a real 'brammer' of a month, like having a second Christmas," he was heard to say.

It was a flurry of importance that the town had rarely seen and, beside the extra business at the market, all the other shops and cafes and public houses fed on the success. The Swan was increasing its orders as the month brought more and more people into town and Daisie enjoyed the excitement and being in charge of the busy place.

When the business subsided to near its usual level, Tommy went to collect the car behind The Swan for its usual run around the town. Desmond saw him arrive and called him in.

"Will you teach Daisie to drive?" he asked. "Don't think I'll ever fancy it myself. And women do drive, I've seen pictures of them."

"She'll pick it up in no time," Tommy assured him.

Tommy was right and Daisie did learn quickly. Several times they were stopped by the local policeman and warned to be considerate, and twice Daisie nearly tipped Tommy out of his seat when she stopped suddenly to avoid being seen by Helen.

Daisie knew she and Helen had to face each other eventually but for those early weeks she was afraid. Then, one day, when, for practice, Daisie had driven the car through the High Street during the market day, she parked in front of the new china shop and, with her heart thumping nervously, she went inside.

Through the summer, Helen had built up the newly opened shop and business had increased steadily week by week. She saw Daisie enter and froze in her seat behind the counter. There was no assistant to send forward to serve. Coldly she looked straight into Daisie's face and demanded to know what she wanted.

"Nothing. I – Helen, I know I'm asking a lot, but couldn't we be friends. I miss you so very much. Desmond misses you. I want us to be friends, like we were." She was halted in her often rehearsed speech by Helen coming swiftly forward and standing in front of her with cold eyes and a tightly clenched mouth.

"It's what you want, is it Daisie? Then you must have it, mustn't you? Daisie always gets what she wants, doesn't she? Whoever suffers because of it!"

The shop door opened and the policeman marched in. "That your car, Mrs Prewitt? Sorry, but I must ask you to move it, causing an obstruction. Should know better you should and on market day, too."

Daisie walked out of the shop without a further word.

A week later whcn Daisie was again in the High Street

she walked past the china shop intending not to look inside. But Helen stepped out and said bruskly, "I'll come to tea on Sunday, if that's what you and Desmond really want."

It was not an easy occasion and Daisie found it best to serve tea and act as waitress and allow Helen and Desmond to talk. Seeing them together made her feel vulnerable and afraid. There was no doubt that they were still very much in love with each other.

By August, when layers of clothes no longer hid the fact, most people knew about Daisie's child. As they expected it to be the cause of much speculation Daisie and Desmond told everyone as little as necessary. It was Helen who broadcast the news, adding that the child was, for Desmond, a longed for joy.

In November, weeks before the child could reasonably be expected, Daisie woke in the night and gave a cry of alarm.

"Desmond. Something's wrong. I feel terrible pains. Oh, there's something wrong. I'm going to lose this baby and all the misery will have been for nothing!"

Desmond was solicitous and panicky. He ran downstairs hastily dressed and went to fetch the doctor. On the way back, running beside the man with his cloak and large black bag, he stopped off and knocked on Helen's door.

"Helen, my love, it's Daisie, something's wrong. The baby it's . . . oh, can you come and sit with her? I don't know what to do."

"Hurry back to her and I'll follow. Just give me time to dress." Helen pushed him on his way and, with a thoughtful expression on her face, went back inside.

Gaynor Prewitt was born at seven the following morning with Desmond walking up and down in the field behind the house followed by a parade of dogs, cats and the duck. Helen assisted the doctor with the birth. Daisie was sleeping when she went home for breakfast before going to open the china shop. She nodded to Desmond.

"You have a lovely daughter, Desmond my dear. Dark haired at the moment, but she'll probably be fair like you when the new hair comes." And fair like Phil Johnson, she thought as she hurried away.

It was two weeks before Daisie was allowed to rise from her bed and come downstairs. The first person she asked to see was Helen.

"I'll send the boy over to the shop and ask her to come at dinner time," Desmond promised. He was so delighted with the new infant he thought to deny Daisie nothing. A daughter with his name, Gaynor Prewitt. At his age it was something he had lost all hope of achieving.

He met Helen at the door and smiled like the besotted new parent that he was and ushered her into the sitting room beyond the Select. Helen held out her arms to hug Daisie and then admired the little girl until Desmond had left them. Then she said softly. "It's Phil's child, isn't it, Daisie? Not Desmond's at all?"

Daisie stared at her, her face fading from its usual glow to a whiteness that made Helen fear she might faint.

"It's all right, Desmond will never know. I love him you see, and I'd never do or say anything to upset him. Never in this world. But I'd like to know."

"I – I didn't know what else to do," Daisie's voice was barely a whisper.

"You could have trusted us, Daisie. Haven't I always taken good care of you? Why didn't you come to me? That lack of trust hurt me almost as much as you blaming Desmond."

"I suppose I was too frightened to risk it. I've never learnt to trust. There was only Mam and Dad. They both let me down. And Phil. Gaynor *is* his child, but he . . . well, you can guess. He isn't the sort to be tied down."

"Funny, I never wanted to tie Desmond down. I thought that we'd stay together without any law and bits of paper to make us. Perhaps I should have married him. He asked me you know, several times. But that's a long time ago." She stood up and her eyes were steely in the lined face. "Just promise me, Daisie, that you'll be straight with him. You'll do nothing to hurt him."

"I took advantage of his honourable nature, Helen. I owe

110

him my loyalty now." But knowing that her secret was out, and to Helen, made the promise harder to give.

There burned deep inside her the tiny flame of hope that, one day, Helen would return to The Swan and Desmond, and she and Phil would . . . But the tiny flame flickered and went out and was replaced by recent memories of the fiercer flames when the house burned and Phil and one of his women had been silhouetted in the glow.

"Phil was a mistake, Helen, and best forgotten. Part of the painful process of growing up." She smiled up at the quiet woman, touched her hand and asked, "Did Tommy ever tell you about the night we set fire to my old house?"

8

One of the first things Daisie did after the birth of her daughter was to bring down her father's pedlar's tray. She placed it on the end of the bar counter and opened its lid to display Dan's remaining stock, oddments of little importance to most but on which their survival had depended.

"Why are you showing that, Daisie?" Desmond asked. "It won't stay clean for long stuck by there."

"It will remind me of how lucky I am," she smiled.

"Best to put it in the living room, then," he replied, "where you can see it. It'll be a while before you're back working in the bar."

"I'm back from tonight," she announced. "I don't want to be a passenger in the business. Gaynor cries whether I'm there or not. Ethel and I will take turns at listening for her and trying to comfort her. That way I can be of some use to you."

"You are useful, Daisie. Looking after our daughter is work enough for the present." She couldn't help smiling at him. He was so pleased at becoming a father it shone from his round face like a light from within, which, she supposed, was what it was. Fired by ignorance, more's the pity, but a shining light of happiness it undoubtedly was.

Daisie ignored his plea for her to stay out of the bar and look after Gaynor and made her own arrangements. It was something he would have to get used to: Daisie making up her mind what she would do and doing it. To help her further she employed a young girl to help with the cleaning and told Desmond afterwards.

As Christmas drew near, Daisie seemed to see the end of

her worries: Ethel Trip, who had a seven year old daughter called Kate, ignored her husband's protests and agreed to help in the bar full-time. She worked well with Daisie and Desmond and was popular with the customers. This gave Daisie time to deal with her exhausting daughter and spend time serving in the bar and preparing food.

Gaynor was not a contented baby. Because she was so fractious Daisie had been afraid Desmond would soon tire of her, but he constantly went to look at her, picking her up and cuddling her with that special devoted smile saved for favourite children.

Daisie's only disappointment was the continuing distance between herself and Helen. She went regularly to the china shop to talk to her one time friend, hoping to wear down her resistance and return to that closeness they had once enjoyed. Although she was well aware of what she had done to Helen and held out little hope. Only her belief in Helen's goodness and generous heart made her keep trying.

She made a regular habit of calling in on Saturday mornings, carrying two cups of tea bought in the market. When Daisie invited Helen to visit her and Desmond at The Swan again, she agreed.

Slowly she began to be a regular visitor, but only during the lunch hour, when they were busy and conversation held no chance of flagging into uncomfortable silences. She sat in the living room beyond the Select and drank tea and talked and admired the baby just like any other family friend. Then, one day when they were extra busy, she helped behind the bar, to Desmond's obvious delight.

"Just like old times, Helen, love," Daisie heard him remark and unexpected jealousy bristled across her skin. She put the baby in her cot and then told the surprised Ethel to take the weight off her feet for an hour. She remained in the bar herself until Helen left, laughing and joking with the customers, handing out insults with the pints and letting everyone know that she was the landlady.

For Helen, the hurt of Desmond's betrayal was still fierce, but it was not in her nature to be vindictive and besides, deep inside her was the hope that one day, when he had become a man for whom Daisie had no further need, he might return to her. Until then she would behave as a friend and support him and his family with dignity.

Living next to Phil Johnson she became aware of the routine of his life. Without really intending to, she noticed, as Daisie had done, that on Sundays he was never seen. He had a horse and a couple of carts and when he might be expected to relax and enjoy the freedom of not having a market to attend, he went out. He left early, long before she rose to begin her day. She would hear the front door close and his footsteps walk around the back of the cottages to the sloping field where the horse lived. Then the sound of hooves, the creak and rumble of wheels crunching on gravel, took him away to some unknown destination. He rarely returned before nine o'clock in the evening. Then he usually went to one of the public houses for a drink with his friends.

Helen began to be curious about her neighbour. She quickly found that questioning him directly was not the way. He was friendly and appeared to reply with frankness but she gleaned nothing. That he had a family somewhere she knew, but a curtain was lowered every time she tried to learn more. With childish glee, she determined to discover his secret.

Stepping out of bed and standing on the cold linoleum was not sensible on a January morning, but shivering with the icy cold she rose very early and watched for him to come out of the house. He was carrying two sacks: one a linen flour sack from the baker and another a newish but coarse sack which held vegetables from the wholesalers. When the flat cart passed a while later, the horse frisky in the shafts, the sacks were on the back together with piles of firewood; orange and apple boxes and crates as well as logs sawn ready for burning.

How could she find out where he went? There was no way she could run after him. If only she could drive.

Desmond had never sat in his new car. It was too much a part of the disaster that ended with him losing Helen and marrying Daisic. He wondered how he could suggest Helen taking it back for her own use. It was difficult to suggest without hurting her feelings. It had been such a generous gift. So he was delighted when, one Sunday morning, she called and asked if she might learn to drive it. He agreed at once, after glancing at Daisie and receiving her nod of approval.

"Tommy will teach you," Daisie said. "Patient and understanding is Tommy. Just what you need."

"Seems I'm going to teach half the village!" Tommy joked when Desmond called in and asked him to give Helen her first lessons.

A couple of hours later he and Helen set off through Cwm Manachlog and out towards open country. When they came to a suitable place he patiently explained the gears and showed her the moves with his hand on hers. After three or four lessons she seemed to have grasped it and one Sunday she set off on her own.

The weather was very cold and although the hood was up the cold January wind found cracks to enter and chill every part of her body. Snow began to fall as she reached the highest point of her intended journey and opening the split screen made the cold almost unbearable. She had been a fool to come so far. But she needed to practice and it seemed such a waste not to use a Sunday. Besides, she had planned that one Sunday, when she felt more confident, she would follow Phil and see where he went.

As she negotiated a turn on the narrow roadway she began to regret her journey. Fear trickled through her veins. Desmond had warned her to stay around the town. Now, with the snow obliterating everything beyond the bonnet, she was frightened. The whole world was white, a moving curtain of spots that seemed to entice her sight away to one side off the road. There were few trees so high on the hills and she imagined any moment to hear unseen rocks tearing the bottom off the car. She knew she had taken a wrong turning somewhere. The town should have appeared before now. She had no idea where she was and how far from habitation. Reports of people dying on the mountainside in snow were frequently heard and she knew that without food or warmth she might become the next.

When she saw a gateway she turned in and drove towards a fairly large house. Tall neglected privet rose on either side of her and the snow was less deep where the straggly trees formed some protection. The house was old and lacking paint. The door stood half open and she thought with dismay that the house must be abandoned.

To her relief someone answered her knock. A frail sickly looking girl about ten years old, stood and stared silently up at her, fear showing in the pale, pale blue eyes. Helen realised that with leather coat, leather hat and goggles hanging around her neck she must be a strange sight.

"Is your Mam in?" she asked gently. "I would like to shelter until the snow eases a little if she'd be willing." Without taking her eyes of the apparition the girl called, "Mam!" But it was Phil who appeared.

"Helen! How did you find me here? What's up? You look frozen."

"Fancy seeing you. Frozen I am for sure. I was driving and the snow, well, I thought it best to shelter for a while. I saw the gate and drove in."

"Driving up to the back of the mountains in this. It's bleak at the best of times and a storm up here usually developes into something far worse than in town. Whatever were you thinking of?

For a moment or two Helen thought he was not going to invite her inside. Then he seemed to make up his mind and with an ungracious shrug stood back and gestured for her to enter. He started to say something, but seemed to think better of it, shrugged again, and guided her through a long, dark passage into a large room at the back of the house.

The snow storm had darkened the day so it was like night time, but Helen could see that the place was poorly furnished. The wood fire was cheerful enough though and Helen sank gratefully into the chair which an elderly woman vacated for her. She rubbed her hands, then held them in front of the flames and began to explain her predicament. The woman made no comment, just stood and listened as if she were only half conscious.

"This is my mother," Phil told her in a whisper when he came in with teapot and cups. As he poured boiling water from the soot encrusted kettle on the hob, Helen looked at the woman before her. She wasn't as old as she had first thought, just shabby and unkempt. Helen realised with a shock that she was probably not much older than herself.

She sensed Phil's discomfort. It was hidden behind a smile but the eyes showed it, reddish in the brightness of the fire they showed his pain. She wondered why. The woman was worn down with work and he might feel guilty about not helping more but that didn't explain his embarrassment. When the rest of the family was presented, they did.

Slowly a second girl aged about twenty and dressed in rather flamboyant clothes glided in. Silently and rather eerily she hugged Phil then draped herself on the couch and watched Helen. No one spoke apart from Phil and he only spoke in whispers. Then a voice called, startling in its unexpectedness and odd wavering tone. It was the voice of an old man from beyond the room in what Helen had presumed was a kitchen.

"Who is it, Jem?" the old man called. "Who is it?"

No one bothered to reply. Helen sipped her tea, glancing at the window in the hope that the snow had miraculously ceased. She wanted to get out. Whatever Phil's secret was she wished she hadn't unearthed it.

"These are my sisters, Helen," Phil said in a whisper that added to the eerie atmosphere. "Mam had seven girls after me but the others are dead. Dad wanted their names to begin with J. So we had Janet, Jacqueline, called Jack, June, Joy, Jo and Jill and Jane." The ten-year-old and the twenty-year-old acknowledged the last two names with a slight movement of their heads then they left as silently as they had arrived came, returning to the unseen man who still asked plaintively.

"Who is it, Jem? Who is it?"

"Jem, Jemima, is my mother," Phil explained.

The tea finished, Helen rose to go. She wondered why he

was whispering and seemed so ill at ease. She didn't want to know. All she wanted was to depart from this strange household.

"It's still snowing heavy, Helen. I think we'd better leave the car and walk back with the horse. He'll guide us. Knows the road like you know your own kitchen he does. I'll just push the car under the some shelter. Wait there, I won't be long."

Helen stood watching the door to the kitchen, smiling nervously at Phil's mother who had returned to her chair and now sat as silently as her daughters had done.

"Is that your husband calling?" Helen asked. "Poorly is he?"

"Never been the same since the accident. Fine he was until the accident." Nothing further was offered and Helen almost ran to Phil she was so relieved when he re-appeared.

Phil fitted Helen with some heavy gum-boots and they set off through the swirling snow. Phil leading the horse, Helen in his wake using the footmarks he had made to make her own steps easier. Once out of the house questions buzzed around in her head like angry bees but even if Phil had wanted to talk the mode of travel made it impossible.

It took them an hour and a half to get home and then Helen insisted on going to The Swan to tell Desmond what had happened. "He'll be wondering, me out in his car and the weather turning nasty."

"You won't tell him, will you? About Jane and the rest?" Helen promised and he smiled his relief. "I'll go in and light your fire, then," Phil said as he led the horse back to his shed and his supper.

Desmond seemed indifferent to the fate of his beautiful car and Helen grieved again for the unfortunate circumstances that had spoilt her wonderful surprise.

"Phil said he'll look after it," she said, "and as soon as the snow clears I'll bring it back."

"No hurry, love – er – Helen. I won't be needing it for a while. Even Daisie won't want to take it out in this weather!"

When Helen returned to her house Phil had lit the fire, made a cup of tea and was sitting on her hearth-rug making toast.

"I suppose everyone will know now," he said solemnly. Helen guessed he referred to his sad family.

"They aren't simple you know," he went on. "It's that they never go anywhere or see anyone and losing all the girls. Little Jill is none too well. She might not survive this winter. They attended so rarely that school gave up on them."

"Your father?" she queried hesitantly. "Sick is he? Your mother said something about an accident."

"He was crushed in a ship wreck. He shouldn't have recovered according to the doctors. It was his head you see. Now all he does is sit in bed near the fire and all he says is, 'Who is it, Jem?' and occasionally re-lives the disaster."

"But, so many children – "

"I know. It's crazy, isn't it? The girls didn't stand a chance, not without a penny of income coming into the house. I go every Sunday and take food, do what I can."

Helen imagined them sitting there in silence, just waiting for Phil's next visit. "What are their names again?" She tried to make the conversation more light-hearted, the pain of it all was showing again in his eyes.

"Janet, Jack, June, Joy, Jo, all dead, and the two that are left, Jill and Jane."

"I won't tell anyone, although I wonder if it might be better for them if someone did. But Phil, if I can help you only have to ask. By the way," she smiled, "how did you escape the J?"

"I didn't," he said wryly. "My first name is John."

Helen deliberately avoided the subject of his unhappy family when they talked, but gradually he began to tell her things, the day to day incidents of any family, like Jill falling and cutting her knee and Jane, proud of making a cake that didn't sink in the middle. From considering him rather unemotional and cold, Helen began to see that within the young man there was the capacity for love. She wished he would find himself a girl and begin a more joyful family life of his own.

One day she dared to ask, "Why didn't you marry Daisie?"

"You know?" He stared at her and she unflinchingly stared back.

"Yes, Phil, I know."

"You know why. If anyone doesn't need an explanation it's you."

"Because of your family? She'd have helped. She loved you. With Daisie you'd have started to build a real family, something to make you forget the unhappiness up there," she pointed through her window to the mountains now clear of snow, shining in the wintery sun.

"I was tempted. Although she was very young, seven years younger than me, I almost proposed. But how could I involve someone with all that?" It was Phil's turn to wave in the direction of the mountain.

During the summer of 1914, as Gaynor grew from a helpless baby into a child who sat in her pram and wailed almost without ceasing, Desmond grew more and more morose. Life with the lively Daisie had been exciting for a while, and the birth of Gaynor was undoubtedly a highlight, but now, with the pub becoming busier and Daisie having less and less time for him, he was lonely for Helen.

The rumblings of war threatened the lives of them all yet there was an enthusiasm for fun during that summer which afterwards was thought of as the need to laugh before it was too late. With several of the local families now owning cars and the charabangs a popular mode of travel, Daisie and Helen organised several trips to the seaside. Leaving The Swan in the care of Ethel and Desmond, they went to the sea in a convoy of cars and the twenty-eight-seater charabang loaded with food for a picnic.

Many of the children had never seen the sea and its expanse was alarming and thrilling. Few had proper bathers, so underclothes were substituted as the children dipped themselves in the cold and frilly waves, then dried on the rocks.

The animal population behind The Swan increased. Besides the dogs, cats, ducks and chickens, someone had placed a goat in the field one night. It was weak with malnutrition and Desmond felt slighted by the fact that, although life was constantly too hectic for Daisie to spend time with him, she found hours in which to coax the small creature back to life. Lonely, used to Helen being always there and available, he developed the habit of walking to the china shop where Helen worked and talking to her.

"That Daisie," he said light-heartedly. "Never still for a minute. Dashing to shop because she doesn't trust the boy, checking everything Ethel does so she might as well do the work herself, and those animals, I swear she cares more for them than for little Gaynor. No wonder when the girl cries so much, mind. Such energy she's got, that Daisie." He was laughing, but Helen could hear beyond the proud boasting and saw the emptiness of his life without her.

"Lucky man you are, Desmond," she said brightly, "and don't you forget it."

The nation held off from war and Gillian's marriage to Waldo Griffiths took place in June. Invitations were sent out only to the more select members of the community. Twenty privileged people received her gold-edged invitation cards but more than treble the number actually arrived at the church and most of them walked back with the invited guests to where Mrs Griffiths, Gillian's mother-in-law, had helped to arrange a dainty spread of ham, chicken and assorted delicacies meant for the polite appetites of twenty-four people.

Mother of the bride, attempting to look serene, almost screamed when she saw the number that arrived expecting to be fed. With appetites that were far from polite, Gillian's friends looked at the spread and waited for the proper food to be brought out. The maid, hired for the day, was sent to buy whatever was available in the shops and she returned with loaves of bread, cheese, bedraggled salads and three dozen eggs.

The eggs were boiled and eaten still warm, the need for refreshment was so great. The elegantly set table was soon a shambles as hands reached for anything edible. Runny egg decorated several shirts as some of the eggs had not been allowed to boil for long enough.

"I think they'll start eating the napkins if Mam and Mrs Griffiths don't find some more food soon," Gillian chuckled to Daisie.

"I think I'd better give a hand," Daisie smiled. She handed the baby to Megan, who looked ill at ease standing beside her fiancé, Arthur, and disappeared in the kitchen. To Mrs Griffiths's horror she hastily cut up bread, cheese and raw onions just as she did for the bar. Some salad was added as a garnish and the plates were enthusiastically emptied.

"That Arthur is sure to tell his mother! What *will* the Huntley-Davies's think of us?" Mrs Griffiths wailed, wishing the helpful Daisie a thousand miles away.

"From the way their Arthur is tucking in, it's the best meal he's had in ages!" Daisie snapped. "You should have ordered more than twice as much if you wanted everything to be fancy!"

"I *would* have ordered twice as much if we'd invited all this lot!" Mrs Griffiths snapped angrily, handing Daisie the joint of boiled ham intended for when the guests had gone. "Where have they all come from?"

"Town it might be, but Cwm Manachlog has the heart of a village and always will have," Daisie grinned. "Here, pass another of those onions, the plates are coming back empty faster than I can fill them!" She turned to the bemused maid. "And you, don't stand there gawping. Pour some more teas. Pity you didn't order more beer, isn't it?" she glared at the unhappy Mrs Griffiths who balefully handed her some more tomatoes and onions.

By contrast, the wedding of Megan and Arthur Huntley-Davies was formal, severe and with a definate lack of fun. The shy gentle Megan who had attracted Arthur, and who his mother saw as a suitable girl to model into the perfect wife, was already beginning to irritate him. For a while he had enjoyed being her strength, had felt masterly and considerate as he guided her through the various occasions they attended during their engagement. Now the sight of her nervous face, her hunched shoulders making the expensive wedding dress look like a rag as she stood trying to become invisible, the way she looked at him before answering the simplest question, made anger swell inside him. If his mother hadn't refused to allow it he would have cancelled the wedding and found someone more suitable to his intended social life among the wealthy.

The reception was held in the one hotel Cwm Manachlog boasted. Small by most standards it had an air of gentility that appealed to the more important citizens. To Megan it was worse than visiting the dentist. She clutched Arthur's hand but he pushed her away. Surely she could have tried a little harder for one day, instead of cowering beside him as if being escorted to her own execution.

The dress Arthur's mother had chosen for Megan was pure white and it made her look sickly and ill-nourished. During the weeks before the wedding she had lost weight and now she was so thin the dress hung on her like a shapeless tube. Her long brown hair, specially waved for the occasion, collapsed from its arrangement before she had reached the church and a fly flew in her eye and had to be rubbed away so she looked as if as she was crying. The gasp from the congregation was of dismay when it should have been of pleasure and delight. Arthur was furious and did not attempt to hide it.

Daisie tried to add some excitement to the day and was at once put in her place. She had gone with Desmond and the seven-month-old Gaynor, 'tucked' for the occasion and wearing her first proper clothes. Daisie had dressed the little girl in a bonnet of satin edged with swansdown and a dress to match. The dress was palest blue with a crotcheted jacket and bootees in white. Everyone admired the child even though she hardly stopped crying long enough to allow them to see her face. It was Megan who calmed her most easily. Glad of having something to do, she took the crying child from a relieved Daisie and nursed her against her thin chest. At once Gaynor stopped yelling and settled quietly to sleep. Megan hummed softly and felt at peace for the first time that day. She was unaware of the stains that marked the front of her dress.

Arthur found her in the room ajoining the hotel kitchen with the child resting against her and showed his anger in a hissed complaint.

"Megan! What are you doing? You should be out there with our guests, not hiding away in here with a snivelling brat!"

"Oh, Arthur, it's all such a trial, and I've been here for ages and no one has missed me."

"That isn't surprising when you refuse to even try to be sociable. What use will you be to me if you can't be bothered to make polite conversation?"

"No use at all, I suppose," she sighed.

His anger greatly increased when he saw the stains of Gaynor's dribble on Megan's white wedding gown. "Get rid of that child and come into the reception room!" It was an order and Megan saw clearly the unhappy future ahead of her.

"What's the matter, Megan?" Daisie came into the small room in time to hear the last few exchanges. "I'll have Gaynor back now, Megan, and thank you for calming her down for me. You have a real talent for making people happy, we've always said so, haven't we, Gillian?" she added as their friend joined them. "Lucky you are, Arthur, and don't forget it!"

Arthur glared and marched out calling, "I've found my shy bride, Mother, trying to get a stain off her beautiful gown. Help her, will you?"

"He doesn't mean to get cross," Megan defended, "but I do irritate him. I can't help it. I'm not as confident as you two."

"Why did you marry him if you knew he was a bully?" Daisie demanded when she and Gillian had ushered her into the ladies lavatories and were attempting to wash her face of its anguished tears.

"You'll have to make a stand, Megan," Gillian said firmly. "Even with Waldo, and he's a dear, I have to make sure he knows what I will do and what I will definitely not do. Start right now."

Gillian was looking particularly beautiful, with a mid-blue dress with wide sleeves and a skirt shaped so it swayed as she swung her slim hips in her inimitable walk. A silver fox fur was draped around her shoulders even though the month made it unfashionable. Gillian made her own fashions and made others envy her style.

"I'll be all right," Megan said after dusting her nose with some powder papers to hide the shine. "Arthur is very fond of me and we'll be happy, I know we will. Once we have adjusted to each other." She stopped outside the doors of the reception room and looked at the solemn throng within. "D'you think everyone has enjoyed it?"

"Of course," Gillian lied with a glance at Daisie.

"And at least I didn't end up in the kitchen!" Daisie laughed.

"Someone else did," Gillian whispered behind an elegantly curled hand and Daisie turned to see Phil standing in front of the kitchen door.

"Hardly dressed for the occasion, is he?" Gillian muttered, sweeping through the double doors with her arm in Megan's. Daisie paused and looked at Phil.

"What are you doing here, Phil?" she asked, amazed at how steady her voice remained.

"Curious to see the better half of the town in their posh clothes. You look fine, Daisie. Prosperous and – "

"Happy?" she finished for him. "Yes, we're happy, me, Desmond and our daughter." Turning away before he could answer she followed her friends into the sober gathering.

Something in Daisie's expression made Helen curious and she glanced at the doorway to see Phil standing there watching her walk away. She waved at him to show him he had been seen.

"Desmond is looking for you, Daisie," she said. "I think it's time to leave. You can't expect Ethel to manage for long."

Desmond waved to his wife across the room. He held his car keys up as a signal they should leave.

"Desmond, would you mind if I stayed a bit longer," she pleaded. "It's Megan, she upset and I'd like to stop with her until she and Arthur go off for their honeymoon."

"That's something we didn't have, Daisie my dear."

"Tosh and nonsense," Daisie snorted. "All that packing

and travelling just to stay in a room far less comfortable than we've got at The Swan. No thank you. We're fine as we are, Desmond."

"Are we?" he looked at her quizzically and her face softened into a smile.

"Yes, we are, and I'll leave Gillian to keep an eye on poor Megan and come home with you. This place isn't a patch on ours, is it? Heaven's above, what an atmosphere for a wedding! Miserable bunch that they are. They'd have had much more fun with us at The Swan. Too scared of what people think of them to enjoy themselves." She tucked the baby more firmly against her, took his arm and they left out. She managed not to look back to see if Phil was still watching. Helen saw that he was.

Megan's honeymoon was a distressing experience for her. Neither she nor Arthur had any understanding of what it would entail. Arthur's sexual knowledge, apart from the impulses of his own healthy body, consisted of what he had gleaned from innuendo and schoolboy-style jokes with a few of his more brazen friends. Megan thought the encounter would be little more than hugging and kissing, both of which she enjoyed.

The shock of his unskilled demands shattered her and she looked into the future and saw a life more dreadful than even the wedding day had disclosed. She would have to accommodate him every night until she carried a child, and once the child was born it would continue and continue.

For the rest of the week in Torquay the days were filled with apprehension and the nights with fulfillment of the dreaded encounter. Later she was to wonder about the place. Was it as beautiful as friends told her? She remembered nothing except the flowers on the wallpaper of their room which she counted time and again. She knew they had taken walks, which Arthur told her would be good for her, and there were vague memories of the cool, tempting sea. She remembered standing looking at its steely surface for hours during the night when Arthur was snoring contentedly. She remembered a huge dining room where she felt conspicuous and unable to eat. Best of all there was a bathroom with a lock on the door where she could relax and be herself for a few precious moments each day. Locked in a bathroom was hardly the honeymoon joy she had expected.

All this she thought while Arthur lay sleeping at last on their final night, all this and a mother-in-law who plans to teach me to become a "social asset".

Upon returning, as soon as she had unpacked her cases and Arthur had gone to his office, she went to see Daisie.

One look was enough for her friend to know she was unhappy. "What's happened, Megan, you've returned to being our little Crying Mouse again and I bet it's that Arthur's fault!" Shushing Megan's muttered excuses she dumped the crying Gaynor into her pram and pushed her outside the kitchen door. Waving the boy away she poured water into the teapot and made Megan sit down and drink. "Pity you won't take something from the other side of the bar, Megan, you look as if you could do with it!"

"I'm just not suited for marriage, Daisie," Megan said, trying to smile. "I didn't expect . . . you know, it was rough and and . . . oh, I wish I'd had the strength to say no. It was his mother, you see, she persuaded Arthur to marry me. She thought I was suitable material to be moulded into the right wife for him."

"You can come here you know. There's a spare room, the one I used to sleep in. It's yours if you find it too much. You don't have to stay with him."

"Oh, I couldn't leave! He'd be so embarrassed. It would ruin him if he had to admit he'd failed so soon. Oh no, I couldn't do that to him, Daisie. Whatever I do, it won't be that."

"What will you do, then? Look at you, the weight has fallen off you like a boiled chicken. You can't go on like this. If a week has done this, what will a month do?"

"Daisie, I know I'm wicked to think it, but someone at the hotel said we're on the verge of war. The shooting of Duke Ferdinand was what started them discussing it. Winston

Churchill is building up the fleet and he wouldn't do that for nothing. Us trying to mediate was considered interference they said."

"Sorry, Megan, but how does that affect you and Arthur?"

"If men were encouraged to join the forces then Arthur might go. Him being away from home would give me a chance to accept what marriage entails, then I'd be able to cope, after a rest. I'd know better what to expect next time. A rest from him, just a rest, that would do the trick for sure."

"A rest might be a good idea, but don't expect the politicians to arrange it for you. A war? Don't be daft, Megan! The government can't even stop Sylvia and Emmeline Pankhurst and their suffragettes from misbehaving. How can they take on countries like Austria and Germany if women can run rings around them at home like they do? God help Germany, mind, if we had an army of women! They'd never dare risk a war then, eh, Megan? Listen to this." And she read reports from recent papers describing the exploits of the women determined to persuade the government to allow women the vote, with pride. She succeeded in making her friend smile a little before retrieving the still crying Gaynor and walking her back home.

"A war, Megan?" She repeated "not a chance!"

9

The war began with a suddenness that startled Daisie. Wrapped up in her busy life that encompassed less than a half mile in radius she barely noticed what went on further afield. The news of it, brought to The Swan on the startled faces of the regulars, shocked her out of her complacency and she began to read the papers avidly. The implications were frightening. There was talk of conscription, a word she had never heard before, and of the possibility of an invasion by armies from far off lands about which she knew nothing.

Her ignorance embarrassed her and she began discussing the daily events with as many as understood them. Desmond only said sadly that, "Things would never be the same", he never tried to explain what he meant and Daisie suspected he knew less than she did. After all, he had never moved out of the town of Cwm Manachlog either, except to go to a cricket match in the outlying villages. She wondered how many people were in the same situation.

Phil was worried at the prospect of being called up "There's the family," he said to Helen. "Who'll look after them? Jane is working full time in the kitchens of the Huntley-Davies's and Jill brings in a little by helping her mother with other people's washing and ironing. Walks across the mountains she does with heavy great baskets to and from the big houses in the next town. But what they bring home isn't enough."

"Mam's not a good manager and she's weary. All that child-bearing and poverty. She buys impulsively and without consideration, easily persuaded to part with cash by the itinerant traders who walk the roads with a suitcase or a tray."

"Loneliness is probably the reason," Helen suggested. "All

those hours and days without seeing a soul. Your mam must be so glad to see a new face she invites them in whoever they are and she buys to make them stay a while. I can understand that."

"Understanding doesn't solve the problems though. I went there one Sunday and was horrified to see the kitchen table covered with cauliflowers and potatoes bought from the local farmer. They knew I'd be bringing the same things from Dickie Daniels on the market. I tried to explain that even if they were bargain prices it was still wasteful to buy more than they could possibly eat and that giving food to someone else's pig was not helping them survive.

"It was easier for her to say yes than to refuse," Helen excused. "And people will take advantage of – " She almost said of the simple minded, but held back just in time.

Helen went with Phil the following Sunday. The skies were clear blue but further into the mountains purple shadows in the folds of the hills were darker than usual, threatening, and, as they neared their destination, far from peaceful. When the horse brought them to the highest point of their journey they saw a circle of low, dark clouds rising in the far distance and Helen likened them to the approach of war and shivered.

As they walked along the dark hall she heard the weak and tremulous, "who is it, Jem?" She wished she hadn't come.

She nodded to the woman sitting beside the fire and went out to speak to the old man. He was sitting in his bed against the white-washed walls in the corner of the large kitchen.

"Who is it, Jem?" he asked, with a look of bright intelligence on his pale face.

"Tell you in a minute," his wife replied as she always did.

To his dismay, Phil found his family all wearing new aprons and useless felt slippers which they must have bought from a travelling salesman with a slick tongue.

"Always the same," he grumbled irritably. "By Friday they're practically out of food and waiting for my Sunday visit. I used to give them money, but not any more."

"Jill said you'd given them to her," Helen said curiously, and Phil raised his pale eyes heavenward in despair.

The subdued people and the sad, uncared-for house added to Helen's depression and she was glad when they were on their way down the narrow mountain road.

"If you do have to go into the army, Phil, I'll do what I can to help your family. But I still think someone should know about them. Someone professional, I mean. They need a constant eye, more than I'd be able to give them."

"The thing that infuriates me, Helen, is that Mam's family could help if they wanted to. Rich they are, see. Plenty of property and money. Landowners they were, sort of gentlemen farmers I suppose you'd call them. In the family there are important businessmen and even a solicitor or two. Would you believe that Mam's brother is an accountant with a big house and servants?"

"But why – " Helen began.

The angry Phil interupted her and went on. "Generations of wealth there's been in Mam's family. Owned property in Aberystwyth they did, in the best part of town and all. But since Mam chose to marry Dad who was from a poor background and without any claim to fame, they cut her right off."

Helen allowed him to continue his harangue but believed it less and less. Phil was lying, of that she was sure. And if he were lying about this, then what else had he invented? Liars rarely made it a once only event.

Hundreds of young men went off to sign away years of their lives, and in many cases their future, believing the politicians when they said it was a glorious war and would save mankind from future wars for ever. They also believed they would be home again by Christmas, full of pride in a job well done, struting around like heros.

For those with less enthusiasm for joining the forces there was the poster campaign: BRITONS, JOIN YOUR COUNTRY'S ARMY; JOIN THE ROYAL AIR FORCE AND SHARE THE GLORY, and many others. One encouraged wives to send their loved ones, WOMEN OF BRITAIN SAY GO! The campaign was effective more for the furore it created among the young women than by convincing the men. A sense of outrage filled feminine hearts when a man was seen in civilian clothes and carrying on as if war was not a reality. Several solitary and peaceful individuals were attacked.

Tommy and Phil were included in the smearing of apparently healthy, cowardly young men who refused to fight. Tommy was not a popular person, even though customers thronged to buy his latest bargains when he appeared at the market. The determination to make money seemed to brand him with mistrust and even those who had benefited from his shrewd business sense joined in the disparaging remarks that labelled him a bit of a fly one, with his eye on the main chance.

Phil arrived at the market one morning driving a new lorry. Tommy went at once to admire it. He had chosen to buy a car for comfort, perhaps a van would have been more sensible. He discussed the purchases with Phil.

"So you found enough money to get yourself something after all," Tommy said patting the shiny new bonnet.

"What d'you mean?" Phil frowned.

"Treated yourself, did you? From the money we made on the department store deal?"

"Nothing left of that. It all went to settle debts and do a few repairs to the house. This was left to me by an uncle," Phil said.

"Brand new, isn't it? Bought it on his death bed, did he?" Tommy shrugged and walked away. If Phil wanted to pretend about the money it was up to him.

Tommy occasionally overheard remarks on his lack of bravery and took them with the stoicism that a healthy bank balance can bring. Then something happened that he couldn't ignore. He and Phil were the victims of enthusiastic supporters of the armed forces.

"Imagine this happening here in Cwm Manachog, Dais," Tommy said when he found his new car, bought only that week, painted with crudely drawn white feathers.

"Park it round the back and I'll help clean it up," she offered, handing baby Gaynor to Ethel Trip. "Glad to have a bit of peace from that one." She smiled ruefully. "Terrible mother I sound, don't I? I do love Gaynor, I really do. But with so much to do and her screaming all the time I am glad when Ethel takes her and I can get away from the noise." She looked at him as she collected cloths and brushes to begin the cleaning operation. "I hope the next one isn't such a squawk as Gaynor."

"Another, Dais? That's great, isn't it?" he questioned, glancing at her serious face.

"It's great, I'm pleased, but I don't know how I'll manage. The boy has left us, gone to look after his son's shop while his son's in the army. Ethel says she wants to leave and do something really useful, like auxilary nursing or ambulance driving and Desmond, well, he doesn't seem to have the same interest, spends more time at the shop helping Helen than here at The Swan helping himself. Sees to the cellar work, mind. Fair play, he never neglects that. The customers would soon complain if the pipes weren't cleaned regular. He knows that."

Tommy didn't say anything. Rubbing at the ugly painting on the door of the car he whistled cheerfully. He knew it was useless trying to involve himself in Daisie's difficulties. Best he stay neutral and then she can always use him as a sounding block when things got too much. Neutral, the word had a different meaning now; he was neutral, siding with the enemy by not fighting for his own nation.

"D'you think I should join up before they makes me, Dais?" he asked several minutes later.

"If you want to choose which service I suppose you should, but that's supposing this will go on for a long time. It won't, will it?"

"Flying a plane might be fun. How would I look in a flyers uniform, Dais?"

"As daft as you look in a suit!"

Phil was woken up at three o'clock one morning by the

policeman knocking on his door. As he opened it, Helen woke in the next house and looked out of the window to see what was happening. Lifting the latch and widening the opening, she heard the constable say, "Are you Philip Johnson?"

"'Course I am, you old fool. Known me for years you have!"

"And the owner of the china shop in the High Street?"

"Yes. Now can I go back to bed or d'you want to see my birth certificate?"

"The shop window has been smashed and from the look of things most of your stock has been taken."

"What! How? Why didn't someone stop them? They couldn't break a great window like that without making a noise!"

"It's possible they broke in and emptied the shop then smashed the window as they left. Either way, you'll have to come along and get it boarded up and the glass brushed away."

Helen dressed quickly and was standing by her door ready to go with him before he had finished arguing with the patient police officer.

"I heard," she said as Phil began to explain. "I'll come with you, I've brought a brush and shovel."

It was dawn before they finished, dawn on a dark, January day. Children walking to school stopped and stared until clouted by their mothers and told to hurry. Business people slowed a little then walked on, pretending it was none of their business. Daisie, stepping out early to go to the dairy for fresh milk, gasped with alarm."

"Helen? What happened?"

"By the daubing inside it seems people around here think Phil should be in uniform."

"Where is Phil? Does he know?"

"I know," Phil appeared out of the ruined doorway and walked across to the two women. "I've a damned good idea who did this, too." He moved closer and whispered, "One of them up on Pleasant View if you ask me. They've all sent their sons to be officers and now they regret it. Inciting others to plague us, that's what they're doing. One of them stopped me as I rode past on my cart last Sunday and demanded that I get into uniform and help the ones who were already facing mutilation and death." He gave a slight grin, "Made it sound irresistible they did, Daisie." He glanced at the quiet Helen and added. "But I can't go."

"Helen and I will look after your family, Phil, if you are made to join up?"

"My family? How did you know about them?" He glared at Helen. "You told her!"

"Helen didn't. Tommy did. He's known for ages and thought I should know, that several of us should know, so you can leave with some peace of mind."

"Leave? Then you think I should go?"

"Soon you won't have any choice! Tommy went to the recruiting office a couple of days ago. He has a medical next week." Daisie turned away, echoing the often repeated remark of Desmond, "Things will never be the same again."

The changes came about so subtly that at first they were hardly noticed. Then alterations to the licensing laws were passed that forbade public houses to remain open during the afternoon. "Damned cheek, telling us what hours we can work!" Desmond complained. They usually closed for a few hours each afternoon anyway but on Saturdays, when the town was full of visitors shopping in the popular market, they stayed open and did as much trade as they managed some evenings. "What's the idea? How can a pub closing in Cwm Manachlog help fight Jerry in France? It doesn't make any sense!"

"They want to make sure the factory workers are not drunk for the afternoon shift," Ethel said.

"With more and more of them women that's hardly likely," Daisie said. "Women don't need laws like that to make them conscientious!"

"*And* it's not allowed for anyone to buy another person a drink any more," Desmond went on, outraged by the interference in his life. "Them up in London say it's to prevent the enemy getting someone drunk and persuading them to pass on secrets, if you ever heard anything so stupid! What secret can we have round here? The best sheep-dip?" The door was propped open to enable the newly washed floor to dry. As Desmond mentioned sheep-dip the face of a ewe peered around the door. "And you can bugger off, too, sacastic sod," Desmond shouted, waving a tea towel at the startled animal. "Time they stopped them sheep coming into the town. This place is like the middle ages."

"What's upset him, then?" Ethel asked.

"The boy leaving means him staying here a bit more and having to neglect his ladylove at the china shop," Daisie whispered. It was the first time she had complained in Desmond's hearing.

By 1916 the residents of Cwm Manachlog were really aware of the distant war. Conscription had come into force, threatening to take every man between eighteen and forty. Many jobs that had always been done by men had women taking them and they complained but managed the long hours and ran a home as well.

The buses that rumbled through the town had women conductors on the steps, the local farms had women tending the sheep and doing a great deal of the heavy field work. Factories making ammunition and store-houses packing food supplies for the forces grew up out of once abandoned sheds and when a whistle blew to indicate the end of a shift, women poured from the doors in greater numbers than the children running out of school.

There were fewer and fewer women at home all day, and older children cared for the younger ones and played until their mother returned from her war work. Even those with small children shared the care of their own and other families and managed to work for a few hours each day. Sundays, always respectfully held as the Sabbath, a day when no work was done, gradually slipped into being the day on which much of the housework was tackled.

Surreptitiously women crept into their gardens and hung

washing on the line, hoping no one would see it and complain of un-Godliness. Steamed up windows revealed where those less brave were drying it inside.

Women served in the shops in positions previously considered only suitable for a man; selling ironmongery, boning and slicing bacon, heaving sacks of potatoes about outside the green-grocers. In the bank the manager, desperate for help, tried to put a woman on the counter, but few would allow her to deal with their business, convinced that no woman could keep from gossiping, so he abandoned the idea as unworkable. There was even a woman working emptying the ashbins.

Ethel Trip found herself employed not as an auxilary nurse, nor a Voluntary Ambulance Driver as she had hoped. Her war was spent delivering coal. Her husband was one of those called to serve in the army and she took over the business. The huge horse and cart moved slowly around the streets obeying whistled or muttered commands and, as Ethel quickly realised, seeming to know without being told where to stop. It taught Ethel a great deal about her husband. Dobbin, completed the round, stopping at every customer and at three of the local public houses, excluding The Swan, where Ethel herself had worked.

Dobbin was one of the fortunate horses allowed to remain in a peacetime occupation. Hundreds of horses were commandeered for work on the Western front. An old man who had lost four of his best mares complained to Desmond but all the sympathy he had was, "Pity they don't take some of these damned sheep!" A few days later a sheep was injured on the road by a lorry and much to Desmond's chagrin became a guest of Daisie's Ark at the back of The Swan.

One of the changes to have a long lasting effect was women taking home pay packets. The prospect of earning money, once little more than a dream, became reality and many silently decided that when the war was won they would continue to find employment outside the home. Support and admiration for the suffragettes grew with a greater understanding of their aims.

"There's me heaving great hundred weight sacks of coal from the cart to the houses and my husband – God keep him safe from harm – expects me to pay meself less than half what he would have paid a man," Ethel moaned, her face a travesty of womanly beauty, covered in black dust, her hair hidden by a bandeau of coarse cloth and eyes red with tiredness.

Tommy continued to run a market stall selling whatever he could find that was cheap and in demand. He had been turned down by the army as being unfit.

"It's my funny eye," he explained to anyone who asked or critisised his being out of uniform, the eye obliging him by twitching in full agreement. "They say if you can't fire a gun with accuracy you're more a danger than a help. Mind, there are those who say I'd be popular if I went along and shot their sergeant!"

"What can we do to help, Tommy," Daisie asked. They were sitting on the wall behind The Swan where Daisie was throwing spare bread to the pigs which, to Daisie's dismay as they were intended for killing, had now joined the rest of the animals. "We'll have to do our bit."

"I'll keep on with the market, but perhaps I'll sell food when I can. What about you, Dais?"

"I can't do more than I am at present," she snapped. "Running this place almost single-handed is enough with Gaynor and baby Oswald, and Desmond doing damn all to help."

"And going up the mountain every week with Helen to see to Phil's family," Tommy said. "Time they were helping themselves. The girls are up in age now and shouldn't be sitting there waiting for handouts like resident tramps!"

"You sound angry, Tommy?" Daisie queried.

"So I should. Entertaining a group of farm-workers they were when I went up on Saturday instead of Sunday. Men, mind, not land-girls. If I hadn't promised Phil we'd look after them I don't think I'd do another hand's turn for them.

"When you say 'entertaining' you don't mean . . .?"

"I mean spending all the money and food I give them on people who should know better than to take it, that's what,

138

Dais." He looked away from her and she guessed he was afraid that the entertaining would lead to something more serious. The girls were obviously a bit simple and there were people who would take advantage of them.

"We have to do what we can but we can't be responsible for them every moment, Tommy," she said.

"I've a good mind not to bother to go up with food this week.

"But we promised Phil – "

"That was when we thought they were helpless."

"Stay away from them," was Desmond's advice when Daisie told him of Tommy's suspicions. "From what you say, it's unlikely they are, er, misbehaving, they're too young and simple for that."

"Since when did intelligence have anything to do with making babies," Daisie demanded, watching Desmond turn away in embarrassment. "There's that mother of his, daft as they come, and she's had seven daughters in as many years!"

"No need to be coarse, Daisie." Desmond sounded as prim as an old woman.

Tommy continued to deliver food to the house on the mountain but the amount was less and less as he could see their prosperity growing. Their new friends had taken the hints Tommy had dropped when he had found them there and they brought farm produce to swell the larder contents.

When Phil came home on leave Tommy intended to explain the situation to him but when he arrived by army lorry a few weeks later he was in no condition to be told anything.

Phil had not been wounded but he was exhausted. Once his landlady put him to bed in his old room he slept without moving for almost twenty-four hours. A week later he was fully recovered. When he heard about his sisters suspected "occupation" he borrowed Tommy's car and drove up to see them.

The house was empty apart from his father calling weakly, "Who is it, Jem?" and his mother sitting silently beside the cold ashes of a fire. After the briefest of examination he knew his mother was dead. He had seen enough death in its cruel and varied forms not to recognise it.

He fed the old man with some soup he had brought, then changed the filthy bed and went to find a doctor. Before nightfall the old man was safely settled in a mental home and arrangements were underway for the burial of his mother. Of his sisters there was no sign. The youngest, Jill, being less than eighteen years old and mentally unfit to cope, was the cause of most concern and the police instigated a search.

They were found in the next town where the oldest, Jane, now twenty-six, had found them a house to rent and on which they had managed to pay a month's rent.

"Couldn't stay, not with Mam dead," she explained defiantly. "Didn't know what to do for her, see."

"What about Dad?" Phil asked softly. "Why didn't you bring him as well?"

"Dad?" She frowned, a faraway look in her eyes, and clenched her jaw tightly, making the look on her face odd and rather frightening. "Dad? He's dead, too, isn't he? We tried to move him and he wouldn't come."

"They've got jobs," Phil told Helen later. "Even young Jill. And from what I could find out they do the work well enough, so there's money for them to survive."

"I'll go over each week as before and make sure they don't want for anything," Helen promised.

"Don't know what I'd do without you and Tommy to help," Phil said.

"And Daisie," Helen reminded him softly. "Daisie does what she can, too."

Before he went back to camp Phil managed to see Daisie alone. She was in the bar raising the ashes of the previous night's fire and relighting it ready for the evening session. Desmond was, as usual, at the china shop helping Helen.

"Off back to fight the Kaiser, then?" she said as he appeared with his uniform over his arm, neatly pressed.

"Yes, I'm catching the morning train tomorrow."

She put down the tongs with which she had been re-building

140

the fire and stood up. "Helen told me about your mother. I'm sorry."

"I won't even be here for the funeral. They had to have an inquest, see, and they won't bury her until tomorrow. Helen's not going, of course, it's men only. But Tommy will stand as my representative."

Daisie moved a little away from him and stood near the bar, fiddling with the contents of her father's pedlar's tray that still stood on the bar top, a memory of what she had been before her arrival at The Swan. "Desmond will go, too, and there's plenty from the market who'll walk behind the coffin. She'll have a send off, don't worry."

His shoulders dropped and she impulsively ran to him and pulled his blond head down onto her shoulder. "It's all right, Phil, we'll keep the grave tidy and respectable and keep an eye on your sisters."

"It isn't that," he said. "I don't want to go back, not to France. They used gas against us you know, when we weren't prepared. Treated us like vermin. Sent us choking and gasping out of the trenches to be shot like rats from a hay-barn. And there we were, being sent back to face it with only a bit of wet cloth across our faces, can you believe that?"

"Now you've got proper gas masks they might not bother any more. It will soon be over, Phil."

"It isn't only the gas. From the moment I return I'll be infested with lice. There isn't anything that will shift them. Can you even begin to imagine that?" He drooped with dismay at the awful memories, trying not to tell her any more but unable to stop. She touched his arm sympathetically and murmured soothing sounds.

"There's an army of rats, glistening with health, that's larger than our army and the Germans put together. They have a better diet than us," he said but dare not put into words what they fed on.

"Machonochie stew and bully beef, that's what *we* live on and we're lucky if it's slightly warm and not filled with disgusting water from the shell holes."

141

Almost unknowingly she had begun to press him against her and when he raised his head and looked at her with eyes large with incipient tears, the rest was inevitable. The kiss, the slow walk up the stairs, past the room she now shared with Desmond, up and up to the small attic room where they had met so many times before.

When they were on their way back down the long staircase, Daisie heard Desmond return. "Now what?" she gasped, her eyes darting around like a cornered animal. "He mustn't find you. There's no explanation he would believe!"

"Go on down you, I'll sneak out through the back when he's out of the way." His lips touched the back of her neck and he whispered, "Thank you, my lovely girl. You were marvellous." Less sentimentally and with a gleam of humour in his eyes that made her heart ache for longer to spend with him, he added, "Like old times this, isn't it Daisie?"

Helen was with Desmond and she looked at Daisie's flushed face and glowing eyes and wondered. She had the look of a woman in love, yet Desmond had been with *her* all afternoon.

"What have you been doing with yourself, Daisie," she asked. "You look flushed. Been busy polishing, have you?"

"Seeing to the fire. *Duw* it's hot when you have to kneel and wait for it to catch, isn't it?"

A few moments later Helen went into the bar and saw that the fire was out.

The war didn't seem to affect Gillian, even though her husband was flying airplanes and dropping bombs on ships far out at sea.

"If I were you, Gillian, don't think I could sleep for a moment knowing the danger Waldo's in," Megan said in one of the rare occasions the three girls got together for a chat. A small café had reopened in the main road, once a popular place for the market people. It had been extended to serve "Teas For Ladies", as its advertisement stated.

"I know I can't help Waldo by worrying," Gillian told them. "So I just pretend he's up in London on business for the shoeshop and I sleep like the proverbial log." She tossed her long, dark hair back and straightened the chic hat on its waves. "I stay beautiful for when he comes home," she laughed. "That's what I call helping the war-effort."

"I'm knitting comforts for the soldiers," Megan said. "I don't seem to have the energy for anything more. I tried going to the first aid post but it exhausted me and Arthur was angry with me for tiring myself out and having to rest the following day."

"Is that why you haven't moved into a house of your own, Megan?" Daisie asked. "All these months with Arthur's mother at your back, I'd have gone mad, wouldn't you, Gillian?"

"No," Gillian laughed, "*She* would!"

Megan had lost three babies in quick succession and Arthur insisted that until she had "successfully brought a child into the world", as he had put it, placing the blame firmly on her inefficiency, they would be better off in his mother's home where Megan could be cared for.

"I hate it," Megan's gentle face folded into a suspicion of a crying session, something she indulged in more and more often in her rare private moments. "I wish I could have my own place, chose my own things and live a life without all the socialising that Mother-in-law insists on. With Arthur in the navy I feel trapped, like a prisoner in some tower waiting for a handsome prince to rescue me."

"Get her," Daisie laughed. "A handsome prince is something we all hoped for and look what we've ended up with! Megan with a bullying mother-in-law and a husband who supports his mother instead of his wife, and me, well, I suppose I'm not really unlucky, but I work hard and have little support from my prince who spends time when he should be helping me, chasing after his previous love." She turned to Gillian, "You're the luckiest of the three of us."

"I knew I would be. I won't let anything spoil what I want from life. You've had two children, one leading you into a marriage to an old man who loved someone else. Oh, don't stop me saying it, it's the truth and you know it. We all know you wanted to marry Phil."

The mention of his name brought back the memory of their brief meeting flooding back. She felt colour rising and hoped her two friends wouldn't notice. She bent her head and talked to baby Oswald as Gillian went on.

"Don't you two think it odd that we haven't had children all this time? I made sure we didn't. I didn't leave it to the man to decide. A child would ruin my social life and that was something I wouldn't want. Pity you two weren't as determined." She raised a hand and the waitress left the customer she was attending to and came to see what she wanted. "See what I mean?" Gillian chuckled. "To be important you have to feel important."

"Megan, why don't you get a job?" Daisie suggested.

"I couldn't. Mother-in-law wouldn't have it. Organising fund-raising is all she'll allow me to do."

"Allow you, Crying Mouse?" Gillian wailed. "What d'you think the suffragettes have been fighting for? So we can decide for ourselves, so we stop accepting rules made by men for their own convenience. And there's you not even willing to disregard the unreasonable demands of another woman!"

"Come and help in the bar. The Swan would soon make you lose your fear of life. A few weeks of that would bring her out of her tower, wouldn't it, Gillian?" Daisie chuckled.

"I couldn't. You know I couldn't. I'm not like you two and never will be." Excusing herself, Megan hurriedly left the café. She had stayed too long. Mother-in-law would be back from her meeting and now she'd have to explain where she had been. Fighting back the unhappiness that threatened to overwhelm her she hurried to the taxi rank and asked to be taken back to her tower on Pleasant View.

To her surprise, Tommy Thomas was driving. "Hello, Megan. Been somewhere nice?"

"Tommy! What are you doing driving a taxi? I thought you worked the markets?"

"I do. And anything else I can get. Thinking of buying a

few taxis and starting a proper business, ready for when the war ends and things start picking up."

He drove through the quiet town where there were still more horses and carts than combustion engines.

"Take your time, Tommy," Megan said, suddenly rebelling. "I'm not in a hurry."

"Go over the mountains to Brynteg and come back into town the other way, shall we?"

Evening was transforming the colours of the hills from the bright sun-touched pink of the heather and the white trunks of the birch trees, into a rich purple and silver pattern among the dark grey shadows.

"It's beautiful," Megan sighed. "I would love a house where I could look up to the mountains. In a valley I feel protected, sort of safe and cosy."

"Why haven't you bought a place of your own if that's what you want?"

"Daisie and Gillian have just asked me that, but it isn't my place to chose where we live, Tommy, that's up to Arthur and at present he wants me to stay with his mother."

"Lots of fellows feel like that, fear of their wives straying I suppose."

"Tommy!"

"It's true, there are plenty of women making the most of having their husbands out of sight."

"That's a terrible thing to say. A wife wouldn't cheat while her husband is in such danger! She'd never live with her conscience."

"Oh, it's all very well for you to get tamping mad and imagine everyone is as obedient and devoted as you, but it's true, there's plenty of troubles to come once this war's over, you wait and see." He grinned at her. "How many men will be persuaded that babies only take six months and not nine, eh, Megan?" He began to whistle then, sorry for being so outspoken. Megan was unhappy at such talk. Being friends with the more worldly Daisie and Gillian hadn't changed her one bit.

He smiled and patted her knee. "Don't change, Megan. So

145

many of us have lost what we had as children. Your charm is partly that you keep a hold of that innocence."

"You mean I'm immature?"

"Give it a fancy name if you like, but whatever it is, don't lose it, eh? It's rare and valuable. Right?"

He pulled up at the gate and watched as she walked down the long drive to the imposing house with its views over the town. She looked small and vulnerable and a longing to comfort her and make her strong and happy flooded over him. Comforting her would be balm to his lonely spirit. Tommy Thomas was financially successful but in desperate need of love.

10

The end of the war was celebrated at The Swan with such enthusiasm that the gaps in the usual crowd were hidden. Three of Daisie's regulars had died and fourteen were wounded and unable to return to the work they had enjoyed before being called up.

Little Dickie returned unscathed and returned to the fruit and veg stall. Billie Beynon had survived but was a sick man, having suffered a gas attack. He was no longer strong but was cheerful, glad to be alive. His dream was to live long enough for his twin sons to take over his business.

The coalman returned and he sat in a corner, his blind eye covered by a brilliant white bandage, discussing with Ethel his return to the delivery round. Their daughter, Kate, now eleven, sat on the porch waiting for them. Their discussion was becoming more and more heated and Daisie called to ask if Ethel would like to help behind the bar mainly to prevent a fight. Ethel was facing unemployment after managing the firm for almost four years, and she was hating it. She was holding a list of customers with the state of their debts and was arguing with her husband about their ability to pay.

"You don't understand, Bob Tripp! A lot of these women have lived on nothing but soldiers pay. How do you expect them to pay their debts right off as soon as their men come back? Besides," she flapped the list close to his determined face, "many of them won't *be* back, so what you going to do about them then? Send all the widows to court? Very popular that would make you for sure!"

The business had been run with exceptional efficiency and Bob Tripp was desperately looking for something about which he could complain. Didn't make sense for a woman to organise a business and work it as well as a man. He gritted his teeth. He'd never admit that Ethel had done just that, never.

In another corner Tommy was questioning Phil about his war and laughing at the exploits of the man who managed to earn more than the officers by grabbing every opportunity to do a deal.

Near the pedlar's tray on the bar Helen and Desmond served the crowd that was increasing daily as men returned, and seeing them together Daisie remembered with a guilt that remained as strong as in 1913 when she had broken them up irrevocably.

She jiggled baby Oswald to get him to sleep, standing in the doorway from the kitchen continuing to watch as newcomers arrived, and split the groups and changed them, like an ever moving pattern. Listening to the buzzing chatter of the amiable crowd her eyes lit on Phil, throwing his head back and laughing. She wondered whether, if she had been stronger, she would now be with Phil, nursing his child, wearing his ring. She sighed. That was something she would never know.

She put Oswald down. At three he was too big to be nursed like a baby but she loved nursing him. She felt a deep need to take every opportunity to hug him and tell him she loved him. Oswald was precious and a delight. Different from Gaynor, who at four was still a miserable child, although Daisie bought her everything she could want in the mistaken belief that happiness could be purchased. Oswald seemed content. He rarely cried and he would go to anyone who opened their arms to him. He woke up smiling, ready for the new day with a cheerfulness that delighted Daisie and made Desmond proud of him. But although Gaynor displayed stamina and sound health, Oswald was not strong.

Dasie left him playing with a wooden train that he loved and went into the bar. "Ethel," she called, "can I have a word?"

"In a minute!" Ethel was no longer polite and respectful. Daisie grinned and said, "Whenever."

Handing the list to her husband and throwing back a final argument, Ethel walked to the bar. "What is it, Daisie?"

"You haven't got a job yet, have you?" Daisie said quietly. When the woman shook her head she asked, "Fancy coming back to work for me?"

"I might. But not as a general dogsbody, mind. I'd want a proper job and no messing."

"Cleaner? A bit of child-minding?"

"No." Ethel's jaw tightened and rose perceptably.

Daisie hid a smile. Ethel was really feeling important after running the coal business for the war years. No wonder Bob looked sick. "Barmaid and help clear up the bar?" she offered.

"I'll think about it."

Daisie's amusement faded. A sense of worth was all very well, but there were plenty of men looking for work. If it wasn't for the fact that Ethel would be cheaper she'd advertise for one.

"I'll give you until Monday," she said sharply and walked away.

Helen still worked in the china shop opened by Phil and on occasions, where there was some special reason for the bar being busy, as tonight, she would come and help in the evenings. Daisie liked this less and less and the reason she wanted Ethel back was so there would be no further excuse to ask Helen for help, excuses Desmond found more and more readily.

"Not jealous of her giving a hand, are you, Dais?" Tommy asked when she told him of her offer to Ethel.

What, of poor Helen? Never. But I don't like her here, people still defer to her instead of me, treating me like an assistant in my own pub."

"She might not be willing to come for much longer, Dais." His eye flickered madly and he leaned to whisper. "Courting she is, mind. Seen her out with that Matt Prosser from the market."

"She isn't!"

"No doubt about it."

"What, him that we have to send home in the drunk's barrow? Never!"

Tommy's eye winked confirmation. "They've been out for walks on a Sunday and he's been to her house for tea. With Ethel Tripp and Mr Power the organist, too, mind. No hanky panky."

"Good luck to her," she smiled.

"See much of Phil now he's home again?" he asked.

"Why should I?" she snapped and began tidying the pedlar's tray on the bar, a sign the question had made her edgy, Tommy realised.

The quiet Helen and the over-confident Ethel seemed unlikely friends, but during the war years they had spent a lot of time in each other's company, sipping tea in each other's homes and, when the weather allowed, walking along the stream towards the mountains. Bob Trip returning home seemed no reason for them to change their habits and the friendship continued.

As the spring of 1919 slowly made way to summer, Ethel handed back the responsibility for the coal business and started back at The Swan. With Helen having less excuse to call there Ethel was carefully pumped by her friend for information about how Desmond and Daisie were getting on.

One day they paused on their walk beside the stream to admire how summer had strengthened the colour on the mountains. A flush of pink clothed the slopes in burgeoning heather blossom, dazzlingly bright in the sun and darker in the shadows made by the few clouds that sailed tranquilly past.

"Beautiful it is," Ethel breathed. "Just beautiful. Makes you glad to be alive."

"I rarely had time to look up, let alone admire the view when I was working at the pub," Helen said and there was sadness in her voice.

"Still miss The Swan?" Ethel asked.

"I'm busy mind and I enjoy the china shop. Phil's easy to work for, but the customers buy and go away instead of sitting to talk. It was like a family, the clientele of the pub. Everyone knew everyone else's business, which can be irritating at times, mind. But there was always someone to listen. There was always someone worse off to be comforted." She kicked at a stone like a small boy, watching it spin off the path and into the shallow water.

The quietly meandering brook was slowed in places with rafts of water crowfoot, no longer flowering, but stretching their elongated leaves with the flow as if struggling to reach the sea. At the muddied edge the tall flowers of water plantain showed with their elegant lilac blooms. The lower banks were alive with small black frogs. The two women stared at the thriving life for a while then turned their steps back to the town.

"Best I get back," Ethel said reluctantly. "The Swan will be heaving tonight once the market closes and with Daisie insisting on keeping the fire going the place'll be like a bread oven!"

"The walls are thick and the windows small. Little sun gets in and without a fire they soon complain of cold," Helen reminisced. "Many's the time I've had to set too and relight it when it's gone out." She quickened her pace. "Think I'll call in tonight as well, if only to avoid that Matt Prosser from coming in and trying to scrounge supper again!"

"Perhaps when the summer visitors start passing through we'll need an extra hand again," Ethel said, patting Helen's arm comfortingly.

Tommy was making a lot of money. There were food stocks that were to be disposed of, legally or illegally, and for the third time in a month he filled a hired lorry and arrived at the market with an enthusiastic Phil to help him sell it. Tins of corned beef and fruit in large sizes that most families would have found difficult to cope with, sausages packed in precious lard and stewed steak, some packages with labels missing and sold as "Mystery Meals" disappeared as fast as Tommy could hold them up on display. The news of it spread and several of the local boarding houses arrived sniffing for bargains.

A couple of blankets were placed at the side of the stall,

ready in case the policemen came past. Best he didn't see and perhaps ask about the origins of the food.

"Are you sure it's not stolen, Tommy?" Phil asked for the third time.

"Well, tell the truth I'm not sure. I didn't ask," Tommy grinned. "Best to be able to tell as near the truth as possible. I don't know with an honest shrug is better than I'm not certain and a guilty wink any day of the week."

Phil shrugged, accepted money offered by a woman who lived on the lower slopes of Pleasant View. "Come on, ladies, stick a couple of these in the back of your pantry and don't tell you're husbands or they'll cut your housekeeping down to half!" The lorry rumbled away empty long before the rest of the stalls finished for the day.

When that lucrative source of revenue ended Tommy had difficulty finding anything as good.

"It's no good, Phil," he said one day when at Brynteg market they offered a few straggly leeks and some duck eggs to disinterested shoppers. "I'm going hire a lorry and take it to London and fill it up with swag."

Phil went with him, taking most of a day to get to South London, arriving at the lane in Houndsditch at four o'clock, stiff and tired. They looked at the stock of the various warehouses before spending their money on a collection of toys and gifts. They filled the lorry with their purchases and saved money by sleeping in it. Surrounded by boxes of toys, and china and glass ornaments they ate fish and chips out of a newspaper package and slept the sleep of the innocent.

The journey home was uneventful and they arrived back in Cwm Manachlog tired and very pleased with themselves. When the assorted goods were sold Tommy had enough money saved to buy himself a second car with which to increase his taxi business. What Phil did with his profit, Tommy had no idea. Whatever deals they pulled off, Phil seemed to show no sign of increasing affluence.

Matt Prosser sold second-hand books and on Saturdays he was one of the first to dismantle his stall and pack away his stock.

He knew that the last rush of customers was almost over and those wandering around were hoping to buy perishable foods cheaply. Books were sold when the spending spree began, when people had money to jingle, not now when it was almost spent.

The boxes of books were stacked on his hand cart and as he pushed his way through the carts and cars in the High Street he stopped and waved at Helen. The china shop was closed and she was waiting for Phil to call and take the money she had totalled and entered in the cash book. She unlocked the door and stepped outside in the warm air of late evening.

"Fancy a drink?" Matt shouted.

"It's too late for me," Helen shook her head. "Did you have a good day at the market?"

"Not really. Phil and Tommy caught the crowds. *Duw* I don't know where they get their swag but they come up with something different week after week. I was at the furthest end as well. Too few customers around for people to browse. You know what it is, Helen, a crowd encourages people to stay, they walk on if they feel too conspicuous. I've asked the Toby for a better spot next week."

"Better luck at Brynteg on Tuesday." She waved and went back in. Matt walked on away from the crowded streets and stopped again outside The Swan. Might as well have a drink before going home to his empty rooms.

The unaccompanied woman in the corner was drawing everyone's eye. In Cwm Manachlog in 1919 it was rare for a woman to go into a public house, and it was severely frowned upon for one to enter on her own. The thin, dreamy looking woman seemed unaware of the curious stares she was attracting. Daisie looked thunderous. Matt, sensing trouble, sat as far from the young woman as possible.

In fact there was a space around her that made the customers crowd into the rest of the space. "They look like scared onlookers at some dangerous exhibition," Desmond remarked.

"And dangerous she is," Daisie muttered. "I think she should be told to leave."

"We can't," Desmond said. "Not without making a scene."

"Three times she's disappeared outside and three times she's been followed by a man. I'm not having that reputation, Desmond. You tell her, now, this minute, or I will."

Desmond began to sidle up to the pale, thin woman who was dressed in what had once been a beautiful voilet dress, with a sailor style collar and buttons down the back to the hips from where a full skirt swayed about her, short enough to show her knees. The beautiful material was grubby and torn in places. As he approached the girl looked up and gave him the most lovely smile. Losing his nerve completely he scuttled back to Daisie. "I can't. People will think that I – that I – I can't, Daisie, and that's that!"

At that moment a stranger stood up, emptied his glass and put it on the table. He looked at the girl and tossed his head towards the door and the girl went out, slowly, seductively. After a few seconds the man began to follow.

Daisie pushed him aside and went through the door, every eye in the room following her.

"You!" she called to the girl who was standing against the side wall. "Clear off and don't come back. D'you hear me? I don't want to see you in here again!"

"What's the matter?" Phil came from the direction of the market, the setting sun making it difficult for Daisie to recognise him at first.

"Oh, Phil. It's nothing, just a trollop I don't want to see in The Swan again."

"A trollop? That's Jane, my sister."

Desmond had followed Daisie out and now he stood staring at an angry Phil.

"Come on, Daisie, if you *know* her, and if she's Phil's sister . . . from what I saw the girl was doing no harm." He smiled self-consciously at Phil. "It's hot in by there," he explained. "The girl kept going out for fresh air, that's all, and Daisie misunderstood, didn't you, my dear?"

"Sorry, Phil. I didn't recognise her. I haven't seen her that often and – " She glared at him defiantly and then at Desmond. "I wasn't mistaken though! She's well, not

154

behaving. I've been watching her. I never trust women who come into a pub on their own. Bad lot most of them are."

Phil handed her a box he was carrying. "Tommy asked me to give you this, said you'd ordered them special. Come on, Jane, I'll take you back home." He glared at Daisie, his pale blue eyes so fierce that it was impossible to imagine them filled with love for her. She was angry at being embarrassed and for the way both Phil and Desmond had blamed her and not accepted the behaviour of the girl for what it was.

"A tart she is, Phil, and be warned, I'll send for the policeman if I see her in my pub again," she said quietly.

Desmond heard her and said with unaccustomed firmness, "*My* pub, Daisie, don't forget it's still my pub."

"Then it's a pity you don't do more to keep it going then!" she snapped, and pushing both Desmond and the embarrassed customer out of her way with the box of tea towels Tommy had sent for her, she stormed back into the pub.

"You were right, Daisie," Matt whispered. "She's living in that old house at the back of the mountain she is."

Daisie thought it politic not to enquire how he knew and nodded her thanks at his support and gave him a free refill. The customer left and after collecting the jacket of his brown suit Desmond left, too, leaving Daisie and Ethel to deal with the full bar as well as serve suppers.

At midnight, when Daisie went upstairs to check on the children, Desmond had still not returned. Gaynor was sleeping curled up in a nest of untidy bedding. It was very hot and the little girl was restless. Daisie felt her head. In the low light from the landing gas light she looked flushed. Gaynor was not a pretty child, even Daisie couldn't pretend that she was. Overweight, full features and wearing the pout in sleep that she constantly displayed when she was awake, did not enhance her. Daisie sighed and pushed the damp hair from the little girl's face. Money and nice clothes will be a good compensation for your lack of looks, she whispered silently. In this world money does the decision making, not pretty faces. Oswald was the sweetest and the most beautiful, and she wondered why this should be. Gaynor had been born out of unbridled love so surely it should be she who showed happiness and joy?

They were both very feverish. Probably just the heat, although little Oswald had been coughing a bit and they might be getting summer colds. She went to the cot where Oswald still slept and looked down at him, his face burning and his breathing rather ragged. She'd get the doctor to the pair of them tomorrow if they weren't any better. He said she fussed too much but better too often than not often enough, she always retorted. She placed a carafe of water and some glasses in case one of them needed a drink during the night.

She lay awake for a long time, rising occasionally to look along the dark empty street in the hope of seeing Desmond coming home. She wasn't worried. She knew where he would be. At Helen's house he was always certain to find a sympathetic ear.

At five she rose, the heat making sleep impossible. The children had woken several times during the night so she moved quietly not to disturb them as she dressed and went downstairs. In the cool kitchen she made a pot of tea. As she sipped she watched the pendulum of the long case clock that ticked the minutes away.

At six she cleaned out the grates, polished them with blacklead and laid them in readiness for lighting the following day. The bar room had that special Sunday morning feeling; still and comforting with its echos of recent activities and its familiar smells. Ethel called in at eight on the way to church and brought some flowers to brighten the room.

"Desmond's out early this morning. What's up with him, the heat kept him awake?"

"Yes," Daisie forced a smile. "Me, too. Only the children can sleep in this weather. Although they were restless during the night and I thought they'd be up before this."

"I'll wake them while I'm here if you like, by the state of your hands you'll be ten minutes getting them clean enough to touch bedclothes let alone the children!"

"Where was Desmond when you saw him?" Daisie called as Ethel began to climb the stairs.

"Sitting in Helen's back garden. I went past the back lane and heard them laughing, popped in to say hello. Just like him to find someone to gossip to, even at this time of the morning."

"Yes, just like him," Daisie agreed.

A few moments later Ethel came hurrying down the stairs, her startled face burst in on Daisie's thoughts. "Daisie, they aren't well. Your little Oswald looks proper poorly he does."

Daisie ran up the stairs and at once saw that Ethel was right. Gaynor was flushed and breathing fast, her face puckering up as she woke, saw her mother and realised she was unwell. Daisie comforted her and ran to see Oswald. He was lying still, his breathing fast, his stomach swelling and falling with every breath. "Ethel!" she shouted in panic. "Go and bring the doctor, fast as you can!"

Desmond arrived at the same time as the doctor and he took one look at Daisie's face distorted with grief and asked, "Daisie? What's happened?"

"You should have been here," she muttered in a held back scream of fear and accusation. "You should have been here."

He stared at her then followed the doctor up the staircase.

Gaynor was sick, but Oswald was dangerously ill.

"Pneumonia, I'm afraid. It can happen like this, suddenly and without any warning," the doctor informed them.

"Will he have to go into hospital?" Desmond asked. Daisie seemed incapable of speech. She just stared down at the flushed and distressed child her hands covering her mouth.

The doctor shook his head. "Best we don't move him."

Two days later, Oswald died. There was a constant stream of people coming to offer their condolences. Phil was among them. With him was his sister, Jane, who wore the same voilet dress and carried a bouquet like a shabby bride. For a moment Daisie wanted to refuse to see them, but need of Phil was always near the surface and now, with the terrible loss of her son and with Desmond seeking comfort elsewhere she was too weak to insist.

"I'm sorry for giving you the impression I was chasing

men," the voice of Jane was so low Daisie had to partly guess what she said.

"It was a misunderstanding," Phil enlarged on his sister's explanation. "She was feeling a bit faint and some men followed her to see if she was all right, like. Jane smiles a lot, but it's friendly she is. Nothing more."

Daisie looked at him, her blue eyes staring into his, saying wordlessly that she didn't believe him. She wanted Phil with an urgency that was bordering on insanity but she couldn't pretend to be a fool.

The Swan had seen many reasons for celebration during the years Daisie had worked there, now it was filled with people gathered for a different reason. Daisie had sat unmoving for most of the days before the funeral. During the night between bouts of exhausted sleep, she sat beside the coffin, and often found Desmond there, staring at the still face of his son. Neither attempted to comfort the other, each grieved silently and alone.

After the funeral The Swan opened as usual but neither Desmond nor Daisie were there. Daisie had taken Gaynor and driven up to see Gillian in her new house on Pleasant View. Megan came and the three friends talked about everything that came into their minds, laughing as if carefree, sober when a serious memory came back to them.

Daisie was defiantly cheerful. She watched Gaynor and determined not to allow her painful grief to affect her more than necessary. She laughed at the little girl's antics when Gaynor was showing off some new trick and was unaware that the laughter had a hollow sound that frightened her friends more than her crying would have done.

Gillian looked blooming. Her clothes were expensive, bought from some of the better shops in Cardiff. Her hair, given one of the new permanent waves, was thick and luxurious and with a hint of red in it that neither of the others remembered seeing before.

"It's fun to make the best of yourself," Gillian laughed when they tried tactfully to question her. "So, it's from a bottle. Better that than the gin bottle, eh?" she laughed. "Although gin's rather nice, too."

Megan, carefree for once, laughed and said, "Mother's ruin the old women call it, isn't it something to help get rid of a child? Not that I need any such thing. I can't keep a baby for more than a couple of months. Although," her shy eyes looked down into her lap as she said, "although, I'm beginning to hope that this time I might be lucky. It's almost three and a half months and – "

The words were lost in the shriek of delight from Daisie who managed to hid her own distress at the thought of her lost baby.

"Well done, I wish you well," Daisie said. "Pity help him with Arthur for a father, mind. But you can't have everything in this world!" She steeled herself to hold back her misery. A baby coming into the world us wonderful news and her own loss mustn't change that.

"Yes, well, if that's what you want, Megan," Gillian said with obvious disapproval. "I couldn't bear the thought myself and I've made damned sure it doesn't happen, but if that's what you really want, to please that miserable husband of yours, well, well done and good luck."

Megan sighed, touching her stomach with gentle stroking fingers. "They don't think I'm a suitable person to be a mother. Do you think the baby is able to hear what Arthur says about me and agree with him?" Her laughter was brittle and Daisie put aside her own grief as sympathy for her unhappy friend was renewed.

"He's a fool if he blames you, Megan," Gillian said.

"And you're a bigger fool if you believe him!" Daisie, always the most outspoken of them, said loudly. Her arms ached to hold Oswald again and the ache entered her heart when she knew she never would. This was the wrong time for this conversation. Absolutely the wrong time.

No one mentioned Oswald until Daisie was leaving. "Today we haven't talked about him, Daisie," Megan said in her quiet way. "But in future we will. It isn't as if he never existed. He lived and was loved. He must never be forgotten." For the first time since her beautiful son's brief illness and death, Daisie cried.

It was as if baby Oswald had been a final link holding the Prewitt's marriage together. With his son dead, Desmond stopped his minimal pretence that he was content with Daisie and the life he led. He spent more and more time with Helen, standing in the china shop and helping her to rearrange her displays, walking down to her small house when there was nothing important to do. When the weather was good they sat in Helen's garden and many reported hearing their laughter ringing out across the lane and the field beyond.

Megan spent more and more time in her room as her pregnancy progressed. She refused any visits her mother-in-law arranged and it was only when Daisie or Gillian invited her out that she made any effort to dress up and leave the large house up on Pleasant View. Even with her friends she frequently made an excuse not to go.

"I'm worried about her," Daisie told Tommy one afternoon when she was at the market buying food. Besides running a taxi service Tommy still had his stall which was filled that day with bundles of firewood.

"I don't see that I can help. I'm not a favoured visitor up there in Pleasant View. Besides, I need to go to London again. There's not a thing round here that I can get cheap enough to make a profit on, Dais. Better this than nothing but I won't make much money today. Want it for nothing they do, those too lazy to go up in the woods and pick up their own."

"If I pay for a few basketful, will you go up and see Megan?" she pleaded. "She refused to come downstairs the last time I called and Gillian hasn't been any more successful. Arthur's going out for lunch without her and his parents will be going to church tomorrow morning. Use the wood as an excuse. If you knocked she might be more inclined to see you."

Tommy agreed. In fact he welcomed the opportunity to spend a part of the loneliest day of the week talking to Megan. He was still far from popular. For most people his exploits were disapproved of and even those who admired his ability to make money without apparently doing much to achieve it, there was a sense of unease and the unconscious stepping back from any attempt at friendliness.

The house belonging to the Huntley-Davises was above that belonging to Gillian and Waldo Griffiths. As he passed the Griffiths' he slowed the taxi and the sound of a gramophone reached his ears. Through the privet hedge he saw that a crowd of young people were dancing on the neatly trimmed lawns. A long table was at the side of the garden covered with a dazzlingly white cloth and filled with food and drinks. Two men in dark clothes and wearing white gloves were standing near to assist the party-goers with their needs. Another stood near the gramophone ready to change records and wind it up. Drinks parties were a popular way of spending Sundays when the public houses were firmly closed.

The women wore flowing dresses in multi-coloured material and their voices and laughter rose on the cool air and to Tommy they reminded him of exotic birds. The men were formally dressed in smart suits that seemed a part of the formal garden with its flower beds and ornamental pond.

Megan's home, with its dark porch, heavy front door and half drawn curtains, exuded an atmosphere of gloom and rigid disapproval of anything merry. It was a startling contrast to the cheerful scene at Gillian and Waldo's. So close to each other geographically yet worlds apart in every other way. Tommy was relieved when his knock was answered and Megan opened the door to him. He took in the pale face, the drooping shoulders and the lank hair that, as usual, had fallen from its grips.

"It's a lovely day, Megan, I've called to take you out." He gestured to the end of the drive where he had left his car. "My taxi isn't needed until tonight to take a few of the faithful to church and back, so let's be off into the wilds of the mountains and find a stream to paddle in. What say?"

Megan was so used to doing as she was told she hardly questioned him, but obediently slipped on a summery cape and some soft shoes and followed him to the car.

161

They walked amid the wild flowers on the hills and followed animal tracks pretending to be hunters, and laughed when they found only a few of the ubiquitous sheep patiently sawing at the soft mountain grass. Streams appeared everywhere and even when they couldn't see one they could hear one gurgling through the ground below the level of the tufted grass.

Tommy was not sure how long Megan would stay, but he had brought a picnic in case she felt hungry. There were pies and meats and fresh salads which they ate with their hands like hungry children.

"Pity life isn't always this simple, eh, Megan?" Tommy said as they re-packed the basket.

They found a clear stream with a gravelly floor and paddled contentedly until a chill wind reminded them that the day was almost gone. In silence they packed the remainder of their picnic and prepared to drive back to Cwm Manachlog.

When Arthur returned from visiting his friends for lunch he was later than he'd promised. Finding Megan absent irritated him unreasonably. He could have stayed with his friends a while longer, the inconsiderate woman! She had refused to come then messed up his day by going out without him. Really, she was the most difficult of women.

His mother had returned from church to where the servants had set out a cold luncheon, but they knew nothing of Megan's whereabouts. It was a sobering indictment of their feelings for her that they didn't worry for her safety, just commented on her inconsiderate behaviour.

His mother's disapproval fuelled Arthur's ill temper and when, a few hours later, she was brought back, laughing, with colour in her cheeks and her hair blown across her face like a brown silken cobweb, he lost his temper and hit her.

Later that night the doctor was called to tell them with regret that once more Megan had lost a child.

Arthur was furious with her. "How could you play such foolish games while carrying a child of mine?" he demanded as soon as the doctor was out of the house.

"My child, too," Megan sobbed. "I did think I was going to be successful this time, I really did."

"Typical of you, wandering around the countryside with an unsavoury character like that Tommy Thomas. My friends aren't good enough for you. Oh, no, you prefer rough uneducated men who live on their wits and by cheating other people. That's who you choose for friends. Well, it isn't good enough, and you're never to talk to him again. D'you hear me?"

Megan was too broken-hearted to argue and as usual he took her silence for agreement.

11

In 1928, Megan finally produced a child. Dylan Arthur
Huntley-Davies was born after a long and worrying labour,
with his grandmother in anxious attendance and an irate
doctor who almost lost his fee by threatening to kick the old
woman out of her own house.

For Megan it was yet another unhappy experience. The
birth was a confused and uncomfortable day during which
she was told what to do, obeying orders instantly; a day in
which accepting pain was as normal a misery as everything
else in her life. Once it was over it was as if she had dreamt
it, that the whole affair had been just another of the dreadful
nightmares from which she suffered.

She remembered thinking it was May, a month when all
the spring flowers came out and gladdened hearts. A month
of maypole dances and celebration, of colour and joy, a
harbinger of a glorious summer. Yet in her heart there was
only winter and the terrible dread that she would never see
another spring.

For a lot of the time she was lost in a world in which people
and the day to day events couldn't reach her. In her more lucid
moments she trembled in fear for the months ahead, when her
mother-in-law would take over both herself and her son. The
thought gave her renewed nightmares which lead at times to
delirious spells and an almost constant depression.

From the first few months of the pregnancy, when
the family began to hope that this child might survive,
Mrs Huntley-Davies had talked about nothing else. Her
droning conversation was partly hope of at last having a
grandchild to carry on the name and business of the family

but also, and more frequently, she warned Megan that with Megan's mental state and her great age of thirty-two, the child was likely to be simple. Every time she spoke to her daughter-in-law she mentioned this fear, blaming the unhappy girl before the event for producing a Huntley-Davies that was not perfect in every way. Megan eventually shut herself off from the painful and cruel words, seeing only the moving mouth and the accusation in the cold grey eyes.

She had tried to talk to Arthur about it, pleading with him to stop his mother from frightening her with thoughts of producing a simpleton, but he only added to her fears by saying, "She's only preparing us for the likelihood, my dear, best to expect the worst then if all is well we'll be happily surprised."

At first Megan was afraid to look at the baby they handed her, wrapped in a white sheet, and she took him and nursed him with as little emotion as holding a doll. Then, coaxed by the sympathetic doctor, who continued to refuse to allow Mrs Huntley-Davies to enter the room, Megan looked down and saw her son. His grumpy face stared out at the world, a deep frown across his brow, eyes slitted against the light as if offended at the interruption from his comfortable and safe shelter.

"Strong and lusty your son, Mrs Huntley-Davies," the doctor smiled. "Though how someone as tiny as you can produce such a monster I'll never know."

"Monster?" she asked, startled, her mother-in-law's words at the front of her mind. "Then he *is* simple, is he?"

"Simple?" What ever gave you such an idea?" He glanced towards the closed door as if he had guessed. "Strong he is and a monster in size, takes after that lump of a father he does for sure," he whispered confidentially and was rewarded with a smile. "But there's nothing wrong with him so far as I can see. A beautiful strong and healthy child you've produced, Mrs Huntley-Davies, never seen one better."

"Thank you. But he'll suffer from having a weak mother like me, won't he?"

"Weak? I wouldn't call you weak, young lady. Gentle and

kindly and having all the attributes of a true and loving mother, those are the words I'd use to describe you," the doctor said. Then he frowned, glanced once more towards the door as if considering the words he was about to utter. "My dear, I think you need quiet for a while so you can get to know your handsome son. I'll tell Mrs Huntley-Davies that you are not to be disturbed by visits, even from her and your husband, for three days. How about that? Eh?"

So for three precious and wonderful days Megan stayed in bed with only the maid servant entering her room. She nursed the baby Dylan and sang to him as she remembered her own mother singing to her and was as near contentment as she had been since she had married Arthur and come to live in Pleasant View.

Outside the bedroom door Mrs Huntley-Davies listened to the sweetly melodious singing and reported back to her son that Megan was, "Off her head, for sure, singing and muttering to a child who couldn't possibly understand, in a frail and deranged manner."

There were family conferences during which Arthur was advised to take the child from his mother and appoint a qualified nurse to ensure Dylan's safety. They ignored the adamant declaration by the doctor that Megan was in good mental health and a loving and adoring mother. Arthur pointed out to his mother that if the way he had been treated since their marriage was an example of Megan's adoration, then indeed the child had better have a nurse and the sooner the better.

Daisie and Gillian both called with gifts for the new child but they were turned away at the door. Daisie wrote two letters, neither of which Megan received. It was Tommy who saw her first when he turned up at the house, again at Daisie's request, with a load of firewood and a pram suit knitted by Helen. Like the others he was turned away from the door, but unlike the others he shouted up at the window where a light burned and was rewarded by the sight of Megan's head appearing and a small hand waving.

"Come down and open the door," he shouted through

cupped hands and she dropped the lace curtain and ran down the stairs. She pushed aside the maid who tried to stop her, raced past her husband who had heard footsteps and come out of the drawing room to investigate, and opened the heavy front door.

"Oh, Tommy, there's a treat to see you. I thought all my friends had deserted me!" She ordered the maid who hovered uncertainly behind her to fetch tea in a manner that cheered Tommy and set his eye winking in frantic approval. To his great disappointment the confidence was not long-lasting.

With Mrs Huntley-Davies and Arthur sitting stiff-backed near them, Megan shrank back to her usual shyness. Their conversation was stilted but Tommy was able to reassure Megan that her friends had indeed called and written during the weeks since the birth of Dylan.

"Why wasn't I told, Arthur?" she asked, and Tommy noted sadly how her voice weakened when she addressed the man who was her husband. He seemed to drain her of energy and spirit.

"Mother and I decided to do what the doctor suggested and allow you to rest as much as possible," Arthur explained.

"Knowing her friends care wouldn't disturb her, make her feel stronger more like," Tommy said sharply. He couldn't understand these cold, unemotional people and wished he could grab Megan and her child and run away with them. With him Megan would relax that stiff jaw, her eyes would lose their painful expression, her wild scrawny hair would again grow soft and thick and shiny: she would sing, laugh and make flesh to cover her bones. He realised that he was almost in love with her, the need to care for her was growing even as he sat there and watched her.

Dressed in poor clothes, a part of his trade persona as he didn't want to look too wealthy, he felt inadequate in the company of these formally smart people but as he stood to go he said firmly, "I will call every day to see you, Megan, and bring messages from Daisie and Gillian in case they can't come." He pointed a grubby thumb towards her mother-in-law and husband. "Don't listen to them, mind, if

167

they say I haven't called. They might refuse to let me in, but I won't miss a day in calling. Remember that will you? We all care for you, Dais, Gillian an' me and don't you never forget it." With a glare at the silent mother and son on their upright chairs he left the room, took his bowler hat from the bemused maid servant, and left, his eye quivering in emotion.

Daisie called for Gillian on the following day and they walked up to the house with bunches of summer roses and a box of Terry's chocolates. With only a moment's hesitation the maid was told to invite them in and they were shown into the drawing room. It was a drab place with heavy lace and dark green curtains covering the large windows and hiding the magnificent view of the town below and the mountains in the distance.

When Megan came in carrying her son the atmosphere lightened a little, with admiring remarks and the presentation of a large number of gifts. But the presence of Megan's mother-in-law meant the three girls were unable to talk freely or indulge in any light-hearted gossip.

"Good heavens, Megan, she's even got me careful not to drop an aitch," Daisie chuckled when the woman disappeared for a brief moment. "No wonder she's got you quaking!"

"Tomorrow you must come into town and we'll have tea in the café," Gillian urged. "I have just bought the most delightful afternoon frock in palest green and I'm longing for an excuse to wear it.

"I don't think – I –" Megan hesitated, looking at her mother-in-law. Mrs Huntley-Davies gave a slight shake of her head and Megan accepted her decision with disappointment. Daisie went home saddened by the visit and worried for the health of her friend.

At The Swan everything was ready for the expected evening rush, but there was no sign of Desmond. "Where's your father?" Dasie called to Gaynor but she received no reply. If he was up in the china shop with Helen she'd have something to say to him. But inspection showed all the work in the cellar was done and when she looked out through the door as she swept the back step she saw him in the field, talking to Arthur Huntley- Davies. Vaugely wondering what they could be discussing so earnestly she went back inside and called again for her daughter.

"I wonder what your father has to talk to Arthur Huntley- Davies about?" she mused.

"Something about an hotel," Gaynor replied vaguely and Daisie went to look more closely at the two men outside. Gaynor was possibly right. They were measuring and Arthur was writing things down in his notebook. She decided to say nothing but wait until Desmond broached the subject.

"I thought to give Ethel a few hours off tonight, d'you think you can help in the kitchen?" she asked without much hope of agreement. Gaynor was a resentful child and always found reasons for not helping.

"Oh, Mam, must I?" Gaynor wailed. They were her favourite words and Daisie almost said them with her.

"What excuse this time?" Daisie sighed.

"I've promised to go and visit Auntie Gillian and Uncle Waldo."

"Funny, I was with Gillian this afternoon and she didn't say?"

"Well, I'm not invited like, but she never minds if I call in. There's always something on in their house."

Daisie noted the disapproving tone and waited for the complaint which was not long in coming. "There's never anything to do here, and with you and dad always working I'm hours on my own, it isn't fair."

"You can feed the animals for a start," Daisie said irritably.

"Oh, Mam, must I?"

With a sigh Daisie gathered the bowl in which the cooked potato peelings and bran had been mixed to feed the hens.

Gaynor ignored her and went on brushing her hair with a look of such boredom on her face that Daisie wanted to shake her. If only Gaynor would do something, anything! Grief and self-pity overwhelmed her as it often did these days. Her beautiful little son, who would have been such delight, was dead. Gaynor, fit, fat and healthy was nothing but a pain. Desmond did as little as he could get away with and Ethel was getting more stroppy by the hour. What an existence!

Carrying the bowl she went to see the animals. She was cheered by the sight of a small donkey leaning over the gate with the patient look of all donkeys, its thick coat full of burrs and small twigs, looking as if it hadn't been groomed for weeks.

"Where did you come from then?" she asked, pulling a tuft of grass and offering it to him. He took it gently, his eyes wary.

"All right if I leave him for a couple of days, is it?" a voice called and across on the far side of the field a small man wearing a misshapen hat waved his arm in greeting. "This is Daisie's Ark, isn't it, missus?"

"For how long?" she asked.

"Two days? Three days? I brought him over to sell on the market but no one was willing to buy him," he explained.

"Come across and we'll discuss it," she said, but he replied that the valuable animal's name was Clancy and he was, "Fine and friendly with women, and you'll love him demented, wouldn't anyone with any heart?" before he disappeared behind the hedge, choosing not to respond to her request for a discussion.

"Well then, Clancy, so you like women. Does that mean you don't like men I wonder," she laughed.

Clancy followed her around while she fed the hens, the rabbits and finally gave fresh water to the last of the horses waiting for their owners to collect them. He stood among the cart-horses, a diminutive shadow in the setting sun, a cartoon of a horse with his short legs, long tail and large head, the pattern of the holy cross on his back. Daisie began to wish that the man had left him for good: Clancy was beautiful, a delight, and already she was dreading him leaving.

After two weeks Clancy was established and Daisie began to believe that the little donkey would remain in the field for always. Every morning she looked out, expecting the owner to have returned and stolen him away during the night to avoid paying for his keep, but every morning when she went down to feed the managerie he was waiting for her, head over the gate, and he would follow her on her rounds until it was his turn to be fed the special treats Daisie had saved for him. As his previous owner had forseen, she "loved him demented".

Daisie hugged his rough coat, now free from tangles, and thought sadly that at least animals loved her. Which was just as well as she had very little luck with humans, including her own daughter.

Then one afternoon, towards the end of May, Clancy showed a side of him that endeared him to Daisie more than ever. The reason the owner had left him became apparent. He loved Daisie, and tolerated Gaynor, Gillian, Megan and Helen but whenever Desmond ventured into the field Clancy turned his back on him and kicked him, hard. Desmond needed to walk through the field on occasions and three times he had met Arthur Huntley-Davies there. He tried watching until the donkey was out of sight then crossing the field, but Clancy was always waiting. Daisie watched one day from the back door and called out a warning, which Desmond ignored.

"I swear the animal was creeping up on tiptoes," she told Ethel later.

Desmond tried to outrun Clancy but Clancy succeeded in outpacing him with insulting ease. He tried an authoritative approach but to no avail. Phil and Tommy were treated the same way and once, to Daisie's deep joy, he butted Arthur.

"Why didn't you tell me you were thinking of selling the field?" she demanded of Desmond, showing no sympathy towards the irate Arthur, who's dignity might never recover.

"It was only a thought. Arthur thinks it could be suitable for an hotel with the stream running through the grounds. I discussed it with – "

"Helen." she finished for him. "You discussed it with

Helen? What about the animals? Where you going to send them? To Billie Beynon the butcher?"

Desmond paused a moment to dream of slow-roasting Clancy. "It was just a thought," he repeated.

"I work twice as many hours here as you do, Helen doesn't come into it at all, so you can at least give me the courtesy of including me in any thoughts you have about The Swan in future. Right?"

"Mam, can I have sixpence? I want some new hair grips," Gaynor called from the upstairs sitting room where she was buffing her fingernails.

"Ask your father! *he* makes all the decisions. I'm just the work horse!" Daisie snapped.

"Can I have a shilling to buy some grips and some ribbon, Dad?" Gaynor called.

"Oh, please yourself. Like your mother, you usually do!"

Megan's joy at the birth of her son faded so fast it was hard to believe that he was hers at all. The pain, the confusion of murmuring people, the messy and ultimately unsuccessful business of her tiny breasts engorging to produce milk, could all have been a part of one of her nightmares. Arthur did not come near her during the first week, even to see his son. His mother brought her flowers which she said were from Arthur, but Arthur himself did not appear. He waited until the nurse took the squealing infant to him in the drawing room. Megan's room was too much like a sick room, he explained.

In the first private and precious few days, weakness prevented Megan from enjoying baby Dylan to the full. Fear of the future, depression and lonelines were quicker to grow than love for him. Even the successs of producing a child did not make her feel anything but a failure. The appointment of a nurse to care for him and the implication that she was incapable, was as clear to everyone as if it had been shouted in the High Street by the town crier.

The two weeks in which the doctor insisted she remained in her room and rested had the opposite effect from what he hoped. Unable to sleep, prolonged isolation and the barely veiled hints that she was mentally unstable, added to her sense of low esteem. The baby was looked after by the crisply uniformed nurse who fetched the infant to her at regular intervals to be fed, but beside those painful and unsatisfactory visits he depended on her for nothing. Bath time was a distant sound from the nursery, heard through the closed door of her bedroom. The nurse dealt with the morning tasks watched by a solemn Mrs Huntley-Davies and occasionally by Arthur, too. Megan was not invited.

As summer faded and Dylan grew into a strong child able to sit up and look around him, Megan was occasionally allowed to walk him in the grounds of the house. She was aware of the nurse standing in the shadows of the great trees near the kitchen door watching her, but seemed not to care. Obediently she pushed the pram around the paths, hurrying through the shrubs so she wasn't out of sight of the watchful nurse for more than a second or so in case she ran to investigate the reason for a delay. Then she would hand the pram back, kiss her indifferent child and return to her room.

Tommy and Daisie were the only ones to produce any animation in her. "Come and look at the mountain," Tommy said one day when he and Daisie arrived together for their almost daily visit. "The clouds have dropped around the peak like an Indian head-dress."

The three of them, with Dylan in his pram, walked across the garden to the place where they could look down on the town and admire the unusual sky. As soon as she had completed the allowed perambulations, Dylan was taken indoors by his nurse. Megan, Daisie and Tommy stayed and watched the sky.

The clouds slowly darkened and covered the distant mountain top in deep purple. They came closer and soon the day was enveloped in the strange colour of an approaching storm. Around them the trees seemed taller and heavier and a sense of isolation drew the three friends together.

"I'd best go, Megan, love," Daisie said regretfully, shrugging herself into her waterproof coat. "My car hasn't got its hood up and I hate fiddling with things like that. Soaked I'll be, like a rat in a storm-drain, if I get caught in this."

Tommy stood with Megan and waved goodbye to Daisie as she backed down the drive and drove off down the winding roads to town. Megan shivered and Tommy said, "Best you go in, Megan, can't have you catching cold, or the witch'll have my head on toast for breakfast!"

"Don't go, Tommy. I'd love to see the storm."

"She'll be out to fetch you as soon as the rain starts, love," he warned.

But she shook her head. "They'll presume I've gone back to my room, they never worry about me."

"Course they do, daft ha'porth."

"Now I'm not feeding Dylan they care even less."

Tommy was worried about her state of mind and didn't know what to do. He knew she should be inside, but guessed that inside meant being alone. A storm could be frightening to someone as alone as Megan.

The rumblings could be heard approaching the mountains, the air was so dark it was almost like night. The wind gushed across the gardens, bending the trees like stage curtains opening before a performance, and he knew that this performance was about to begin.

The rain fell with sudden ferocity. The first violent crack of thunder filled the air. The fir trees under which they sheltered gave sufficient cover for them to avoid the worst of the rain and the remembered warnings about not standing under trees in thunder storms were nothing more than added excitement. The smell of new grass as the rain touched the earth teased their nostrils. Needles on the pines sent forth their scent to add to the clean earthiness and the world was filled with exotic perfume.

The rain formed a curtain that separated them from everything but the sound and scents of the storm. Megan couldn't put her feelings into words, she just knew she was happy.

The flashes of electricity that lit the sky, and the cracking and rumblings of thunder were so frequent, they knew the storm was overhead. Megan's face was glowing with the thrill of it. A sudden crack that made Megan squeal and Tommy nearly jump out of his shoes, was followed by the groaning of splitting wood and between them and the house they watched as a birch tree tilted and slowly slipped sideways, down and down, until it fell in a shuffling of branches and lay still.

"Oh, Tommy! Isn't this exciting?" Megan had to shout above the sound of the thunder and the rain. She turned to him as she spoke and he clutched her in his arms. The intensity of the rain made water filter down through the tree at last and onto their shoulders. As the rain soaked them they kissed and it was as if the thunder was within them, their need of each other a storm so violent that it had cracked the sky.

12

Gaynor watched as her mother lit the fire in the bar room. Daisie was wearing a long black skirt which was protected with an apron which in turn was protected by a coarse wrap-around length of sacking which reached almost to her ankles. She had on an old pair of leather gloves and was giving the bars of the fire a final polish with a long thin brush with a handle on its back. The bristles were worn flat and she looked at it and shrugged.

"Best I buy a new one on Saturday when the market opens, this one is nearly down to the wood."

"I'll get you one over in Brynteg if you like, Mam," Gaynor offered, placing her straw hat on her long, straight, light brown hair. She had tidied her bedroom, brought her washing down and thrown it on the pile in the back kitchen as a sop to her conscience. Now she was going out.

"Want anything else at the shops. Mam?" she asked, with fingers crossed, hoping the answer was no. "I thought I'd call for Bronwen and go into Brynteg on the bus. The market's there today and I need some curlers and a new comb."

"All the way to Brynteg for curlers? You can get them in the High Street. Just an excuse to get out and away from the jobs you should be doing. This is a business, not a playground."

"I've fed the animals and seen to my bedroom," Gaynor pouted.

"You can fetch me some dark grey wool. Helen's offered to make your father a new pullover for the autumn and I said I'd buy the wool this week." Daisie looked at her daughter and said in chorus with her the usual whine. "Oh, must I?"

"Well," Gaynor added, "I'm sure to chose the wrong shade."

"There's a piece of wool in the sideboard drawer, and the pattern's with it so it shouldn't tax your poor brain too much. And," Daisie added firmly, "I want you back here by three o'clock at the latest so no slipping off to the park when you get back. There's the washing to be ironed and that's your job, remember."

Gaynor slouched against the bar and glared at her mother's retreating back. She was still overweight, the baby plumpness which people referred to as puppy fat had never left her. Lack of exercise and being spoilt with the wrong foods had strengthened its hold. Her face could have been pretty but wasn't. She seemed resentful of what life had given her and the scowl that was an almost permanent fixture did not improve her looks. She tried valiantly to dress her long mousy hair but it fell away from any attempt and Daisie refused to allow her to have a permanent wave, another excuse to complain about her life.

She tried to hide her figure with long full dresses, but in her case bunched up skirts and layers of blouses, silk scarves and cotton jackets emphasised rather than disguised the excess flesh.

Since leaving school almost a year before she hadn't found herself a job. Appearing to try, she was more than content to stay at home and not have to face rising early and spending hours of boredom in work she didn't want to do. She would wait, she told her parents, until she decided what she really wanted, then give it all her heart.

The truth was that life around the pub, helping when she had to and avoiding the more tedious tasks by the simple expedient of disappearing at crucial times suited her perfectly and she was the envy of her few friends. Becoming a lady of leisure was what she was suited for, like Auntie Gillian whom she envied and admired. She dreamed of marrying a wealthy man and living a life devoted to pleasure.

The real reason for the proposed visit to the next town was the market, the butchery stall in particular. Since the sixteen

177

year old twins, Billie and Eric Beynon, had started to help their father she had become more interested in helping with the shopping. Each Tuesday she found some excuse to go to Brynteg market. Every Saturday she actually volunteered to go with the weekend shopping list and carry it back. The fact that Billie Beynon frequently carried the loaded baskets for her had not escaped Daisie's notice.

"Started early, hasn't she?" Desmond said when Daisie remarked on it, "her not fifteen till November."

"I suppose she has. Not enough to do, that's Gaynor's trouble. She should be still at school, making a career for herself instead of making sheeps eyes at boys!"

"What does she want with a career? Girls get married don't they when they find a man to care for them? Looking after a family that's what she'll be doing before long."

"Pity help them then, with her hardly able to boil an egg," Daisie chuckled. "Won't learn, no matter how I coax her, and with her appetite you'd think food was a priority, wouldn't you?"

Gaynor didn't call for any of her friends. Most worked in a shop and they only had a few hours off on a Wednesday afternoon which was half day closing. Today, instead of complaining about her lack of company she was glad to be on her own. Billie Beynon was becoming very attentive and without the encumberance of a friend, he might be more inclined to talk for a while. Big he was, like his father, and she really liked big men. "They make you feel safe and protected," she told her friends.

The market was held in an area behind the main road in Brynteg, in what had been a small community of houses. Demolished some years ago, the uneven remnants of the buildings were now used just once a week for the stalls.

The Toby was in his office, the door of which was clearly marked Market Superintendant. His office was a disused shed and when Gaynor approached she could see him arguing with a man who was complaining about the position he had been given. The man was shouting and gesticulating wildly towards a cart that had set up near the entrance and out of line and was effectively blocking his stall from view.

"How much did he slip you, then?" The man demanded. The Toby stood up threateningly behind his untidy desk, making the man back away.

"Finish the day but don't bother to come back next week because there won't be a tober for you. Nor the week after. You can forget markets in this town till my memory fails me!"

The market was a large one with four lines of stalls, the centre two back to back. To save the effort of searching for the butcher's stall, Gaynor braved the wrath of the two men, knocked on the open door, ducked under the arm of the angry stall-holder who had been rendered speechless, and asked, "Is there a butchers here today, superintendant, if you please?"

The Toby smiled and directed her. Then, the smile wiped swiftly from his features like a wet duster crossing a blackboard, he returned to his argument with the irate stall-holder.

Waldo Griffiths had opened a market stall where he sold cheaper shoes and slippers as well as daps, the local name for plimsoles, and other inexpensive footwear. There was a great shortage of money and three of his four shops were now closed, their windows boarded up and used as leaning posts by the growing number of unemployed.

"Hello, Uncle Waldo," Gaynor smiled. "Never knew you were a market person?"

"I'm not, I'm just setting things up. In fact, I'm looking for someone to help run the stall, I don't suppose you'd like to help for an hour or two each week, would you?"

"Me? Good heavens, no, Uncle Waldo. Mam would never have it. I'm too useful at home," she laughed.

She waved and went on, stopping to say hello to Little Dickie Daniels on the fruit and vegetables, Matt Prosser the bookseller who already seemed weak in the legs from drink and unable to concentrate, and several other traders she knew. Work on a market stall? Not me, she thought with a shudder.

Billie and his twin, Eric, were experiencing a lull in the business of the day and when she walked up and smiled Billie spoke briefly to Eric and came to greet her.

"Gaynor Prewitt, well, fancy you being here again. Want a glass of pop?" he led her to the rear entrance where a stall was busily selling cool drinks and sandwiches to customers and stall-holders alike.

The white overalls and the blue and white striped apron Billie wore were a familiar sight, together with the straw hat that was a badge of his calling. When he removed them and slipped on a beige linen jacket she felt a brief disappointment. Although by no means diminishing his size, some of his importance went when the uniform was shed. His short hair was scraggy and ill cut. The back of his neck shone deep red with sunburn and his hands, stained from the meat, were far less attractive than she had imagined.

They drank the lemonade he bought then hand in hand wandered through the stalls. There was a large oak tree on the path near one of the exits and beyond it a meadow where sheep grazed peacefully in the warm sunshine. The grass was cropped, a contrast to the field beyond where the sheep were not allowed. There, amid the swaying grasses, multi-coloured wild flowers grew in glorious abundance: poppies, cornflowers and scabious, with a few corn cockle and ox-eyed daisies and the plumes of meadow-sweet making a carpet of such beauty that even Gaynor paused to admire it.

Billie led her up through the sheep and over the gate into the long grass of the hay-field and sat down, pulling her down beside him where they were hidden by the luxuriant growth.

Billie kissed her, gently at first, then as she offered no resistance, with greater enthusiasm. Soon his passion was filling her with feelings that were bordering on fear as he grew more and more fervent, his strength alarming. Yet soon fear retreated and gave way to a wonderful perception of her own power, far more potent than her physical weakness.

His thick fingered hands were caressing her shoulders,

pressing her against the soft earth, then sliding delightfully down her back, measuring the length of her against him and filling her with an awareness of his need that she did not fully understand. She was more than a little relieved though when he said in a panting whisper that he couldn't stay long.

"Can't leave Eric on his own, see," he explained. "Dad's gone for a pint and won't be back till later." Reluctantly he rose and he walked back to the gate, stopping once or twice to share a more chaste kiss. Billie didn't climb over the gate but opened it for her to walk through. She felt like a duchess. He held her for one last kiss leaning against the open gate between the sheep field and the hay meadow. He didn't bother to close it. The sheep wandered up and ambled into the hay field and began to graze.

When Billie returned to his butcher's stall where a crowd had gathered and were impatient to be served, Gaynor headed for the bus stop in a dream. She wanted to get home and into the privacy of her room and think about Billie and what he did to her. She hesitated when she saw Phil with Tommy helping him, selling the usual assortment of china and linen and stood for a while, amused by his fast patter and the semi-juggling skills of his display. Then Phil left the stall with a rather furtive expression on his handsome face. Curiosity made her follow him to the same entrance she had used with Billie.

A young woman was waiting near the oak tree and together they walked up the same hill, past the same sheep into the same hayfield. As soon as they lowered themselves into its privacy, she began to turn away, a knowing smile on her fleshy face, then a yell made her turn and she saw Phil jump up, a dark stain covering his white trousers. She didn't hear his expletive but guessed, with complete accuracy.

"Oh, shit!" he shouted.

"Quite!" his companion said with a loud laugh.

When Gaynor was sitting on the bus, dreaming about Billie, she was still chuckling over Phil's disaster. The picture of his dismay on finding the sheep-mess on his trousers reminded her of sheep. Sheep reminded her of wool and then she remembered the wool she had promised to get for her mother. Idly she began to invent an excuse.

Gillian and Waldo Griffiths enjoyed their life but Waldo's contentment was marred by the fact that Gillian and he had never produced a child. He knew nothing about the means used by his wife to prevent it happening and after the first ten years of their marriage they rarely mentioned it. Gillian filled the house with friends, arranging a party whenever an excuse could be found. He couldn't say he was unhappy, yet, when Megan visited with her small son, Dylan, he felt the swell of half submerged resentment at what he considered his failure.

The shoe shops were not doing well. As with other tradesmen, he was experiencing a slump as unemployment increased. The market stall venture, recommended by Tommy, was an attempt to recoup some of the lost trade. Griffiths's shoe shops had always had a name for selling only the best, but the market stall would fill the needs of those too poor to be fussy. He hated the very idea of dealing with the lower end of the business. It was another failure to add to the inability to produce a child.

He kept the worst of his worries away from Gillian. When he closed the shops and sacked the staff, he made it sound like good business sense. "Shops will be selling for next to nothing soon," he told her, "and we'll have the pick of some choice sites for less than they're worth now. It's good economics. No matter what hardships people face, they'll always need shoes, won't they?" Although, in that he was wrong.

During the years that followed, as men were laid off and women pleaded for the most menial of jobs to earn enough to fill their childrens' stomachs, many families went barefoot to school and older brothers and sisters shared shoes and took it in turns to go out dressed up, feet being scrunched into boots and shoes far too small or stuffed with paper to disguise the fact they were too large.

Waldo noticed that the coalman was wearing a style of inexpensive boot that his shops didn't stock. "I had to buy them second hand over in Melinbanc," the coalman explained. Waldo pretended surprise to hear that the man was short of money. Businessmen always pretended to be doing fine even if their weren't.

"Coal is a good business isn't it? When will people not want to buy coal? It's as certain as shoes, is coal. How can you tell me you're hard up?" Waldo asked.

"Where you been living, boy?" the coalman demanded. "All my customers owe me money and there's a fat chance of me seeing any of it before the spring. They try to pay a little off the balance each week but with winter coming they won't manage even that."

"We don't allow credit," Waldo said a little stiffly.

"Lucky for some!"

"You got to be firm, and that's easy enough when it's something people can't do without."

"There's plenty of other coal merchants willing to take on my customers and when that happens there's no chance at all of my being paid what they owe."

"We have a scheme where people who are less fortunate can join a club and pay weekly, but they don't have goods until they've paid," Waldo said. "It isn't much but it helps. And it discourages those who don't know any better, from spending money they don't have."

"Your conscience is nice and clear then. In your sheltered world with friends who're able to conserve wealth by sacking workers and persuading those left to do more, you can choose to be unaware of the realities of the time. So it's pity help the rest of us. Sod 'em all, keep the workers down where they belong. That's your attitude!"

The speech was not Bob Tripp's usual style. Waldo decided he was one of the new socialists and wished he hadn't begun the conversation. "Ethel's still enjoying her job at The Swan, I hear?" he said to change the subject.

"Just as well. I don't have enough to keep Kate and her in comfort these days. What with the debts and people trying to manage on less fuel." He sighed, his eyes bright in the black-stained face. "Damn me, the horse eats better than I do!"

Waldo was embarrassed by the reminders of other people's problems. He remembered the death of Bob Tripp's brother, a farm labourer who had had two sons. One one had been killed during the war and the other had lost an arm. Bob Tripp gave his sister-in-law a set amount each week to help her to cope.

"Sorry, Bob," he said. "I know things are hard. Tell you what, you can fill our coal barn up when you have a day spare, and I'll give you the money straight away, no need to send out a monthly bill."

Megan was a regular visitor to Gillian and Waldo. She never attended their parties but often arrived in the afternoon and shared a jug of fruit juice with Gillian. It frequently happened that Tommy Thomas called in, too, on his way back from one market or another, and after a brief word and the offer of tea, Gillian would leave them to sit and talk and play with the baby, who was crawling and entertaining them, giving them an excuse for their bright eyes and cheerful laughter that was really the result of their being together and in love.

Although her health was fragile and her happiness built on Tommy's visits, Megan seemed to blossom that summer.

"It's as if today is all we've got, Gillian," she told her friend one afternoon when they waited in the garden for Tommy to call. "Dylan is only a baby and already he's entered for private school. He'll be at a boarding school when he's eleven. I can't look into the future and plan lovely things. I have to grab the moment, like children do. Christmas is too far away and might never come."

Gillian didn't know how to cope with such melancholy thoughts and was glad when Tommy arrived. The couple seemed so right together, laughing and talking and playing with the baby like children themselves. Gillian wished Arthur would go away and leave Megan with Tommy with whom she seemed to find that happiness which had eluded her all her life.

Tommy and Megan met at other places besides Gillian's house. On Sundays, when the servants were given a day off having prepared all the food for the day and dealt with the routine tasks of fires, bedmaking etcetera, Megan was blissfully free.

Mrs Huntley-Davies went to church and then for coffee with friends. Arthur invariably went out to lunch. Tommy called for Megan and with Dylan in the pram, they walked, singing at the tops of their voices, heard only by the mountains and the birds. Tommy frequently forgot the words and whistled instead or invented his own, which made Megan's merry laugh ring out.

Megan's whole life revolved around her meetings with Tommy. His face would appear before her whenever things were difficult. She felt him beside her when Arthur was particularly demanding or his mother over critical. She imagined his arms around her, comforting her and encouraging relaxation and sleep as she settled into her bed. He was a tonic to her flagging spirits even when he was not with her. Tommy Thomas, with his red, spiky hair and those intensely blue eyes was her reason for living.

Then came an event which changed things for both of them. In 1933, when Dylan was five and already at school, the unbelievable happened and at the age of thirty-seven Gillian produced a son.

Motherhood was such an unlikely event that it was not until three months before the baby's birth that a terrified Gillian and a surprised and delighted Waldo were told by their doctor that a baby was on the way.

The next twelve weeks went past in a flurry of activity as a nurse was chosen, a nursery decorated and stocked, and a frightened Gillian constantly reassured by, of all people, the nervous Megan.

"It is unpleasant, I wouldn't pretend otherwise," she soothed, "but it's soon over and once the baby is born it's finished and can be forgotten. Oh, Gillian, you'll love being a mother. I didn't at first, when no one trusted me with my own child, but once Tommy had made me feel stronger and more able to cope, well, it's wonderful, really it is."

"I'll never fit any of my lovely dresses," Gillian wailed.

"And look at my brassiere, it's big enough to carry coal in!"

"You'll get back to as you were before, don't worry. Anyway, Waldo will be so pleased he'll buy you as many new dresses as your wardrobe will hold."

"Megan, I'm frightened. I know I'm too old for this. I might die."

"Nonsense."

"Will it hurt very much?"

"More than toothache and less than being run over by a goods train."

"Oh, why did this have to happen now?"

"When the pain gets so you think you can't stand it, that's when it's quickly over, I promise." Megan smiled. "Think of me, poor old cowardly Crying Mouse. If I can stand it, you can for sure." For Megan the role of the strong capable person was a novelty and one which she enjoyed.

By concentrating on the vision of both her figure and her life returning to normal, Gillian coped well with the last few weeks and once the pains began, she concentrated even harder on what Megan had said. A doctor and nurse had been engaged and Megan stayed in the room with her for as long as they allowed and was the first to see the child. Waldo was at the Cwm Manachlog shop, snapping at all his best customers, threatening his assistants with the sack and inwardly crying, convinced his adored Gillian would die.

"You were so right about me loving the role of mother," a glowing Gillian said when she held up her son for Daisie to admire. "From the first sight of our little Michael, I adored him." For her and Waldo it was not going to be the end of anything but a new beginning. A life as full but twice as exciting began on that September day in 1933.

Tommy found he was as moved by the event as anyone else. He and Megan continued to meet at Gillian's and seeing the new baby brought on strange longings. He began to question his own life and wondered if he would ever experience the joy of holding his own child. Suddenly, and unexpectedly, he wanted to.

He loved Megan and thought that was something which would never change. He also knew she could never be his wife. Could he marry someone while he felt such strong love for another? The first move was to end the relationship with Megan. He talked it over with Daisie.

"See, Dais, I know it's impossible. Her and me, we'll never get together, not while Arthur lives and he's likely to reach a hundred the way he looks after himself. I don't think I can face the rest of my life without someone of my own, someone truly my own."

"I agree that you and Megan are a lost cause. But you can't just go out and grab a wife like picking up a bunch of bananas from Little Dickie Daniels's fruit stall!"

"I know that, Dais, but there's Ethel Tripp's daughter, Kate. She's twenty three, young enough to have children and old enough to consider marrying me."

"You'd marry someone you don't really love?"

Tommy looked at her, the knowledge that she had married Desmond Prewitt to give her child a name hovered in the air between them but the words were not spoken.

"Better than being alone, eh, Dais?" he said.

"Yes, Tommy, much better. But Kate Tripp? She's a stuck up piece that one. Real 'Icky'. Thinks herself better than the rest of us for all her family's lack of riches! And what makes you think she'll even consider you for a husband?"

"I've got money, Dais." He spread his fingers as if to count off his attributes. "And apart from my face and my hair and the rest of me I'm quite handsome!"

"You'll have to tell Megan in a way that lets her down gently. She loves you. Your love makes the rest of her life bearable, you know that, don't you?"

She's stronger now than she's ever been. She'll cope. I know she will. I won't just abandon her, Dais. We'll still be loving friends."

"I hope she'll understand and be glad for you. Such a pity things don't work out as we hope. She's so much better now, but her contentment has always been on a slender thread."

*   *   *

Ethel Tripp's daughter, Kate, worked in a small office that dealt with the marketing of wool and wollen material. There wasn't a cattle market or a wool merchant in the town and all the wool went to a central area to be graded and sold. It was Kate's job to write dockets and send the wool off by rail, receive payment and pay the farmers for the wool that passed through her hands. Once the shearing was finished, the rest of the year was spent handling the yarns and fabrics that were sold in the shops owned by the firm she worked for.

Kate was always dressed neatly and when she wanted to she dressed with exceptional skill, chosing clothes and accessories that added to her rather formal appearance and changed her into a very attractive young woman.

She was not very tall but, because of her choice of styles and her confidence, she appeared taller than most. Kate was a quiet young woman, but not shy like Megan, more self contained, and Tommy was amused at the sharpness of her tone when he said something she disagreed with, like when he had once stopped and offered her a lift.

With the intention of making her acquaintance and hopefully to court her before the year was out, he made use of every opportunity for meeting her. One day he saw her setting off up the winding road that led up past Pleasant View to the mountain. He called in to see Gillian briefly and managed to be driving out of the Griffith's gateway when Kate was striding past, dressed in a well fitting tweed suit and strong brogue shoes.

"Hello, Miss Tripp. Can I offer you a lift?"

"Not unless you're *twp*! I'm out for a walk, Tommy. What's the point of having a lift back home when I've walked half way up the mountain for the pleasure of walking back down? Now go on with you and take that noisy car out of my way."

The fact that the noisy car was a brand new Morris Cowley saloon that cost a hundred and ninety-five pounds did not impress her. He watched as she climbed over a fence and strode off down the hillside through the springing heather, waiting for her to turn back and wave. She didn't.

Tommy used to meet her sometimes as she walked to the

Post Office make her way through the busy street to put the money into the bank.

"Fancy a bite to eat?" he asked one Saturday when she stepped out of the bank into the cold of a November morning. "There's usually a good pie and mash at The Swan."

"I don't go into public houses, Tommy Thomas. What d'you take me for? Mam might work in one but that doesn't make it right for a woman to go into a man's domain!"

"All right, stupid of me, Kate. What about the café?"

"If you like, but what brought this on?"

"Just watched you walking down the road and thought it would be nice to have a chat," he said, wishing he could think of something smart like Phil Johnson always managed.

"Me walking down the road would be a most stimulating start to a conversation," she said adding to his dismay. Then her expression softened and she said, "Come on, then, yes, I'd like to have lunch with you. But not the café. What about the hotel instead?"

So their courtship started with a meal at the hotel where Tommy felt conspicuous in his shabby market clothes, but Kate had a manner that made such things unimportant and soon they were talking as naturally as two friends who had known each other for years instead of being more or less newly acquainted. Tommy's view of his future grew more rosy with every minute that passed.

Megan still saw Tommy regularly at Gillian's house but there was something lacking and the visits slowly reduced in number. Instead of three times in a week it dropped almost imperceptibly to two and then one. She remarked on it and Tommy said, "Dark nights, see. Always the same in the winter. There's so much to do and so few hours of daylight to do them. I work three markets and there's me chasing round the countryside searching for gear to sell every chance I get. Better when the spring comes round again." He avoided her eyes, afraid of the doubt he would see in them. He was a coward for not explaining about Kate and he knew he must tell her soon. He did mention seeing her occasionally and Megan joked about the young woman's stiff and formal manner.

"That Kate was always a bit of a madam, wasn't she, Gillian?" she laughed, hugging Dylan who had fallen off the bicycle Arthur had bought for him. "Never approved of anyone, talk about looking down your nose, she was a master of it!"

"Mistress you mean," Tommy said.

Gillian whispered, "Now then, there's a slip of the tongue!"

"Come on, she isn't that bad," Tommy said, ignoring Gillian's quip. "Kate's got a good sense of humour when you get to know her."

"How do you know? You can't know her well, Tommy?" Megan frowned.

"Oh, they meet at the market. Tommy knows everyone in Cwm Manachlog, don't you, Tommy?" Gillian said quickly.

Tommy nodded but the warning was there, he had to tell Megan, and soon.

One Saturday evening when Tommy and Kate were eating in an hotel in a place beyond the mountains, he began to hint at something more than friendship between them. Kate thought it time she made her position clear and brought up the subject of Tommy's work.

"Surely you don't intend to run market stalls all your life?" she queried. "Now you're set up financially you'll want something better for sure."

"Why?" he asked. "I like the work and I do very well at it."

"I couldn't marry anyone who worked in such a hand-to-mouth manner," she said casually. "It's all right for you I suppose, being a single man, but to marry you'd have to get a proper job, wouldn't you?"

"What d'you suggest, supposing I wanted to change course?" he asked, joining in the game of pretending to talk generally, when they both knew it concerned themselves specifically.

"I don't know, but if you wish, I'll give it some thought."

They continued to see each other frequently walking, going to the theatre and for car rides, stopping at tea shops and occasionally taking picnics, but Tommy knew

190

she was holding back until he had made his decision. He had to have something better to offer her than the role of wife to a market trader. It made him miserable. He loved his job and would find it hard to give it up, especially for one that entailed staying in doors for the best part of each day. And earning far less money!

Daisie had noticed that Tommy was more friendly with Ethel Trip and seemed to be well acquainted with Ethel's rather haughty daughter. She said nothing to either Tommy or Ethel. When he came to tell her he was considering asking Kate to marry him, she feigned surprise.

"You, getting married, Tommy? Never! Who is she then?"

"You must have seen me with Kate Trip, Dais. I've been courting her this ages."

"It's a surprise to me. I wouldn't have thought she was your type at all. Stuck up she seems to me. Though why when her Mam works in the bar and once worked on the coal cart."

"We get on great, really, Dais and, well, I've got enough money to buy a good house. Nothing fancy, mind, I don't want to live with them up on Pleasant View, but big enough for us and perhaps a couple of kids."

Daisie looked at him, his face somehow hollow and sad, serious and vulnerable. His eye was twitching like fury and she recognised for the first time his loneliness. "Go on, Tommy, she can only say no, and why should she do that? A good catch, that's what you are, Tommy Thomas."

"Will Kate think so?"

"Any single girl with sense would jump at the chance of marrying you. But," she added, "what about Megan. What will you tell her?"

"I thought that you and Gillian might . . .?"

"No. That's something you'll have to do for yourself. But we'll be there, for Megan's sake. Let us know when you mean to talk to her and Gillian and I will be there."

"Megan is stronger now. She'll cope without me," he said without conviction.

"Crying Mouse she'll always be, Tommy, we both know that. She's strong only because you've been holding her up."

191

"What can I do, Dais?"

"You want a family, a home and children, don't you? Things Megan can never give you. If you decide to marry Kate you must accept that Megan will be hurt. If Kate accepts you then you must tell Megan a firm goodbye."

"Couldn't we stay good friends then?"

"It's not easy."

"We only have one life, Dais, I don't want to see mine slip away without experiencing all the normal human joys."

"God 'elp, Tommy, I'm the last one to talk about moral issues with my history. But start straight, for Kate if not for yourself. Otherwise this marriage is doomed before you've even got it started."

Kate met Tommy one evening. She was smiling and bursting with news. "Tommy, I've had a word with my boss and he's prepared to offer you a job in the firm. Selling it will be, and that's something you're very good at, so there shouldn't be a problem."

"I don't know, Kate, love. Wool, isn't it? What do I know about wool?"

"Forget wool. Just think about selling. You'd have a telephone and a desk and an office of your own and someone to deal with all the details so you are free to deal with customers."

"You mean sell over the telephone?"

"Most large shops have telephones these days, Tommy. It's the civilised way to do business. There would be some calls of course. The smaller shops like the personal touch. But much of it will be by letter and telephone."

"Kate, I couldn't stay in one room all day. It would kill me. I'd feel like I was choking if I was to be shut up."

Kate didn't argue but there was a decided coolness about the rest of their time together that day.

It was December before Tommy spoke to Megan. Sunday was the only day of the week Daisie and Desmond could be free and as Christmas Eve fell on that day, Gillian and Waldo had decided on a party. Daisie and Desmond were among the first to arrive with Gaynor looking determinedly bored, convinced she would be the only young person there. Then Bob and Ethel Trip arrived with her daughter, Kate, who looked splendid in a woollen suit of forest green with touches of red, woollen stockings and cosy ankle boots in dark green leather. Gaynor admired her at once. Kate knew how to wear clothes and perhaps she might pass on a few tips. She sat beside the young woman and flatteringly told her how much she admired her taste.

Megan had persuaded her husband to come with her and Daisie noticed at once how lacking in spirit Megan was, with the sombrely dressed Arthur beside her. She saw the pale face glance constantly towards the door, watching for the arrival of Tommy. Was Arthur aware of his wife's feelings for Tommy Daisie wondered, and if so, did he care?

There were several of Waldo and Gillian's business friends and acquaintances to make the number up to a comfortable twenty. The decorated room, the gramophone playing in a corner and the huge log fire created an atmosphere of celebration and the guests took no time at all to begin to laugh, flirt and enjoy themselves.

Old Billie Beynon arrived with his twin sons, Billie and Eric, to Gaynor's undisguised delight. Daisie was amused and relieved to see her daughter's face breaking into smiles.

When Tommy arrived Daisie could see he was distressed. He had spoken to Megan earlier that day and she had refused to accept what he was saying, pretending to misunderstand. Now, his intention of announcing his engagement to Kate was wavering and he looked to Daisie for support. Waves of excitement, anticipation, joy and impending tragedy, wove themselves into a strange mood.

By nine o'clock the room was crammed with lively dancers, their faces glowing with an excess of exercise, food and alcohol. Several other couples had arrived unannounced to bring gifts for the following day and were easily persuaded to stay.

The heat of the rooms necessitated opening the windows and allowing laughter and music to escape and spill out onto the crisp, frosty lawn. Billie and Gaynor managed to slip outside and before they froze to death, or had Daisie calling them inside, they enjoyed a few kisses and some shared words of love.

Megan sat with the solemn Arthur and watched the rest of the party, having fun. Apart from a couple of stately dances during which she pleaded with her eyes for Tommy to change partners, she seemed numb and lifeless. Arthur determinedly ignored the exciting rag-time melodies and danced only a slow foxtrot.

It was almost midnight before Tommy managed a private word with Megan. "Megan, my dear love. What I said earlier is true. Don't pretend it isn't happening. Kate and I are going to be married at Easter. Please, please be happy for me."

"Don't tease me, Tommy. I can't stand being teased. Not today with Christmas and everything."

"It's no joke. You and I will always be lovers. But we can never marry or even boast about our love. I want a home and a family of my own."

"So do I, Tommy. Dylan belongs to the Huntley-Davies'. He isn't mine. The house belongs to them, too. I haven't a home or a family."

This was harder than Tommy dreamed of even in his worst moments. "You and I can't marry. You won't divorce Arthur, or I'd wait for you, you know I mean that."

"He'd be so embarrassed for people to know our marriage had failed. I couldn't do that, Tommy."

"Please, Megan, please understand that my marrying Kate doesn't mean I don't love you."

"Don't leave me, Tommy," she whispered as Arthur returned.

As the clock touched hands on the hour of midnight, Tommy cast a last agonised glance toward a stricken Megan, and held up Kate's hand.

"Friends," he said proudly. "I am happy to tell you that Kate has agreed to become my wife."

It was as if someone had announced the end of a war. Everyone shouted at once and crowded round them to offer their best wishes. Jokes and advice, both polite and ribald, flowed with the drinks. So no one noticed Megan leave.

The party dispersed soon after and the guests made their noisy way home. Daisie and Desmond and a glowingly happy Gaynor had hardly climbed into bed when there was a furious knocking at their door. Daisie went down and saw a fraught Arthur standing there.

"It's Megan," he gasped. "She's threatened to kill herself. Come and help me look, please!"

"Have you told the police?"

"Yes, of course. She left me a note. Please hurry. You might know where to start looking. Help me, please!"

Daisie called Desmond then hastily dressed. "Best we go and tell Tommy," she said as she hurried out of The Swan's front door. "He knows her well and might guess where she might be."

"Not him. He's the cause of this. Don't think I'm unaware of what's happening!" Ignoring his words, Daisie hurried to where Tommy lodged and quickly explained the situation.

Tommy got into his car, his trousers half buttoned, no tie, his collar hanging by its back-stud and waving about like a cartoon butterfly around his scrawny neck. His eyes looked wild. She was going to die and it was his fault for playing with her emotions like the imbecile he was!

Megan was carrying one of Dylan's teddy bears. She walked along the bank of the stream unable to see through her tears, her feet bare, her nightdress dragging on the cold hard earth. She knew she shouldn't be here, she knew Arthur would be cross. She was living a dream. Helen was walking beside her and Helen was soaking wet, telling her it was best for everyone. Far off a distorted image of Tommy's face called, "No." Helen guided her along the path beside the stream to the point where Helen herself had once slipped into the cold water. She hurt her foot on a sharp stone and gave a cry. Helen said, "Never mind."

Tommy was driving towards Pleasant View. She must be near

her home, perhaps in the garden of Gillian's house where they had so often met and been happy. He had to find her and make it right. It didn't matter what Arthur thought. He had to take her away. Forget Kate, it was Megan he loved and Megan who needed him. Below him in the town he imagined Arthur and the others had fanned out, running throught the deserted streets calling her name. They mustn't find her. It had to be he who took her in his arms and promised that everything would be all right.

A tramp was sleeping in the rotting remains of Daisie's burned out old home. The wall remained and a part of the corrugated iron roof, now red with rust, was a partial cover for the living room. He had lit a fire in the grate and had settled to spend his Christmas in its warmth.

He went to the fire-damaged doorway and threw down the last empty flagon and was startled seeing Megan's ghostly figure walking beside the still water. Her feet below the long nightgown were hidden by the frost rimed grasses and in his inebriated state she appeared to be floating just above the ground. He screamed. Megan woke out of her trance and turned back towards town, arms held high, the teddy in one hand like a banner.

Conscious now of her undress and fully aware of the intense cold, she ran blinded not now by tears but by panic, across the field behind The Swan, through the lane and out into the High Street.

Tommy approached the Griffiths's house and jammed the brakes on hard. Fool that he was, it was the stream! That was where Megan would be heading. If he hadn't been so drunk he would have thought of it sooner. He turned the car, scraping the polished paintwork against the hedges as he turned in the narrow road.

Reaching the town he went past the church. He turned the corner and went up on the grass verge and slithered off. His actions were clumsy and he rose up onto the grass verge again and hit the church wall. The car bounced off, he hit the other side of the road and scored the paintwork on a lamp post with a harsh squealing sound. The car stayed on the pavement as Tommy struggled to correct the steering. He went down the kerb, skidded, over compensated, and went back up on the pavement. He had to drive to the nearest point to the stream to save time. He had to find her before it was too late. Careless of anything but his need to find her, he started the engine again and, still on the pavement, speeded along the road to the other end of the main road. In an effort to concentrate he slowed to get the wheels off the pavement then picked up speed again along the High Street.

Then he saw the strange apparition gliding along the pavement and in his drunken state took a few precious moments to realise that she was about to run across the road.

He hit her as she darted across and in disbelief saw her pushed before the squealing car as he pressed and pulled on the brakes. The car stopped and silence fell. She lay crumbled between the front of the car and the wall of The Swan. He knew she was dead even before he stepped out of the car.

13

Gaynor had been looking out of the bedroom window of The Swan. The sound of the racing car engine was frightening in the still night. Then she saw it happen. First the car careering wildly on and off the pavements, its headlights blazing. Then her eyes were drawn to the street below and the small pale figure running into its path. She saw Megan running out into the road, arms held high, and heard the dull thud of the impact. The figure seemed to float in slow motion, taking an age to be lifted like a rag doll before falling to the ground. The car skidded and pushed the tiny figure against the wall.

She screamed then ran back to her room. She ought to go down, see if she could help. Trembling, she made for the top of the stairs, went instead to look again through the window and saw that Tommy was standing over Megan, that people were running from several directions towards them. On the pavement that sparkled with midnight frost, a shadow was slowly surrounding Megan's head and shoulders, flowing towards the gutter in a slow river, black in the light of the street lamp. Gaynor knew it was blood. Then she heard the low wail that rose in eerie animal-like ululation and knew the sound came from Tommy Thomas. She ran to her room jumped into bed and covered her ears. A few moments later she was sick.

Arthur arrived at that moment and, pushing Tommy out of the way, went to stand by the body of his wife. His face was a mask of disbelief. He stared at Tommy, a frown distorting his features, but he didn't see Tommy. He saw the small, shy young girl he had married and wondered how it could have ended like this, in a gutter near a public house in the middle of Christmas Eve night.

Daisie stopped him from disturbing his wife. "Best we leave her, Arthur," she said softly. "Just sit with her and let her know you love her." Arthur did as Daisie told him and, with an arm across Megan's thin shoulders that were exposed under the torn nightdress, he sat and slowly began to sob. He tried to repair the torn cloth, pulling the broken ends together to hide her back. He tried to tell himself that she wasn't dead, that the doctor would make were well again. But the stillness was frightening and he knew the fallen statue would never breath again.

Tommy stared at the still form of the dead woman. There was silence all around him, silence that buzzed in his ears, a complete deafness. Around the frail body of Megan there was nothing but darkness. The world was empty except for the two of them. Megan was dead. He had caused the death of someone he dearly loved.

All around the silent tableau people gathered as they waited for the police and the ambulance to arrive. Unheard, doors and windows opened, footsteps approached and people hovered in a great circle, not speaking but making their sympathy clear.

Phil was one of the crowd and he managed to touch Daisie's arm and nod to show he shared her grief. Daisie wanted to hold him and feel his arms supporting her against the horror of the past moments. But she couldn't. Desmond was beside her and he was holding her other arm in a trembling grasp that revealed his distress. She wanted support but instead, as usual she thought with rising sadness, she had to give it. Belatedly she remembered that Gaynor might still be awake and she ran up to her room to find her trying to clear the mess from her bed.

"Sorry, Mam, it was such a shock. I couldn't help it."

Daisie hugged her daughter and for a rare and precious moment they felt need and love for each other.

"It's all right, my darling girl. Mam's here. Go and wash yourself and I'll soon have this lot sorted." But they remained, standing with their arms around each other for a long time before they set about their tasks.

Gaynor was soon asleep in a freshly made bed, but Daisie busied herself, first with making food and tea for the people that had gathered around the accident, talking to the police, then preparing for the new day. She had no need of sleep. The shock had pushed aside the languid contentment they had all felt at the end of Gillian and Waldo's party. The normal everyday tasks, instead of being a comfort, seemed artificial, as if she were pretending that life could go on in the usual way, with Megan dead and Tommy bearing the guilt.

At eight o'clock in the morning she had come to the end of the work she could find to do. Unable to be still, she glanced in to see Gaynor still sleeping, made breakfast for Desmond, and drove up to see Gillian and Waldo. The police had been there and had taken statements so she didn't have to break the sad news. She couldn't talk unemotionally about the actual events yet, so they sat near the fire in silence, the gaudy tree and the brightly wrapped presents an inpertinance on such an occasion. Their few murmured comments were the wish and need to do something to help.

"I've already written a note offering to have Dylan on the day of the funeral," Gillian said and after that there seemed nothing more to add.

They sat together for less than an hour, drank tea none of them wanted, then Daisie went. As she drove through the gates she saw Arthur on the road examining the wall on which scratches showed like recent wounds, where Tommy had carelessly reversed his new car. She rolled down the window to speak but he turned away in the direction of his house.

She returned to The Swan and it wasn't until she stepped inside and saw the holly decorating the bar that she remembered it was Christmas day.

After she had cleared the breakfast things that Desmond had abandoned, Gaynor helped her to prepare a light lunch, both pretending that 25 December 1933 was a day just like any other. The goose she had intended to cook remained on the kitchen table. Desmond took it to Helen and asked her to cook it and give it to a needy family.

The inquest looked bad for Tommy for a while. "Wanton and Furious Driving" was the charge Arthur expected and which could mean two years in prison. He wanted it very badly. It was Daisie and Gillian who gave evidence of Tommy's love for Megan, and hers for him, and the explanation that he had been frantically heading to the stream to save her that convinced the magistrate it was a case of accidental death.

Arthur was furious and had to be led from the court room by two officials. He seemed determined that Tommy should suffer and Daisie knew that much of the unfortunate man's distress was embarrassment as the news of the state of his marriage was revealed. She felt a deep pity for him.

Tommy saw the man and wanted to share his grief. He called on Arthur but was told he was not welcome. "I loved her, too," Tommy said.

"And look what your so called love did to her!"

Tommy left the silent house and wandered disconsolately off across the fields, his feet crackling on the brittle, frosty grass, towards the top of the mountain. When the cold forced him to abandon a vague intention to walk down the far side, he went to see Kate Tripp.

They hadn't met since Christmas Eve when they had announced their engagement and he was puzzled, although not unduly alarmed. Some women were not good about showing emotion.

She opened the door to him but stepped back when he went to kiss her. He didn't think anything of it. Kate was not a very demonstrative woman and besides, she had to move away to allow him to enter the small hallway. She moved away from him again when they were inside her parents neat and orderly living room. Then, when he held his arms out in invitation, she turned away and asked him if he would like some tea.

"Hell, no, Kate! I want to hold you and ask if you've missed me these past days." There was no response and he was hurt by her casualness, wondering why, in the days since Megan's death, she had not contacted him to offer her support and sympathy.

She clearly wasn't going to explain *her* absence, so he said, "Sorry I haven't been to see you but I can't get over the shock of what happened."

"Me neither, Tommy. Best we forget it all, don't you think?"

"Forget it? How can I forget it? I drove a car and killed Megan."

"Oh, I don't mean to forget that. I know you never will," she said softly. "I mean our engagement. Best we forget it happened."

"You don't blame me for her death?"

"Yes, I suppose I do."

"But she was demented, she ran out into the road without giving me a chance to stop!"

"I know, Tommy, but you were the reason she was running. You were the cause of her wanting to kill herself, weren't you? I couldn't live with a man who did that to a woman who loved him." She ushered him out efficiently and closed the door on him before he realised what she had said.

When her words had sunk in he walked away through the lively Saturday market that no longer seemed to have any relevance to him, unaware of the friendly shouts of the stall-holders and the harassed figure of the Toby demanding to know when he'll stop messing him about and let him know whether or not he wanted a stall. On he walked, stopping when he reached The Swan.

"Can we talk, Dais?" he asked and at once Daisie left the bar where she had been tidying the pedlar's tray, and beckoned him to follow her up to the sitting room above the bar.

Like Tommy, Daisie needed comfort. Desmond had closed up his mind to the affair and refused to discuss it. In desperation she had gone to the china stall and asked Phil to call and see her. He came an hour later with some food for the animals. She went out into the field to see him, wrapped in her old cloak for warmth. But Phil had refused to let her talk about Megan, threatening to stay away unless she let the subject drop.

"I'm sick of the misery of it," he had explained firmly. "Everyone in Cwm Manachlog is talking about nothing else. I came to you for fun and a bit of a laugh, not to listen to any more long-faced grieving for a woman who was so unhappy she's probably better off dead." He apologised almost at once, seeing from her stricken face that he had gone too far. "I'm sorry, Daisie. I shouldn't have said that, even if I was thinking it. But, well with you sending for me, I thought, you know . . . You and I, we're partners for laughter, a bit of flirting and some relaxation from all the worries of business and sickness and the frustrations of life. There's no room for grief and misery in our precious time together. And it is precious, isn't it, Daisie my love?"

"Am I? Am I your love?" she asked.

"Need you ask?" He kissed her. But lips were unsatisfactory and she pulled away. This wasn't the way to deal with Megan's death.

Phil was shaken. She had disturbed him. Although they had no intense love affair, he had always loved her. So many barriers in the way had made it stupid to even hope that one day they might become a couple, yet even when he was with one of his other women, it was always Daisie who was on his mind.

Daisie and he parted with both of them feeling restless and unsatisfied. Meeting had only reopened a wound. Phil decided to find a woman with whom he could spend the evening and perhaps the night. What was the matter with him that a woman like Daisie could get to him after all this time?

Daisie had a bubble of disappointment worrying away inside her created by his reminder that she was only a bit of fun, that she wasn't important to him other than for a laugh and a good time. While trying to be a good wife to Desmond, she had spent a lifetime loving Phil. She felt angry with herself for her weakness and was only a little sorry when she saw Clancy emerge from his shed and run silently as a shadow, then turn neatly to kick Phil as he was about to climb over the fence.

Although the inquest had given the cause of death as accidental, Tommy still faced hours of questions from the police. Arthur seemed obsessed. He was searching for new evidence and each time he had a theory or a fresh discovery of damage showing the careless way Tommy had driven that night, he went to the police station or to his solicitor. Slowly a file against Tommy grew and fattened.

One Sunday, while Desmond was with Helen and Gaynor was having tea with Billie Beynon, Tommy arrived in the field behind the house with a load of hay.

"How much do I owe, Tommy?"

"Nothing. It's a gift, I had it given to me."

"Again?" she said. I don't know when I last paid for hay or food. And the vet rarely accepts payment when he comes. People seem to enjoy sharing in Daisie's Ark."

"Arthur is determined to blame me for Megan's death, Dais," he said as, white faced, he began to haul the load into the hay barn.

"Now, Tommy, don't get depressed. Losing her is bad enough, without you expecting to take the blame as well."

"But I *am* guilty, Dais. Arthur's right about that."

She looked at Tommy who had a drawn look he had worn since the accident, his red hair like a flame against the pale skin. She prepared to wallow in sadness and memories. They both needed it. Collecting a coat she said, "Let's go to your place, Tommy, there's no chance here to talk in peace."

They walked through the cold streets, through the crowds of people flooding the stalls looking for bargains and into the cold uncomfortable rooms Tommy rented. Daisie lit a fire and made a tray of tea and sat beside him on the one comfortable couch. "Now, Tommy, my love, let's talk."

To her surprise his first words were not about Megan but Kate. "She's left me, Dais. Kate won't marry me after all. Megan's death needn't have happened. I could have taken my time, let her down slowly, eased my way

204

out of her life without giving her a moment's unhappiness."

"What a lot of old lol! Megan died in an accident. Going out to kill herself she was and ending it under a car instead of how she'd planned wouldn't have made any difference in the end, would it?"

"Killing herself because I was abandoning her," Tommy said. Daisie believed the same but she argued loudly.

"You weren't abandoning her for heaven's sake. She was a married woman. You were just announcing your engagement to someone Megan knew you were courting, not saying goodbye for ever like a hero in *Peg's Paper*!"

"Daisie, I think she had headed for the stream."

"So? Drowning is not an uncommon way to commit suicide."

Daisie's heart was racing as she talked so matter of fact about Megan, but she knew she had to for the sake of Tommy's sanity.

"But," he said slowly, "she was coming away from it. I think she had recovered her senses and had changed her mind. When I hit her with the car she had changed her mind about dying."

"You don't know that." White faced Daisie stared at him.

"Sure of it I am."

The fire crackled as the sticks caught and the coal shifted and slipped to where the smallest amount of red showed through the black. It needed more sticks to save it. The wood must have been damp, Daisie thought stupidly. She looked at Tommy, his eye fluttered in the parody of a wink. What was there to say?

Impulsively she moved and put her arms around him. He responded and within seconds they were kissing, their need for comfort fast becoming sexual. Minutes later they lay on the floor with the fire collapsed and showing nothing but a few useless sparks. It was as if they had just found each other and, ignoring the coldness of the room and the time marching on, they loved and comforted each other in a way Daisie had lacked all of her life.

When Daisie finally prepared to leave, they both knew it would never happen again. They had been in desperate need. It had been a momentary insanity which would enable them to get on with their lives as before. But Daisie wondered whether they could ever be close friends again.

In the street outside, a tall, rather self-assured young woman walked past without glancing at the door. Kate Tripp didn't have a car but the day was crisp and dry, the walk would be beneficial. Through the town she walked at a steady pace that didn't slow as the road began to climb up and out of the town towards Pleasant View. Sufficient time had passed, it would be considered correct now to go and offer her condolences to Arthur Huntley-Davies.

It was February 1934, snow lay across the pavements edged by grey heaps where the traffic had pushed it from the roads and householders had cleared it from their doors. Daisie woke with a start and looked at the clock. Eight o'clock, she had overslept! She threw back the covers and reached under the bed with her toes to find her slippers. The air struck cold and she quickly grabbed her dressing gown from the end of the bed. Strange Desmond hadn't woken her.

She spent as little time as possible in the bathroom, where ice made convoluted designs on the window panes and a small mound of snow had gathered at a point where the woodwork had rotted and the frame was distorted into a curve. She dressed and went down to find the door unlocked and no sign of Desmond. Probably gone to shift Helen's snow for her. Never interested in helping me, she thought irritably.

The kettle took for ever to boil and when the tea was made she found she didn't want it. She gathered the food for the animals and went out. It was bitterly cold, yet when she returned to the house she was sweating and a few moments after removing her coat and loosening her cardigan she was sick. There wasn't a moment of doubt after that. She was almost thirty-eight and she was carrying a child.

Dismay fell around her like a dark, wet cloak, engulfing her in tearful self pity. As if her days weren't hell enough.

206

How could she manage to support and love another child at her age? Oh why was life so cruel? The irony of it.

Her first calm thought was the hope that it wouldn't be a boy. She didn't want a replacement for her lovely Oswald. The second was to wonder how Desmond would take the news.

Helen and Desmond were sitting in front of her fire eating toast and home-made marmalade. The fire was making Desmond's face as red as snow-clearing had done. Helen smiled at him, spread thick butter on a freshly toasted slice, and put it on his plate.

"Desmond, my dear, are you sure?"

"I should have done it years ago. Daisie and I are completely unsuited and, as you know, she manages very well without my help. I know she wants to do everything for me to help compensate for my loss of you. She's not insensitive. She understands about us. But by being so damned efficient and hard working she's made life harder for me. When was the last time she even asked my permission to do anything, let alone needed my help? She manages my affairs so well I feel like a lodger in my own home."

"But she won't be able to keep The Swan if you leave."

"The Swan will be sold. I've already spoken to that Huntley-Davies and he will come next week to measure up and start looking for a buyer." He looked at her and said ruefully, "I did try to leave her some time ago. Remember when Huntley-Davies came to measure the field? I changed my mind that time, couldn't go through with it. Megan's death made me realise how short life it. This time it will really happen."

"Next week? Then we'll be together before the end of the summer?"

"We'll be together as soon as I've told Daisie. Today, as soon as I get back, I'll tell her I'm leaving her and coming back to you, my love."

"I can't wait," she sighed.

"If Daisie choses to go straight away, then you and I will

run The Swan as we did before, won't we? Until it's sold of course, only until it's sold."

They sat for another hour discussing their future and planning where they would live. Then, seeing it was almost opening time, Desmond rose and kissed Helen and promised he would be back later that day to report on Daisie's reaction to his announcement.

As soon as Desmond returned, red-faced and cheerful from his visit to Helen, Daisie said she had something to tell him.

"I have something to discuss with you, too," he said seeing her through a haze of euphoric joy. "But you first," he said generously.

She told him. And the shock he suffered frightened her. "It's all right, Desmond, I'll be all right. The Swan will have to manage without me for a few weeks that's all, but Ethel will help out. We'll manage." She saw the colour drain from his face and wished she had broken the news more gently. She led him to a chair and poured him a brandy. "Heaven's above, Desmond, it's more of a shock for you than for me and I've got to have the child!"

"Are you sure?" he said, his voice no more than a croak. "I'd have thought you were too old."

"So would I. But I think the doctor will confirm."

He didn't seem able to discuss it, although that was nothing unusual, Daisie knew that it was to Helen he went when he had something he wanted to talk about. It was the same now. To her annoyance and humiliation he said, "I must go and tell Helen."

"Helen? What's it got to do with her?" His words hurt her more than at any time in the past. "Oh, Desmond, surely at a time like this it's me you want to talk to?"

He didn't reply, didn't see her tears. He gathered the coat he had just taken off and went out, leaving her standing staring after him.

"What is it, Mam?" Unseen, Gaynor had come into the room. She poured herself some tea and sipped sleepily.

The anguish at the casual way Desmond had taken the news filled Daisie with the need to tell someone, get some reaction that was less painful. Gaynor was twenty now, old enough to understand. And although she would normally have not told her until the event was no longer able to be hidden, she blurted out, "I think you're going to have a brother or sister."

"And you'll be a granny at the same time," Gaynor said calmly. "I think Billie Beynon will marry me, mind. So it won't be so bad, will it, Mam?" For the first time in her life, Daisie fainted.

"No, Gaynor, you can't be married in a white crinoline!" Daisie sighed and looked at her pouting daughter, who glared then swept out of the room and up the stairs. "A white crinoline indeed. And in her condition. Whatever next!" She and Ethel Tripp were cleaning the glasses and ornaments over the bar and Daisie turned away from her daughter's retreating figure and dusted the packets of pins and other faded items in her father's old pedlar's tray.

Behind her Ethel Tripp chuckled and said, "If she leaves it a bit longer she can have matching dresses for her and her baby!"

"It's no joke, Ethel. There's me trying to bring sanity to this wedding and she's sitting there dreaming about crinoline dresses. Pity she didn't think of crinolines sooner," she shouted so her daughter could hear. "Too late for fancy weddings now, three months or more too late!"

"Never mind, she'll have a good start with the Beynon's. They aren't short of a copper or two."

"It wasn't what I'd hoped, Ethel," Daisie sighed.

"When is it ever?" Ethel stretched up and put a glass tankard back on its hook. "When is it ever? There's that daughter of ours turning away from Tommy and setting her cap at Arthur of all people. God'elp, imagine me having him calling me Mam!"

Billie Beynon's father had agreed to the couple living with him and Billie's twin, Eric. With his wife dead he was quite happy to give up a bedroom and share the rest of the house with a woman who, presumably, would look after them all.

Most couples started their married life living either in two rented rooms or, when the bride thought she could get on well enough with her mother-in-law, living what was locally called "through and through", sharing the house and having only a bedroom they could call their own. Although even that was not strictly private territory against invasions from the rest of the family.

Gaynor's wedding was threatening to be a farce. "More like a flaming circus act than a wedding," Desmond, who was becoming more and more irritable, complained. "Why don't you make the girl behave?" He was very touchy since his plans to leave had been shelved and he was very worried about Helen. She was rarely seen, hating Daisie for wrecking her life for a second time. There were occasions when she refused to answer his knock and, although he had a key, there was no way he could argue with the heavy bolts across the doors.

The reason for his most recent complaint about Gaynor was the way she walked. Although she was fat and able to hide the fact she was carrying a child, she began to walk with that backward lean many woman used in the later stages to ease their uncomfortable backs.

"Desmond is right, she does it on purpose, to bring her condition to everyone's attention," Daisie complained to Ethel Trip. "What's wrong with young people today? They've no pride. There's me determined to hide it until it's like a mountain inside my frock and she's, well, she's flaunting it!"

"With you two it's the difference in age," Ethel said, rubbing a glass until it shone. "Young people think they're the only ones to have a bit of you-know-what."

Gaynor knew that this wedding was the one and only time she would feel important. She had seen it so often, an engagement and everyone makes a fuss as if it were the first time a ring had been placed on a third finger to sparkle in tawdry splendour. Then the wedding and presents and a party and all the town wishing the bride well, making jokes about the night to come and generally making the girl special. Then the first baby and again it was cause for celebration. Then it would be, "Oh, having another is she?" in a bored voice. And that would be that, you were miraculously transferred to the next generation and all hope of fun was gone for ever.

She had missed the engagement, although Billie promised her a ring one day, and the wedding was not going to be a beautiful affair in the church with bridesmaids, bells and organ, and a posh do after. But she would make it memorable, if only for her audacity. She bought a wide, white ribbon in the market and planned to wear it tightly around her waist to emphasize her condition. That would make all the old miseries pop their eyes in disapproval and she would be remembered long after some of the more coy and conventional brides. She smiled to herself as she pictured her mother's face as she lurched into the register office on her father's arm.

On the day of the wedding it rained. Bob Tripp had agreed to drive her the short distance to the register office so that wasn't a problem. But her father was.

"I'm not walking down the road with you in that outfit so you can forget it." Desmond glared at Gaynor, his face red with anger. He removed the jacket of his new suit and sat down near the table.

"But Dad!"

"Dad nothing. I'm not going with you unless you change so don't waste time. If you want to be married this morning you've only a minute or so at most."

"Tommy will give me away," she said defiantly. "Or Bob Tripp."

"No they won't. Got more sense than that! Go and change at once or I'll walk down now this minute and cancel the whole thing."

Gaynor was frightened. She had never seen her father so angry. His face was flushed and his eyes were deep and glittering. She knew she had hurt him, trying to make an exhibition of herself to shock the old busy-bodies of the town. She had hurt him terribly.

"I'll change," she said, capitulating under his glare.

So she stepped out of the be-ribboned car with her father

and walked to meet Billie, who was resplendent in a slightly small navy suit, a white shirt that didn't quite meet across his large stomach and a blue tie. His shoes were shining like glass, the smile on his rosy face hardly less dazzling.

Gaynor looked pretty in a surprisingly demure way in a long straight top over a full, narrowly pleated skirt in a pale grey and trimmed with blue. The white ribbon, her banner of defiance, was across her shoulder as if depicting her as the prize winner of a beauty competition, flowers were pinned to it across her bosom and waist. She carried her mother's small prayer book.

In the crowd that gathered Kate stood with her mother and Arthur Huntley-Davies, his son and his mother. Kate was carrying the small boy, lifting him up for a better view. Bob Tripp was behind his wife, waiting for the family to finish shaking hands and accepting congratulations before driving the newly married couple back to The Swan for the wedding breakfast. He was hungry and he knew that however simple the wedding, the food at The Swan would be plentiful and good.

Phil was there, a melancholy expression on his face. His two strange sisters wandered around the road watching people, smiling in their innocent and friendly manner and Daisie wished they would go away. She wondered if Phil was thinking of the bride who was his own, unclaimed daughter. Perhaps, like her, he was thinking that in happier circumstances he would be the one leading her down the aisle.

Daisie looked around at the smiling faces and thought of the simmering dissatisfaction those smiles were hiding. Many who had discontent in their lives would look at these people and envy them their apparent joy. Life, she thought finally, was a cheat and a liar.

Tommy spoke to no one. He watched the wedding party as if they were strangers and only with Daisie did he share a wan smile. She invited him back to The Swan but he didn't think he would go. Kate would be there but she was firmly ensconced at Arthur's side these days. No, he'd hand Gaynor and Billie the bale of household linen he had brought for them then, he thought sadly, he would go home.

Helen didn't attend although Daisie had sent her an invitation. She sent a parcel which, when Gaynor unpacked it, was a knitted pramset and a couple of home-made bibs. Daisie wondered if it was kindness or sarcasm.

"Whew, what a hectic few months this has been," Daisie said to a rather over imbibed Desmond as they packed up after the guests and the newlyweds had finally departed. "Since Christmas Eve so much has gone wrong: Megan's death; the inquest; my disaster – " she patted her swelling belly, "and Gaynor's! Now a wedding." She smiled at him sitting there with a scowl on his normally placid face. "Perhaps the wedding will be the start of better times, eh, Desmond? With our Gaynor settled and two new babies to be welcomed, Helen to help us when needed, we can look forward to some really happy years. You'll love having a baby around again, won't you? Helen will be pleased, too. She was always good to Gaynor and to little Oswald for the short time we had him." She frowned. "I didn't see Helen at the wedding? She hasn't been here for weeks. She isn't ill, is she? I've been round there several times but she doesn't answer the door. I haven't seen her in the china shop either. I hope she isn't ill. I hope she'll help out when I have my baby."

"Your baby messed things up good and proper," Desmond muttered.

"It's not what I'd have chosen," Daisie said amiably as she wiped the surface of the bar. "But it won't mess things up. I won't let it."

"*You* won't let it! *You'll* cope! It's not what *You'd* have chosen! Well, surprising as it might seem to someone as selfish as you, Daisie, other people are affected besides *You*!"

"Don't pretend it will add to your workload, Desmond Prewitt!" Daisie snapped. She was tired, and having tried to bring him out of his foul mood by talking about his lady-love was suddenly exasperated and in no mood to listen to his complaining. "Everything here is my responsibility. How can my having a baby affect you? You hardly do a hand's turn here

213

and I can't see that a baby will alter anything. I'll have it and I'll look after it. You haven't made a decision since the day I married you!"

"Oh, haven't I? Well you might be surprised to hear that I made a decision that this baby of yours ruined!" Emboldened by drink, still angry at the way Gaynor planned to behave on her wedding day, he said, "I had decided to leave you. There, what d'you think of that for a decision then? I was going back to Helen, where I belong. Then you spring this baby on us and I, fool that I am, thought my duty was to stay. Twice you've messed up Helen and me. Twice."

Leaving Daisie staring after him in a mixture of disbelief, hurt and sick disappointment, he lurched across the room and stumbled up to bed. Daisie followed a while later but she passed their bedroom door and went up to the attic room she had used when she had first arrived at The Swan as a frightened child.

14

Desmond spent more and more time in Helen's small house at the end of the High Street. One day, as they sat in the window, looking out onto the early spring garden where crocus speared their way through the untidy grass and snowdrops rang their silent bells in the gentle breeze, he touched her arm and said, "Helen, my love, I've come to a decision."

"You can't leave Daisie, not now," Helen's eyes pleaded with him. She shook her grey head and added, "We can't build our happiness on the misery of others, Desmond, dear. That would never work, not for people like you and me."

"I know I can't leave her. Not now another baby's on the way. But I want to make sure you're comfortable. Arthur Huntley-Davies is interested in buying these houses, including the one where Phil Johnson and Tommy Thomas rent a room. I think I'll sell. I'd be rather pleased to kick Phil out anyway. I've never been very keen. I don't like the way he looks at Daisie. Then I could buy us a better place to live and one day . . ." He didn't finish the sentence. "One day" was too far into the future now with a baby arriving in the autumn. He was sixty-one and the future looked too fragile to hope for a happy ending to his and Helen's love story.

"I like this place," Helen said, patting his hand. "We've had some happy hours in this garden and although it's small it's plenty big enough for you and me. Sell by all means if that's what you want, but not to please me. You don't have to do anything to please me, my darling."

"The Swan will be yours when I die," he added. "I've made sure of that."

"Oh, Desmond, don't talk of dying on such a lovely

morning. Let death and sickness wait a while. Think of the wonderful summer we'll have and then, in the autumn, well, another life bearing your name, that's something wonderful."

"Is it? I'm too old to be a father. And becoming a grandfather at the same time. There's daft I feel. I'm afraid I won't be here when they need help. How can I be, I'm an old man."

"Nonsense, Desmond!"

"Sorry, but I'm feeling morbid today."

"I'll look after Gaynor and the new baby if I'm spared – if that's what you're trying to say."

He stared at her and smiled. "Talk about reading my thoughts. I know Gaynor is a grown woman and married to Billie Beynon and going to be a mother herself, but for all that she's still a bit helpless. I think she'll need carrying for a long time yet."

"I'll see she has all the help she needs. Daisie and the new little Prewitt, too. Now, can we leave the subject of death and enjoy the rest of the hour you have to spare for me?"

Instead of going home after leaving Helen, Desmond went first to see Arthur Huntley-Davies at his office and arranged for the sale of his properties. Arthur's eyes glowed with delight even he couldn't hide. "No, there's no need to tell Phil and Tommy, I'll deal with it all," he said. "You needn't worry yourself about a thing. Leave Tommy Thomas to me."

Desmond didn't tell Daisie of his intentions so it was with alarm that a few days later she met Tommy coming into The Swan demanding to know why his belongings had been thrown outside his rooms and the locks had been changed on the house.

"The shed in the yard, too," he complained. "All my stuff to sell at next Tuesday's market in Brynteg is out in all the weather! Daisie, why didn't you warn me I was going to be evicted?"

"But there must be some mistake. Desmond hasn't said anything about it."

"Selling the houses, so Phil tells me. *He* knew, so why didn't I?"

216

It took a while, but with Daisie and Ethel Tripp helping, Daisie driving the car and Ethel helping with the loading, Tommy transfered his belongings to a couple of rooms in a nearby house and managed to rent a barn for his stock. The barn was further away from town than he liked but he decided that for the moment it would have to do.

"There's no lock on the barn," he complained when he and Ethel had filled it with the linen and clothes he planned to sell, "but it should be safe for a few hours until I can come back with a padlock and a couple of window locks."

"What's in these boxes?" Ethel asked, helping to heave several tea chests against the wooden walls of the barn.

"Glass and china." He lifted the nailed-down lid on one or two with a claw hammer to show her the plates and other items they contained. "I won't be able to shift that lot mind, not until I find a spot where Phil isn't breathing down my neck," Tommy said. "The market superintendants won't have a second china stall, with Phil attracting so much trade they don't want to send him elsewhere to avoid a rival."

"Make him drop his prices, mind. Pity he doesn't drop them as often as he drops his trousers." Ethel grinned, her face almost as dirty as when she sold coal. "Still, Tommy, this is good stock and not perishable so it won't suffer for keeping. Perhaps you could try over in Pontypridd? Ponty's is a big market and that's a place Phil doesn't use."

"Yes, I'll think about it," Tommy said, kicking one of the tea chests holding the china. "I want to shift it, even if it isn't perishable. Money lying idle that is, Ethel."

A few days later, Kate Trip and her mother, dressed smartly for the occasion, were invited to tea at the Huntley-Davies's and as soon as Arthur's mother had poured them a second cup of tea from the gold-rimmed china teapot Arthur asked Ethel, "That Tommy Thomas has found himself another place, then?"

"Yes, a couple of rooms and a barn for his stock. Helped him move I did. Felt sorry for the poor man."

"Poor man!" Arthur looked at Kate as if they shared a

secret. "That 'poor man' as you call him killed my wife and almost broke your daughter's heart."

"Well, whatever. He's suffering now isn't he? And for what was only an accident, after all." Ethel glared at Arthur, daring him to disagree.

"Where is he storing his rubbish?" Arthur asked.

Ethel explained the position of the barn and the weakness of the walls. "It'll have to do for now but he'll be looking out for something better." Her face cleared and she said, "Of course, you being an estate agent, you might find him something, mightn't you?"

"I might," Arthur said, turning away, his expression showing the unlikelihood of such a happening.

A week after Ethel had talked to Arthur, Tommy arrived at his barn to find the police waiting for him.

"Oh," he groaned, "don't tell me I've had a break-in? Not surprised, mind, the place is as full of holes as a granny's dishrag."

"It's we who have broken in, Tommy. And very surprised we were at what we found."

"You broke in? I don't understand."

The sergeant held up a vase, sparkling with rainbows of colour in the afternoon sun. Tommy took it and frowned "Good for me this is. Crystal it is for sure and worth a lot more than the market customers would pay. No, sorry, that isn't mine. Where did you get it?"

"From your lockup, Tommy." The two policemen went inside the barn and Tommy saw at once that there was more stock than he had placed there.

"Wait a minute, this stuff isn't mine. Look there's something going on here that I don't understand. Ask Daisie Prewitt and Ethel Trip, they helped me move this stuff. They'll tell you what was here."

"Stolen from a warehouse in Brynteg it was, only the best stuff was taken. Someone knew what he was doing, don't you think? In Brynteg over the weekend, were you?"

"I was there, on, let me see, on the Tuesday. Right until the market closed, as usual. Then I came back here and put

218

back the stuff I hadn't sold and went home. I was here in Cwm Manachlog on the Saturday and on Monday I was getting my stuff sorted for the week's work. Five tea chests there was here. Five and no more." His eye was blinking furiously, the policemen considered it a certain sign of guilt.

"It's the weekend we're interested in, Mr Thomas. Saturday you were in the market, but what about Sunday?"

"I went to see Huntley-Davies, then I just walked the hills."

"Alone, Mr Thomas?" The policeman allowed a moment of silence then went on. "The warehouse was broken into with a claw-hammer, very like this one," he pointed to one on the floor. "And what was worse, much worse, the warehouse watchman was hurt bad. Hit, he was, with a claw-hammer so the doctor thinks. A claw-hammer very much like that one."

"There's no point in my telling you that isn't mine either, is there?" Tommy said, showing them his own, thrown in a corner behind the tea chests. White faced and trembling, he was led away.

No one could confirm Tommy's whereabouts during the Sunday. He was far from certain himself. Distressed by Megan's death, his own guilt and the enquiries still being made, he walked for miles over the cold hills, seeing nothing, always alone and scarcely remembering where he had been.

Daisie and Ethel were questioned, Ethel was asked to describe what Tommy had stored in the barn and was strongly insistant that the number of teachests had been less than those found by the police. Unfortunately there was an eye-witness who remembered seeing a man running away from the warehouse and although it was night and he admitted to being short-sighted, he was certain the man was Tommy Thomas.

The police decided there was a case to present to court and he was taken into custody facing several charges: one of burglary, plus grievous bodily harm against the injured watchman.

There was also new evidence to suggest that his wild and erratic driving the night of Megan's death could have been caused by his haste in getting away from the scene of another crime, which threatened to changed the verdict on Megan's death. There was a more ominous side to his haste that night if the new allegations were true. If he were found guilty of the robbery, then Wanton and Furious Driving would be the least of it.

Daisie and Ethel walked from the solicitor's office frightened by the suddenness of Tommy's changed circumstances.

"He's always hated the thought of being locked up," Daisie said when they stood outside the grey building.

Arthur stood behind her, arm in arm with Kate Tripp who ignored the presence of her mother, considering her foolish for speaking up for a criminal. A crowd had gathered outside the police station to see Tommy being led away.

"There is justice after all," Arthur said grimly. "The punishment was owing to him. He committed murder and got away with it. Got my dear Megan out of the way when she became a nuisance and yet he wasn't punished." There were a few murmurs of agreement and a number of derisory remarks aimed at Arthur himself.

"Come on, Arthur," Kate said, "Don't upset yourself any more."

"Tommy asked you to marry him," Daisie shouted, swinging round and barring their way. "How can you be so indifferent to his plight? Scared stiff he'll be, locked up in a cell for years. And all a mistake."

"It was I who made a mistake," Kate said. "Lucky escape I had, I only hope mother doesn't try to help him any further. People are already suggesting she was involved."

"You don't really believe he was guilty of theft? And of attacking an old man?" Daisie demanded.

"He involved my family. Involving mother in his futile attempt to prove his innocence he has caused rumours to be spread about her – "

"Mam," Daisie corrected irritably. "You've always called her Mam."

"If he can do that to my mother," Kate insisted, "then I wouldn't be surprised at anything, would you, Arthur?"

"You're saying that spreading rumours is the same as bashing an old man? What a lot of old lol you talk, girl. If you want my opinion it's Tommy who was the lucky one, escaping for someone as unfeeling as you. Prison would be a better fate than being married to you." Daisie was shaking, the baby felt like a burden of lead, it was all so stupid. Tommy wouldn't have robbed a warehouse, he valued his freedom too much and besides, he didn't need the money. She thought there must be something she could do but felt helpless. It was as if she were tied up and struck dumb.

"That Arthur was pleased," she said to Desmond when she went back to The Swan. "You'd think he planned it to punish Tommy for Megan's death."

Desmond only nodded. It was what he suspected.

Although Gaynor was married and living with the Beynons, she spent many hours of each day with her mother. Daisie tried to coax her daughter to cook and clean, even going to the house and helping her, but she soon learnt that it would be her doing the work and Gaynor getting the praise, so she stopped.

"Sorry, Gaynor, but carrying a baby isn't an excuse for nine months of idleness. Look at me. Running this place and with your father more out of the place than in it. No pot-boy and only Ethel to help."

"But it's different for you," Gaynor wailed. "I'm not like you. You're strong and I'm not well and – "

"Get home and have a meal ready for Billie and his brother when they come back from the market. Here, take these potatoes already peeled, all you have to do is boil them. For goodness sake stop thinking of yourself as one of the idle rich and get on with things."

Daisie felt like a bully trying to make Gaynor into something she was not. All her childhood she had spoilt her, believing that by giving her all the things she had lacked as a child she was giving her a good start in life. Now she expected her to miraculously transform herself into a capable wife and housekeeper.

"All right, Gaynor," she called as her daughter went out of

the door. "Bring them all here tonight, I'll cook for us all."
It was hardly noticeable to cook for the three men and her
daughter with everything else she had to do.

With the baby due in less than a month Daisie was tired,
irritable and more than a little sorry for herself. She was
lonely even with the busy pub to run and Gaynor hanging
around all the hours of the day. There was no one to call her
own, no one who cared to listen to what she had to say.

In September the weather became very warm and she
grieved for Tommy still shut away waiting for his trial to
begin. She missed him more than she would have expected.
He hadn't been a regular visitor to The Swan, not since their
momentary lapse in January, but he was at least a friend. She
still felt the absence of Megan, too. And Gillian and Waldo
were so wrapped up in their little boy, Michael, that they
hardly had time for anyone else. Phil hadn't been to see her
for weeks. Life, she thought, was absolute hell.

At the end of September, leaving Desmond and Ethel,
assisted by Helen, to cope with The Swan, Daisie went by
trains and bus, to see Tommy. She was shocked to see that
he was thinner, greyer and looked weak and ill.

"Tommy," she said with an attempt to hide her distress,
"you look like a doll with all the stuffing pulled out. Aren't
you pleased to see me?"

"Course I am, Dais. But don't come again. I can't bear to
see you carrying our baby and looking so beautiful and being
stuck in here unable to help. Oh why is life such a pig?"

"What? What did you say? *Our* baby?"

"Never doubted it for a moment I didn't. Not after that day
just after Megan died."

"But . . . don't be daft! It's Desmond's child. Married we
are even if he spends most of his time down with Helen it's
my bed he shares and . . . Tommy, don't even think it!" But
Daisie knew in her heart that he was right.

He gestured to the door leading to the governor's office
that was guarded by a prison officer. "Go and see the
governor before you leave, Dais. There's something he
wants to discuss. Got to go now, I can't watch you walk

away. Forgive me, Dais, but I got to go." He shuffled out through the distant door like an old man and Daisie wondered if she would ever see him again.

The governor was a small man, dressed in a neat tweed suit and with his hair combed down over his forehead. He had a clipped moustache and there was about him a military manner. He was softly spoken and kindly in the way as he invited Daisie to sit and take a cup of tea to refresh herself. His eyes were bright with intelligence and he seemed to have a way of seeing into her mind as he handed her a letter and explained that Tommy wanted her to have his car.

"The repairs are done and details are all here and the forms signed," the man said. "There are also his possessions, his, er, stock, held by the police at present I believe. He would like you to arrange for a Mr Philip Johnson to dispose of it and put the proceeds into an account for his – ahem – for a child due to be born to you in about three weeks time."

"*My* child," Daisie said firmly. "The child my husband and I expect in a few weeks is nothing to do with Tommy Thomas. If he thinks it is then he's demented."

"Just so. Well, if you would attend to these matters? I think a solicitor should be involved just to make sure everything is done properly."

"No." Daisie stood up awkwardly and glared at the man. "I have no claim on anything belonging to Mr Thomas and I think his things should be sold and the money put aside until he's released."

"If convicted I'm afraid he is facing a long sentence, Mrs Prewitt."

"It will end, though. Everything comes to an end."

"He wants you to have it, Mrs Prewitt. He wants that very much and if he's, well, mistaken about his – er – your child then I believe he still wants the child to have the money."

"No."

"It affects men in different ways, being in here," the govenor said quietly. "Cut off from the world, losing their freedom and the threads of their lives, having no say in anything that affects them. Even the toughest of them, and

I don't think we can class Tommy as one of those, even the hardest villain needs to have something to think about, some event going on beyond these very high walls, regardless of their absence. Something they can think about and take an interest in, a pretence that they are involved. It can be the difference between survival and mental breakdown, Mrs Prewitt."

"All right," she said. "I owe him something as a friend. I'm sure my husband will fully understand. I must do it if it will give him hope."

"It will, Mrs Prewitt, it will."

"It will be kept intact for when he is released, mind."

"That isn't what he, er, as you think best, Mrs Prewitt."

Daisie's second daughter, whom she called Alice, was born a week later. She weighed a little over four pounds and had a round face, round blue eyes and bright red hair. Small she was but the doctor declared her fit and well able to survive. The realisation that she was on the way had been a disappointment at first but now Daisie wanted desperately for her to live. In some way, the child's strength was tied up with Tommy's. If Alice was strong then Tommy would be, too.

Desmond came and held the tiny scrap with endearing tenderness and Daisie felt a surge of hope. Perhaps Alice's arrival heralded a happier stage of life for them all.

To add to her delight Helen returned to The Swan to help while she was laid up. With Ethel working as many hours as were needed, the daily routine ticked along without any hitches. Daisie's feeling of contentment grew, a sense of repose settled on the household. Even so she was honest enough to wonder if Desmond's beautific smile of goodwill to everyone he met was due to baby Alice or the presence of Helen at The Swan, like old times returned.

Gaynor came daily and sat to be waited on, making Helen and Ethel long to tell her what they thought of her behaviour.

Daisie had said little about her visit to Tommy and when the letter came from the solicitor stating the amount in baby Alice's account, to her relief Desmond gave it to her unopened. She placed the bank book and the letters in a shoebox at the bottom of the wardrobe and tried to forget the matter. One day she would tell Desmond, but not now, when everything was as near perfect as she dared hope.

A week after Alice was born, and while Daisie was still confined to her room, Gaynor gave birth to a son, Gareth. In a household of three men, she had gathered around her several women to assist and managed to exhaust them all. After a fortnight during which she refused to do anything, even feed the child, she arrived at her mother's door demanding to be looked after.

Billie Beynon followed with his twin brother Eric. Almost without Daisie realising it they moved in. Old Mr Beynon had taken himself off to live with a sister in Cardiff, fed up with the spoilt young woman and her demands. Daisie's brief period of tranquillity was over.

Daisie brought up both Alice and Gareth while Gaynor wandered around seeking sympathy and returning, in spirit, to the position of daughter and not wife and mother. Billie didn't complain much although Daisie caught the occasional look of exasperation on his face when he was unable to find a clean white apron and trousers, or his shirts were still in the washing basket crumpled and dirty.

Daisie took over their washing, too, and apart from when Ethel helped she did most of the ironing as well, walking from the scorched-marked sheet on the blanket-padded table to the fire to change a cool iron for a hot one, until her ankles felt like over-stuffed cushions about to burst into flame.

She was tired but her determination to shame her daughter into doing her share was failing. Gaynor was more and more the spoilt daughter and less and less the wife and mother.

Helen continued to help in the bar and Daisie wondered vaguely why this was so. There was no real need. It didn't help Desmond, he did little enough anyway. And surely, after all that had happened, Helen didn't feel kindly enough towards her to want to ease her burden? It was puzzling but Daisie was too exhausted to worry over much, she was just grateful that she was there and keeping Desmond happy.

Alice was a contented baby and, by the time she was twelve months old, she was fitting into the routine of the busy household with little difficulty. She endeared herself to everyone, walking at ten months, talking in a lisping, high-pitched voice and friendly with everyone she met. In an attempt to say her name she called herself Lally and the nickname stayed with her.

Tommy's trial was over before they were aware of it. He had asked that they were not informed in advance and, not knowing the procedures or how to get the information for themselves, Daisie and Gillian knew nothing about it until they read the account in the paper.

His sentence was harsh and Daisie, who believed that he would be released, was horrified to read that he had been given four years. Reading the account in the papers she couldn't believe the man they referred to was her dear friend. Tommy, whom she had known all her life and had always been there when she needed him, was no longer free.

Daisie wrote to Tommy at the prison once a week but after six months her letters were returned, stating he had moved to another prison and did not want his whereabouts disclosed. Daisie put the letter with the others in the shoe box at the bottom of the wardrobe and told herself that another of her friends was lost to her.

In April 1936, when Lally and was about eighteen months old, Clancy died and at once Daisie replaced him with another donkey, a small one that soon became Lally's best friend. The two little babies were often to be found sitting together in the field, Lally chatting as if the animal could understand, the donkey wearing an expression that suggested that he did. Where most children played with toys, Lally seemed to find her happiness among the animals of Daisie's Ark. There were always chickens there, many having far outgrown their usefulness and just sleeping and eating, two ducks had found their way there and refused to leave. A goose, given to Desmond as payment of a loan and which they were unable to kill and eat, was contentedly strutting about the place like a sentinel, warning them when anyone approached. Unlike little girls from other reasonably wealthy homes, Lally spent her life not in dresses but in home-made dungarees.

One summers morning Daisie dressed her little daughter in a new dress and pink coat and shoes, pleased to see her looking like a girl for once, and drove up to see Gillian. She was forty but felt fifty. Gareth went with them as Gaynor insisted she was too tired to look after her son.

For Daisie, being responsible for the two children was the same as having twins, although they were completely unalike in appearance. Lally was still small and dainty, red-hair like a flame framing her round face. Gareth was a miniature replica of his father, dark, thick set, solid, like a little barrel and with a deep voice to match. With Gillian's son, Michael, not much older, the three of them played contentedly while the two women talked. Daisie brought up the subject of Tommy and explained about his gift to Lally.

"I suppose he hasn't any children and needed to feel there was someone outside thinking of him. At least, that was how the governor of the prison explained it." Daisie said. "We've always been close and probably because I was there when Megan died and supported him then, he thought of my child rather than yours."

"He loved Megan, didn't he," Gillian said. "So why was he talking about marrying that awful Kate Tripp?"

"He couldn't ever marry Megan. Can you imagine Arthur letting her divorce him? Too shamed he'd be for people to know he had failed. If he *had* agreed Megan wouldn't have been able to cope with such an ordeal. She had never really changed from being our little Crying Mouse, had she? Seeing you and me settled with a growing family affected Tommy I think. He was old enough to feel the lack of and needed a home and a family. Poor Tommy."

"Poor Tommy," Gillian agreed. "What will he do when he

comes out? Come back here d'you think? Did he give you the money to be sure of a place to go?"

"No, not now. He's cut himself off completely. He doesn't write and my letters are returned. I've pleaded to know where he is but he asked the prison not to forward his address to anyone who asks. I think he'll go somewhere where he isn't known and begin all over again."

Gillian waved goodbye as Daisie took her two charges and piled them into the car. She waved as the car set off down the hill, then shook her head. Tommy must believe Lally is his, she decided firmly, or why else would he give away money he would need to start again when his sentence was over?

The Swan was busy that evening and Daisie was angry. The children were in bed, Gaynor had half heartedly prepared the food for the evening meals and was now listening to the radio. Desmond and Helen were out and Daisie and Ethel were serving the steady flow of customers. It was so unfair of Desmond to take the evening off at the same time as Helen. It left them very short-handed.

"If that Gaynor would help just a little, we'd manage without him altogether," Ethel said when Daisie complained. "Useless he is mind. So slow young Lally could jump over his head if she was only tall enough to reach the taps!" They chuckled as they imagined the toddler serving drinks.

"Quicker she'd be for sure," Daisie agreed. "The speed he goes, it's like he's driving with the handbrake on!"

In an irritable mood, Daisie looked up and saw Phil's sister Jane entering the bar. The little she heard about the woman was far from pleasant, male visitors being the gist of it. Having her in the bar would soon earn the place a bad name. She threw down the cloth she was using to wipe spills and walked across, her finger pointing.

"Out!" she said. "I've told you, I don't want women like you in my bar!" Too late, she saw that Phil was behind her, holding the door for her.

"She wanted to talk to you, Daisie," Phil said and within seconds his anger matched hers. "I didn't think you'd be so wild that you refuse to speak to her."

"Sorry," she snapped, furious at Jane for putting her in such a position. "But the rule remains. I don't want wives worrying when their men come here for a peaceful drink. She doesn't enter my bar. If she wants to talk to me then she must arrange to call when the bar is closed."

"Damn," she muttered as Phil departed, taking the bemused Jane with him.

"Wanted a job, she did," Matt Prosser told her quietly. "She's back at the house on the mountain, plenty of 'callers' I hear. Phil's trying to get her a place where she'll be looked after."

"Good luck to him." Daisie's anger showed no sign of fading. "If he thinks I've got time to watch over her as well as two children, feed nine people and run this place, then he's dafter than I thought!" Everyone is leaning on me but there's no one to even ask if I'm all right, she thought in a moment of self pity.

When Desmond returned at eleven o'clock that night he dropped another bombshell. "I'm staying over tomorrow night, Daisie. Being a Saturday, there'll be no rush the following morning and Helen needs a bit of a hand in the garden."

"Get her!" Daisie said rolling her eyes in disbelief. "Get her!"

For the rest of the summer a routine developed and continued. Helen helped at The Swan but on Mondays she and Desmond took the evening off to go to the pictures, and on Saturday, when Desmond walked her home, he stayed, returning after lunch on Sunday.

With Daisie putting on a show and ignoring the comments of those who quickly became aware at the unusual situation at The Swan, weeks passed in relative calm. Daisie began to leave certain jobs to Desmond and noticed they were done without complaint. Helen, too, took over certain tasks and managed them with her usual efficiency, taking almost as much interest in the running of the place as she had when she had been in charge.

"It's all very odd, but at least it's peaceful," Daisie

explained to Gillian. "Yet I have the uncomfortable feeling of waiting for the second boot to fall. It's as if we're all quietly holding our breath expecting something to happen."

Daisie rose early on Sundays the same as every other day. She made a cup of tea before walking across the field to feed the animals and talk to the shaggy coated Clancy II. One morning she saw Desmond climbing the gate and running across the field towards her. It can't be that he's so pleased to see me, she thought wryly. It must be fear of the donkey. The animal had inherited the same tendancies as its predecessor and she smiled as the animal's eyes widened and began to position itself for a hefty kick, but she held its head and prevented it from misbehaving as Desmond hurried up.

"Helen isn't well," he gasped. "Go down will you, Daisie, see if you can help?"

Daisie was alarmed at the sight of his sweating face which looked grey and drawn. She suddenly realised he was getting old.

"All right, give me a chance to fetch a coat. Go back to her and I'll follow."

Helen had a feverish cold. In fact, Desmond looked sicker than she did. Daisie forced back irritation and suggested an aspirin and a cup of tea before returning to The Swan.

Desmond didn't come home that day, but the next morning he returned, started on the cellar work, prepared for the delivery of barrels and flagons and talked about nothing else but Helen.

"I didn't like leaving her, Daisie. Proper poorly she is. Won't eat a thing. She shouldn't be on her own."

He seemed unable to manage the crates and empty barrels, and she found herself helping to lift and roll them to where they would be collected. He was red-faced and he constantly stopped and burped loudly as if suffering from indigestion.

"For goodness sake, Desmond, why don't you go back to her," Daisie said softly. "You'll wear yourself out worrying. Best you're there in case she needs a doctor called." She spoke sympathetically and after serving the hastily prepared meal of bubble and squeak and cold meat, she began to prepare a tray of attractively displayed food to coax the woman's appetite.

"Take her this food, stay a while," Daisie said.

"I will go back to her," he said, jumping up from the table in a rage and startling her with the sharpness of his retort, "and sick as she is she'll have a better meal for me than this muck!" He pushed the plate away in disgust and Daisie stopped it as it was about to fall on the newly washed floor.

"Calm down, Desmond. There's no need to get yourself in this state." She forced herself to stay calm. "Stay till she's better, we'll manage here all right."

He was red faced and furiously angry as he grabbed his coat and left the house.

"Desmond, I've made her this food," she called after him. She was worried, but not about Helen. Desmond seemed so tense she thought it was he who would need a doctor if he wasn't careful.

When he arrived at Helen's house she took one look at him and insisted he went to bed.

"Look how hot you are, your face is like a beacon it's so red. Getting my cold you are, and we don't want it to turn to 'flu. Come on, love, just settle down under the covers and I'll fill a hot water bottle for your feet."

"Stop fussing me," he surprised her by shouting. But he did as she asked.

He got up and ate a meal at seven o'clock then he slept again. The next morning when Helen woke it was to find him beside her, as cold as a marble statue and with that still greyness that left no doubt. She sat with him for hours before calling the doctor and going to tell Daisie.

15

The fear of being alone made Daisie grateful for the presence of Gaynor and her family in the weeks following Desmond's death. With Lally and Gareth practically her sole responsibility she was needed and had people to care for. She had moments of panic when she watched Lally playing happily, remembering how suddenly her darling Oswald had died and she would drag her thoughts away from such dark imaginings.

The humiliation of Desmond being found in Helen's bed had caused much laughter in Cwm Manachlog. She might have laughed, too, if it had been someone other than herself involved. She felt momentary sympathy for Helen, but it faded as quickly as it came. Even with all her activities filling the hours she felt his absence.

She kept busy and concentrated on those who needed her especially the animals, which included an injured fox, a confused pigeon and even, for a while, a hedgehog that had been hit by a cart.

There was need, however, of an occasional flight to freedom, to escape from The Swan and be on her own, reassured by knowledge that she had people waiting for her when she returned. She often drove up into the mountains and several times she passed the house where Phil's family had lived. The house was empty now, both young women settled in jobs on the other side of Brynteg, although she had heard reports of Jane occasionally staying there.

One day she noticed that the window of a bedroom was wide open and bright curtains swung in the breeze. She ought to go and check that everything was safe, although she admitted to herself it was an excuse to be nosy. She slowed the car then abandoned the idea and drove on. Phil would probably make regular visits and she would hate him to find her there.

Helen stayed away from The Swan until the day of the funeral and then she arrived in time to travel with Daisie, Gaynor, Billie and Eric Beynon. The two children were left with Ethel. Silently, Daisie moved up in the hearse and made room for her between herself and Gaynor. In a town where funerals were always "men only" occasions their attendance caused gossip and disapproval.

Most of the town turned out and a long procession wended its way back from the bleak cemetary to The Swan where Ethel and a few temporary staff were waiting to serve food and drink. Helen had hardly spoken to Daisie even though they were in close proximity for most of the sombre day. She was still there at ten o'clock that night when the bar was all but empty and the last customers were being encouraged to leave by Ethel.

"I'm sorry to have to break this news to you, Daisie," Helen said nervously, "But The Swan is no longer yours. Desmond left it to me and although you can stay here until you decide what to do, I want to sell it as soon as things can be arranged."

"What are you talking about, Helen?" Daisie looked at the small, grey-haired and tired-looking woman with alarm and unease. She must be demented. In a state of the shock after finding Desmond dead beside her. "Come on, Billie will walk you home. We'll talk about it tomorrow, right?"

"A night's sleep won't change anything," Helen insisted quietly. "Desmond told me years ago, before your Lally was born. I promised him I'd look after her, he wanted that made clear."

"I look after my children. I don't need your help!" Daisie felt a rage beginning to. What was the matter with the woman? What ever nonsense Helen had in her head, this wasn't the time to listen to it. Not now, having just dealt with the funeral. She felt tired and unutterably weary. After the shocks and emotion of the past days she was not able to cope with this. "Tomorrow," she said firmly. "We'll talk tomorrow."

"He loved me, he always did, even when you spoilt things for us. The Swan is mine. All his other properties are sold and the money is in an acount in my name."

Suddenly Daisie knew it was true. She stood up, took the cup and saucer from Helen's hand, and lifted the woman out of her chair. She was so calm, sitting there telling her she had no home and no money after the years of back aching work she had put in.

"Get out. Now!" she said. "You might have acted like a tart and persuaded Desmond, *my husband*, to give away what I have worked for, but I won't have you sitting there drinking my tea and swallowing my food while you tell me about it!"

"You'll know for sure when the will is read," Helen looked at her almost sadly as she added, "I won't see Lally without, mind. Loved that little girl he did."

Daisie was so bewildered at this new revelation, so hurt, she wanted to hit out at someone. She wished Desmond back so she could watch his face as she told him who Lally's father really was. She sat down then, in the chair recently vacated by Helen and cried, ashamed of her thoughts when Desmond, whom she had used and whose happiness she had ruined, was just laid to rest. It was Helen she should hate. But even that idea refused to take root.

She didn't go to bed but rested in the armchair, dosing and watching the light of a misty dawn seep through her eyelids proclaiming a new day, a day on which she would lose her livelihood and her home. She stood up and closed the lid of the pedlar's tray, tucking in the shoulder straps, tying the tapes and preparing it for storage. She wondered idly if she would ever display it again.

Helen did not appear that day and at five o'clock, leaving the patient Ethel in charge, Daisie went to see Phil. She had to talk to someone and he surely wouldn't turn her away now?

"You'd better come in," he said when he opened the door of his house in Coombe Street. She thought there was a shifty look in his eyes as he hastened her inside and closed the door.

"Hang on. Don't pull me inside as if I'm a bit of illegal swag for the market."

"Well, with you a widow now, we don't want people talking, do we?"

She stared at him, then turned away to re-open the door. "Get you! All the women you take up in the mountains and in any shady corner you can find *you're* afraid of *me* ruining your reputation?"

"You might as well know it, Daisie," he looked away from her. "I'm going regular with someone."

Daisie didn't move. What was wrong with her? How could she have lived for more than forty years and still have no one she could rely on?

"Anyone I know?"

"A woman called Phyllis Rees who lives in Brynteg."

"Oh, I see," Daisie gradually recovered her wits and said, "and because of this oh so fragile relationship you can't talk to me when I'm in trouble?"

"Sit down. Tell me what it is."

"Don't bother!" she pushed him out of the way and fumbled for the door latch in the dark hallway. He held her firmly and her struggles ceased, her shoulders drooped. She had no energy left for fights.

"Oh, Phil, Desmond has left The Swan to Helen. I'm without a home, after all the work I've put in. Homeless and without the means of earning my living. Can you forget your Phyllis long enough to tell me what I can do?"

"How could he have done that!" Phil's anger was balm to her shattered nerves and she began to wallow in self-pity.

"Loved her all these years he has. I tricked him into marrying him, you and I both know that. I suppose this is my punishment."

"I let you down then, didn't I?"

"Yes, you did, and I was only seventeen." She heard herself then, she was whining and moaning. She took a deep breath and said in a firmer voice. "That was then. This is now. What can I do?"

"Wait until you see the solicitor. I'm sure Desmond wouldn't have arranged for you to be thrown into the street. There'll be time, and probably money. You could start again, The Swan isn't the only public house in Cwm Manachlog."

"On my own I wouldn't get a public house, you know that. Not with plenty of men applying. Besides, I don't think I'd want to. Perhaps I'll do something different. A market stall perhaps?"

He held her close, his cheek resting on the top of her head where grey had faded the red hair to a more subdued shade. "Or a tinker?" He grinned, and she felt the creases of his face on her head.

"Now there's an idea," she replied.

She was calm enough to joke as she left him, opening the door a crack and peering out and whispering, "There's a man over by there reading a paper, d'you think he's really a spy, sent by your Phyllis?" Then she turned and still smiling added, "Phyllis? Oh, you couldn't! Phyl and Phil, it would be too silly."

Phil had been lying about having a regular girlfriend. Phyllis Rees was the first name that came into his head. He was afraid that, with Desmond no longer there, Daisie might presume they would get together. That was not possible. It never had been possible. There would certainly be gossip though and that was something she could do without.

He felt ashamed after she had gone. She was in trouble and if he couldn't be a friend to someone he had been half in love with all his life then he was a poor specimen.

That evening he went to The Swan and sat in the corner near the door to the kitchen where he would have the opportunity to talk to her. Ethel was busy at the bar. He looked through the kitchen door and saw Daisie washing dishes.

"Aren't you serving?" he asked. "It isn't like you to be in the kitchen when you can be in the bar. Why not give us a tune, we could do with a sing-song."

"Get you! Sing? In the mood I'm in? Know any durges about woe and misery do you?"

"Helen been in today?"

"No. I haven't heard a word."

"Seen the solicitor?"

"No fear. There's no hurry to hear bad news."

"Then tomorrow you must sort something out. I'll go with you. Honestly, Daisie, I'd have thought that was the first thing you'd do."

"I haven't been thinking straight since all this happened."

"Whatever happens, you'll cope, Daisie, my love. Always able to cope."

His words seemed more depressing than cheering. "'Daisie will cope, Daisie will manage'" she said aloud. "It seems to me that the better able you are, the less people are inclined to help." She left the dishes, went to the stairs and called Gaynor down. Time for a few new rules if she were to survive the approaching unheaval.

She couldn't hang on to Gaynor and her family simply for her own needs. They needed a home of their own. She had to help her daughter to stand firm and deal with everything life handed out. With a husband who earned reasonable money on his stall and a brother-in-law who helped financially she had no worries. But, as Daisie knew only too well, tomorrow might be another story. Gaynor had to be made strong. "Dishes." she said to her daughter firmly, "and tomorrow we'll talk about where you and your family are going to live when I leave here. Not," she added firmly, "*not* with me! Right? Stand on your own two feet you will, my girl. You've got Billie and Eric and your little boy depending on you now, mind."

Sitting on a stool beside the sink, Phil winked his approval and for a moment Daisie remembered Tommy, and all her determination faded back to misery. "Life is hell, isn't it?" she whispered.

Phil came at ten o'clock the following morning to keep a ten-thirty appointment. They walked together through the High Street and Phil didn't seem to mind people seeing them together, much to Daisie's relief. They were invited to wait in the small formal room across the room from the solicitor's office where a fire burned brightly and a table displayed magazines, which they both ignored.

"I'm glad you called me, Mrs Prewitt," the man began. "It was my intention to write to you, but I decided that a few days for you to recover – er – your composure was best."

"Can you just tell me my position, clearly and concisely, please." Daisie was stiff with anxiety and Phil found her hand and squeezed it comfortingly.

The solicitor had a pen in his hand and he ran the end of it down the pages in front of him to pick out the relevant sentences.

"Er, now let me see, er, the properties at the far end of the High Street have, er, been sold as you know and the monies from the sales is, er, in your husband's account. Er . . ." He scratched his head above his ear with the end of the pen. Daisie, in her tense state, felt an urge to giggle.

"The Swan," he went on, frowning with concentration, "is, of course, yours outright with no mortgage or any other entailment to worry about, so far as I have yet discovered. There's only the formality of, er, probate to be gone through, which shouldn't take very long, and then everything will be, er, plain sailing, shall we say?"

"The Swan is mine you say?"

The solicitor looked slightly embarrassed, he picked up the pen again and began scratching. Unfortunately he now held it upside down and the ink smudged his face.

"There was a previous will, Mrs Prewitt, but it was made before Mr Prewitt's marriage to you, so it is null and void. There isn't, to my knowledge, another will, so everything he owned will be yours. It was surely what he would have wished."

"I thought it was Helen's and . . ." Her voice faded and she stared at Phil. "Helen said Desmond intended – "

"The previous will was in that lady's favour," the solicitor confided, scratching at his dandruff and adding more ink to his scalp, "but as I say, she was not his legal spouse. So

238

unless he went to another solicitor, er, after your marriage, and that I doubt, the facts are undisputable. I must say I find it surprising that you expected anything different, Mrs Prewitt?"

"Life is filled with surprises," Daisie said holding a hand to her chest against the breathless racing of her heart. "Not all of them unpleasant."

There were a few more details to be discussed then Daisie had some business of her own to settle. Phil sat beside her and said nothing until it was all finished. Then he congratulated her on her new position in life and wished her well.

"Thanks for coming with me, Phil," Daisie said as they walked back to The Swan. "I wonder, will you do one more favour for me?"

"You want me to tell Helen," he guessed.

"Come with me at least."

"Best we do it now, then," Phil said.

Passing the place where the market was held, it looked unfamiliar. The pavements were wide and empty, characterless with the lack of noise, the crowds and stalls missing, as colourless as a faded photograph. They walked down to Helen's small house and knocked on the door. She opened it but did not invite them in.

"You have hidden Desmond's will," she said quietly, when Daisie briefly and gently explained. "Well, don't think any good will come of this, Daisie Clements."

"Prewitt is the name and has been since nineteen thirteen, and no, I have not seen any will, as well you know." Daisie spoke as calmly as Helen, but she wasn't holding back anger, she felt genuine compassion for the woman. "If Desmond intended to leave The Swan to you he unfortunately did nothing about it." She took a deep breath before continuing, "Helen, besides The Swan, which is my home and my livelihood, the house you live in is mine, too, as soon as probate is granted. I have instructed the solicitor to transfer ownership to you as soon as this can be arranged.

"Giving me what's mine by rights!"

"Goodbye, Helen," Daisie walked away, the sound of

the slamming door echoing in her mind for the rest of the day.

Gaynor, Billie and Gareth, with Billie's brother, Eric, a rather self-conscious addition, continued to live at The Swan. Daisie knew she had to persuade them to leave. She overheard arguments between Gaynor and Billie who wanted a home of his own, one which they could share with Eric, his twin and business partner, and not be under the roof of his mother-in-law.

When a house went empty at the far end of the village near the road leading up to Pleasant View, she went to see it. It was for rent and, although small, it would accomodate them all in reasonable comfort. She mentioned it to Billie before telling Gaynor.

"We're going to move into it," Billie said firmly. "I'll tell Gaynor straight away."

To his and everyone else's delight Gaynor seemed pleased with the idea. But it was Billie, Eric, Phil and Daisie who cleaned it and decorated it and arranged the furniture that Gaynor had bought at great expense.

When they were settled into their new home, Daisie missed them. For weeks Daisie cooked too many potatoes, tins of cakes no one wanted. She bought huge joints of meat that ended up feeding someone else's family and was often seen transporting pans of soup down the road to feed Gaynor.

"This is ridiculous," she grumbled to Ethel. "The amount of food needed for myself and Lally is pathetic and hardly worth the bother."

Gaynor seemed content and able to manage and for a while Daisie was relieved. Then a few rumours began to disturb her. Although the house was reasonably tidy and clean, it was not Gaynor who did the work. Billie and Eric did most of the cleaning and some of the cooking. Gaynor spent her time visiting friends or sitting smoking and listening the the wireless Billie had bought her as a reward for accepting a house of their own.

Daisie pretended not to know. They had to sort it out themselves, she had interferred too much already.

In 1939, when Britain was on the verge of war with Germany, Daisie was invited to a meeting at the school to discuss arrangements for accommodating some evacuees from the London area.

"The war hasn't even started and here we are in the thick of it" she complained. "I'm too busy to attend, Gaynor, you'll have to go for me." To her dismay her daughter returned a couple of hours later with two small boys in tow.

"I thought it was preliminary discussions" Daisie frowned. "Well, I can't help and that's that!"

"You have to, Mam, evereyone must do their bit. This is Peter and Paul," Gaynor said shamefaced. "Anyway, I sort of agreed that you'd take them."

Daisie took hold of the boys' hands, smiled sweetly, told them they were lovely, and took them back.

The hall was like a noisy battleground, with children talking and crying, a group of well intentioned women trying to place them with families, and the doubtful women who had come to volunteer homes for one or two. The loudest voice was that of Mrs Huntley-Davies and second was Kate Tripp who appeared to be her assistant.

"I don't know what Gaynor was thinking of," Daisie said without preamble, handing the boys back to a harassed looking lady holding a clipboard and a list. "A pub isn't a place to bring up strange children. Busy I am *all* day, not just when the pub is open, mind. I can't be watching them every minute."

"Come and see what we're up against," Mrs Huntley-Davies said, opening the door into the large assembly room.

The double doors swung open and the noise was greatly increased. The hall was filled with groups of children, each wearing labels tied to their buttonholes, carrying small suitcases, carrier bags and other bundles of possessions, one or two had dolls and all had a gas mask in a case. They were bewildered by all that had happened to them, waiting

241

for someone to offer them a home. Older brothers or sisters, some only six or seven years old, were in charge of smaller siblings and were trying to look calm and grown-up. They all talked loudly and looked terrified. Daisie's heart went out to them. She bent down to talk to Paul and Peter.

"I'd love to have you, really I would. I think you're a lovely pair of boys, without doubt the best two here. I'd have chosen you two from among this lot for sure, but I run a big public house and it isn't the place for youngsters like you, honest it isn't. I'll come and see you when you're settled, pretend I'm your Auntie Daisie. How will that be?"

The boys nodded, a more hopeful look grew on their tired young faces. Perhaps if they had an Auntie Daisie things might not be so bad.

"We got lots of auntie's back home," one of them said.

"Farsands," the younger one agreed, which Daisie translated as thousands.

"Good heavens," she laughed, "I'll have to learn your language if I'm going to be your auntie!"

Phil's sister, Jane, drifted in and offered to look after a few of the children, she was politely refused. "Thank you Mrs um, Johnson, did you say?" one of the harassed organisers said, "Very kind, I'm sure, but we'll let you know, right?" The organiser raised an eyebrow at Daisie with a what-ever-next, expression.

Miss Johnson, Daisie almost corrected, then she saw that the girl wore a wedding ring. Really, the poor thing was more than a bit simple. She dressed up and pretended, just like a child.

Dylan Huntley-Davies, Megan's son, was standing near his grandmother who sent him to reassure one of the boys who was refusing to put down his gas mask.

"Mum said I must keep it with me all the time," the four-year-old insisted. "Them Germans might send gas any time."

"Not here," Dylan explained with all the authority of a boy of eleven. "This is Wales and we have such strong winds that any gas would be blown straight across to England.

242

That's why you're here and not in London," he said with indisputable logic. "Now, leave it by there and come and have something to eat. The food's in the classroom where you'll be coming every day. You can chose a desk." Dylan led the boy away, dropping his gas mask with the pile of assorted bundles in a corner of the large hall.

Daisie stared after Dylan in admiration. Megan's mother-in-law might have been a bit of a dragon but she was making an excellent job of bringing up her grandson. Megan would have been proud of him.

"I'll send some crisps and some bottles of pop," Daisie promised Mrs Huntley-Davies. "It's all I can do," she said sadly.

The children took a while to settle to country life. Many had not seen fields or mountains before and the automatic closing of farm gates took a while to learn. Sheep wandered through the town as they had done in Daisie's childhood. A cow from the farm beyond the old cottage where she had lived wandered along the stream in the warmth of a summer's day, strolled through the main street and got stuck in the doorway of the florists shop.

Boys and girls fell out of trees, soaked and ruined new shoes playing in the stream. Boys stole from the fruit stalls having been dared to by the local boys, and suffered a few clouts around the ear. Girls scrounged wooden boxes to make prams for their dolls and used cardboard boxes to make dolls houses. Boys were bitten by dogs, usually because they teased them to pretend they weren't afraid.

Daisie kept her word and visited Paul and Peter, usually with Lally and Gareth, who were almost five. The four became friends and all benefited from learning of a life so different from their own.

One night in November 1940 a storm rose over night and several trees came down and blocked the roads. Daisie still slept in the top room of The Swan and she looked out, hearing the screeching and tearing of the great branches and saw that besides two great beech trees falling the roof of the shed where Clancy II and three goats sheltered was about to collapse. There was nothing she could do alone so she ran for Phil.

While she led Clancy to the relative safety of the coal store ajoining the house, Phil wrestled with the corrugated roof. "There's nothing I can do until the wind drops," he panted, when he had abandoned his effort to wrench the roof from the remaining nails and lower it to the ground. "The shed is no more. You'll have to give it for scrap, make an aeroplane propeller or something," he joked.

A few days later a shed arrived, it consisted of wooden sections which bolted together. It wasn't new but was in good condition. The council had already taken the scrap metal, the remnants of damaged wood had been burned, and Phil came soon after the shed and began to errect it.

"Where did you get it from? Who do I pay?" Daisie asked.

"No charge. The vet sent it," he said, his teeth tight over a couple of small washers. "Now, hand me that spanner will you? Then stand well back in case this lot falls down." Daisie handed him the spanner and went behind the section to hold the bolt firmly in place with a screwdriver. "Stand back I said. I don't want you harmed."

"Oh shut up, and don't talk with your mouth full," she grinned.

Daisie was puzzled. All the years she had been looking after animals, the vet had rarely sent her a bill. Now, according to Phil, he was giving her this shed. She knew he admired the way she cared for unwanted animals but this was too generous. She telephoned him later and he admitted that it was Phil Johnson who settled the account each month and who had bought the shed to replace Clancy II's storm damaged home.

"Well, I couldn't do anything else to help and I know Desmond didn't like spending money on Daisie's Ark," Phil said when she faced him with it. "I'm fond of you, you know that."

"How fond?" she asked, her head on one side.

He looked at her quizzically. "Very fond."

"Why don't we get married then?"

"Daisie!" He frowned as the thought battled within him. It was what he wanted, but it was not possible.

"I can't," he said. "I love you but the answer has to be no."

"But why? Can't you tell me why?" she pleaded.

"It's money for the most part," he said. Then, being coaxed, he explained. "Dad being ill all these years has cost a hell of a lot of money. The doctors said there was little chance of him getting back to as he was before the accident but I had to try. You can understand that, Daisie, I couldn't leave it when there was another treatment or another doctor with another type of care. I had to try everything."

"I can understand that," Daisie said sympathetically.

"And there are still the debts from his businesses, they have to be paid unless I'm content to let him die with all those people complaining about the money he owed. I have to do it, Daisie. For his good name. I can't abandon my responsibilities."

"Wasn't your father a seaman? I thought there was an accident on board a fishing boat?"

"Oh, he was a seaman all right. But he owned the firm who ran the ships. Now and then he would go out with the men, share their dangers. One day he faced a storm with them and, well, you saw how the storm left him."

"Why didn't you tell me all this before? We could have shared it, Phil. I'm not without money and – "

"It's a debt of honour, see. It has to be me who clears it."

He was tight-lipped as he turned away and finished putting the roofing felt on the new shed. The explanation was unsettling and Daisie couldn't decide why. Was it true she wondered. She shook off the doubts, wanting to ask more. But a glance at his face told her the subject was closed.

When he climbed back down the ladder a while later he came to her and held her against him in silence for a long moment, and in that familiar way leaned his head on hers, his cheek touching the top of her head. "I wish things could have been different, Daisie."

"Is it because of my financial situation?" He didn't reply and she went on. "If it's because I'm not short of a pound or two then it's crazy. How many lives have been ruined for fear of what people will think? Perhaps if I hadn't married Desmond for fear of what people would think of me my life would have been happier."

"We'll never know. We can never go back to the cross roads of life and try the other track, can we?"

Several times each week Daisie called to see Helen. Friends had told her that Helen was unhappy, lonely and in need of something to brighten her life. Daisie felt responsible for her, believing that Desmond would have expected her to take care of the woman he had loved. There was also the residue of guilt for the way she had changed Helen's life irrevocably, twice.

As she knocked the door one bright afternoon, Daisie hardly expected a reply. If the door was opened, a sharp rebuff was all she could hope for. But least she would be able to see for herself how the woman was. But Helen not only opened the door, she smiled politely and invited her inside.

"You might not have invited me in if you knew what I want, Helen," she said briskly. "I've come to ask for your help."

"Oh yes?" Helen gave nothing of her feelings away.

"I need a barmaid. Experienced and efficient and one the customers like. Will you come back to The Swan?"

"Don't waste time in preliminaries, do you?"

"You know me, I never did. So, will you come?"

"I suppose I could give you an hour or so."

"Thanks, Helen." Daisie went home wearing a wide smile.

The war changed the field behind The Swan as much as the rest of the town. There were more than thirty hens in low temporary buildings, simply made from an inverted V of woven fencing strengthened at each end and to which a wire-netting run was added.

"For eggs, only, mind," Daisie insisted. "I'm not breeding chickens for the oven, Hitler or no Hitler!" Her own hens, in varying stages of infirmity, continued to live contentedly until the vet decided they were no longer enjoying life and took them quietly away. In one corner were three pigs in a corrugated sty, owned by Billie and his brother. These *were* registered and were intended to end up as bacon, and Daisie tried to pretend this was not so.

The market thrived, each stall-holder buying whatever he could and selling it with ease as shortages began to effect the people of Cwm Manachlog. Food was less of a problem for Daisie than some with the rations allowed for catering and growing a lot of her vegetables in a part of the field and with a son-in-law selling her scraps of meat on occasions. She fed her family without the difficulties faced by most.

Everything seemed set for them to survive the war without too many problems. Daisie didn't have a husband or a son to go to war, and Billie and his brother were in safe occupations, or so she thought.

She was standing outside the school playground talking to Lally and the two evacuees one morning when Gaynor ran towards her shouting something unintelligable.

"Calm down," Daisie laughed. "No need to tell me there's a war on, I know."

"Mam, Billie's been called up. He and Eric both. They'll have to leave the market stall and go into the army!"

After seeing Lally safely into school, Daisie went with Gaynor to talk to Billie.

"Why do you and Eric have to go, Billie?" Daisie asked. "I thought being a one man business and dealing with food you'd be exempt?"

"I have to go," he said simply, and Daisie thought that like so many men, he was anxious to serve his country. But the need to go was to get away from his wife, something he could hardly tell Daisie.

Since the early days of their marriage, it was Billie who had done most of the cooking. His brother, Eric, did the housework, while Gaynor was rarely in. She spent most of everyday out of the house, leaving Gareth with Daisie, and told no one where she went.

247

Almost immediately the twin brothers, looking enormous in their uniforms, confident of victory and frighteningly strong, went off to fight. It was with disbelief that less than three months later, the news came through that Eric had died. Apart from a few tears and the relief that it had been Eric and not Billie, Gaynor seemed unaffected.

While the war raged on, bringing news of more and more tragedies to the small town, life in Cwm Manachlog seemed, for Daisie, to be as tranquil as any time she had known. Phil was a regular visitor to The Swan, sometimes his sister was with him, and Daisie insisted they sat in the room beyond the Select, out of sight of the increasing number of women who now came into the bar.

Daisie began to play the piano in the bar again. She ran talent competitions and encouraged singing as a foil to the miseries of rationing and the heartbreaks as previous customers were reported missing, wounded and killed. When it was possible she also arranged coach trips for customers at The Swan, as it was not easy for anyone to get away on a holiday.

She found an unexpected ally in Mrs Huntley-Davies and helped her to organise games, outings, picnics and sports days and dances for children and adults in the long summer holidays, trying to compensate for the absence of fathers and brothers and uncles. Both Lally and Gareth involved themselves in the entertainment. The extra children in the area added to the fun at other times of the year. In the winter there were enthusiastic snowball fights, street gang against street gang. Large parties went tobogganing on the mountain slopes beyond Pleasant View. Bogie cart racing developed into an art and street games kept the children outside until long after darkness had fallen. Huge skipping ropes were often swung across the road while upwards of a dozen children skipped, caught up in the rhythm of it, chanting incomprhensible rhymes.

Passing the school yard one day, Daisie stopped to listen as Paul and Peter with several of their friends decided who would be "on it" for a game of hide and seek.

Icka licka bicka sicka,
Minga monga moo,
Acka lacka backa sacka,
Out goes you.

The children stared in surprise when Daisie joined in the last two lines. It was one she had taught Paul and Peter when she was showing them how to skip. She walked away wondering if they would even be able to return to a London that was being bombed almost out of existence. She had never been anywhere further than Cardiff and was unable to imagine the size of London, which she pictured as a town similar to her own.

"Surely," she said to Ethel, "there can't be a building left standing after all these bombs?"

Her fears were confirmed one day in May 1941 when news came through that during a severe air raid, Paul's and Peter's parents, aunts and uncles and cousins, had perished with more than a thousand others. The family to whom they had been allocated were quite elderly and Phil said at once, "Why don't you have them, Daisie? You're fond of them and you've plenty of room. You'd like having a couple of extra kids around. Perhaps later on, if it works out, you could keep them. I know how you like to have your Ark filled and London kids would be a change from chickens."

"Well . . ." she hesitated.

"It's yes, I can see by your face."

"I'll think about it." Then she made up her mind and said, "I'll do it and the sooner the better. Tomorrow Billie goes back off leave and this time Gaynor might come and ask if she can come to live back home while he's away." She reached for her coat. "Paul and Peter will be much more fun!"

16

Daisie enjoyed having her "two men", as she called Paul and Peter, living with her at The Swan. The young Londoners fitted into the routine of the busy house with ease and were soon helping with some of the chores, enjoying the tasks and making them fun. The fact that they volunteered and were not pressured into helping made it fun for her, too, and she loved them for it.

They slept in the small attic where she had begun her days at The Swan so long ago, but there had to be a few changes. One night she found them hanging out over the windowsill high above the ground, looking at the stars, and she decided to have bars on the windows.

"They aren't naughty boys but a bit daring," she explained to the workman who came to fix them.

"Protect them from one danger and they'll find two more," the old man said. "Don't tell me about boys, I had five of them, lost two in this war already and the others are still out there fighting. Makes you wonder why we bothered, only heartache they bring. Only heartache."

Daisie soon got used to David Johnson coming in each day and discussing with her any problems he had met on the butchery stall. Billie had found him to run the business while he was absent and he ran it with skill. He was popular with the customers who knew he always did his best for them in difficult circumstances. Gaynor didn't help although she did try to count coupons and enter the amount in the Ministry of Food forms. She soon got in a muddle, leaving the job for too long then finding it difficult to remember where she had left off the previous time. So it was Daisie who counted the customers who had registered their ration books and ordered the meat and argued with officials when there was a dispute over the amounts sold.

"I quite enjoy it, David. Winning an argument with the faceless men in those offices is a treat," she admitted one day when she came off the phone having won an extra supply of corned beef they weren't entitled to. "Heavens above, we've got to have *some* fun out of this war."

The shortages became more of a problem as the war years rolled slowly on. Women would queue for hours for a length of coconut matting or a few white and often poor quality cups and saucers from Phil's stall. Leaflets were issued giving recipies for fatless, or eggless cooking, and how to disguise vegetables so the family thought they were having meat. She often wondered how they would have managed without Bisto, Oxo and dried egg. Other leaflets showed how old clothes could become new ones, there were ways to patch children's worn garments and decorate them at the same time. Make do and mend was a way of life. Daisie thought she would never have another spare moment. Whenever she sat down her hands reached for knitting or sewing and if it hadn't been for Helen and Ethel, and for Phil's regular help, she thought she'd never get through another day she was so tired.

Posters of every kind were on display throughout the town, asking people to save crusts to feed pigs, save fuel by walking instead of riding, save rubber on tyres by driving carefully. There was DIG FOR VICTORY and SHUT THAT LIGHT OFF. Newspapers were recycled, metal taken for making planes, guns and tanks. Bones were collected to make fertiliser for crops. The picture of the Squander Bug was a familiar sight and Daisie though it was staring straight at her.

Many young girls who were earning more money than they had dreamed of, in munition factories or driving buses and delivery vans, happily ignored all the pleas for restraint and bought any luxury they were able to find. They bought utility clothes with coupons and enjoyed the spending as a compensation for the sometimes tedious and often dangerous work.

Air-raids were a frightening occurance that fortunately

troubled them less often than many other places. Sometimes the war seemed a long way from their town which, with no serious targets, received only a few bombs dropped by aircraft lightening their loads on their way back to Germany.

It was the costal towns with their docks and factories and supply dumps that suffered the worse damage. Though the seven houses and three casualties in Cwm Manachlog were enough as well as the reports of the death of men and women from the small town which Daisie read in the papers.

In spite of the harships and the worries Daisie thought it was a happy time in many ways. She saw Phil frequently and Billie was still safe. Gaynor seemed happy enough in her own home looking after Gareth and working four hours a day in a factory. What she did with the rest of her time was impossible to discover. David Johnson looked after Billie's stall, and was managing to make a success of dealing with the shortages by filling the stall on occasions with rabbits and a few game birds and, in spite of having less to sell, was making a profit.

Daisie thought of Tommy Thomas and wondered how and where he was. How he would have enjoyed all this chasing around for something to sell. The effort of searching for food was constant and Little Dickie Daniels and his son were often to be seen setting off on their small cart to beg the farmers and small-holders to sell them a portion of their crops. They were often successful and returned with a load of tomatoes or cucumbers or sacks of potatoes and greens, but Daisie knew that Tommy, with his unerring nose for profit, would have done far better.

What could be found had to be carefully used or put by for another, less fortunate day. Along with all the other women in the town Daisie dried food and bottled it and made jam and preserved eggs and waited for it all to be over.

Petrol was more and more difficult to obtain but she managed to drive out over the mountains sometimes, to relax and breathe the fresh air. Paul and Peter, Lally and Gareth went with her and rolled and tumbled in the fresh grass and they all returned refreshed. Passing the house where Phil's family had lived one day, Daisie noticed the house was obviously occupied. Jane couldn't be living there alone and she presumed that another family had taken it over. She saw Jane wandering around the market one Saturday and asked her where she lived.

"Wherever you see me is where I belong," The strange woman smiled her most beautiful smile and walked on, leaving Daisie, mouth half open, preparing another question.

In 1945, as celebrations were in full swing for the end of the war in Europe, Daisie thought things could only get better.

"Once the men are back we'll have a great party," Daisie said to Gaynor one morning in late May, her blue eyes filled with excitement at the picture of it. Then the glow faded. If only it could be a celebration of her marriage to Phil, but there was no sign of that happening, even though he often told her how much he loved her. She wondered if it was still because of his need to look after his family, or whether he had become so used to his life he no longer thought about changing it.

Putting aside her dream of marrying Phil she determined that nothing should ruin the joy of knowing there would be no more deaths and no more worries. Life was good, she reminded herself, and ahead was only contentment and peace. Billie would be back and Gaynor seemed to be running her own home and settling down at last. The money given to her each week by David Johnson was sufficient as she no longer came to ask Daisie for more.

Then Gaynor shocked her out of what was almost complacency by announcing, "I'm leaving Cwm Manachlog, Mam, and before Billie comes home."

"Leaving? What are you talking about?"

"I've sold his business and I'm going to live in Swansea."

"What are you talking about now, you stupid girl! You've sold Billie's business? What will he do when he comes home? Go on the dole with hundreds of others? Gaynor, what are you thinking of?"

"I sold it to a man called Appleby, the papers will be signed soon and then I'm off."

"Who is dealing with it?" Daisie demanded.

"I won't tell you. You can't spoil this for me. It's a chance to get away and stand on my own two feet like you're always telling me. Mam, I won't let you – " But her mother was already reaching for the phone.

"I, er, don't think you've anything to worry about, Mrs Prewitt," the solicitor said. "It is true your daughter approached me and discussed the sale of her husband's butchery business but unless her husband agrees and signs the necessary papers, er, there's no way I can proceed."

"Why didn't you tell me, or someone?" Daisie's voice was almost a shout.

"I thought it unnecessary to worry, er, Mrs Prewitt. I thought it would simply blow over, er, like the other times."

"She's tried to sell the business before?"

"There have been times, when she's made enquiries."

Daisie put down the phone and stared at the open door though which her daughter had just disappeared. That the girl was lazy and useless she had to admit and she blamed herself. But was she deranged as well? Or just plain wicked? She thought of Phil's sisters and the odd behaviour of his mother and father. His fears of having a family who would develop the same unbalanced character came home to her then. Gaynor was Phil's daughter and perhaps, like his family, she was not mentally strong.

Her first reaction to the new thought was, as always, guilt. She had forced the girl to go away from her, refused to help on the mistaken belief that she would be better made to cope. Now she knew she had been wrong, dreadfully wrong. Leaving Helen to attend to the early customers she hurried off to find Gaynor and persuade her to talk.

There seemed no other solution but that she asked Gaynor to come back to The Swan. She had to have her where she could watch her and prevent her making any more stupid attempts to ruin Billie's business. What else was the girl doing about which she knew nothing?

Gaynor's return to The Swan with her son, Gareth, seemed like an end to Daisie's contentment. She was a disrupting influence, even upsetting Paul and Peter who had remained

254

there since the beginning of the war and considered it their home. Gareth, too, seemed as resentful as his mother and, like her, treated the two cheerful and patient evacuees like interlopers.

Daisie found it difficult to talk to Gaynor. As mother and daughter they should have found it easy to be friends, but they had nothing in common. Daisie was interested in everything and enjoyed discovering new opportunities for learning. Gaynor was bored with everything she faced. Daisie was slick and efficient, getting an enormous amount of work done in a day, while Gaynor sloped off at the first opportunity.

Where she went or whom she met Daisie didn't know. Her one consolation was that her daughter managed her money without difficulty and kept Gareth and herself well clothed.

The same inability to communicate applied to the friendly and out-going Lally and the morose and disgruntled Gareth. Gareth was bored with the animals, bored with living in a public house, and bored with the prospect of working for a living. Lally was growing up into a happy, loving girl who enjoyed every day. Cousins they remained but at eleven years old they were no longer friends.

Phil began to travel up to Stafforshire frequently to buy the seconds of quality china direct from the factories to sell on his stalls and in his shop. All the best china went for export but the plain and sometimes patterned second quality ware was gratefully bought by women who had not been able to replace their stock during the war years. During one of his absences, his sister Jane was arrested for soliciting. Phil bailed her out on his return and promised to see that someone kept a firm eye on her.

"Which means me," Daisie said with a sigh when Phil came to The Swan and explained his predicament. "I'm not going to search for her, I don't have the time, Phil, but I'll watch out for her when she's in town. That's all I can do."

David Johnson, who ran Billie's business with such efficiency, was a regular visitor to The Swan, coming to explain any difficulty, keeping Daisie in touch with Billie's business in a way that Gaynor could not understand. He was a quietly capable young man and his honesty and dedication to Billie's business appealed to Daisie, who welcomed him into the group of people who formed her family at The Swan.

Billie came home at the end of June and Daisie used his return as the excuse for the party she planned. There had already been street parties in the town, each vying with the rest for the award of Best Decorated Street to be presented by the local newspaper as their contribution to the town's celebrations. Phil managed to buy some good quality mugs, one for each child in the town, which were paid for by the council.

With food still rationed they had difficulty making the long trestle tables look festive, but with flags rescued from attics and bunting cut from old clothes, flowers both real and artificial and assorted sandwiches and cakes, both children and adults thought it was magical. Surely this was the end of austerity and making do? For a day, at least, it was.

Someone had illegally killed a pig and they had pork sandwiches like they hadn't tasted for years. Chickens, not from Daisie's Ark, were cooked in The Swan's ovens, wrapped in margarine paper as there was no spare fat. These made more sandwiches and pans of soup for the lucky recipients of the bones. Several dozen eggs and some blackmarket cheese from a couple of the local farms helped, and the food was talked about for months after the event.

A food inspector walked along the heavily laden tables with glazed eyes and said nothing, convincing himself that it had been a fantasy or a dream brought on by deprivation.

Jane wandered past, smiled her slow smile and stopped to talk to him, and another fantasy was promised. He was more reluctant to turn away from that one. He and Jane walked away to where he had parked his car without Daisie seeing them. Jane smiled at him and directed him to where they could be alone.

When Billie returned to Cwm Manachlog he went first to the house where he presumed Gaynor and Gareth lived. He was told by the new tenant that she was at The Swan. He arrived, exhausted after days of travelling and found her sitting in a corner of the bar with David Johnson, their solitary room in a mess and the only food the bar meals cooked by his mother-in-law.

Billie stayed three days, saw no sign of an improvement, and left her. "Sorry, Daisie," he said when he told his mother-in-law he would not be returning to his wife. "I've had a bad war, I've lost Eric who was my pal and partner as well as my brother, I come back and find I've got no home, no wife and if Gaynor had been cleverer I'd have had no business, either. Thank goodness I chose David Johnson to look after things or I wouldn't even have that!"

"She can't help it, Billie, I realise that now. There's some inborn weakness in her, something she inherited, perhaps. I've tried to help her but I'm afraid she'll always be the same." She couldn't say more. She didn't want it made known that Gaynor was Phil's daughter, more for Gaynor's sake than her own: Phil Johnson, whom she loved and would have married careless of any risks, whose sisters and mother were far from bright and who had obviously passed on that weakness to Gaynor.

Paul and Peter, the two evacuees, went back to London soon after Billie returned. The Citizen's Advice Bureau, together with the Salvation Army, traced some distant relatives and they were welcomed back to a house not far from where they had lived before the war. Glad though she was to see then safely returned to their family, Daisie missed them dreadfully. She had always needed lots of people around her and laughter and fun in her life. The two boys had supplied it.

Daisie saw them to the station where they were met by a cousin and his wife who had travelled down from London and were going to give them a home. After the train drew out of the station, Daisie didn't want to go back to The Swan. She felt as if a part of her had been wrenched away and left a raw wound.

Driving through the town, waving at several of the many people who knew her without really seeing them, she went up to Pleasant View to call on Gillian. But the house was empty. Disappointed she drove on without any clear intent, up over the top of the mountain, until she saw Phil's parents' house in the distance. On impulse she stopped and knocked on the front door. The house had been abandoned for years, yet there were fresh curtains at the windows and she was curious. She had only been there with Phil in the past and even when he had asked her to keep an eye on Jane, he had told her Jane and her sister had never returned to the house after the death of their mother.

There was a lorry in the drive but there seemed to be no one at home. The door swung open in the breeze that was rarely absent from the high position on which the house was built. She stepped inside and found to her surprise that the house was now fully furnished. It was cheaply done and the colours were almost childlike; the walls were white, the floor covering was pale blue, but these were obliterated by cushions and covers of cheerful pinks and orange, scarlet and deep maroon, all mixed up in glorious but startling combinations of brightness that hurt the eye and gave a restless feeling to the room.

She heard sounds coming from above but didn't call. She felt like an interloper and began to prepare her excuses for being there. Footsteps came slowly down the stairs and Daisie turned, expecting to greet a stranger. But it was Gaynor who walked into the room.

"Gaynor? What on earth are you doing here?" Daisie was frightened. Immediately came the thought that Jane was here, too.

"I was just visiting to see if Jane was all right," Gaynor said. "Someone said she was ill, so I thought . . ."

Daisie knew she was lying. Gaynor concerned over someone else was unlikely to say the least and there was something in her manner that would have made her doubt her words anyway.

"I'll give you a lift back," she said. "As long as you're all right, Jane."

As she led Gaynor from the door she looked up and thought she saw a curtain move. Curious, she darted back inside and ran up the stairs. A man was coming out of the front bedroom.

"Who are you?" Daisie demanded.

"Don't tell my husband, will you?" Jane said in her low, gentle voice.

"I think you'd better go," Daisie said to the embarrassed visitor and she looked at Jane.

"How long has Gaynor been coming here?"

"Oooh, ages and ages," Jane smiled. "She helps me look after my other friends."

Sickness like bile filled Daisie's throat as she hurried to the car and drove her daughter home. She was waiting for Phil the moment his van appeared in the main road.

"I can't accept responsibility for Jane," she blurted out. "She's a prostitute and there's no use you denying it. I've *seen* her, half the town knows what she is, so stop pretending." She added as he began to protest, "And what's worse, she's got Gaynor up there doing the same thing. The house must be as well known as the town hall!"

"She does have a lot of men friends."

"Stop it. Stop it, Phil! You shouted at me once before when I told you this and I won't take it now, not now she's got Gaynor on the game."

"I'll go and see her."

"Do that. And tell her she must leave Cwm Manachlog. She should never have been allowed to return." She was bursting with the need to cry. What a failure she had been. To have had a daughter and see her end up like this. What on earth had she done wrong? Even the possibility it was a weakness inherited from Phil's family didn't console her. Gaynor wasn't weak. She had just been brought up by a mother who hadn't cared enough. A mother who had spent too much time building a business and making a life for heself to give sufficient time to her daughter. It shouldn't have happened. Gaynor was her failure, a burden she would have to bear. She glanced at Phil's pale face, his eyebrows so fair they were almost invisible, his eyes dark shadows in the failing light. Yes, Gaynor was her burden, a burden she had to continue to bear alone, from the stubborn look on his face.

"Why won't you accept what she is, Phil?" she asked. "You don't help anyone, especially me, by pretending."

"I'll go and see her," he repeated. "She'll explain. Jane will always talk to me."

Daisie remembered the girl's gentle, soothing voice, "Don't tell my husband," she had said.

"Phil, Jane isn't married is she? Or lost a husband? Or boyfriend?" She thought that such a loss, in a person too timid to cope, might be the beginnings of an explanation.

"Jane, married?" Phil laughed bitterly. "What do *you* think!"

Gaynor moved out of The Swan once more and this time she left Gareth with Daisie. She left no address and Daisie went up to the house on the mountain to see if she had moved in with Jane. As before, the front door was unlocked and she went inside. Jane was asleep, lying across the couch with such a sweet smile on her face Daisie didn't wake her. She was clean and sweetscented, her dress one of the billowy styles she so often wore. Daisie closed the door as she left and tiptoed to the car after making sure that there was no sign of her errant daughter there.

A letter arrived a week later and Daisie tore it open in haste to learn that Gaynor was safe, well and happy and she said that Daisie and Billie weren't to worry any more.

Gareth disappeared a week later. He left a note telling Daisie he was going to visit some friends in Cardiff and that he would be in touch. He told Lally he was going to London, but that she was not to tell anyone.

Daisie was frantic with worry. He was only a child still and in need of someone's care, but she couldn't find him even though she went through his discarded address book and contacted every name in it.

Phil did not mention anything further about Jane and Daisie found it impossible to broach the subject. Gaynor was another person best not discussed, and they let things settle, although the worry about Gaynor and her grandson never left Daisie's mind for a moment.

Billie returned to his butchery business and placed money in a bank account each week for his son whom he hoped would return to him one day. Business boomed, even with the continuance of rationing, as Billie and David made rabbit pies and pasties. Faggots and peas, cooked meats and peas pudding extended trade further.

David Johnson worked well with Billie and at the start of the fifties, was made a partner. Between them they ran a newly acquired butcher's shop in Brynteg and, after the shop closed, worked the market stall selling pies and sausage rolls. The Toby quickly complained and insisted they opened all day or cancelled their tober altogether. Not wanting to lose the opportunity to build the cooked foods business, they asked around to find an assistant to help.

"Mam, can I help Billie and David?" the sixteen-year-old Lally pleaded. "I'd love to, it would be such fun."

"Everything you do is fun," chuckled Daisie. "It'll be hard work, mind. And your college work mustn't suffer."

Lally ran to the market and asked Billie if she could be the one to deal with the morning customers. He had already found an elderly man to take charge so he accepted her offer.

"Only if your sure your Mam agrees, mind," Billie smiled. Lally was such a light-hearted child she made everyone who saw her smile.

"She's willing and if you need someone else then can we ask Michael Griffiths? He'd be glad of some extra pocket money. Auntie Gillian and Uncle Waldo wouldn't mind I'm sure."

So, on Saturday mornings, while Billie Beynon and David Johnson sold meat in their new shop, Frank Flowers, assisted by Lally and Michael, opened up in Cwm Manachlog market, serving customers with pies and cooked meats until lunchtime when Billie and David took over.

Michael Griffiths was a disappointment to his parents. They had a chain of shoe shops again and interests in several local businesses besides. Michael did well at school, was pleasant and cheerful as well as highly intellligent and seemed set to take over the family firm, but he refused. Instead he left school at fifteen and did a variety of jobs, including bus cleaning at the local depot, school caretaker, pot-boy at several pubs including The Swan, and eventually, assisting a jobbing builder.

It was as a jobbing builder that he earned his small wage when he came to help Lally at the market that sunny autumn day in 1950. From then on they were rarely apart.

Michael became a resident of Daisie's Ark, spending his spare time there and making himself useful in a number of ways. It was Michael who fixed extra shelves in the large kitchen and made floor and wall units to extend Daisie's storage space. Lally was his willing assistant and they worked together with an ease that made Daisie's heart swell with delight. What more could she want for Lally than to be happy in love?

It was in the same year that Dylan Huntley-Davies returned to Cwm Manachlog. He had served in the Royal Airforce during the last few months of the war, ending up as an administrator as the camps and training centres were gradually disbanded. It was his intention to return to the town and his grandmother's house and the family firm with as little delay as possible. The absence from home had not affected him as much as some, being away at school from an early age. His father and his step-mother, Kate, now lived in a new house in the same area of town as his grandmother, but he had no intention of going to live with them. The house on Pleasant View was his home as it had always been.

He saw Lally when he stopped at the market for a coffee before finding a taxi to take him up to his mother's home on Pleasant View.

"Lally? Good heavens, you look just the same as when I last saw you," he exclaimed.

"Thanks, Dylan!" she laughed, throwing her head back with enjoyment. "Plaits, ankle strap shoes and cotton socks, pimples and a fringe that went into my eyes! There's glad I am that I haven't changed."

He smiled a little sheepishly. "I knew it was you, so you can't have changed much," he defended with a slow smile.

"Here, drink this coffee, your brain's dehydrated," she chuckled. "Tell me, what have you been doing since we met? Out of short trousers I see."

"I'll come and see you later and tell you all about my little war effort, shall I?" he said.

"Yes, that would be nice."

"That wasn't old Sobersides Huntley-Davies was it?" Michael asked as he wrapped two meat pies in white paper. "Got tall, hasn't he?" And he cheerfully turned to serve yet another impatient customer.

Lally watched Dylan pass through the throng, taller than most and surprisingly attractive. They had teased him when he was a child for being ponderous and dull. He was still ponderous but with a self assurance that made him seem anything but dull. The war had certainly changed him.

Daisie and Gillian sat in the empty bar and drank the tea that Gillian had bought "off ration" in the market.

"Floor sweepings!" she said in disgust. "And they charged a shilling a packet!"

Daisie laughed and poured the brew away and made fresh with some of her rations. They sipped appreciatively when the tea was poured and began to reminisce. Daisie touched the dusty items in the pedlar's tray that had belonged to her father so long ago and smiled.

"Remember how I lived when I was ten?" she said. "A house that might easily have fallen in on me, a father who was regularly brought home from this pub in a barrow, drunk without a leg under him. And all the time I dreamed of the wonderful things that lay ahead of me."

"You haven't done badly, Daisie," Gillian replied. "In those days I couldn't have imagined you owning this. A job cleaning or in a laundry, or working behind a shop counter was the height of ambition then."

"All I wanted was to be married and have a house where I could look after a family," Daisie admitted. "There wasn't anything else I wanted."

"That's the dream we were encouraged to have, though. Generation after generation of women refused a voice, frowned on if they dared to pass an opinion on anything. Men expected to do their thinking for them; make the decisions that affected the whole family, and then demanded obedience in everything. Fat chance of a woman following a career. That's why we didn't dream of better things, Daisie. If you married a successful man you contributed, not in his work place but by darning his socks."

"Thank heavens for Emmeline, Christabel and Sylvia Pankhurst and their supporters. Even though their battle came too late to help us. Came a bit too late for our children, too," she added sadly. "Gillian, what did I do wrong with Gaynor?"

"I don't know where I went wrong with Michael," Gillian sighed. "I didn't want a child as you know, I enjoyed my life too much for it to be interupted by having a baby to care for. Yet when he arrived I loved him dearly. I was happier then than I could have imagined. A different sort of happiness, mind, but truly wonderful.

"Michael was my life from the moment he arrived. I did everything I could to give him a good start in life. He had the shoe shops there ready and waiting for him, he went to the best schools, met the right sort of people, yet he works like someone with nothing better to hope for. He refuses to join the firm, did you know that?" She looked at Daisie to share her frustration. "Much to Waldo's disappointment, he won't even consider it. Now he's working as a jobbing builder of all things! I don't understand it, neither does Waldo."

"Megan's son is well-educated and is joining his father in the family business. A self-assured young man is Dylan. Of the three of us, Megan's son is the most successful and, pity help her, she didn't live to see it."

"Successful? I'm begining to wonder how that's measured,"

Gillian frowned. "Michael questions what we mean by success. He says no one can ask more out of life than that he's happy. Your Lally is happy, Gaynor wouldn't be if she had a million pounds, a houseful of servants and sunshine every day."

"Perhaps Michael is right. Yet I feel that happiness has evaded me. My happiness has always been tied up with Phil and he won't marry me."

"Why?" Gillian asked. "Why in all these years have you two never married? Was it fear of producing backward children?"

"He'll never admit it, but that must be part of the reason. We both know what his mother and father were like. And there's that sister of his, Jane, who talks daft and entertains men. Phil refuses to admit that, too." She hesitated to mention Phil's other reason, some part of her was uncertain of the truth of it, but she said, "There's money worries, too, or so he says. Me having enough and him without any. Some family debts or something," she explained vaguely.

Melancholy settled over Daisie's shoulders after the conversation with Gillian. She had seen herself as that young girl, ragged and with so little food that people brought scraps to her and glowed when she showed them how grateful she was. Now, at the age of fifty-four she was still dreaming of a future filled with happiness. Would she still be looking forward with hope when she was eighty?

Idly she wondered if she would marry Phil if he ever asked. She patted the dusty pedlar's tray and smiled. Of course she would. He was the one thing her life lacked. She was too busy to be unhappy, yet there was always that yearning for Phil to join her and share the good days and the bad. In spite of The Swan being full, sometimes to bursting, she was often lonely and loneliness was something that had followed her all her life. Only Phil could release her from that.

17

Michael Griffiths arrived at The Swan almost daily. One day he approached Daisie with a suggestion. "How d'you fancy having a paved area at the back where you can sit a few customers on nice sunny days?" he asked. "We could plant a few trees and the old drunk's barrow would look good filled with geraniums in the summer."

"A beer garden? In Wales? What an idea! Umbrellas we'd need and not to keep the sun off," she joked. The idea took root however and the work was quickly begun.

Billie decided to give up the market stall he had worked since he was a child. David Johnson wanted to take it over and the two men came to discuss it with Daisie.

After allowing them to talk over their plans, Daisie asked, "David, you're a cousin to Phil. What d'you know about the family up on the mountain, Jane and her parents, did you know them when you were small?"

David looked puzzled. "The family on the mountain? I don't understand, Mrs Prewitt. My family all live in Brynteg, lived there for generations they have."

"I'm talking about Phil's parents and his sister, Jane," she smiled, preparing to tease him for his rare absent-mindedness.

"They aren't his parents. Their name is Jones, not Johnson. Jane isn't his sister, Mrs Prewitt, she's his wife." Daisie's reaction to David's revelation was firstly disbelief. Surely he couldn't have kept such a thing from her all these years? She remembered all the intimate moments they had shared. Yet even then, when he was telling her she was his only love, and only family problems were between them, he was holding back an enormous lie. There must have been other lies, too.

"Oh," she managed to say to David, who was completely unaware of the bombshell he had landed in her lap. "He's looked after the Jones family for so long I thought they were his own. I'd forgotten that Jane was his wife. It's such a sad affair, isn't it? When was it they married?"

"They were both very young, I don't think Jane was more than sixteen."

There was small consolation in the fact that he hadn't married Jane while she was meeting him, producing his child and forcing herself to marry Desmond Prewitt. That would have been the final insult.

She asked David about Phyllis Rees, who didn't exist. The accident that had injured Jane's father was mostly lies. His father had been a seaman, working on a trawler, but he hadn't owned the business and neither was his family uncaring or rich. She was shaken to learn that even the seven sisters lived only in Phil's imagination: Janet, Jacqueline, June, Joy and Jo and been inventions, but for what purpose she couldn't imagine. There had only been Jane and Jill.

"Phil romances a bit, mind," David said, a polite way of telling her he knew Phil was a liar.

Somehow she managed to survive that day, dragging the shock of it around with her like a trailing cloak of despair and humiliation. For the first time she felt her age. Fifty-four and ever since she was seventeen she had believed in Phil's love and later his story about his sister and his unhappy, confused family. All the time, she wailed inwardly, all the time it was me who was confused and so stupid that I didn't question a word he said. Didn't query for a moment his reason for not marrying me.

Hurt and humiliation were replaced with anger and the need to hit back. She telephoned the police and suggested they looked at the house on the mountain, then realised that her own daughter was more than likely there with Jane, entertaining heaven knows who. Fury changed to panic. She shouted instructions as she put on her coat and, leaving a confused Helen and Lally in charge, she drove up to the house at the back of the mountain.

The first person she saw when she pushed open the door was the last person she wanted to see, Phil.

"Is Gaynor here? I want to talk to my daughter." She pushed past him, wiping the welcoming smile from his face and making him stagger back against the wall.

"Daisie," he whispered like some eighteenth century actor hamming up a part. "What are you doing here?"

Ignoring him she went into the back room where the sun rarely shone and the bright colours were a pathetic attempt to compensate. The house smelled of damp and decay and she wondered in those few seconds just how much neglect the cheerful furnishings and pictures were hiding.

Jane was standing near the window looking out at the windswept garden. There was no sign of Gaynor, yet some sixth sense told Daisie she was near.

"Where's Gaynor?" she demanded. Phil had followed and he tried to assure her that Jane was alone. Pushing him out of her path once again, Daisie ran up the stairs with Phil following. Gaynor was in the front bedroom. The bed was neatly made and there was no sign of another person having been there. Daisie told a nervous Gaynor to get down and into the car, then, with Phil watching and following her like a demented puppy, Daisie opened the cupboards and looked under the bed. Phil wondered if she had lost her senses.

"What are you looking for for heaven's sake!" he demanded at last.

With a perfectly timed flourish, Daisie threw open a built-in wall cupboard that had been papered to disguise its presence and revealed a sheepish looking, elderly man. Without a word, or even a glance at Phil, Daisie marched out and got into the car.

"I didn't know. I swear I didn't know," Phil called after her.

An hour later the police made a check, found nothing and decided the call had been made by a crank.

*　　*　　*

Gaynor was unwell, coughing and suffering what seemed like the onset of flu. She had lost weight and seemed to get worse as the day progressed. Brighter in the mornings, by each afternoon she was quite feverish. Daisie put her to bed on the day following her return and coaxed her appetite with trays of attractively displayed food. She didn't mention where she had found her or the man who had stood trembling with embarrassment and fear as she had dragged her daughter out of the room.

"Sorry, Mam, it was just a bit of fun," Gaynor said a few days later. "Jane does it for fun, that's all."

"Pity she can't find something useful to do if she's bored," Daisie snapped and Gaynor knew she meant herself and not Jane.

"Will you ask Billie to come and see me?" Gaynor asked. "He might know where Gareth is. He's never written to me but he might have been in touch with his father."

"He hasn't," Daisie told her. "I've asked but Billie hasn't heard a word."

"I thought he was at an address in Cardiff," Gaynor said. "But I've written and had the letters returned. I went there to see if I could find a trace of him but no one knows anything. Heaven knows where he is or what he's doing."

"I've tried every way I know, but if he doesn't want to be found there's not a thing we can do," Daisie said sadly. "Cheer yourself with the thought that he must be all right. He'll be home fast enough if he is in need of help." Overwhelming pity for the silly girl who was her daughter made Daisie run to the bed and hug her. "I'll go and fetch Billie straight away, after I've got the pots washed from breakfast and seen to the grates," she promised.

"D'you know, Mam, you've never done anything for me straight away in all my life. It's always been 'in a minute', or 'when I've seen to this or that', or dealt with someone else. Everyone was dealt with before me. I've never felt important. Never."

"How can you say that?" Guilt made Daisie's voice louder than she intended. "You have to remember this is a business house, not a normal home with the mother spending all the time she wants doing things for her family. I've carried the weight of this place, done most of your father's share besides my own, while he was wandering off, sitting chatting without a care in the world to Helen."

"Oh, Mam," Gaynor said wearily. "I know all the excuses, I don't want to know *why* you haven't been available, I've heard all the excuses a hundred times. I just want you to know what it's been like for me."

"Are you saying it's my fault, you running up to that house and entertaining men with Jane?"

"No, Mam. That's not what I'm saying. The fault, if there is any, is all my own."

"I'll go and catch Billie before he leaves for work." Daisie pulled her overall off and folded it as she added, "He'll come this evening then for sure."

"What about the dishes?" Gaynor asked with a touch of reproach.

"They'll wait. I'll see Billie first."

Daisie never found out what happened between Gaynor and her estranged husband, but she guessed Gaynor had asked him to try again. That he had refused was apparent from the drawn and tearful face Gaynor wore after he had gone.

"Everything all right?" Daisie asked.

"Please try and find Gareth, will you, Mam? Ask anyone who knows him and try to find out where he's gone."

Daisie tried over the following weeks but heard nothing. Gaynor recovered from her illness but seemed empty, as if the sickness had gone inward and would never clear.

Daisie tried to hide her misery with enormous amounts of work, erasing Phil from her mind by exhaustion. She cleaned the house from the attic where she had shared a bed with him down to the cellars. The pipes and taps shone, the floors were spotless and the walls had the whitewash replenished long before it was needed. She cooked mountains of food, sacked the washer woman and did it all herself. With Gaynor

270

once more back in The Swan and under strict supervision, she was constantly on edge and she didn't need Helen's gentle warnings to know that if she didn't calm down she would break.

The Swan was still referred to as Daisie's Ark and the comfort of attending to the animals helped her. Clancy II was in charge of the field, less inclined to kick now he was getting older, but he still needed to be watched. There were, at varying times, hens, ducks, geese, rabbits, two goats, five cats and two dogs, besides the temporary lodgers, like the deer, the owl and the fox with a broken leg. She loved them all and needed their need of her.

"This place is well named," Helen said one day. "People and animals are sure of a welcome at Daisie's Ark."

"Does that include me?" Phil said coming through the door.

"Hello, Phil, you're too early for a drink."

"Can I talk to Daisie, in private?" he asked.

"No he can't," Daisie said swiftly.

"There's something I want to tell you," he insisted.

"I already know!"

Phil looked puzzled. "You know about my new van?" he said.

"Oh no, I'm not talking about your new van, although I knew about that, too. With Helen sitting in the corner and taking in every word, The Swan is more efficient than the Ministry of Information. No, Phil, I'm talking about Jane, who isn't your sister but your wife."

Helen slipped quietly out of the room and closed the door. The statement was news to her. Startling news and she shamelessly listened at the door.

"I've tried a hundred times to tell you." Phil turned away, head low, his voice a murmur. "I've tried, really I have."

"Get him! In nearly forty years he hasn't managed to remember to tell me he's a married man."

"I almost forget it myself at times."

"And what else have you forgotten? How many children do

you have? I don't mean the ones being brought up with other men's names."

"I'm sorry, Daisie. I knew within days of the wedding that Jane was, well, you know . . ."

"No, I don't know. Tell me."

"She was so beautiful and sex was a strong urge when I was young."

"Only when you were young? Get him!"

"She seemed to offer a life of perfection. Then I found out that she was little more than a child in other respects."

"But you stayed married to her."

"I was tricked into marrying her. They kept her true personality a secret from me. I was young and gullible. They gave me money, too, enough to start my china stall. I was grateful and when I did find out what she was like it was too late."

Listening to him, Daisie knew for certain that this too was more lies. No matter how many stories she disproved, he would invent more.

"I accepted responsibility for her," he continued in a dull monotone. "With the start they gave me, what else could I do? Jane and her family, they lived a better life with my help than they would have had without it. What they gave me to make a start, was every penny they had in the world."

Lies, Daisie shouted silently. More lies. She watched him as he went on, staring at the man she had loved and seeing a stranger.

"I knew I could never divorce Jane and marry you," he said. "You don't know what it cost me to walk away from you when you were expecting Gaynor, my only child."

"But you *didn't* tell me. You let me think I was just another unfortunate and stupid young girl without the sense to avoid trouble. Stupid, unclean and utterly worthless, that's how you made me feel."

"I'm sorry, Daisie, you'll never know how sorry."

"Go away, Phil. Daisie's Ark is closed."

Helen moved away as he came towards the door, but not before she had heard Daisie say that Gaynor, who Desmond

272

had believed to his, was Phil's child. She had always known, but hearing it said aloud opened the old wound afresh. Desmond needn't have left her. But what was the point of getting upset? It was all too late. Yet because of Daisie and Phil's predicament she had lost the man she loved and who loved her. They had deprived her of The Swan, taken away all she had.

Gareth turned up at The Swan one day and, fielding questions neatly, said very little about where he had been or what he had been doing.

"Aimlessly wandering it seems to me," Daisie told Helen. "He's mentioned Bristol and Cardiff and London but without giving any reason for being in any of those places. How can he live without a base to come back to each night?"

"He's just exploring the world a bit. More than we ever dared to do, Daisie, they're more restless," Helen said. "That must be a good thing, seeing other places, learning about how other people live before deciding how and where you want to spend your days."

"What a lot of old lol. I don't know what's the matter with the boy. He's got no need to travel rough like he's been doing. He's got a home at The Swan and now his mother's living here as well you'd think he'd want to stay."

Gareth stayed only a few days and the morning after he had caught the train to some undisclosed destination with a vague promise to write, Daisie went in with Gaynor's breakfast tray and found the bed empty. Without a word Gaynor had gone, too.

Daisie made enquiries but could find no trace of her daughter. What had she done wrong this time, she wondered? She had waited on her, spoilt her and tried to make her feel loved and wanted. Leaving without a word was a painful reminder that her earlier failure to make Gaynor secure in her love could never be changed.

After a week of fruitless enquiries she was told that Gaynor was back with Jane, in the house at the back of the mountain.

She drove up there and pleaded but Gaynor refused to return to The Swan.

After leaving secretarial college Lally found herself a job in the offices of Arthur Huntley-Davies. In 1951, Arthur welcomed his son Dylan into the firm and Lally became Dylan's secretary. The work was interesting and the business increasingly successful as more and more people were buying their own homes.

There were several boyfriends both during her time in college and afterwards but it was Gillian and Waldo's son, Michael, and then Dylan Huntley-Davies who were her most frequent escorts. Daisie was amused to think that history was repeating itself and her daughter was friendly with the sons of two of her closest friends.

"I can't see it ending in marriage, though," Gillian said to Daisie one day when they sat in her garden and sipped pre-dinner cocktails. "It's gone on too long. Any magic there might have been has faded by now into the pleasant, mutual affection of dear friends."

"She and Michael are inseperable at times," Daisie said hopefully. "And he's talking about building a house. Perhaps one day they'll look at each other with different eyes."

"Rose-tinted spectacles are for the heroines of novels not a down-to-earth young lady like Lally," Gillian laughed.

"I've been trying to persuade her to travel," Daisie told her friend. "She has that money left to her by Tommy but she hasn't used a penny of it."

"Poor Tommy. I wonder what happened to him?" The friends sat, each thinking of the lively Tommy Thomas and imagining how he might have spent his life. After a long silence Daisie revealed that their thoughts were running parallel by saying with a chuckle, "Whatever he's doing, I bet he's not short of a copper or two!"

Someone else who seemed not to lack a copper or two was Gaynor. Although her daughter never came to The Swan, Daisie went to the house on the mountain most weeks, but usually left without seeing her daughter. By surreptitious searching she guessed that the two women were still using the house to entertain men. She saw to it that the pantry was well stocked with food and she even left money on occasions, but knew she could do nothing more. Gaynor lived the way she wanted to live and there was nothing she could do to change things. Trying to help would create more trouble and alienate her further.

People who did see her from time to time reported that she looked far from well, thinner and showing signs of weakness. Daisie left notes asking, then begging, her daughter to call and see her but she never came.

Gareth returned on rare occasions, visiting for a few days then departing without telling Daisie or anyone else where he had been or how he earned his living. Sometimes he left without even seeing his mother in whom he seemed to lack any interest. It was unsatisfactory but there seemed to be nothing they could do to persuade him to stay.

The fifties slipped away with life and attitudes changing, the machine age bringing many marvels such as washing machines and refrigerators and televisions. Modern cookers, record players, food-mixers and other time-saving items entered many homes. The gradual freedom from the drudgery of hand washing, simple improvements like squeegy mops easing the task of floor washing, improved surfaces that needed no polishing; all these combined to persuade people they were living in luxury. There was talk about the new supermarkets that were to transform shopping and in the small crowded corner shops patient customers longed for the competition that they imagined would give them better service and cheaper prices.

It was a changing world and many believed they had more say over how their lives were lived than their parents, yet most remained in the same places, doing much the same jobs and, with a few exceptions, like eating scampi and spaghetti bolognaise and minestroni soup, living in much the same way.

Lally enjoyed helping young couples to chose their future

home and took a keen interest in finding something to suit their requirements. One day, when a statement from the building society reminded her about the money invested for her so many years ago, she decided to buy a place for herself. Before mentioning the idea to Daisie she discussed it with Dylan.

"Why do you want a place of your own, Lally?" Dylan asked. "You're happy with your mother at The Swan, aren't you?"

"We'll soon be in the nineteen sixties, Dylan," she laughed. "Today young people don't have to stay at home if they don't marry. She hadn't been completely honest with him. She felt she was in a rut. And there was the problem of Michael Griffiths. Michael was still talking about building a home for them but had done very little towards achieving it. Her thirtieth birthday was ominously close and it was time she had a place where she could display her own artistic preferences and her own personality.

"Will you be able to afford to pay a mortgage," he asked hesitantly. "Please don't think I'm prying but your wages aren't the same as a man's and once you commit yourself you have to keep up the payments whatever disasters befall you."

"I have some money and I've been thinking that now more and more people are buying their own homes, it might be a good way of investing it. I might not need to borrow very much, or even any mortgage at all."

They were walking from the office past the site of the market where the stalls were surrounded by the lunchtime rush of customers.

"Look through the brochures in the office and if you see one that interests you let me know, we could view after work on Monday."

"You'd come with me?" Lally said showing her delight.

"Having a man about gives a greater impact. I know," he added with his slow smile as she was about to protest. "I know all about women's equality, but if you wish, and only if you wish, I'll come with you and make sure you aren't persuaded into agreeing a purchase or a price about which you aren't completely certain."

Lally thanked him again. She was breathless with excitement. Imagine Dylan going with her to choose a house! Lally went into The Swan to tell Daisie.

"Do you think it's a good idea, Mam?" she asked when Daisie had returned a casserole to the oven after thickening the juices.

"A house? You, buy a house? Whatever for? There's me with this great barn of a place rattling around me, Gaynor gone, Gareth gone, and you're thinking of leaving as well?"

"I won't want to stay with you for always, Mam. To have a place of my own would be something to enjoy. A bit of garden perhaps where I could sit and admire my handiwork." She crinkled her eyes in a gentle smile and pushed her red hair from her eyes. "I could make cakes and invite you to tea."

"What if you get married? You do want to marry, don't you? Well then there you are," she said as Lally nodded. "A man wouldn't want to move into a ready made home. You'll marry and buy a place you both like and enjoy building your home together, sharing the fun. Why move away now while you're still fancy free and able to go where you like and do what you want to do without responsibilities? They come soon enough."

Lally tried to explain that it was what people did now.

"You'll have to talk to Michael won't you? I thought he was building a house for you and him to live in? Doesn't that mean you and he will marry? He won't want you and Dylan choosing a home for him."

"No, I don't want to tell Michael. He'd persuade me not to do it. Michael's answer to everything is to do nothing. I want to explore this idea, Mam, and I don't want Michael spoiling it with doubts. I might not buy after all, but I want the decision to be my own."

If Daisie was upset, she tried not to show it. She loved her youngest daughter dearly and would never have discouraged her from anything she wanted, but this meant another person leaving the house. What would she do with no one to cook for and clear up after? Then she laughed.

"Do you know, Lally, I think your suggestion has brought me to my senses. All my life I've wanted nothing more than to look after a family. When I lived in that old shed of a place on the bank of the stream my dream was a nice house, nice husband, nice children and the leisure to look after them all and be the perfect mother. Now here I am, a grandmother and still wanting the same things. I've spent my life looking forward to something that I'll never have and now it's too late for them to happen. I should have moved on, accepted what I had, or wanted other more attainable things."

"You would have if you hadn't been the landlady of The Swan, Mam. You'd have found other interests, developed skills and enjoyed hobbies. But limited by this place, with the unsocial hours and the rare days off, how could you be anything else but what you are?"

"I could have taken days off, but I never wanted to."

"Glad I am that you've stayed the way you are. I realise how lucky I am, having a loving Mam and a constant safe place to come back to. Daisie and her Ark. You've made a place people love to come to, and I don't just mean to buy drink and eat your food, either."

"But I neglected you, didn't I? Always saying wait a minute, I'll do it later, let me just do this first – "

"Neglect? What a funny thing to say, Mam. You were always there. Busy, for sure, but always there. I couldn't have wished for a happier childhood." Daisie hugged her but her eyes were sad. Two daughters, the same upbringing, but with reactions to it so very very different. Poor Gaynor, she thought with a sudden longing to see her. The people she had wanted to share her Ark with were Lally, Gaynor, Gareth and Phil. None of them wanted to be there.

Lally tried once more to persuade her mother to talk about the man who had left her the money. "Won't you even tell me his name, Mam?" she pleaded. "Or tell me if he's alive or dead?"

"Dead he is, for sure," Daisie said with conviction. Tommy

would have turned up at The Swan by now if he had lived. Years since he was released from prison and not a word. He must have died, in despair, probably, after suffering imprisonment all those months.

"He was a friend. That's all you need to know. A family friend who went away and wanted to leave something for you to benefit from. I don't think he would have liked it, mind, knowing the money was taking you away from me."

"Mam, I'm not leaving Cwm Manachlog. Down the road I'll be."

"Wait till you get married, love. Plenty of time then to find a house of your own."

"Michael has asked me to marry him," Lally said. "I don't think I will."

"Michael Griffiths?" Daisie said, feigning surprise "There's lovely," she said, relieved, "friends we've been all our lives, me and his mother. Gillian and Megan and me were inseperable when we were girls. Marvellous it would be if you married Michael. Gillian and Waldo would be pleased, too. They love you and they've always hoped you'd be their daughter-in-law one day."

"Mam, you're not listening. I said I don't think I will."

"But you aren't saying no for definite, are you? Not for definite." She smiled at Lally. "Fancy, us three friends, Megan, Gillian and me, and now you working for Megan's grandson, Dylan, and almost engaged to Gillian's son, Michael. My life has always been as stormy as a witch's cauldon but it's beginning to make sense at last."

"Mam," Lally said patiently. "Don't pretend not to hear me. Michael has asked, I haven't said yes."

"But you will, I just know it. Out of all the traumas and disasters some good is flying towards us at last."

Lally became thoughtful as her mother left the room. Michael was a problem. Since they were children they had been close friends. An engagement was imminent and she was frightened by the prospect. It was an engagement they were drifting into and one which held little excitement.

Buying herself a house was a way of postponing the event

or even taking away the inevitability of it. Michael was still working as a builder and dreamed of creating a magnificent house for them both to move into one day. She was young enough to be happy at the thought of being a bride and having gifts and good wishes in abundance. But deep within her was the secret hope that someone else would come along and, if not a handsome knight on a white charger, then some modern equivalent, to show her with flattering impulsiveness that she was desirable. In her mind's eye the man on the charger was Dylan Huntley-Davies.

One morning, when Lally was at work, Daisie went to find Michael. She drove up to the house at the foot of Pleasant View and found Gillian sitting in her modern living room embroidering a cushion cover.

"Don't laugh, Daisie," her friend said, putting away the sewing. "I'm making a couple of cushions for when Lally and Michael decide to get cracking on this wedding that's been in the air for years. D'you think there's any hope?"

Daisie looked around the well appointed room with its elegant armchairs and the french windows with the magnificent view of the mountains. "Not a lot," she sighed.

"Perhaps we've made our children too comfortable," Gillian said echoing her sigh. "They aren't in any hurry to leave and make homes of their own, are they?"

"I didn't think so, but now my Lally is talking of buying a house of her own and, what's more, living in it."

They discussed this item of news for a while, then Daisie asked Gillian where she could find Michael. "Someone has to try and wake him up if he wants her. She's unsettled and even if she doesn't buy a house she could surprise us all by marrying that Dylan."

Gillian told her he was working in Brynteg, not far from the market site there. "Fool that he is," Gillian complained. "There's my Waldo getting older and needing some help and Michael messing about doing odd jobs. Now he's talking of taking on a market stall would you believe? Selling tools and garden equipment. We should never have allowed him to work with Billie and get the excitement of the market in his blood. It's so exasperating. There's no need, Daisie. He's got a job here with his father. What's the matter with young people today? We never argued with our parents, did we?"

Daisie chuckled. "I can hardly remember my mother. Never caught my dad sober enough to talk to let alone argue with. Remember how Dad used to come home as lively of two pen'orth of cats meat, flat out in that barrow? The drunk's barrow they called it. Still there it is, at the back of The Swan, but filled with marigolds now not drunks. They go home by taxi these days. How times have changed."

"Your Lally will pull him together, won't she?" Gillian said returning to the subject of Michael. He'll make her happy, too, he's a dear boy."

"I think a prod in the right direction might be needed if he isn't to lose her."

"Then prod away, Daisie, prod away!"

Daisie found Michael in Brynteg. He was re-pointing the stone frontage of a cottage not far from the market.

"Hello there. What you doing round here? If you've come for the market you've got the day wrong," he joked. "Nothing on offer but three empty boxes and a dead cat."

"Put that trowel down and come and buy me a cup of tea," she shouted up at him. He ran down the ladder and led her to a small café, where he ordered tea and doughnuts. When the waitress had placed the food in front of them he sat smiling at her in his good-natured way.

"Did you know that Lally is thinking of buying a house?" she said.

"Why would she want to do that?" he frowned. "No, you must have got it wrong."

"She told me not to tell you, mind. But she and Dylan have considered some already. There's one near the foot of the mountain, below Pleasant View, not far from your Mam and Dad's place. She's quite interested in it I believe. They've looked at it twice and they're going again this afternoon for a third time. Dylan thinks it's lovely." She thought a bit of embroidering of the truth was justified.

The frown deepened, then cleared. "I know what it is!"

"You do?" Daisie said doubtfully.

"It's me. She's trying to tell me to get cracking and start this house of ours. She's getting restless and this is just her way of telling me to get on with it. She's right, mind. I've dawdled about for long enough."

"So what are you going to do?"

"That's partly up to you." He looked at her, bit into his doughnut and, his mouth surrounded with sugar, asked, "Will you sell me a bit of the field?"

"For your dream home?"

"The plans are already drawn. Lally would have something to do then: planning it all, choosing bathrooms and kitchens at first, then furnishings. She could have anything she wants."

"And you think she wants a house behind The Swan?"

"I'll tell her tonight."

Leaving Michael fired with enthusiasm, Daisie drove away. She sympathised with Lally and her hesitation. Michael was a dear boy as Gillian said but perhaps Lally wanted a more positive man she thought wryly.

To return to Cwm Manachlog from Brynteg meant turning the car around. Instead Daisie drove through the small town and up onto the mountain road. This way she would pass the house where Jane and, presumably, Gaynor still lived.

Passing the house with its overgrown garden and the partly open door she shuddered to think what her daughter was doing to earn her living. The few reports she had of her had been that she had lost weight and looked ill.

Daisie slowed the car as she passed the end of the drive where gates hung drunkenly on rotting posts. There were two cars parked near the house, half hidden by the tall untidy privet. Slowing down, tempted to try once more to talk to Gaynor, Daisie saw that one car belonged to Phil. She turned her head, pressed the accelerator, and hastened away.

Later that day she heard that the second car had belonged to the doctor, Jane had been taken to hospital. Her first thought was that Gaynor was up there on the mountain alone.

"I'll go and see her," Helen offered, "she'll be more

inclined to answer the door to me," and she ordered a taxi. She returned a while later alone.

"Where's Gaynor?" Daisie asked. "Wasn't she there?"

"She's in hospital, too. Daisie, they have tuberculosis, the pair of them. Consumption we've always called it."

Going to the hospital was a dreadful experience for Daisie. Gaynor was seriously ill, her face small, reminscent of when she was a child. It was no surprise to be told that there was little chance of recovery, the first glance had told her that.

Gaynor was in isolation but Daisie sat for hours watching and waiting for a sign of movement. Phil came to enquire after his wife and Daisie backed away out of his sight as he approached. She didn't want to talk to him, not now. It was Jane who had brought Gaynor to this, of that she was certain. She longed for a comforting presence, but Phil no longer qualified for that position, and never would again.

18

During the first week of Gaynor's illness, between visits and the necessary work at The Swan, Daisie searched for Gareth. He ought to be with his mother. She needed him now to help her get well. Despite asking people who might know of his whereabouts and writing dozens of letters she couldn't find the slightest trace of him.

She hardly looked at a newspaper or heard a radio newscast or she might have been aware of the protesters who marched out of London to Aldermaston. The news was full of descriptions of the Aldermaston Marchers, the Campaigners for Nuclear Disarmament, who walked in the hope of persuading the government to stop manufacturing, stocking and testing nuclear weapons. If she had looked at the papers that week her search for her grandson would have been easier.

Gareth's face appeared in several newspapers. In one he was grappling cheerfully with a policeman, in another he was marching with the protesters. No one in Cwm Manachlog expected to see anyone they knew in an incident so far away and reported in a London paper, so no one saw his picture. Besides, his beard would have made it difficult for anyone to recognize him had they been looking for his face.

Daisie knew Gaynor was seriously ill and she had to stop pretending it was not so. She walked into the hospital ward one morning in the second week of Gaynor's stay and begged the doctor to answer some questions. "What are you doing for her?" she asked.

The doctor knew she didn't want details of his treatment, the words would fade from her mind the moment they were spoken. He knew her need was to draw him into conversation so she could ask the one question to which she really needed an answer, a question too painful to be brought out without preliminaries.

"We are treating your daughter with two antibiotics, Mrs Prewitt, Isoniazid and Streptomycin, possibly with the addition of a third, Para-amino Salicylic Acid. These often have encouraging results." He looked at her and she could see the sadness in his brown eyes. She'd cope, but she had to know the worst.

"But?"

"But the prognosis is not good. The disease has reached a dangerous stage."

"Why didn't she seek help before things became so critical?" she asked, anger covering her need to cry.

"The disease often goes into recession and for a while she may have though she was returning to good health. Then the symptoms re-occur and she became too ill to care. Another brief time of feeling better follows during which she again believed she was well or at least recovering. It's an insidious illness, one that creeps up, often without giving the sufferer much of a warning."

"She's had a cough for a long time. She's got so thin . . ."

"If she had consulted a doctor about it we might have found out in time to cure her but," he looked at Daisie's frightened face and asked, "you wish me to tell you the truth?"

"Please," she said quietly.

"The disease has travelled from her lungs through the windpipe and is now affecting the larynx. There have been several haemorrhages, like the one that brought her to us ten days ago. I'm afraid that the next might signal the end of her suffering."

Stunned by the shock of having her fears spoken out loud made it impossible for Daisie to visit her daughter. Surely the knowledge of Gaynor's impending death would show on her face, as clear as words written for her daughter to read.

She left the hospital after assuring the kindly doctor that she was all right and, getting into the car, she drove up through the mountains. The beautiful end-of-summer colours of the grasses and heathers passed in front of her eyes unseen. All she could see was the face of her daughter through the stages of her life: a baby, cranky and restless; a toddler, demanding everything she could see and mostly getting it; a school girl who blamed the teachers for her failure to achieve; a young bride walking out of the church with a smiling Billie Beynon; the young mother who gladly left much of the work to her own mother; and latterly, the memory of dragging her out of the house at the back of the mountain where she lived an immoral life with Jane. Did I ruin her chances of happiness? Daisie wondered sadly. Would her life have been different if I had given her more time and fewer compensations for my lack of it?

She drove slowly home and went into the bar. Tidying the tattered pedlar's tray she wondered anew why Gaynor had been her failure and why fate was robbing her of a second child.

Now it was certain Gaynor would not recover, Daisie tried even harder to contact Gareth. He ought to be there to say his farewells to his mother even though they had had very little contact in recent years. The police tried, and the Salvation Army, she even tried a private detective.

Gaynor died a month after being admitted to hospital. Billie spent most of these last days with his estranged wife and grieved for what might have been. In her illness her face had returned to how she had looked when he had courted her, rosy and almost waxen in its smoothness. Memories flooded back and ached inside him. After her death he cried with Daisie for the girl they had loved who had been lost in the woman they hardly knew.

Lally walked from the hospital with her mother after seeing her sister for the last time and decided that she could no longer continue with her plan to leave home. Her mam needed her now. Plans to buy a home of her own and leave The Swan would have to wait until they had all recovered from the loss. She had lost a sister although she admitted to herself that Gaynor had never seemed that close. A sister was someone with whom you could share secrets and unhappiness and joys.

Gaynor had been more like a disinterested aunt who popped in and out of her life at intervals and left little trace. But the feeling of loss was still strong and rather frightening, a reminder of her own mortality.

The funeral was not as large as when Desmond had died, although many turned up to follow the coffin or called in to The Swan to show their regret and sorrow and support for Daisie. None of the businessmen who had swelled the cortege for Desmond came for Gaynor and only a few of the younger people who would have once been her friends. She had separated herself from most of those that knew her and for Daisie the small gathering, the few cars and flowers, the emptiness of the church, reiterated the sad story of Gaynor's life.

Phil was there, standing behind her, his voice swelling with the hymns. She wondered what his thoughts were on seeing the body of his daughter prepared to be lowered into the earth, a daughter who had lived and died without knowing him. She hated him in that moment, wanted to push him out of the church. He had no right to mourn someone he had refused to acknowledge. Then the flare of anger subsided. This was not the place nor the time for anger. Regrets were enough to bear, for herself and for Phil.

Daisie had flouted tradition before by attending her husband's funeral. This time if there were disapproving faces she was unaware of them. She hardly noticed who was present, seeing only a haze of familiar faces, close friends she had made during her long years in Cwm Manachlog, but she did notice a stranger there. Among the half-seen, half-recognized faces she saw a man at the back of the church near the door, sitting sideways as if already regretting coming and anxious to make his getaway as soon as possible. He was tall, very thin, pale and bearded, looking too small for the clothes he wore. In his shabby suit and a trilby, which he replaced the moment he left the church, he hurried away, head down, anxious to be gone. He was observed by many but none admitted to knowing him. Daisie stared briefly and, in the conflicting emotions of grief, bewilderment and disbelief and thinking ahead to the food she had to supply, forgot all about him.

She didn't expect Phil to come back for the spread but watched him from the corner of her eye as he walked through the churchyard to where cars waited. It was a great relief when he got into his car and drove away from the town.

There would be plenty of people coming back to the Swan. Daisie wished it were over. She would encourage the mourners to leave as quickly as was polite. Today she needed time alone to face the awful emptiness of saying goodbye to her daughter, something a mother never expects to experience.

In the weeks that followed, while Jane lingered on in hospital and life at The Swan continued with the strange hush that accompanies mourning, Michael began digging the foundations of his house in the field behind the Swan. All through the winter he used some time every week on the untidy site. Sometimes Lally would help, mostly he worked alone. He and Lally had not announced their engagement and, as winter burst into spring, Lally began to see more and more of Dylan Huntley-Davies. If Michael was aware of her long absences he seemed not to mind. Or, Lally thought, even to care. He just went on digging the foundations in the field accompanied by the assorted animals, and ordering the materials for the first stage of their dream home.

One day Daisie was sitting outside the back door waiting for the last of the Welsh-cakes she was making to brown, when Dylan Huntley-Davies came to see her.

"It's about the money Lally inherited, Mrs Prewitt," he began when she had greeted him and offered tea. "She says she doesn't know where it came from, but that someone left it to her? Is that person dead? Can you possibly tell me who that person was?"

"Why should I," she asked with one of her straight stares. "And why have you stopped calling me Auntie Daisie?" He ignored the second question and said, "I might as well tell you. I am thinking of asking Lally to marry me."

Daisie went inside and took the last of the round flat cakes off the hot girdle with the wide icing knife so ideal for the purpose. She didn't answer him until she had carried the heavy circle of metal outside to cool against the wall. She gestured to some chairs and invited him to sit. He sat upright in a chair that was meant for lounging and his solemn face was a mask of secretiveness. He wouldn't give a hint of his emotions, she thought sadly. His formal speech, his formal behaviour, how could lively, outgoing Lally accept him as a life-long partner?

"And you think she'll say yes?" she said at last. Her heart fell with a thump of disappointment as he gave a brief nod.

"I know most people consider me dull, Mrs Prewitt, but we get on so well that I don't think Lally would support that belief."

"Oh, I see. But why do you want to know where her money came from? Isn't it sufficient to know that someone loved her enough to leave it to her?

"I do not like secrets, Mrs Prewitt."

"Amen to that! Secrets cause nothing but trouble." Her thoughts flew to Tommy Thomas and all the years that had passed. That was one secret she wanted to remain. No one believed Lally to be anything other than Desmond's daughter, the time for rumours to spread was long gone. Perhaps it was time to tell Lally who her benefactor was, a dear family friend. That the friend believed he was her father was irrelevant. It was time, too, for Dylan to accept that his mother had tried to kill herself and had not been killed by a careless driver. Yes, now seemed a good time to clear a few of the cobwebs from the attic of her mind.

She stared at Dylan for a long moment before saying, "If I tell you, will you promise me not to tell anyone else?"

"But we've just said that secrets are – "

"There are secrets and secrets," she interrupted.

"If you think it best."

"I do. I don't want old stories raked up and sifted. That often results in people getting only half the story and usually the wrong half." She touched his hand in a calming gesture and said softly, "You do remember when your dear mother died?"

"When she was murdered by that drink-crazed motorist you mean."

"No, Dylan, that was not what happened. Best you accept the truth. Your mother was my dear friend, rather beautiful in her way, but she was always lacking in confidence and self-esteem. Her marriage to your father was not a success. He expected her to miraculously lose her shyness and become a socially extrovert wife. It made her frightened and very unhappy. One day, she, well, she admitted to loving someone else and when that someone else told her goodbye, for a while she was demented with anguish. She went out determined to kill herself."

"That is not true! My father said – "

"What your father said was to protect his *own* anguish, Dylan. How could he cope with believing he had made her so unhappy that she preferred death to life with him?"

"Go on," he said icily.

"Tommy Thomas loved Megan, your mother. He told her goodbye in the hope that it would help her reconcile herself to staying with your father. He wanted her but believed that the right thing for her was to try again to be the sort of wife your father wanted. Instead, she went out that night intending to end her life."

"He was a drunken and careless driver. He ran her down in the street like a stray dog. She wasn't planning to destroy herself. *He* destroyed her!" Dylan stood up, his eyes blazing and glared at her. It was the most animated Daisie had ever seen him. It was apparent that Arthur had brought him up to hate Tommy.

"Dylan, love, she was running around the town in the middle of the night on Christmas Eve wearing only her nightie! Not even slippers on her poor little feet. She was holding a teddy bear aloft like a flag. Just like a frightened confused child, she was. Crying Mouse we used to call her. Did you know that?"

290

Daisie knew she had made a mistake, a dreadful mistake. She had hoped to talk about his mother's death in a way that he would see that poor Tommy was innocent.

"That man. It was *he* who gave money to Lally? Then she mustn't accept it. I won't allow it. She must give it away. I don't care where she gives it but I won't have anything to do with it!"

"Isn't that Lally's decision?" Daisie asked quietly.

"Not if she becomes my wife it isn't."

"Tommy didn't kill your mother, Dylan. He loved her and was driving towards the stream desperate to find her before she succeeded in ending her life. You must believe that. It's my only reason for telling you about the money, so you'd understand and forgive. Your father has told you his version and now you must at least consider another."

"Forgive the man who murdered my mother? How can you ask it? Believe that my father drove her to suicide by his treatment of her? You expect me to accept that?"

Daisie watched him go with anxiety in her heart. What had she done? In an attempt to ease Dylan's pain she had only increased it. And as for Lally, she had probably ruined her chance of marrying him, if, she thought cautiously, if that was what Lally truly wanted.

"What did Dylan want, Mam?" Lally called from the field where, unnoticed by Daisie, she had been filling the water troughs and washing down the shed floors.

"Oh, nothing much," Daisie called. "He was just passing."

Lally turned to where Michael was half hidden in the deep trough he was finishing off, his head appearing with regularity at the same time as a spadeful of earth sprayed out around him. "Come and take a break, Michael," she called. "Mam's made some Welsh-cakes."

The young couple walked towards her, both were wearing jeans and open necked check shirts. Michael's face was red with his exertions, the dark hair falling almost to his chin. Lally looked cool even though she, too, had been working hard, her red hair a halo around her smiling face. What would marriage to Dylan do to that lovely face, Daisie wondered.

Would he reduce her to an unhappy shadow? She and Michael looked carefree and comfortable, so right together. And yet as soon as they had eaten some of the spicy cakes and drunk some coffee, Lally went to the phone and spoke to Dylan. Michael smiled, shrugged a little wryly, and went back to his digging.

"Why doesn't he propose and announce their engagement?" an exasperated Daisie asked Helen as they cleared the dishes later that day.

"He's probably afraid that, like all the other creatures accepted into Daisie's Ark, he'll be asked to have a check up at the vet!" Helen laughed.

Dylan disappeared from the town some days after Daisie's revelation about Lally's inheritance. He told no one where he was going, but arranged for his father to deal with his appointments and the day-to-day running of the business. Lally was disappointed at his lack of communication but not unduly alarmed. Business often took him away from Cwm Manachlog, although she usually knew where he could be contacted. He returned after about a week with the vague explanation that he had been researching his family background. He had only been home a few days when he went off again. This pattern continued for months. Any suggestion that he wanted to marry Lally had faded out of sight. Whatever was keeping them apart was becoming an obsession. He spent hours in his office poring over papers in a file, which he promptly hid when she approached.

The only clue Lally had was a couple of used train tickets which suggested he had been in Bristol at one stage, in London at another. When she discussed his erratic wanderings with Daisie her mother tried to hide her fear. Dylan was looking for Tommy Thomas, of that she was certain. But what did he intend doing when they met?

She was worried about Lally growing older and unmarried. She could see the inexorably moving tide of life taking her quietly on until she reached the age when she was unable to have children, still waiting for Dylan to make up his mind and marry her. Oh, why didn't Michael have a bit more *go* in him! To hide her anxieties she rounded on the absent Dylan.

"I thought he was a man who didn't like secrets. Then he goes off without a word. Ages it's been with him going away for days at a time, doing God knows what with God knows who, God knows where!"

"He'll tell me when he's ready to talk, Mam," Lally defended.

"How can you be so casual? Your youth is slipping away." Daisie demanded. "He doesn't even explain when he reappears after one of his vanishing tricks. Is this the man you want to marry, love? Take care if you do. If he hides things from you now, what will he keep from you when you're wearing his ring?"

"It's a ring on my finger, Mam, not through my nose." Lally laughed. "I trust him."

"That's more than I do then."

Michael said nothing about Dylan's behaviour. He went on digging the foundations, frequently changing his mind and the plans, much to the frustration of the council planning department and Daisie.

If he was worried about Lally's devotion to the often absent Dylan, he didn't show it or even mention it. When Daisie questioned him he just shrugged and said, "It's up to Lally. She'll make up her mind one of these fine days and then we'll all know what we're doing."

"And you're prepared to wait?" Daisie was close to beating him on the head to stir him into some kind of action.

"It's up to Lally," he smiled. "I'll leave it to her. No use rushing her, she has to get Dylan out of her system before she'll be happy with me."

"Get him," Daisie muttered, "talk about patience in a coma! And there was me expecting to have another grand-child one day."

While Dylan was out of town one Friday in February 1965, there was a terrible storm. It began in the early afternoon and increased as darkness fell. By midnight, trees swayed as if they had no more strength than pipe-cleaners, gutters ran with thick, muddy water and gurgled around drains too small to cope.

Daisie couldn't sleep and went downstairs and sat in the bar and looked out of the window. By two o'clock water was running down the High Street like a river and she feared that the stream had over-flowed. Hurrying to the window overlooking the back she saw the dull glimmer of water almost covering the field. Calling for Lally to help, she hurriedly dressed in Wellingtons and an old Mac, and went to rescue the animals.

She was relieved to see Michael appear out of the dark night and they soon had the dogs, cats and chickens on high ground. The rabbits in their hutches were outside the back door with the goats standing beside them, nibbling the wet hay that poked through the cracks. An injured goose waddled up behind Daisie and hissed his disapproval of the fuss. The ducks had disappeared.

Michael remembered a hibernating hegehog and carefully lifted it out of its vulnerable position and placed it in a box to be returned to its home later. They were still sorting things out when dawn broke, beautiful and calm, behind the mountains with a brightness that seemed like an apology. Voices called from the street where men and women were out assessing the damage and the market's Toby was deciding how best to safeguard the market area in case of further rainfall. Somehow he had managed to obtain some sandbags and was organising the traders into making a wall on the most likely area to be flooded.

As the light strengthened and the damage became more apparent, they could see that the stream had indeed broken its banks. Worse, the footings of Michael's house were filled with water. Swimming serenely along the new waterways, were seven ducks.

The night of the storm brought several changes. Michael gave up on his plans to build in the field. It had never flooded before in living memory, "But the storm might auger a new pattern of weather that makes flooding a regular risk," he told Daisie sadly.

Michael spent days considering other sites and discussing alterations to his plans with Daisie and Lally, but the second change resulted in his abandoning the idea of building completely.

Lally announced her engagement to Dylan Huntley-Davies. Before telling her mother Lally went to find Michael. Although neither had spoken of it in any official terms, it had long been presumed by themselves and most of their friends that one day they would marry. He was shocked by her news, convinced that when she thought carefully about being married to Dylan she would return to him and everything would be all right.

"It's because we have allowed things to drift for so long," Lally explained when he asked why. "I suppose I love you and always will, but there has to be some passion, some urgency for us both."

"I can show you passion," he said with a shy grin. "Oh yes, just give me a little encouragement."

"I don't doubt you are a passionate and loving man, Michael, but we seem to be stuck in a groove. Good friends, loving friends, but never meant to grow up and become lovers."

"And Dylan, you reckon he's passionate?"

"He loves me."

"Can you explain why he's taken as long as me to do something about it? Funny passion, mind, if he can put it on hold for when he's got the time to deal with it!"

"How different has it been for you?"

"I had to wait for you to get him out of your system. Damn it all, Lally, I love you."

"Why didn't you tell me?" she asked quietly. "Why didn't you say? Love was in me but neglected and over grown. It's lost its sparkle."

He put an arm around her and kissed her gently on the lips, then held her tight. For a long time neither wanted to move.

"Be happy my lovely girl," he whispered against her ear. "Be happy."

19

On the day following the storm a man entered the bar, dragging a collection of bags, and stood hesitantly at the door. Daisie glanced up and began to prepare to send him away. A tramp he was for sure and even though she felt sympathy for them she knew their presence in the bar caused irritation and would drive some of her customers out.

"I want, Can I – " the man mumbled.

A second look made her squeal with shock. The shabby man was her grandson, Gareth. At once she ran to him but stopped short of hugging him. He was filthy and even in those first moments she saw that he was infected with head lice.

"Gareth, you can't stay here looking like that. And," she added snatching his bags from hands that were grimed with dirt, "the only place for all this is outside!" She threw his bags out through the door and, holding him warily by an ear, dragged him through the bar and up the stairs. He followed and made no protest. In the bathroom she told him to strip and talked to him while he did it, not friendly chatter, just mild disgust at the state of him and the clothes he had obviously worn for weeks.

In all this time Gareth hadn't said a word. And even as she pulled at his clothes to hurry him he said nothing, just glanced at her from time to time through eyes that were glassy and feverish. Once he was down to a pair of underpants, the colour of which she couldn't hazzard a guess, she told him to stand where he was and she ran down to get a box in which she put all his ragged garments. She took them down and set fire to them. If there was anything he valued it was too bad.

Before running a bath and while he stood there shivering

she cut off his hair. "You can go to the barbers later and have it tidied up. One of them crew cuts it'll have to be, mind. Like them Americans used to have." As the water ran into the bath, dirt came off his feet in dark strands and Daisie shuddered at the thought of how long he had been living rough.

"Gran, I – "

"Later we'll talk," she interupted. "Now I want you clean and fit to be seen!"

She left him then and hoped that the soap-flakes she had poured into the water would be sufficient to restore his skin to a normal pink. She held back tears with difficulty. She had to be strong, efficient, make him start the road to recovery from whatever devil had driven him away. She would feed him then let him sleep before telling him that his mother was dead. She scrubbed the kitchen table while she waited for him, a physical escape from the overwhelming need to howl.

It was half an hour later when he came downstairs, wearing the dressing gown she had put ready for him.

"Gran, I – "

"Cup of tea and some lightly poached eggs on toast, ready for you in a minute." She busied herself at the stove. "Now, tell me, Gareth, where have you been and what on earth have you been doing?"

"I want to come home," he said.

"And what d'you want to do?" she asked, grim expression on her face but tears in her heart. She had to be harsh with him if he were to recover from this most recent stage in his lazy life.

"I want to work at the Swan as your pot-boy," he said.

"And?"

"And, Gran, could I have a room here, just for a while, until I find myself a room?"

"This is your home, Gareth, you needn't ask me that."

"And Gran – "

"What else," she asked.

"Can . . . can you lend me some money so I can buy some clothes?"

She laughed then, laughter that swiftly turned to tears. "Oh, Gareth, love," she said when she had recovered. "I think I'll say no to that. Think of the trade you'd drum up wearing only those underpants!"

Once he had eaten she put him to bed and he slept at once. Leaving Ethel to keep an eye on him she hurried to the market to buy extra food.

There was a stranger in the market that day, a thin, elderly man selling what Daisie guessed were religious pamphlets from a battered suitcase. He didn't seem to be attracting much business. Cwm Manachlog was not the place for new thoughts on the Bible, most were satisfied with the old, and when they had troubles they had the well known and comforting faces of their ministers and vicars to help solve them.

It wasn't unusual to see newcomers with something to sell. There was often a queue before the market opened, people waiting for the Toby to decide whether he had a place and to which trader he should award it. This man looked familiar. Daisie stared at him but couldn't put a name to the face. With a half memory tormenting her, she walked back to The Swan.

Daisie was restless. Gareth was still sleeping and she could only wait and hope that when he woke he wouldn't gather some food and leave again, his plaintive request for a job faded with the sleep.

Helen's quavering voice called her from the room beyond the Select. "I wouldn't mind going up the market for half an hour if you could take me, Daisie."

Daisie agreed without complaint. She never refused to take Helen for a walk. Helen was now living off the Swan as she was getting on in years and Daisie knew how much the old lady missed getting out. She had to depend on customers sharing any news, whereas she had once been the centre of gossip. Women entered the public houses in greater numbers each year, although few came without their husbands or sons to keep their image respectable. Many of Helen's old friends visited and sat beside her in her favourite seat in the corner near the tattered remains of the old pedlar's tray. But Daisie

298

knew that for Helen it was not the same as being involved in the daily life of Cwm Manachlog.

Their progress was slow, with Helen hanging on to Daisie's arm and stopping to greet every familiar face. The old man was still there when they eventually reached the furthest stalls.

"Who's that man talking to the Toby, Daisie?" Helen asked in a penetratingly loud voice. Daisie shrugged and helped Helen to a chair beside the food stall. "He was at Gaynor's funeral," Helen went on. "Sat at the back he did, then galloped off before I could find out who he was." There was complaint in the old woman's voice as she remembered her disappointment.

Daisie looked again at the man. "The funeral, of course, that's where I've seen him. I half recognised him earlier." She walked towards the man intending to take a better look. The man turned his head, saw her coming, grabbed his suitcase and darted off through the crowd. "Who was that?" Daisie asked one of the stall-holders.

"They call him Twicer, but I don't know any more than that. He's often around."

On the following Saturday, when the market returned to Cwm Manachlog, Daisie found him again. Selling tracts and a few booklets he seemed to be earning a few shillings. Hardly enough to pay for a small room and some simple meals, Daisie thought. She walked towards him, determined to find out who he was. Again he ran away when she grew close enough for him to see her coming.

He seemed to vanish during the week, appearing only at the market with his battered suitcase. The Saturday market was her only hope. Then she thought of Michael.

She found him at home with Gillian and Waldo and told him of her suspicions. "That man selling religious pamphlets," she said. "I think I know him from somewhere. Michael, he couldn't be selling them drugs, could he? Religious tracts indeed! Who'd buy them when the church offers all you need for free? Will you come with me when I talk to him?"

299

"Best to leave it to the police," Michael advised.

"Come with me to the market and help me get close enough to talk to him, will you?"

Michael agreed and they went to join the busy throng searching for bargains among the assorted stalls. Michael moved casually through the crush of people while Daisie worked her way carefully around behind the man with the battered suitcase. Walking along the backs of the stalls, carefully avoiding the guy ropes that threatened to trip her, Daisie came out beside him and caught hold of his arm before he could move. He turned with a jump of fright and she stared into his face.

"Tommy Thomas!" she gasped.

"Please, Dais, go away. Pretend you haven't seen me."

"What are you doing here? Why didn't you come to see me? Oh, Tommy, you look so – " her throat filled with pity as she looked at the almost unrecognisable face of the once lively Tommy. His chin was covered with a scrubby beard. His eyes, once so bright with enthusiasm, were dull and watery. Of the red hair there was no sign under the trilby hat he wore.

"Please, Dais, go away. I don't want anyone to recognise me, not now."

She turned away, her eyes unable to see because of the tears that flooded them. She couldn't bear to look at Tommy's sad face and his shabby, uncared-for clothes. First Gareth, now Tommy.

She thought of past days when she, Tommy, Gillian and Megan had been young enough to dream about a glorious future. What had happened to them all? Only Gillian could honestly say she'd been happy. Megan dead, Tommy living like a pauper, and herself? Well, apart from Lally who would soon be gone, she was alone, just as she'd always feared.

And where had Tommy been all these years? What was he doing now in Cwm Manachlog, the place he had left in disgrace so long ago? The questions rolled around her troubled mind and the most hurtful was why Tommy hadn't been to see her.

In the bar that evening every time the door opened she

looked up expecting Tommy, but she was always disappointed. Hours passed and she had difficulty holding herself back from running outside and shouting his name, begging him to come.

Lally returned from a brief shopping trip and this made it even harder. She couldn't involve Lally in all this. She tried to smile and act normally as Lally began to chatter. And all the time she was weeping inside for Tommy.

"What's the matter, Mam?" Lally asked when her mother didn't respond to a question.

"A headache, love, just a headache."

"I'll make a cup of tea and put a couple of cloves in it, shall I?"

"When I was a child," she told Lally as she sipped the tea, "the stalls stayed opened until well into the night. Sheep wandered around our feet eating what they could find, and dogs and cats were too hungry to worry about fighting each other. The stalls were lit up with flares and later, electric lights. It was wonderful after dark on winter nights. There was always a man selling hot chestnuts. We used to warm our hands on the brassier. Another sold snails although I never fancied trying them. There was often someone singing or playing some music trying to earn a few pence. Oh, the street was transformed into a magical place in the market after dark.

"The crowds increased the later it got, not like now, with everyone racing home to watch television. There were always people hovering, waiting patiently to get the lowest prices as the vegetables became limp and bedraggled and the meat darkened and attracted ever increasing swarms of flies."

Lally hugged her mother and asked, "Mam, why are you so melancholy? You aren't sick, are you?"

"No fach, not sick. Just remembering the good old days that we thought were awful, yet were in some ways the best. It's like that old saying that to travel hopefully is better than to arrive. Well, I've travelled and I've arrived, I won't be making many changes, this is where I am. And I think the journey was the best part. There is hope as you make your way, but once you've arrived you have it all, the good, the bad and the Gawd'elp us, as Desmond used to say."

At four o'clock Lally went to meet Dylan and Daisie was unable to contain herself any longer. She made the preparations for the evening hardly aware of what she was doing. Then she went out again into the street.

Many of the stalls were closed. The Toby, once so insistant that they stayed until the official end of business, no longer had his way. By five o'clock the street was empty and the rubbish neatly stacked for the ashmen to collect. There was no sign of Tommy Thomas.

Lally had a lot of spare time on her hands as Dylan continued to spend a lot of time absent from the town. He gave meagre explanations of his activities and Lally waited patiently for the time he was ready to explain. She spent a lot of time helping at The Swan and Michael was more and more frequently working beside her.

Once or twice she and Michael went for a walk over the hills and she was glad of his uncomplicated company. Michael surprised her by bringing a picnic on one occasion, not a box of sandwiches and a flask of coffee in case they found themselves hungry and far from a town but a wicker basket that had belonged to his mother and was filled with delicious salmon and chicken treats. There was salad as crisp as any she had eaten and an assortment of fruit. A bottle of wine in a cool-box gave the meal a celebratory air.

As they ate Michael looked at her strangely, his eyes fascinating her and making her very aware of him. It was as if he knew a secret and was waiting for her to discover it, too.

She was a little confused when, on Monday morning, she went to the office. She was restless but unable to understand why. The weekend with Michael had been fun. She realised how much she had missed having him around and the first sight of the office with the gloomy decor and minimal comfort made her want to run straight back out.

She went into the small kitchen at the back of the building and made a pot of tea. It would be all right as soon as Dylan returned. She loved him. There were no doubts. Michael was just a familiar friend, someone who was from that other part of her life, a family friend.

Michael again became a regular at The Swan using Gareth as an excuse. He helped behind the bar, attended to the cellar work and encouraged Daisie to take a few hours off. He knew the routine and seemed to enjoy coping with it all. As a family friend, Lally told herself time and time again. That was all he was, just a dear friend. Seeing him and sharing an intimate picnic was strangely pleasant. But a happy interlude was bound to create some confusion.

She looked at the solitaire on her third finger. It was Dylan she belonged to. It was only his absence that made her feel this way. Once he came into the office and smiled at her everything would settle into its right place. She had almost convinced herself by the time he arrived. Almost, but there was still a niggle of doubt that refused to be squashed.

20

When Dylan returned from his latest visit to Bristol, as soon as he stepped from the car Lally saw that he was in an angry mood. It was Monday morning and she felt the edge of his tension even as she watched him from the office window. She tried to build up a false excitement, told herself how much she loved him, pretended that he would sweep her into his arms and tell her he had missed her. She realised she did this often, even when, as now, she knew from Michael that he had been home since Friday and had not contacted her. He stepped through the door bristling with over efficient demands for work to be completed.

"Darling, I'm so glad you're back," she said, walking to greet him and raising her face for a kiss. "Was your visit a success?"

"Oh, Lally, my dear. I'm so glad to be back with you. Will you take this pile of letters? I want them typed this morning and sent off before the midday post."

Chastened by his casual greeting she took the sheaf of papers and returned to her desk. "I've missed you all this week," she said softly. "Didn't you miss me a little?"

"Of course. We must meet tonight and catch up with all that you've been doing. Did anything interesting happen while I was away?"

It was not the greeting the affectionate Lally had hoped for but, she told herself, she had to accept that effusiveness and outward displays of love were not in Dylan's nature. She wonderd, a little sadly, if she could ever become used to his formal manner. Shyness might explain his hesitation when they were in company, but when they were alone, surely then he could display his feelings?

"Nothing exciting, dear," she said, sitting at her desk and beginning on the correspondence he had ready for her. "Did you succeed in what you wanted in Bristol? When did you get back, last night?"

He took another sheet of paper from his briefcase, put it before her and tapped it impatiently with a finger. "Phone these people will you? Tell them the contracts are here and ready to be signed this afternoon." The subject of his absence was closed before it was opened.

During that first hour she tried to arrange for them to meet after work, suggesting a film, the theatre and even a walk, but to each invitation he shook his head. Work, he told her, had piled up in his absence, and in the words there was a hint of critisism, as if the fault were hers if they were unable to meet socially. She should have done more to ease his burden.

The atmosphere in the office was one of cool business-like orderliness and after an hour it seemed to Lally that it would never change. If she married Dylan this is what she must expect, calmness and orderliness and strictly no frivolity. She had always believed that she could wear down his formality and persuade him to relax and enjoy life more, but her confidence was wavering.

Dylan went out at ten o'clock to meet a prospective buyer at his bank and as soon as he disappeared out of the door there was a phone call for him.

"It's about a Mr Tommy Thomas," the voice explained. "I have traced him again. Will you ask Mr Huntley-Davies to call me back immediately?"

"Oh, a relation is it?" Lally asked. "I understand he has been searching for lost relatives."

"No, er, that is . . . you'll have to ask him, miss. Just get him to ring me."

Curious, Lally wrote a note on her pad with the time of the call and the man's telephone number. An hour later she rang the number and was told by a delightfully soft and soothing west-country voice that she was speaking to the Avon Detective Agency. Without speaking she replaced the phone. So, it *was* about his relations and none of her business. But why the secrecy? She smiled then. Being Dylan he wouldn't want anyone to know about additions to his family if they were not acceptable and respectable.

Michael Griffiths had given up the idea of having a market stall. He had imagined it would be as much fun as when he and Lally had helped Billie Beynon. Like everything else, nothing was fun without her. He was being forced to accept that Lally had abandoned him. While he was waiting for her, she was waiting for Dylan.

He had been patient to the point of lethargy, yet what else could he do but wait and hope? He had this plan deep in his mind, unspoken and rarely even considered these days. It needed Lally to make it work. There was no other woman he wanted so, as there was no alternative, he would continue to wait. One day, surely, she would tire of Dylan's pompous and frigid manner? Then would be the time to come out with his plan. He hoped it wouldn't be too late when she did.

Apart from the jobs he had promised to do he looked for no further work. He was often at The Swan fixing new shelves or doing small repairs. He enjoyed helping in the bar, too, chatting with the customers easily, fitting like a well worn slipper.

Gillian was worried by his lack of purpose and tried again to persuade him to join his father in the shoe shop business. Michael only shook his head. He would wait a while longer for Lally to give up her plans to marry Dylan and come back to him.

"I don't know what to do, Daisie," Gillian sighed when she met her friend in their favourite café one Saturday morning. "Michael says so little about what he feels, in fact, when I asked him outright what's the matter, he smiles as cheerful as an eager puppy and says everything is, 'Great, Mam. Just great.' I know it's your Lally. She's set on marrying Dylan and he's devastated, and worse, keeping it to himself.

306

What's taken them so long, Daisie? That's what makes me wonder."

"Who'd have believed it, after all the years when those two were inseparable, that she should fall for Dylan of all people!" Daisie snorted in exasperation. "Handsome in his own way, I suppose, and wealthy. But like his father before him, as dull as last week's newspaper he is and always will be. *And* he goes off for days at a time and doesn't tell her what he's been doing."

"Never!" Gillian gasped. "You mean she doesn't even know what he's up to when he's out of town?"

"Comes back and carries on with life without a word of explanation."

"What a start to a marriage."

"You ask what's the matter with your Michael," Daisie said sadly, "well, I wonder what's up with my Lally. There she is with two men dangling. Or," she amended, "one man dangling and another dangling her more like."

"She must know where Dylan goes?" Gillian asked.

"The only thing he's told Lally is that he's researching his family. But if that were so, why doesn't he take her with him or at least talk about his discoveries?"

Daisie didn't stay in the café long. The morning was overcast and humid and she was very tired. Running The Swan was becoming harder. Time she thought of selling and finding herself a small house and a neat garden. If only her dear Oswald had lived and was able to take on The Swan. But, she thought as she gathered her handbag and umbrella, dreaming never brought changes, only action could do that and there seemed none she could take.

After saying goodbye to Gillian she walked back through the stalls, so different from when she was a child. New faces, most of them strangers, Little Dickie Daniels waved, and the young men who had taken over the butchers stall from David Johnson. Phil had given up the stall and had installed a manager in the china shops, of which he now had three. He spent his time sitting talking to other old men either in The Swan or the reading room of the library. Of Tommy there was no sign.

Today everything was strange and alien. No familiar faces to greet her as she strolled through the crowds. She felt old and out of touch with the world in which she lived. It was time for change, she felt that deep in her bones, but she had no idea how to achieve it.

She climbed the steps and entered the pub and without stopping to remove her coat, went up to the small attic room and looked out over her field and to the fields beyond where the stream flowed so peacefully.

She had vague memories of a time when she had been a happy child. She remembered a small house filled with people; brothers, neighbours, dozens of "aunties" who were no relation but who loved her as much as if they were. And a mam and dad. There was warmth and good food and laughter and always people milling in and out of the door and sitting on the long couch against the wall opposite the fire. She remembered her father pulling the couch around close to the fire on wintery evenings and one of the friends bringing a small concertina to accompany their singing. She had once been given a small toy piano which she had treasured but which had been sold along with so much she had valued.

The Swan seemed hollow, empty of all human presence, lost in the mist that surrounded it, echoing around her as her thoughts flew back to that small, barely remembered overflowing house. She had tried to fill her Ark so she could re-create the happiness and security of those hazy days. Now she never would. Perhaps she would talk to Dylan and ask him to find a suitable house for her and she would retire, let someone else fill the place with noisy children as she had failed to do.

Whatever happened, there was something she had to do first. She had to find Tommy. She didn't take off her outdoor shoes, she was going back to the market later. The day being a gloomy one, Daisie knew that many of the stall-holders would leave early. She went back as soon as the lunchtime crowd had departed and The Swan was in its afternoon quiet.

As before she walked around the back of the stalls, slowly and carefully making her way to where Tommy stood, his open suitcase at his feet. She managed to grasp his arm before he saw her and she held on to him desperately while she persuaded him not to leave. Ten minutes later she was still holding his arm in a vice like grip and leading him up the steps and into The Swan.

Dylan stood at the window of his office, having told Lally he would be working all afternoon. He looked out into the High Street and saw the dreary shoppers walk past with their dripping umbrellas and empty baskets, and return with their purchases. He knew now that Lally's money had come from Tommy Thomas, the evil man who had murdered his poor mother. He had telephoned the police and reported the man as a vagrant. Soon he would be gone and after the warning he intended to give him, would never come back. He would tell Lally to dispose of the money she had received from the man and he would start to arrange their marriage. They would be free then of dark secrets. It was worth the delay to get the matter of Tommy Thomas cleared up. Alice was her real name, he mused. He would insist she used it once she was his wife. Lally was no name for a Huntley-Davies.

Tommy sat with Daisie for a long time and listened to her news, saying little but wanting to hear about all that had happened in his absence. Then he insisted on returning to the room he had rented. He was pleased to see Gareth and agreed with Daisie that the boy was ready to give up his wanderings and return to a more organised existence. Promising to see them again soon, he stepped out of The Swan and stood looking around him at the slowly empty-ing street.

He saw the police car stop across the road and noticed the way the men stepped out of it and strolled casually towards him. He wondered vaguely where they were going and was startled when they stopped him and held his arm.

Daisie stood, helpless with horror, as a policeman held Tommy, who made no effort to free himself. Running out she demanded to know what was happening. On being told he was being arrested she ran indoors for a coat prepared to follow.

"Best you wait a while, Mrs Prewitt," one of the officers told her. Give it half an hour then we'll know more of what's happening."

"But what's he done?"

"Half an hour, is it?" the man repeated.

"Don't come, Dais," Tommy pleaded. "Please, don't come."

The Swan was empty. Helen was asleep. Gareth and Michael were in the cellar whitewashing the walls. The place was like a tomb.

Lally came back from a shopping trip at six and found her mother walking up and down, still wearing her damp coat and out door shoes. In despair, Daisie told her what had happened.

"Surely he'll come back here, he hasn't anywhere else to go," she wailed.

"Who is this friend of yours, Mam? What's his name?" Lally asked.

"Tommy Thomas, a dear friend who I thought was dead."

"Mam," Lally asked hesitantly, "it wasn't Tommy Thomas who left me that money, was it? Dylan's been making enquiries about him, I think."

At nine-thirty on Monday morning, Tommy walked into The Swan.

"Tommy! Thank goodness you're all right! There won't be any charges, will there?"

"Not this time, Dais," he smiled and for a brief moment Daisie saw the old ebullient Tommy behind the grey face.

Daisie and Lally prepared lunch and food for the bar while Tommy explored the building. When they were ready to eat they took their trays into the room behind the Select and Daisie asked quietly, "Where *have* you been all these years, Tommy? Why haven't you once been to see me?"

"Oh, round about. I heard about Desmond dying and thought you'd marry Phil Johnson. So I went to London and

310

worked the markets there, but I didn't make much money. My heart wasn't in it somehow. All our grand plans, eh, Dais?" he grinned.

"But religious pamphets, Tommy. There must be something more profitable than that."

"I usually sell linen, like I always did, but the trade isn't the same. Too many ways of buying goods now. There's these catalogues where you buy now and pay later, while those with money prefer to go to one of the swish department stores and choose from a dozen shades of every colour. It was never like that on the markets, was it? Bargain prices and who cared about the colour?

"When I came back from Gaynor's funeral I wanted to stay, see how you were all getting on. Damn me, it was as good as reading the sequel to a much loved book, Dais, finding out who was who, and seeing children I'd never met already grown up into men and women.

"Disappointed in Megan's son, mind. Dylan they called him. The same name as one of our cleverest poet and him turning out as boring as a rusty old bucket. Did you know he's been spending every spare hour and Gawd knows how much money, searching for me?"

They had forgotten Lally was sitting near them and were startled by her saying, "He's never met you but he hates you because that's what he's been taught."

"What a way to spend your life, hating someone you don't know and planning revenge for something they didn't do," Daisie said. To her relief Lally seemed to agree.

"Dylan and I were never suited, Mam. I don't think he'll ever be happy." She smiled at Tommy. "I hope you'll be happy here. You know, I've talked to a lot of people about you. Dylan is the only one who considers you were guilty of Megan's death. None of your friends believe it."

"Oh, I did it, Lally. I killed my lovely Megan even though I was trying to save her from death. Ironic wasn't it, Dais? Me the drunken prince on the shining black motor hoping to rescue a damsel in distress and ending up killing her. There isn't a night I don't wake and remember. Best Dylan blames me rather than think his mother was so unhappy she wanted to kill herself, eh?" He pushed the tray of food aside, his appetite gone. He thanked them for the meal, and returned to the room he rented in the house where Helen had once lived.

Lally and Michael visited him often and listened to his stories and shared his memories of a time when Daisie and he had been young. It was they who heard of his intention to leave Cwm Manachlog after a week or two. When they told Daisie she went to see him.

"Tommy, we're both past love affairs and all the hassle of courting and the rest, but I want you to consider coming to live at The Swan. I'm not offering you charity so don't look like that," she chuckled as he opened his mouth to protest. "If you want to you can help around the place, the animals take a lot of our time. You'll earn your keep that way and a little besides. No strings, mind," she added as he again threatened to refuse.

"Lovely idea, Dais, but I think you'll be having enough changes at The Swan without me coming and adding to the confusion."

"Changes? What changes? Heaven's above, Tommy, what's happening now?"

"Look over by there."

Daisie looked through the window where he was pointing and saw Lally walking past with Michael. They were arm in arm and both laughing happily. In front of them walked two dogs and a few cats, behind them, five ducks, a noisy goose and, taking up the rear, an ageing donkey, probably wondering whether he dare show his authority over the menagerie by butting Michael, Daisie thought with a chuckle.

"What changes?" Daisie repeated. "If you mean Lally and Michael, it's friends they are and nothing different, more's the pity."

"I had a talk with Michael the other day and persuaded him to admit what he really and truly wants to do with his life."

"That's more than Gillian and Waldo have managed to do."

"He wants to run The Swan, Dais. With Lally helping him he'd make a good job of it, don't you think? They're coming to see you this afternoon to discuss the idea." He looked at Daisie's startled expression, saw it transformed, watched it glow with pleasure.

"What will you say, Dais? Be glad to hand over to someone younger? Or are you going to be like Queen Victoria and hold on to your crown until it's too late for them?"

"Tommy Thomas! Five minutes you've been back and already you're shuffling us about as if we were a pack of cards!"

The Swan welcomed its new owners with a party. Daisie had insisted.

"A party is how we always celebrate at The Swan," she said, as Michael finished painting the wall near the front windows. "A lick of paint is fine but it isn't enough."

So a party was organised, which Daisie arranged under the critical eye of old Helen who sat in her corner near the pedlar's tray and checked details of the arrangements like the suspicious old matriach she was.

The party wasn't like the earlier ones. These days there were plenty of places to go beside The Swan. Many families had a car and could get to places far from Cwm Manachlog for an evening's entertainment. Many houses had a television which kept them indoors, even though Daisie had one fixed on the wall. The laughter at the celebration was genuine, but no one wanted ordinary things like Daisie strumming a tune on the piano and joining in the old familiar choruses. Pop music was the folk songs of the young. The juke box was the accompaniment to the bar-room chatter. This was the time to be young, a time when nothing over three months old was of any value.

"A throw-away society," Daisie complained. "And I'm heading for the rubbish tip any day now."

"Stop your moaning, Dais," Tommy whispered. "Here's our Lally and you don't want her to think you're unhappy."

"All right, Mam?" Lally smiled. "Michael's gone to feed

the animals. He says we need a new shed for the goats, there's another kid expected soon, and the new lot of hens will be glad of the old building."

"Goats, chickens, rabbits and another donkey to take the place of poor old Clancy. You and Michael married and bringing in fresh business among the young. Gareth out of our hands for a while, but at least safe and in touch. Ethel still popping in to see us all, and Helen living here with me and Tommy. The Ark is filling up nicely. How could I be unhappy, my lovely girl?"

"There's Phil, too," Tommy said when Lally had gone back to her bar. "The richest man in Cwm Manachlog some say. He comes in regular these days to sit and look at you and wish he'd made a few different decisions."

"Oh, I suppose that's something we all do, Tommy. Live to regret. You know, on the whole, I think you and me ending up at The Swan and watching others do most of the work isn't a bad ending to our story."

Tommy reached for her hand. His blue eyes met hers and they smiled at each other like two conspirators after a job well done.